TABOO AVENGED

7/31/98

To Rick;

Glad an way!
[signature]

TABOO AVENGED

By Griffin T. Garnett

BRANDYLANE PUBLISHERS
White Stone, Virginia

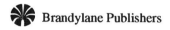 Brandylane Publishers

P.O. Box 261, White Stone, Virginia 22578
(804) 435-6900 or 1 800 553-6922; e-mail: brandy@crosslink.net

Cover art by Dill O'Hagan.

To Harriet and Bobbie

CONTENTS

ACKNOWLEDGMENTS

Thanks to my reading committee: my two sisters, Alpha Lee Smith and Ann Temple Balbirnie; Dr. Robert Emma; Jerry Kesten; Robert M. Cockrill; Ben R. Coles; and my wife, Harriet.

This writing would never have reached submission manuscript stage without the efforts and patience of Barbara Graves, my secretary for so many years.

Last, but not least, I appreciate the continuing confidence and work of Robert Pruett, my editor and publisher.

Griffin T. Garnett

Part I

Greg and Caroline

1

Caroline McFarland Morgan was sitting at her dressing table fastening an earring to her earlobe.

She turned to her lawyer husband and asked, "Greg, do these earrings you brought me from Bora Bora go with this dress?" Gregory T. Morgan was standing behind his wife, looking into her large oval dressing table mirror as he clipped on his tux tie.

He glanced down at his vivacious brown-eyed mate of sixteen years. What he saw he not only liked, he adored. Her figure was still trim. Her face was angular and youthful, her brown eyes as mischievous as ever, and her naturally wavy hair was styled in an upswept hairdo. The dark blue cocktail dress she wore was chic. The V-neck of the garment was not dangerously low cut, but it did reveal the cleavage of her firm breasts. The Garfield's couturier product was strapless and portrayed her comely molded shoulders and upper back. She needed no necklace to emphasize her beauty. He mused how fortunate he was to have her stand by him through the thick and thin of those sixteen years. And, there had been a lot of thin during WWII.

Then Greg looked at the distinctively designed beaten-silver earring with the dark blue cat's-eye stone in the center. "Honey, the earrings go well with your dress. Wear them. I'm gonna' wear the matching cufflinks tonight. Two minds with a single thought."

Caroline, adjusting the earrings, looked up at her husband, "So, you remembered too."

"I'll never forget," he said.

Caroline Morgan was excited. She loved the theater in any shape or form; from burlesque to Shakespeare, amateur songfest to opera, and the Steppe Brothers to the Bolshoi Ballet. Though she had not majored in theater arts at Goucher

1

College, she had appeared in many of its amateur productions. Once, before she met Greg, two years her senior, she had seriously considered a stage career.

Tonight, 25 October 1954, they were to be the guests of their friends and neighbors, Frances and Will Barton, at a packaged fund raising deal benefiting the Greenspace Environmental Foundation. The foursome was going to the Willard Hotel to attend a gala cocktail buffet, and then on to the National Theater to see a performance by the Southwest Pacific Dance Ensemble.

The ensemble had been appearing at the famed D.C. show palace for five days before standing-room-only audiences. This night would mark the beginning of the dancers' last week of performance in Washington. From there, they would head for New York and an extended Broadway run.

The *Washington Post* had recently run a lead story and review about the island dancers in its Sunday theater section. That story told how not long after WWII, the Southwest Pacific Dance Ensemble, blessed by the French Colonial Government, had originally been formed in the Society Islands as a tourist attraction. The sponsors of the troupe were not identified, but the article did relate that the artistry of the unnamed Polynesian lead dancers, backed by the solid performance of the other troupe members, and highlighted by the stunning choreography, had catapulted the ensemble into ever widening recognition. This was the first American appearance after a very successful western European tour.

The paper reported that the troupe performed a series of dances depicting Polynesian history and culture, particularly the culture and history of the French Society Islands. The story ended by saying that the overseas rave reviews were justified.

Greg and Caroline had read that story as well as the theater reviews of the dancers in other D.C. papers. They were looking forward to a most pleasant evening.

The couple's only child, thirteen-year-old Gregory T. Morgan, Jr., affectionately known as "J.R.," was a spitting young image of his brunet, energetic dad. He would be spending the night with his friend, twelve-year-old Tim Polk, son of their back-fence neighbors, Walter and Ann Polk.

As the Barton's drove past the entrance posts onto the driveway that encircled the Morgans' attractive Arlington, Virginia, rambler, J.R., with his overnighter packed, opened the Morgan's back door and yelled, "I'm gone to Tim's. Have a nice time and don't do anything I wouldn't do. I'll see you tomorrow after school."

Greg, walking the hallway from the master bedroom to the kitchen, replied, "OK, Son. Don't you and Tim completely clean out the Polk's refrigerator." The back door slammed shut. Greg knew that J.R. and chunky Tim had bottomless pits for stomachs. Those two had been known to completely decimate the contents of their parents' refrigerators on various occasions. He wondered just what was in J.R.'s mind when he said, "Don't do anything I wouldn't do." And, Greg reminded himself to tell his son not to slam the back door shut so hard each time he entered or left the house. J.R. and Tim had a secret hole in the back fence to shortcut the otherwise two block walk to the front of each of their houses.

2

While driving on the Fourteenth Street Bridge over the Potomac River, the dividing line between rational southern living and Federal government fantasy, affable Will Barton said, "I'll take you three to the Pennsylvania Avenue entrance of the Willard Hotel. Then I'll park in the parking lot behind the District Building. Wait for me at the hotel entrance."

"Don't do that," said Greg. "Just go to the lot. It's not far to the hotel. We can walk from the parking lot. After supper, we can walk to the theater. It's only a block away."

"I agree," said Caroline, "Even in high heels, I'd enjoy the walk on such a lovely night, now that Hurricane Hazel has at last spent her fury here and moved north."

Blonde Frances Barton, seated in the front passenger seat of their Lincoln Premier, pouted up at her husband. She preferred being driven to the hotel's front door. She loved a stage entrance anywhere, particularly at the Willard where a liveried doorman would open the car door for her and escort her to the entrance stairway. But, it was three to one, and she would have to walk.

3

The big lounge off Peacock Alley (the famed first floor corridor of the hostelry) was crowded with patrons, members and guests of the foundation as the foursome entered. There were representatives from the State Department, various embassies, and the armed forces, as well as many local citizens like the Morgans and the Bartons-- about three hundred party goers in all. The assemblage was in evening attire.

Waiters wandered through the crowd dispensing drinks. Caroline, taking a bourbon and soda from a tray, looked at Frances Barton and jokingly said, "I don't see any Polynesian dancers, do you?"

"Maybe you can't tell if they're in street clothes," said Frances.

"I guess not. But, I'm disappointed," said Caroline.

Frances tittered. She always tittered when she couldn't think of a response.

Greg and Will sauntered up to their wives, each with a small glass plate stacked with buffet food. "The oysters-on-the-half-shell and the steamship round are delicious," mumbled Will through a mouthful.

"Pigs," said Frances, as her eyes played the crowd. "You two didn't even look to see who was here before you hit the trough."

"Didn't even get a libation," chided Caroline.

"We're hungry, we didn't have time for a snack at the ninth tee during our golf game today. As soon as we finished the round, we had to rush home and dress for this affair," said Greg just before he bit into a large roastbeef sandwich.

Caroline glanced over the shoulder of her husband and saw a handsome, copper-skinned male staring at her from about fifteen feet away. He was short, trim and wore his tux as if it was an everyday suit. His eyes met hers with a fleeting glance. Then the sturdy bronzed individual continued his unabated stare at the side of her head. Caroline looked at Frances and said, "Let's visit the buffet table. I'm getting hungry too." She turned to Greg, "We'll be right back, Hon. Fran and I are going to get a bite to eat. Wait here."

"It's too much trouble to wander through the crowd with these plates," said Greg.

Caroline and Frances went to the long food filled table. Each took a plate and began to make selections. Caroline was nervous. She looked up frequently, peering over her shoulder to see if her observer was near. Frances saw her actions. "You trying to find somebody, dear?"

"No," said Caroline, "Just looking at the crowd." After several views of the party goers in her vicinity, she relaxed. Maybe it was my imagination, she mused. Caroline and Frances, carefully balancing the food on their plates, inched their way back to the spot where their husbands stood munching and conversing.

Greg spotted several of his legal cohorts and waved to them. Caroline saw Mrs. Wrightfield, her parents' next door neighbor in Wesley Heights, D.C. They chatted. Soon it was show time. The Morgans, the Bartons, and most of the party guests, after reclaiming their wraps, strolled from the hotel to the National Theater.

4

The two Northern Virginia couples entered the playhouse, had their tickets cleared, were each handed a multipage playbill and were seated in "H" row, center orchestra seats, five minutes before curtain time. There was a hum of anticipatory conversation throughout.

Caroline opened her evening bag and took out her opera glasses, placing them on her lap. She also took from her handbag the small flashlight she carried to look at the playbill during the performance, if need be. "Please hold this for me. The clasp on my bag sometimes doesn't stay closed. I'm afraid I'll lose it," said Caroline as she handed Greg the little light. He put it in his tux pocket.

The house lights dimmed. The pit orchestra began its overture. Greg had never heard most of the melodies. But one he recognized, "The Hawaiian War Chant." The piece was played in the manner and style he had heard on the French Southwest Pacific island of Bora Bora during the war, quite different from the usual stateside version. The melody slurred from key to key, fast-slow, soft then thunderous. The beat began stirring memories hidden within the former Landing Ship Medium skipper. The overture ended -- applause -- the stage was aglow with soft lights -- the pull curtains parted -- the filmy drop curtain lifted silently, and the show was on.

5

The female dancers in the first numbers wore knee-length pastel pink gowns. The male dancers wore similarly colored tight-fitting, knee-length pants. The bronzed male upper torsos were quite a contrast to the pastel color worn by the troupe.

Greg noticed that all of the dancers were barefoot. That's an emphasis on realism he thought, and immediately became aware that the two lead dancers, one male, the other female, were taller than the other members of the troupe. The lead female dancer's straight, iridescent, black hair flowed down her back, almost to her waist. He observed that she was lithe and regal with the moves of an accomplished ballerina, at least as far as he knew about ballerinas. Dance, in any of its forms, wasn't really Greg's cup of tea. He admired grace in all sports, and he had a keen eye for movement detail, but the only time he really cared about dancing was when he had his arms around his beloved Caroline, and was swinging with her to the music of a big band.

There was something about the female lead that attracted Greg's attention. He was puzzled as he watched her graceful movements -- as if he had seen them before. But where?

6

Taboo, the routine before intermission, began. Greg watched with increasing interest as the stage scene changed in a rush. There in a clearing of coconut trees was a partially disassembled Quonset hut, painted Army green. The female dancers entered from the right wing and danced to center stage. They now wore multicolored calico ankle-length skirts and white, off-the-shoulder, linen, slipover tops. The males entered from the left stage wing, they wore multicolored calico shorts. To the soft, low strains of "The Hawaiian War Chant," the lead female dancer swirled from backstage through the troupe to front center stage. She wore an even more vividly colored calico skirt than the other female members of the ensemble. Her hair now hung in two long braids with a little white bow at the end of each braid. Greg gasped quietly. The scene was beginning to be all too real. He reached into his pocket for the little flashlight. He hadn't looked at the playbill. Now his heart was thumping as the memory of an episode he had witnessed in December of 1944 was struggling to emerge -- apparently being revisited on stage. He opened the playbill and shone the flashlight on the inside first page. The first name he read was "Jacques Montagne, Ensemble Manager." Greg was truly surprised. That was the name of his Polynesian friend from Bora Bora, the chieftain's son, the educator. He looked up to the stage. From center rear, through stage mist, appeared a mock up of a gray Navy jeep driven by the lead male dancer who wore a tight-fitting takeoff of a U.S. Naval officer's summer fatigue uniform. The lead female dancer leaped toward the dancer in the jeep. "Jesus!" said Greg aloud. Caroline cast her concentrating husband a sharp critical glance. So did Will Barton. Oblivious to his wife sitting on one side of him and Will Barton sitting on the other side, he stage whispered to no one in particular, "I can't believe what I am seeing." His wife eyed him this time with deepening uneasiness. Greg again flashed the little light on the playbill and thumbed the pages quickly until he reached the vignettes of the dancers. Under "Female Dancers" he read the name at the top of the page, "Mary D'Quino Montagne, leading female dancer and wife of ensemble manager, Jacques Montagne." The memory that had been struggling, now surfaced with a fierce impact. He felt a chill race through his body, much the same as he had when he watched the real episode unfold ten years earlier on Bora Bora. Greg was sure that the lead female dancer was Mary D'Quino -- native of Bora Bora, a graduate nurse from L'Hospitale de Tahiti, and sole perpetrator in the weird event. She was still svelte. Greg was absorbed, as if he was centered in land between dream and reality. He saw the troupe dancers swirl away leaving Mary D'Quino and the male lead to portray, in an engaging routine, the very gripping happenings that had ultimately led to the beaten-silver gifts he and his wife were wearing that night.

Caroline, engrossed in the dance, now realized the cause of her husband's apparent bewilderment. She was seeing unfolding on stage Greg's story of the Bora Bora wild episode, and the resulting severe injury to Lieutenant Benjamin I. Feldman. Without looking at her husband, she raised her right hand to her right earlobe and felt the earring.

Greg watched as if in a trance as the series of events that led to the near castration of Lt. Feldman and to the islanders complete ostracizing of him was interpretively danced gracefully, but fiercely. At the very end of the dance, Mary D'Quino (now Montagne) reached down, picked up limp Alberto DeFrances, the lead male dancer, and placed him in the passenger seat of the jeep with the same grace and ease she exhibited when she picked up an unconscious, tattered, uniformed Lt. Feldman, and casually placed him in the passenger seat of the base jeep. Just as in the real incident, Mary D'Quino entered the drivers seat and the jeep disappeared into the back stage mist. The music rose to a crescendo -- stopped -- the filmy curtain descended -- the stage went dark. The audience roared its approval as the house lights flooded the theater for intermission.

7

Never had Greg expected to see a replay of the macabre occasion he had actually witnessed. To most of the audience that last dance before intermission was a fierce, artistic routine with a certain subtlety, the true meaning of which was obscured from them. To him, the dance represented stark tragedy, from start to finish.

8

Greg Morgan, ex-executive officer of LSM 460.5 (a small amphibious ship of the WWII Sandscraper Navy) sat glued to his theater seat and remembered an afternoon, in early December, 1944. Pharmacist's Mate Eugene Foyle had been requested by the pharmacist's mate of the fuel base to leave the ship and come ashore to aid him. Foyle returned to the ship later that night. He related to Greg and Larry Stapleton, skipper of the 460.5, the physical condition of Feldman, the autocratic base exec, when Mary D'Quino brought him into the infirmary, slung over her shoulders like a big bunch of island bananas. Greg remembered the first version of how the accident happened as told by Mary D'Quino to Lt. Commander Ralph Farqua, the refueling base CO. She had told her story in the presence of Foyle. Among other things Foyle related, "She said the ram goats of the island flock must have attacked him when no one was in sight." But, Greg knew differently, knew it was a lie, because earlier in the day he had received a message from ashore saying that his friend, Jacques, the chieftain's son, requested that he come ashore immediately and meet Jacques at the base gate. Greg, not on watch, had done so. Jacques was in his father's yellow jeep. He appeared quite nervous. He asked Greg to get in the carrier. Immediately, they took off and raced up a rough trail. Jacques never said a word as Greg held on to the grab bar and wondered what the hell was happening. Jacques stopped the jeep behind a large clump of low Palmettos. He got out, put a finger to his lips, then beckoned for Greg to follow him. Jacques stopped walking and quietly pulled back a palm frond. They were at the MASH site. He and Jacques then saw the entire, bizarre episode from their position behind the Palmetto clump, not more than two hundred feet from a partially dismantled Quonset hut. And, the event happened with lightning swiftness. Greg had seen Feldman, the base exec, several times from a distance, but never met him formally. When Feldman drove up in the base jeep, Mary was supervising the dismantling of the MASH unit. The workers, upon seeing Feldman, vanished, seemingly swallowed by the ground. Yet every Palmetto clump within a hundred yards of the Quonset hut appeared to be growing glaring black eyes. As soon as the jeep stopped, Mary, with coiffure and clothing almost identical to her stage appearance, climbed into the passenger seat and started to embrace the startled officer. The duo struggled, rolled out of the jeep onto the ground. Feldman banged his head hard against the left front wheel as he strove to break the Amazon's grasp. With one hand, Mary succeeded in grabbing Feldman by his testicles. She squeezed with such tenacious ferocity that the redheaded Lieutenant howled, then went limp from excruciating pain, and lapsed into unconsciousness. She proceeded to rake him from head to foot with the fingernails of her free hand, almost tearing Feldman's clothes to shreds. Greg felt revulsion at what he witnessed. Jacques appeared stunned and embarrassed. As soon as the episode was over, Jacques, without a word, had immediately driven Greg back to the base. With the briefest of goodbyes, Greg left the yellow jeep and headed back to his ship. He was disgusted and upset with his friend. Why hadn't Jacques intervened?

Greg remembered he was even more perturbed as Foyle described, at the base infirmary, how time and again Feldman would regain consciousness, look up, and see nurse Mary D'Quino standing over him. According to Foyle, Ben, upon seeing Mary, would immediately become hysterical, roll into a fetal position and lapse into unconsciousness.

9

Greg also remembered that early the next morning, while he was standing on the main deck of his ship, he saw a PB4Y land in the water beyond the inlet coral reefs. The small gray base tender, with several personnel on board, hastened out of the harbor to meet the plane. Lt. Feldman, strapped in a body basket, was transferred from the tender to the flying boat. The Navy air ambulance then flew off into the sunrise. That morning, the whole end of the island, almost surrounding the lagoon where the 460.5 was anchored, seemed to relax.

10

God, how well he remembered the final scene. That same day, shortly before his ship refueled and prepared to leave the harbor, he received an urgent message from the base to meet Jacques at the base gate as soon as possible. Greg initially decided not to go, but then changed his mind. When he arrived ashore and went to the gate, there was his friend in the driver's seat of the yellow jeep. Mary D'Quino was in the passenger seat.

That's when the regal female told him she committed the act to prevent further deterioration of relationships between the islanders and the Navy. The request for the interdiction had been made to her by the island elders, and she whole-heartedly agreed to be the instigator. She told Greg that he, unwittingly, had been made a witness by Jacques so that Commander Farqua could be cleared of any implication if there was a Naval investigation. She said Farqua had no knowledge that the episode would occur. And, Mary D'Quino, seated in the jeep, told Greg she later had gone to Farqua and spoke the truth about the entire happening. Greg was surprised at Mary's calm candor and bravery. He remembered Jacques' quiet gesture of apology for having him as an unwitting witness to the taboo. Jacques got out of the jeep and gave Greg a little box wrapped in French linen, requesting that he not open the box until Greg's ship was at least ten miles at sea. He kissed Greg on both cheeks, re-entered the jeep and drove off. Later that day at sea, when Greg took the linen wrapper off, there was an exquisite, small, silver box. He opened the hinged lid. On top of cotton was a card: "For you and your lady. Remember the Isle of Everyman. Your friend, Jacques." Underneath the card, nestling in the cotton, were the distinctively designed and beautifully crafted beaten-silver earrings and matching cufflinks, each with a dark blue cat's-eye stone in the center. Greg did not know that the earrings and cufflinks were among the prized possessions of Jacques' parents. At their insistence, the gifts came through Jacques to Greg because of what the chieftain knew about the taboo and could not then reveal, even to Jacques.   The gifts were Jacques' parents' attempt at atonement.

11

Greg, still seated, recalled that a couple of days before the tragic performance, Stapleton had, as a matter of courtesy, invited Farqua to have dinner aboard ship. The base CO accepted with such gusto and quickness that Greg and Larry were truly curious as to the reason for such a speedy response. That night, at the wardroom table, after Farqua had downed a couple of jiggers of brandy and relaxed, he told how he had lost his former exec as the result of a serious refueling accident. And, "Shortly thereafter, that arrogant, son-of-a-bitch-trade-school-lieutenant, Feldman, reported for duty as my new exec. That bastard has, in no time, completely disrupted the relationship between the islanders and my little refueling base. The natives are fuming at my new second in command. His obnoxious manner in dealing with the Polynesians, particularly those who work dismantling the former MASH unit, has incensed them. But, despite my pleas, I am unable to get him to listen to reason concerning his dealings with the island workers. God knows what's gonna' happen."

Greg sighed. The apparently gentle Polynesians had endeavored to solve the problem by "Taboo," a Polynesian ritual performed in numerous ways, whereby, among other results, a person may be set apart, ostracized, demeaned in the extreme. Greg believed Feldman had suffered much more than just being ostracized.

12

Will Barton arose from his seat. He looked at Greg. "Man, you're white as a sheet. Have you seen a ghost?"

Greg looked up at his rotund-featured host, "Would you believe not just one -- but several?" he replied.

"From a dance recital?" asked Will.

"You've got no idea what was behind that last dance," said Greg. "I do. I'll tell you about it someday."

Caroline Morgan was standing. "Hon, let's get a drink in the lobby," she said as she held out her hand to her husband.

Greg smiled, took her hand and headed for the aisle. As they stepped onto the ramp heading to the theater lobby, Caroline slipped an arm under her husband's arm and eased close to him. "I know you never expected to see that dance and neither did I. I can only imagine its impact on you. I know the events as a story told by you. Just watching that performance gave me the shivers." She shuddered.

"That episode happened a long time ago," said Greg soberly.

13

When they reached the lobby, Greg stopped, pulled out his wallet, and took from it one of his business cards. He commented to his wife, "I'm gonna' send a note backstage to Jacques. Maybe we can see him and Mary D'Quino after the show."

"Oh, Greg, that would be exciting. I'd love to go backstage and meet Jacques and his wife," replied Caroline. As she stood and observed her slim, wiry husband, she could tell from the flash of those black eyes and the slight tension of his jaws, something was truly disturbing him.

Greg turned the card to the blank side, placed it on his wallet and wrote: "Dear Jacques, I would like for you and Mary to meet with my wife and me after the show. Can that be done? Your friend, Greg Morgan." He went up to a nearby usherette. "Miss, would you please deliver this card to Mr. Jacques Montagne, he's the ensemble manager. I think he is backstage. Tell him I'd like for him to give you an answer. I'll wait here until intermission is over. If you get the answer after intermission, I'm in H row orchestra, seat eleven. And, here's five bucks for your effort."

The young lady grinned, "I've met Mr. Montagne. He's a lovely gentleman. Sure, I'll be glad to deliver your note to him. He is backstage tonight. I'll get you his answer pronto." With that, the usherette walked briskly down a side aisle. Greg watched her until she opened a door at the lower end and disappeared.

14

Caroline said, "Greg, you stay here and wait for an answer to your note. I'll get us a couple cups of orange juice and be right back."

Greg grinned acquiescence, but he was troubled. More than once after the war he had wondered if, at their meeting, Mary had told the truth as to the cause of the taboo episode. He wondered if Farqua's verbalization about Feldman masked some other reason for his apparent dislike of the red-headed lieutenant. Could the whole scene have been concocted to hide an evil operation, a set of circumstances the principal players in the taboo, including Jacques, did not want known. If so, Greg realized he had really been taken in, because he initially believed what he had been told by Mary. And, Greg wondered why had Mary D'Quino given up her nursing career? What had happened to Jacques' first wife? How long had Mary D'Quino and Jacques been married? He remembered that Mary was graceful. He was struck by her bearing the first time he had seen her directing the dismantling of the MASH unit buildings in the coconut grove on the island. But, where and when had she mastered the art of dancing? Even his untrained eye could tell she was an accomplished ballerina. What had happened to Mary as a result of her disclosure to Commander Farqua? What had happened to Farqua? What had been the lives of Jacques and Mary since the war? Had Feldman recovered?

Greg's adrenalin was flowing, partially in anticipation of the answers to those questions, but primarily from a deep gnawing sense of guilt for never having made an attempt, after the war, to determine the true consequences of the bizarre episode he had witnessed on Bora Bora (The Isle of Everyman). Time and again, the events had troubled him, but his preoccupation with the future had all but blocked out that past. Now that past was present.

15

Caroline returned with two plastic cups. She offered one to her husband. "Try a sip of this 'Florida Gold.' It'll help calm your nerves."

"Thank's, Hon. I hope you are right. But, I just have a feeling of foreboding -- warning -- call it what you will."

"You and your intuitive sixth sense have gotten us in a pack of trouble before," said Caroline.

"And out," replied Greg with a sly grin.

"OK, and out," quipped Caroline. She wondered just what in the name of God was her husband considering. She thought, whatever it is, please drop it. For a while, just let me lead the life as wife of an up-and-coming young lawyer. That's screwy enough. Caroline's brown eyes met Greg's and held them long enough for her to realize there was no way she could prevent his going forward with whatever plan he was formulating. True, he would tell her soon. But, that wouldn't be enough this time. She had on the earrings that resulted from an emotional, wild episode, maybe a continuing one. She was intrigued. This time she wanted to be a part of whatever was going to happen.

16

The lobby lights dimmed, signaling the audience that the second act would start in three minutes. Greg and Caroline met up with the Bartons in the lobby and headed toward their seats. Frances and Will entered the row. Just as Greg was preparing to do so, he felt a tap on his shoulder. There beside him was the usherette. She smiled at Greg. "Sir, here are the replies to your card," and she handed him two small folded sheets of white paper.

"Thanks so much," said Greg as he took the notes, and slid passed the theater goers already seated.

Caroline, standing in the aisle, waiting for Greg to enter the row, saw the exchange. Once they were seated, she turned to her husband, "What's Jacques' reply? I'm anxious to know."

Greg unfolded one of the notes, took the flashlight from his pocket, and directed its beam on the paper. He and Caroline read:

Dear Greg,

I am delighted that you and your wife are in the audience. I was sure it was her when I saw a beautiful young woman wearing my family crest earrings earlier in the evening at the Willard Hotel. They are the only set to have ever left the island. But, before I could introduce myself, I was interrupted on a matter of business. When I was able to look again, she was gone. I did not see you.

Show this note to Mark Tuft, doorman inside left aisle stage area entrance door. He has been instructed to escort you and your wife to my office. See you soon.

Your friend,
Jacques

"I'll be darned, so that's who he is," said Caroline. Greg eyed her curiously. "I'll tell you later, Hon," and then she added, "I've often wondered about the design on the gifts from Jacques." She hesitated, then said, "It'll be exciting to go backstage again."

Greg grinned in response.

"Who's the other note from?" she asked as Greg unfolded the second small white sheet.

They read:

Dear Greg,

I read your note to Jacques. He does not know I have written a separate response. I have taken your office phone number from the card, and will call you at 9:00 a.m. tomorrow. Trouble dances with the troupe. Jacques is so naive. He does not recognize how unstable, how degenerating, trouble may be.

I need your help. If something odd, untimely, should happen to me during our stay in D.C., or later, tear the Lit'l Trouper apart.

Hurriedly,
Mary D'Quino Montagne
P.S. Do not mention this to Jacques when we see you and your wife after the show.

"What in the world does she mean, Greg?"
"I have no idea at this moment," responded Greg.
The house lights dimmed.

17

Caroline nervously twisted her shoulders a bit as she and Greg watched the first dance after intermission, "To the God of the Waters." The music was a rolling, ancient, Polynesian sea song. The costumes were ocean blue in color. The dancers with the two leads in the center, were in line rhythmically bowing, emulating the rise and fall of waves. Caroline picked up her opera glasses to get a good look at the troupe. The female dancer next to Mary D'Quino caught her attention. The young ballerina was not as tall as Mary, but in Caroline's opinion, the dancer exhibited a grace and dance mastery equal to that of the female lead. There was just that little indefinable attitude of her entire body that caused Caroline to train her glasses on the face of the young ensemble dancer, and then on the male lead dancer to the immediate right of Mary. Greg's wife leaned over and whispered in his ear, "What in the world is wrong with Mary D'Quino?"

Greg looked at Caroline in surprise. "Why do you ask?"

"I sense revulsion on the face of the dancer on either side of Mary when they look at her, as if Mary has offensive B.O."

"Let me take a quick look."

As Caroline passed the glasses to Greg, the line broke up and spun off into pairs. Greg focused on the young female dancer. He observed no such expression. She had the typical pasted smile of a dancer concentrating on a difficult routine. He did notice a small mole on the left side of her neck. "Damned if I see anything unusual," said Greg as he handed the glasses back to his wife.

"Wait until the next time they're in line," said Caroline as she placed the viewers in her lap. The number ended.

18

Greg became increasingly apprehensive as he viewed a smooth quick change of scene, "Homage to the Volcano God." The music was offbeat and loud, and there, in the stage background, was the extinct volcano on the north side of Bora Bora. Greenery reached almost to the top. The low mountain appeared like a mound of dark pistachio ice cream with chocolate sauce on top. The male lead, in a flaming red leotard, leaped onto stage from the right wing. From his hands hung long, thin, red and orange streamers. He began to whirl them in a rhythmic, artistic manner depicting the eruption of the volcano -- himself. From the left wing, Mary D'Quino seemed to flow on stage in an island green, trailing gown. She had part of the train gathered in her right hand. She was the green growth of the island supplicating the volcano to calm down. As Greg watched her, he noticed a hitch in Mary's step, to him completely out of character with her usual fluid motion, and certainly not a part of the routine. He reached and took the opera glasses from his wife's lap. His first focus was on Alberto DeFrances, the lead male dancer. He saw fear and bewilderment in the eyes of the muscular Polynesian. Then he focused on Mary D'Quino. She was perspiring excessively. The neckline of her gown and the area under each arm pit and from there down each side of her dress was being stained a much darker green. Her face was not only dripping perspiration, but her jaws were clenched and the muscles of her neck stood out as if she was struggling to control her body. Her eyes were two black orbs evidencing excruciating pain and stark terror. Though her teeth were clenched, her lips were open. She was gasping for air.

Greg leaned to his right and spoke softly to Will Barton, "Will, please take Caroline home when you and Frances leave. I've got a feeling that the second unpleasant act of *Taboo* is about to begin, and I've got to get backstage. A couple friends of mine are there."

Will looked incredulously at Greg, "Sure, Greg, anything you say. But how do you know something is going to happen?"

"Watch," said Greg. He then turned to Caroline, handing her the glasses and whispered in her ear, "That old sixth sense has kicked in. I'm sure that all hell's gonna' break loose in a couple of minutes. I've got to reach Jacques. The Bartons will take you home. I'll call as soon as I can."

Even without the glasses, Caroline could tell something was out of kilter on stage. "Greg," she replied gently, but positively, "Not this time. I'm a big girl now. The war is over. These are my earrings. Jacques invited both of us backstage. I want to be a part of whatever happens."

Greg gave his wife a scowl and shook his head. He didn't want to get in a verbal hassle with her in the middle of the National Theater.

"I'll see you later, Frances. But, don't wait for us if we're not back when the show's over," said Caroline as she put her opera glasses in her bag and slid out of her seat to the aisle. She was followed by Greg. The Bartons cast bewildered looks at their two guests. Several playgoers seated in nearby seats turned and watched the duo hasten up center aisle toward the lobby.

19

Caroline let an irritated Greg take the lead. As they were walking rapidly down the left side aisle toward the stage area entrance door, she caught up with her husband; her dander was up also, "Just this one time, Greg. I won't get in the way. And, I do know something about theater backstage. I've been there before. Maybe I can be of some help."

Greg's anger cooled as he listened. He admired her interest. He knew it was genuine, even if she couldn't help, but he was concerned for her if there was real trouble. "OK." He hesitated, "I'm sure from watching Mary that something's made her ill, just how ill we'll soon find out."

As Greg reached to open the backstage area door, he and Caroline heard a moaning gasp flow through the audience -- silence -- and then a swish as the stage pull curtains raced shut. The door closed behind the duo and they saw Mark Tuft, guardian of the stage area door, in a straight chair that was tilted back against the corridor wall. His fedora was pulled over his face. He was sleeping soundly. Greg went up and patted him on his shoulder. The aging, ex-club, welterweight, with his flattened, bourbon nose, came awake with a start. His hat fell to the floor. "The show ain't over," he growled as his bleary, beady, blue-green eyes tried to focus.

"One never knows," said Greg. "Where's Jacques' office? We've got to see him now. It's urgent." Greg showed him Jacques' note.

"I already know about it," said Mark, as he wiped a drool of tobacco juice from his chin with his scarred right hand, and spat a thin stream of juice into a small spittoon on the floor by the chair. He reached down, recovered his hat, looked at Greg and said, "Come on, I'll show you." The two front legs of the chair hit the terrazzo corridor floor with a resounding swak!

20

The trio headed down a dimly lit corridor and almost collided with a stage hand and a wild-eyed tuxedo-dressed Jacques as those two were racing the corridor to the right side stage entrance. Jacques passed Greg, started up the three steps to the wing area, did a double take, looked back over his shoulder and shouted, "My God, Greg, it really is you. Mary has fainted on stage."

Mark Tuft left. Greg and Caroline followed Jacques up the three steps and entered the wing area with the hot, brilliant, overhead Kleig lights beaming down. Greg's nose was tickled by the smell of heated, freshly-painted scenery, mixed with the pungent scent of perfumes and body sweat from the dance troupe. Caroline gave a little cough.

The stage was bare except for three figures. On center stage was the crumpled green-draped figure of Mary D'Quino. Kneeling beside her was a deeply concerned Alberto DeFrances, the lead male dancer. Kneeling on the other side of the unconscious, but convulsive, Mary D'Quino was the young female dancer Caroline had seen in the line dance -- the one who had constantly glanced at the star ballerina. The young dancer was gently stroking Mary's head.

Greg walked on stage and dropped to his knees by the side of the fallen dancer. He saw her convulsive movements and the froth sliding from her mouth down her right cheek to the floor. He looked up and yelled, "Caroline, find a phone and call for an ambulance."

A stage hand in the right wing saw the words were addressed to the stunning woman in a blue evening dress standing nervously by his side. He looked at Caroline and said, "Follow me, lady. The nearest phone is in Mary D'Quino's dressing room."

Kneeling by his wife's side, Jacques stared in utter disbelief at what he was seeing. He moaned, "Mary, Mother of Jesus, Mother of Jesus, what is happening?" He was momentarily in such shock at the horror he was witnessing, that all comprehension and color had drained from his normally coppertoned body. He appeared to Greg to be a yellow grayish waif, lost thousands of miles from home.

"Is there a couch anywhere near?" asked Greg.

"There's one in my office," mumbled Jacques.

"Let's get her there quickly," said Greg. "Help us please," he said to another male dancer who was now standing by the fallen figure. The four men carefully lifted Mary from the floor and that was no mean feat because of her continuing convulsions. As they were lifting her, Greg saw a slender Polynesian, also in a tux, enter the stage. Jacques recognized him and in an attempt at control said in a husky voice, "Maurice, tell the audience that Mary has become ill. There will be a brief intermission. The show will continue with Linguette in the role of lead female dancer. Take over for me, *s'il-vous-plait*?"

Maurice nodded acceptance and left the stage to assume his duties.

"Holy Mother of Jesus, how could this happen?" sobbed Jacques, holding Mary's head, and leading the way to his office.

Most of the female dancers, gathered on the far side of the stage, were weeping openly. As Greg was leaving the stage, helping to carry Mary, he glanced over his shoulder and saw the female dancer who had been at fallen Mary's side approach the shocked group and appear to be talking to them in a calming and authoritative manner. She seems to be quite a leader, he thought.

21

The stage hand led Caroline to Mary's dressing room then left. Caroline entered the small, brilliantly lit room without at first noticing any of its contents. She was concentrating on finding the phone. She saw it on the marred, dingy, white dressing table. She sat on the flimsy table bench, picked up the receiver, dialed "O," and heard the other phone ring twice. A southern female voice drawled, "Operator."

"Operator, this is Caroline Morgan backstage at the National Theater. One of the members of the dance troupe has become seriously ill. Will you please send an ambulance to take her to a hospital?"

"Which hospital?" asked the Operator.

"George Washington," said Caroline without hesitation.

"Which entrance?"

"What?" exploded Caroline, her temper beginning to rise.

"Which entrance of the theater shall the ambulance come to?"

"I don't give a damn if it comes through the roof, just get here quickly," yelled Caroline over the phone. There was silence on the other end. Caroline realized she'd been unduly sharp and now spoke evenly. "Please have the ambulance come to the front of the theater. Someone will be there to direct the emergency personnel backstage."

"Thank you, Ma'am. The ambulance has been ordered. Bye."

22

Caroline tried to calm her nerves. Greg had warned her. Now she was beginning to understand why.

Did she really want to be a part of this? Did she really have the stomach for such happenings? This wasn't like PTA or a Sunday school teachers meeting or even an amateur theater production. This was backstage, the backside of the closed curtain of life she had never seen before. Greg had been her shield from much of it. She was truly grateful. Now she was in this episode. She had insisted. What else could she do to help? She sighed. She quickly gazed around the room and saw that it was small and plain, hadn't been painted in years. The once white walls were a dusty gray. On one side of the room was a pole that stretched from wall to wall. It was almost filled with costume changes on hangers. Mary's? There was one dilapidated boudoir chair, pale blue. There was a single faucet, white, porcelain sink set into the dressing table. The dressing table top was covered with various jars of makeup, cold cream for removal, shades of powder, powder brushes, various colored lipsticks, a large comb, a set of hair brushes, and a box of facial tissue. Also on the dressing table top, next to the sink, was a large iced tea glass with about an inch of what, at first, appeared to be orange juice. There were lipstick marks on the top of the glass. Next to the glass was a half-filled bottle of Orange Crush with a cork stuck in the top.

She couldn't help but think: This might have been my life, if I was lucky; a dingy dressing room like this, here, or anywhere, and night after night stage calls, sweaty performances under glaring lights, brief applause, lonely hotel rooms, maybe a friend here or there, occasional visits home, wondering about reviews, competition, unending competition, to constantly, creatively portray roles and yet retain a healthy perspective on real life and living. My, God, how tough, how dedicated good performers have to be. For me, or most of me, I made the right choice years ago. But, a little of me still tingles at the sight of a stage.

She rebounded to the present. Her excitement had left her throat parched. Before she reported back to Greg she just had to have a quick drink of water. She looked for a fresh drinking glass but all she saw was the tall glass with the remnants of the orange drink. She took the cork from the Orange Crush bottle and poured the remaining contents of the glass into the bottle. She noticed she had spilled a few drops on the dressing table top. Then, she washed the glass with the tap water from the sink, reached over, took tissue from the box and wiped the glass, removing the lipstick smears from the rim. Hurriedly, she wiped the spilled drops of the orange drink from the dressing table top, balled up the used tissue and stuck them in her evening bag. She would dispose of the soiled tissue later. Caroline filled the glass with tap water and drank two long thirst-quenching gulps. She sighed in satisfaction, then heard someone enter the room. She rose, with the glass in her left hand, turned, and was face to face with the young dancer she had observed through her opera glasses. There was a look of genuine surprise in the eyes of the ballerina.

Caroline held out her right hand. "I'm Caroline Morgan. I just came in to make a hurry up call for an ambulance."

The young dancer momentarily stood in the doorway as if rooted, regained her presence of mind, and shook Caroline's hand. A slight smile lit her face. "My name is Linguette. I am Mary's understudy. I have to rush a change. We have duplicate costumes on the rack in here, in case I have to fill in for her. Excusez-moi while I change. The curtain will go up in five minutes." The young dancer walked over to the hanger-draped pole, took down a green costume and placed it across the boudoir chair.

As she approached the dressing table, she looked at the glass in Caroline's hand and then at Caroline. Caroline saw the look and said casually, "I was thirsty. I just had to wet my whistle. The water tasted so good." She continued, "I'm going. I've got to find my husband and Jacques and tell them the ambulance is on its way."

"Sure, sure," said the young dancer as she started to disrobe. She stopped, looked seriously at Caroline. "What in the name of the Holy Mother has happened to Mary?"

"I wish I knew," said Caroline. She replaced the glass on the dressing table, left the room, and headed down the corridor in search of Greg and Jacques.

23

A young grip was walking toward her. "Have you seen Mr. Montagne or his wife?" asked Caroline.

"Yes, Ma'am. They just carried Mary D'Quino into her husband's office. It's the third door on the left after you turn the corner. She's a mighty sick lady."

"Thank you," said Caroline and she hastened her step.

When she reached the office, she knocked on the closed door. A bewildered Jacques opened it. "The rescue ambulance is on the way. It's coming to the front entrance," blurted Caroline.

Jacques reached to his desk, picked up the phone and dialed two digits. Caroline heard someone respond, " Box Office."

Jacques spoke excitedly. "Belinda, when the docteurs arrive, have someone direct them to my office. Make sure they bring a stretcher." He hung up.

Caroline entered the room. Her husband was kneeling by the couch. He was gently wiping the face and forehead of the stricken dancer with a small wet towel. Mary D'Quino Montagne was stretched out on the couch, lying on her side, and facing the door. Though she made no sound, her body shook and convulsed. Caroline's knees buckled just a little when she realized Greg was continually washing away droplets of saliva and blood that trickled from the dancer's lips.

"For God's sake, can they not hurry," moaned Jacques.

"Thanks, Hon." Without turning his head Greg added, "Caroline see if you can find a coat, a blanket, anything that we can throw over Mary. Her convulsions are being made worse by chills. God knows what's happened. I've never seen anyone in her condition."

Caroline put her evening bag on Jacques' desk, looked around the office, and saw nothing. Then she remembered the costumes on the rack in Mary's dressing room. "Greg, I'll be right back," and she raced down the corridor to the star's dressing room. No one was there when she entered. She went to the rack, grabbed several costumes off the rack, glanced at the dressing table as she left, and hurried to Jacques' office. As she approached the office door, there was Mark Tuft fending off a man and a woman in street clothes. She heard him say, "I don't give a shit if you were in the audience and are reviewers from the *Post*, you can't go in there now."

"But, we have a right to know what has happened to Mary D'Quino," said the demanding woman reporter. "We have. . ."

"In a pig's ass you do," interrupted the bristling ex-pug. Not only did he bar the door, but he grabbed each reporter by an arm and, despite his small size, rapidly propelled the two news representatives down the corridor toward an exit door.

Caroline quickly entered Jacques' office. Greg took the costumes and spread them over the increasingly pale Mary D'Quino.

24

Greg looked pensively at his Polynesian friend. He took another business card from his wallet, turned it to the blank side, wrote out his home phone number, and handing the card to Jacques said, "My home phone number is on the back. When the ambulance arrives, go with Mary to the hospital. As soon as you know her condition, give me a call. I don't care how late it is."

"Oh, thank God you were here tonight, Greg. Of course, I will call." Jacques took the card.

"Where are you staying?" asked Greg.

"The troupe is staying at the Harrington Hotel, just a couple blocks from the theater. Mary and I have a small, but comfortable, suite there, Room 502."

25

Mary's condition had bothered Greg from the moment he had seen her struggling for control on the stage. When he knelt on the stage floor beside the fallen dancer, his observations of Mary really triggered a warning. The so-called "ferret instinct," attributed to him during WWII by Colonel Washburn, his relative by marriage, surfaced.

Greg looked up at his distraught island friend, "Has Mary ever had any other spells like this one?"

"Never, Greg. She has constantly enjoyed good health and takes no regular medications. She has used her medical knowledge to help maintain her vitality and youthfulness. You have seen evidence of her strength, even tonight. All during her nursing career, before and after the war, she maintained a regime of physical exercise, including her ballet workouts. Why do you ask?"

"I'm just curious," said Greg. He was silent for a few seconds. "Does she have any enemies? Some one or more who truly dislike her? Would do her harm?"

Jacques looked disconsolately at his stateside friend, "Greg, Mary is a woman among women on our island. She has been a dominant figure, a true leader. I am sure there are some islanders who are glad she is on tour, but none I know of who would seek to harm her." He hesitated, "There is the episode you know about, Lieutenant Feldman and Commander Farqua."

"What about Feldman and what about Farqua?" interrupted Greg.

"Well, there was an investigation."

"When?" asked Greg.

"Shortly after the war ended and. . ."

26

There was a sharp knock on the door. Caroline, who had been standing near the door, listening intently, reached out and opened it. Two emergency specialists entered the room and unfolded a gurney. The blonde, heavyset one walked over to the couch, knelt and felt for Mary's pulse. He took the stethoscope from around his neck, placed the listening device on the side of her neck. He next listened to her heart, and observed the blood-tinged saliva still trickling from her mouth.

"Billy, rig me an IV now," said the attendant. Billy opened a medical box, pulled out an IV bottle and tube. He quickly attached an extension rod to the gurney. The thin black man knew his stuff and Mary soon was receiving fluid from the IV.

"She's not in the best shape," said the blond to Greg and Jacques. "Help Billy and me get her on the stretcher. But be careful. She's fibrillating wildly. Billy, when we reach the rig, radio the G.W. emergency room and have the trauma team stand by."

Jacques had noticed the name plate on the jacket pocket of the blond spokesman. "Warren, I am Jacques Montagne, husband of your emergency patient. I would like to ride with her to the hospital, *s'il- vous-plait?*"

"Sure, sure, Mr. Montagne. I don't blame you for wanting to ride with her. Ordinarily I would say no. But, tonight we're a man short. Billy may need your help on the way. As soon as we tie her down, let's get rolling."

27

Caroline was watching as the four men lifted Mary from the couch onto the stretcher. The dancer had never opened her eyes. The little droplets of blood continued to form at the corners of her mouth. The stress of what had occurred and the sight of the pathetic dancer, as she was lifted limp onto the stretcher, made Caroline nauseous. She leaned heavily against the desk.

Greg saw her movement, saw that she was pale and struggling to keep from blacking out. As the two emergency crew wheeled the loaded gurney from the room, followed by Jacques, Greg walked over to his wife and helped her to the sofa just vacated by Mary. "Hon, sit down, lower your head between your knees." Greg joined her on the couch, a little shaken himself.

"You gotta' be kidding!" mumbled Caroline.

"No, I'm not kidding. Do as I say before you really do pass out."

"OK, OK, Mister Hot Shot," feebly responded his wife as she drew up her evening gown, spraddled her legs and lowered her head. She gagged once or twice.

"Breathe deeply," said Greg.

Within a minute or two she raised her head, looked up at her husband, and quietly asked, "Where in the hell did you learn that trick? In a courtroom?"

"Naw, the Navy," said her grinning husband. "Do you feel better now?"

"Much, much better. Thanks."

Caroline straightened her dress, patted her hairdo and sighed. "Greg, this has been a night. I'll never forget, never."

"I'm sorry you got caught up in this mess," said Greg, as he looked at his wife with concern.

"I asked to be. I'm not sorry. I only hope that Mary is going to be OK."

"Don't bank on that."

"What do you mean?"

"Caroline, when I first knelt by Mary to try to help, I was reminded of your remark when you saw her dancing in line."

"What remark?"

"When you said that the dancers next to Mary had odd looks on their faces when they looked at her."

"So?" questioned Caroline.

"I don't blame them. When I knelt by Mary, one of the most weird, nauseating odors I have ever smelled oozed from every pore of her body -- worse than when someone runs over a squashed skunk on the highway. I think she's been poisoned."

"You don't really mean that, do you?" Caroline's eyes were wide with surprise.

"Hell, I'm not positive. But remember Jacques said Mary was in good health, didn't suffer from physical episodes of any kind. There, on the stage she really reeked, was unconscious, and in convulsions. Something odd had to have happened."

Caroline looked beseechingly at her husband. "Greg, let's get out of here before I get sick again."

"You're right, Dear. We've had enough for one night. Jacques will call us when he knows something."

28

Caroline picked up her evening bag from the desk, made sure the clasp was tight, then arm in arm she and Greg left the office and headed for the front entrance. The ensemble was still performing, but it held no fascination for the Morgans. For them, the show was over. Exhausted from their tension and efforts, they hailed a cab.

29

"My, God, how good it is to get home," said Caroline as Greg unlocked the front door and held it open for her.

"This has been a weird night,"said Greg.

Caroline turned up a table lamp, and crossed the living room to the antique Maple low-boy-on-stand. She opened the middle drawer and dropped her evening bag into it. The drawer held her pocket books and bags for all occasions; shopping, bridge, evening and everyday doings. Bags were her major idiosyncracy. She had plenty of them. At one time in the past, it had been hats, but hats were out. Now it was bags.

As the couple undressed for bed, Caroline asked Greg, "Who would want to poison Mary, and why?"

"You heard what Jacques said. She was a woman among women on the island. Maybe someone there had it in for her. Maybe Feldman, maybe Farqua. Maybe Linguette, the dancer on Mary's right. Maybe even Jacques. Who knows? And, who knows why?"

"Oh, I don't think it was Linguette or Jacques. They were too distraught," reflected a somber Caroline.

30

When she finished putting on her white silk PJs, she said, "Greg, when you check the house, please get me a fruiter of milk and a couple of grahams to sooth my nerves before I try to sleep."

"Sure," said Greg as he pulled on his robe and headed for the kitchen. While he was there, the phone rang. Caroline picked up the extension on the bedside table. A quiet, sober voice asked, "Is this the Morgan residence?"

"Yes, this is Mrs. Morgan speaking," and Caroline heard the click on the phone as her husband picked up the extension in the kitchen.

"Mrs. Morgan, this is Jacques. Get Greg on the line for me please."

"I'm on the line, the kitchen extension. How goes it, Jacques?"

There was momentary silence on the other end, a moan, followed by, "Mary is gone. She died moments ago."

The stunned couple heard Jacques' soft weeping.

"What should I do? A representative from the D.C. Coroners Office is here. The hospital and the coroner want an autopsy. Oh, Christ, an autopsy on that lovely body. What should I do?"

Caroline whispered, "Oh, no."

Greg said, "God, how tragic." After a brief period of silence, he continued, "Because of the way Mary died, the authorities have a right to an autopsy. If you don't agree, they can get a court order for it. I suggest you consent to the request. If you have nothing to hide, the procedure may help reveal some answers you would want to know."

"I guess you are right," said Jacques. "I will do it as soon as I hang up."

"Jacques, get the emergency room doctor to give you a sleeping pill. You've done all you can do tonight. Go to the hotel and try to get some rest. I'll pick you up at the hotel entrance at exactly 9:30 a.m. tomorrow morning. And, Jacques, don't speak to a soul about tonight until after we talk. Not a soul, do you understand me?"

"You have my word. Thank you for all your help, goodnight," and the shocked, saddened, weary husband of Mary D'Quino hung up.

31

When he entered the room, Caroline was sitting on the bed, her arms were wrapped around her drawn legs and her chin was resting on her knees. Her hair was in pink rollers and her youthful face was taught with nervous fatigue. She appeared to Greg as a new pink haloed angel who had just escorted her first arisen to the Pearly Gates. She had gotten through the procedure, but God alone knew how.

Greg handed Caroline the small glass of warm milk. She sipped silently, then nibbled a graham cracker. After a minute or so he said, "Caroline, you did well tonight."

She stopped sipping, "Only because you were there. Greg, I had no idea what to do. But, you do get involved in the damnedest messes."

"And now you're in this one," said Greg with a faint smile.

" I know," she said quietly.

Caroline finished her milk and cookies and turned out the bedside light. The couple pulled up the covers and settled into their king-sized bed. Greg was lying on his right side. Caroline, lying on her right side in front of Greg, backed up against his chest, and ran her left hand down his left arm until her fingers intertwined his. She drew his arm across her body, placed his hand on her breast, and then put her hand on top of his. She softly said, "My, your thermostat is always set on such a lovely temperature, your body just radiates a calming warmness."

Greg gently kissed the nape of his wife's neck.

Caroline wriggled a little closer to Greg.

32

Outside the open bedroom window, in a little thicket of yews, a ground-nesting bird inched closer to her mate. He softly chirped, "Poor-Will, Poor-Will." The night lament wafted gently over the Morgans' open bedroom window sill. Caroline heard and drowsily whispered her reply, "Poor Jacques, poor Jacques." Then, except for the occasional sigh of the night breeze and the rustle of falling oak leaves, all was silent and soon the Morgans were asleep -- in troubled sleep.

Part II

What About Feldman?

1

He knew that the eight-year-old hated the name "Izzy" ever since Izzy's sister, Rebecca, had so nicknamed him. He saw Izzy on a hot Sunday morning in July, playing in a park. Most of the Gentiles were at church or Sunday school. Sixteen-year-old Rebecca was doing the sitting chore, and only because she could surreptitiously sit on a park bench with Ivan Bososcov. Ivan was two years her elder and the one person she had been forbidden by her family to see. Her mother (what was her name?) had caught the two in early throws of sexual experimentation three weeks before. Caught them on the back seat of her dad's four-door Cadillac convertible, in the steamy double garage. Rebecca's mother was bringing some old newspapers into the tin-roofed shed to add to the stack neatly piled in a corner. Periodically, she would take the accumulated stock to a scrap house and negotiate a sale. She was a frugal woman for all her husband's affluence. She would never outgrow the instincts instilled in her by her struggling parents who had immigrated from Poland. Just as she stepped quietly through the open side door to take the papers to her neat pile, she heard heavy breathing and giggles. She went over to the auto and discovered her daughter on the back seat, with no bra and her blouse pulled up to her neck. Young Ivan was excitedly nuzzling the nipple on one of the developing breasts of her willing young daughter. The discovery was a shock to all three; Rebecca went into hysterics, Ivan fled wildly, and Rebecca's mother was horrified and astonished to learn her daughter was maturing. She had seldom given a thought that Rebecca would pass through the same growth stages she had experienced what seemed like so long ago. Dutifully, she had told her husband about the episode. He had damned out his wife for being so lax. When Rebecca came downstairs for supper that night, her papa (what was his name?), without warning, had dealt his daughter a heavy backhand slap across her face, called her a Jewish slut and loudly forbade her from ever again seeing that young Russian bastard or he would kill them both. Rebecca had screamed, more in defiance than injury. Her mother had wept at her stupidity in telling her husband.

Now, he saw Rebecca on the bench easing up to Ivan as Izzy was running through the park with Janice Witherspoon, the seven-year-old blond Izzy had met there weeks before. Her nanny was sitting on another bench quietly crocheting. Jan had been the one little person who truly liked Izzy. She was Izzy's friend. He knew Izzy's feelings for Jan encompassed what should have been Izzy's feelings for his sister. But, Rebecca seemed so much like their papa. He also knew Izzy's feelings toward his father were tinged with fear and dislike. On that hot July morning, as he saw Izzy chase Jan around the English boxwoods, that gave off a wonderful pungent odor, the ground would seem to roll every now and then. Suddenly, Izzy tripped on a root and fell sprawling. He heard someone yelling, screaming in pain. Was it Jan? Was it Izzy? He opened his eyes.

2

"So, you finally decided to pay us a visit," said a smiling blond man dressed in white with a lightweight white coat over his clothing. He had an odd apparatus hanging around his neck.

Lieutenant Benjamin Feldman's eyes portrayed his feeling of absolute terror. "Where am I? Who are you?" he moaned.

The man standing over him smiled.

"Lieutenant Feldman, you are on board the hospital ship, *Southern Cross*. I am Commander Russell Williams, a Naval physician."

"You addressed me as Lieutenant Feldman?"

"Yes. You are Senior Lieutenant Benjamin I. Feldman, aren't you?"

"Lieutenant of what?" asked Feldman.

The doctor raised his eyebrows just a little. "The United States Navy."

Feldman's terror was not lessened. "You say you are a doctor and that this is a hospital ship?"

Doctor Williams sat on the edge of Feldman's bunk and began to study his patient. "That's right," he said.

"And, where are we going?"

"To the U.S., to the San Diego Naval Base," replied the doctor.

Feldman began to gasp for breath. All he could remember was seeing Izzy playing in the park with Jan. "I don't remember any Navy. Where do you say I am?"

"Take it easy, son. You've come through a rough episode. Your memory should come back soon."

Feldman tried to turn. He realized his arms were tied down by his sides. He felt two belts across his body, holding him snug in the bunk. Something was attached to his right arm. And a tube ran up from there to a clear bottle above his head. With that slight movement, a severe pain shot through his groin. He winced as he saw a lightning flash.

"My, God, what is all this about?" he shouted. Perspiration was rolling off his brow.

3

The doctor reached over. Ben felt a tingle in his left arm, then an encompassing warmth. Once again he saw Izzy in the park. This time with Izzy's mother. She was short and slim. She looked pretty. Her cheeks were aglow with color and her brown eyes beamed excitement and expectancy. Izzy became engrossed watching two gray squirrels chase each other 'round and 'round, up and down the trunk of a large oak tree across from where Izzy and his mother sat. She had brought with her two bagels and a small thermos of milk. She would share both with Izzy.

Izzy glanced at his mama and saw her peering toward the walkway that led to the park entrance. Izzy looked and there came Sven Olson, the tall, raw-boned, bald-headed, Swedish owner of the fish market that sold carp blessed by Rabbi Yeskovitz. Izzy's mother visited the market once a week, sometimes more, to buy carp.

He knew Izzy had noticed that his mother seemed more alive, pert, as she was about to make a trip to the fish market, or just after she made such a trip. At least until his mama later saw Izzy's papa.

Sven approached the bench. "Rebecca told me I would find you here. I decided not to wait for you to come to the market. I delivered the fish to your home."

"Mr. Olson, you are so kind. You didn't have to come here to tell me you delivered the fish." But, she knew he would.

"I know. But it's such a lovely day, I don't blame you for coming to the park. May I sit?"

Izzy saw his mother's face glow even brighter.

"Oh, that would be nice for a few minutes," said Izzy's mother as she shoved Izzy tighter against the bench arm to make room for the fishmonger.

Mr. Olson put his hand down as he sat. Izzy saw Olson's hand covered his mother's hand on the bench. He saw his mother inhale quickly.

"There are so few lovely days like this," said the tender-gruff voice of Sven.

"You're so right, Mr. Olson."

And, Izzy saw that Izzy's mother's eyes were caressing Mr. Olson. Her eyes said, "My dear one." Izzy was no fool.

The two squirrels scrambled down the oak tree and chased off to another oak. Izzy joined the squirrels in the chase. When they rushed up an adjoining oak, he watched from the ground until they disappeared in the foliage. Then he shuffled back to the bench, took his seat, and kicked at the small green acorns on the ground in front of him. Olson and Izzy's mother sat in silence that seemed to need no words.

Shortly, the Swede arose, "My dear, I must get back to my duties." He smiled. Izzy's mother was radiant.

"Thank you very much for the fish and the visit," said Izzy's mother.

As the tall, bald, Swede stood up, he looked at Izzy. His brown eyes bore into Izzy's innards. "Benjamin, be good, look after your mother. She loves you." From that moment on, he knew Izzy had wished the fishmonger was his papa. Olson respected Izzy, had called him Benjamin, not Izzy-you-red-headed-brat.

4

Someone was shaking him gently by the shoulders. "Lieutenant, wake up. You've visited us once before, now's the time to put in another appearance." Doctor Williams was watching Lieutenant Benjamin Feldman, saw him open his eyes. "Good," said the doctor. "We're going to change you. Can you help us a little? Roll over on your right side." Feldman did as he was told and felt someone wipe his ass with a cold cloth. "Now, turn over the other way," said the doctor and Feldman saw the copper-toned corpsman who was taking the diaper away and placing a new one around his lower torso.

Feldman felt ashamed, embarrassed. "Christ, doctor, how long have I been like this?" he asked in a weak voice.

"A little over two weeks," was the prompt reply. "For a while, we didn't know whether or not you'd recover. But, the last couple days, you showed evidence of rousing. You're a lucky young man."

"And you say I am in the Navy?" inquired a still doubting Feldman.

"Just believe me, Lieutenant, you are. How about trying a little liquid nourishment. You've been on nothing but IV for over two weeks. Before we start to figure it all out, you need some real food. Would you like some beef broth?"

Feldman was too weak to resist. He felt weird. He really didn't know whether or not he was hungry. But, he was willing to try anything to shake the feeling he was floating, headed somewhere he had never been before.

"Rudolfo, get the Lieutenant a cup of hot beef broth. Bring a bent straw. Hold him up enough so he can swallow, not choke on the stuff."

"Aye, Sir," was the response of the Philippine corpsman, and he was off for the broth.

So began the physical rehabilitation of Sr. Lieutenant Benjamin I. Feldman.

5

On the first day after returning to full consciousness and in his struggle to come to grips with reality, Lieutenant Feldman had Doc Williams sit by his side. With the aid of the doctor, Ben reviewed and defined the various parts of his body: arms, legs, feet, hands, ears, ass, eyes, penis and testicles, and their functions. He truly needed reassurance he wasn't noncompos. When they were finished, the doctor looked at the Lieutenant with a grin. "Good, now that you know them, try to use them regularly -- all of them. It'll help you to recover quicker and make our work much easier."

Two days later Ben's arm restraints were removed. That's when he found he was wearing a suspensory. He investigated and, by God, his nuts ached, were black and blue, and horribly swollen. How did that happen? He had no idea. Who was he? A wave of panic nausea again swept over him. Why was he where he was? Then he remembered Doc Williams admonition, "Let's get some strength before we start to figure it out," He tried to relax.

Soon the diapers were off. He was using a bedpan and a bunk-hung urinal. Rudolfo, the corpsman, came by less frequently. Most of the men in his area, whoever they were, were very quiet. They were being fed by IV. Seldom was there a word from any of the poor bastards, an occasional moan or scream, then the place resumed its cemetery silence. Ben couldn't tell whether it was day or night. The lights remained the same.

He guessed it was morning when Rudolfo awoke him. "Sir, let's change from that gown to PJs. I'll help you." It was a struggle. Ben not only felt weak, he was weak. Just that little effort caused him to breathe heavily and perspire. When they finished, Rudolfo smiled. "We're making progress; here's your robe," and Ben put on the blue bathrobe. "See if you can stand." Ben sat up, swung his legs over the edge of his bunk, put his feet to the floor, and with the aid of the corpsman, tried to stand. Fierce pain gripped his groin and his nuts ached like no pain he had ever felt before. He gritted his teeth and stood. "We'll be able to make it," said Rudolfo. "Sit back and wait for me." The corpsman disappeared. In a few minutes he returned with a wheel chair. "Sir, you've been promoted. You're leaving intensive care and going where there's real life, to the rehabilitation area. I'll take you. You'll like it. At least you'll be back in the real world."

Don't count on that. How can I return to the real world when I don't know who I am, where I've been, where I am or why I am? Feldman thought to himself. But, he dare not let the corpsman know. "Let's go. I'm ready," he said with a twinge of uncertainty in his voice. He wondered how he knew the words to speak, to understand, when he couldn't remember a damned thing about the past.

6

He was wheeled to an elevator, it went up. How far, Ben didn't know. Then he was wheeled down a corridor to a door marked Unit 4C. The corpsman set the brake on the chair, the ship had a slight roll. Rudolfo opened the door. Sunlight streamed through a porthole into the four bunk room, two uppers and two lowers. One lower bunk was empty. "That's your home 'til we get stateside," said Rudolfo, pointing to the empty bunk. He wheeled Feldman to the bunk and was helping him from the chair to the bed when Iris Welling, an ensign Navy nurse, entered the room to aid the corpsman. "Good luck to you, Lieutenant Feldman. From now on you'll be under the care of Nurse Welling. This is Ensign

Welling," said Rudolfo as the nurse stepped to the side of the bunk. Feldman looked up at the tall, black-eyed brunette and immediately passed out.

When he came to, a bright-eyed young man was leaning over him, wiping the perspiration from his brow. Feldman was finally able to focus on the man. He too was dressed as Doctor Williams had been.

"I'm Lieutenant Commander Daniel Rutherford, M.D. Just what happened?"

A shaken Feldman looked at the doctor. "Who knows, I don't." And Feldman's lips quivered in hidden terror. For a moment, Feldman's eyes left the doctor and saw bewildered Nurse Welling standing in the background. He gasped at the sight. The doctor followed his glance, saw the nurse, nodded to her, and she left.

"Why, Lieutenant Feldman? Why did she frighten you so?" the young doctor's question was calm and forthright.

"I wasn't frightened," said Feldman, whose eyes betrayed his feelings. The doctor looked steadily at the distraught figure before him. Then tears streamed down Feldman's face. "Yes, I was frightened, frightened shitless, but, Doctor, I have no idea why."

"Take a couple of these pills and this glass of water. Rest awhile. One of your roommates will wheel you to supper. Try and make it. You need strength and real food." As he was leaving the room, the doctor turned to the other three occupants. "Guys, I know you like Welling, but I think we'll make a change for a while."

Feldman heard mumbles of discontent as he once again returned to the park.

7

"Hey, buddy, wake up," and Feldman felt a firm hand shake his shoulder. He opened his eyes to see a tousled-haired, heavy-set guy in PJs and robe standing by his bunk. He wore an eye patch over his right eye. His right arm was in a sling. His uncovered blue eye twinkled.

"You can't sleep your life away. I'll help you into your wheely and to the officers' mess. You can make it. My name is Karl Schmidt. I'm one of your cabinmates. I know yours is Feldman."

Feldman couldn't help but grin. He shook Schmidt's left hand. The guy reminded him of a good-natured Captain Hook in *Peter Pan*. Now, how did he know about Captain Hook and *Peter Pan* when he didn't even know who he was? "I'll try," said Feldman.

8

For the first time in God knows how long, Ben didn't stay in bed. He sat, albeit in his wheel chair, and had supper at the mess table. To his great surprise, he was hungry. He wolfed down his food. Karl, seated beside him, watched. "My you're skinny, but you sure are making up for lost time."

"I guess I've got a lot of time to make up. How much I don't know," said Feldman.

"And what's that supposed to mean?" asked Karl.

"I don't really know who I am, where I've been, or what is going on."

"Jesus, I wish I was you," and Karl's cheerful countenance faded. "It was hell," he said. Karl put down his fork and shuddered.

"I'm sorry," said Feldman as he continued eating.

"I wonder what my wife will say when she sees me in San Diego?" murmured Karl. "She's so damned squeamish about appearances. I'm afraid I'll scare her away."

"Not if she loves you," Feldman said bluntly and he again felt terror. What did he know about love? Where had the word love come from? Did he, Feldman, have a wife? Where was she?

"You're right, Buddy," said Schmidt. "She knows I've been hit, but not how badly. She'll soon find out. Five more days and we'll be there." Feldman wondered what other wounds Karl was concealing.

9

The next morning, with the aid of a corpsman, Feldman took the first shower he could remember.

Damn it felt good. At least he was alive with all of his parts -- and functioning, he hoped. His groin and testicles hurt less. He could now walk a kind of straddling wobble. Even with the suspensory, each time he nudged his testicles with a leg, he saw lightning flashes as the pain seared through his stomach. It was bearable though.

Karl pushed him to lunch. "I ain't gonna' do this much longer," he said as they returned to the cabin. "Doc Rutherford says he's going to take your wheely away from you this afternoon."

"Oh, shit, I've loved the luxury," said a smiling Feldman.

Just as they were settling in for the afternoon rest, lively blonde Navy nurse Rose Greely swept into the room. "Hi, guys," she said, and then she turned to Feldman. "Lieutenant, Doc Rutherford wants you to read to me."

"Do what?" asked a surprised Feldman.

"Read to me."

"Go ahead," said Karl with a big grin, "Read her *Little Red Riding Hood*." The other cabinmates guffawed.

"Don't be a smartass, Lieutenant Schmidt. You've got your problems. He has his," said Nurse Greely.

Schmidt, smiling, nodded in agreement.

She handed Ben a piece of paper. He looked at the print and felt an odd tingle race through his body. He was excited. Had he forgotten how to read? Could he focus on what was written? He concentrated on the words. Then looked up and asked Nurse Greely, "You mean I should read this?"

"Aloud if you can."

"The little red fox jumped over the moon," read Ben.

The room exploded with laughter.

"What idiot wrote that? The animal that jumped wasn't a little red fox, but a damned old cow," Schmidt said with a wide smirk.

"That literary gem wasn't written by just any idiot. I'll bet it was our shrink, Gertzman," said a deep voice of another cabinmate.

"Don't be disrespectful," said Nurse Greely. Then she giggled.

"Thank goodness you can read, Lieutenant Feldman," she said. And Feldman realized she knew a good bit about his troubles. "Read this, but not aloud." She handed Feldman a brief note. He read:

> *To Lieutenant Benjamin I. Feldman: You are to report to my office at 1600 hours this afternoon for an interview. Corpsman DeLong will come to your cabin and escort you.*
> > *Frank C. Gertzman*
> > *Commander U.S.N.*

"Do you understand the note?" asked the nurse.

A wave of apprehension swept over him.

"I'll be there." he responded.

"See you boys later," said the cheery nurse as she left the room.

10

Accompanied by Corpsman DeLong, and after a torturous walk, Ben Feldman knocked on the office door of Commander Gertzman. It was exactly 1600 hours.

"Come in, Feldman," said a deep, gravely voice. The lieutenant entered the room alone. It wasn't what he expected, not Navy grey. The bulkheads were a soft blue. The sofa against one bulkhead and matching easy chair were a bright yellow. The easy chair was in front of a metal desk. The desk was painted the same color as the bulkheads. Sunlight streamed in from a porthole on one side of the desk. There were small yellow drapes around the sides of the porthole. Doctor Gertzman arose as Feldman entered. He is tall, my God, he is tall thought Ben Feldman as he reached out and shook the hand of the doctor. The doctor's grip was firm and comforting. The face behind the hand was craggy and lined, partially hidden by a large black mustache. Two piercing, steely grey eyes peeked out from underneath bushy eyebrows. What a contrast he presents to the decor of the room thought Ben.

"Please be seated," said the doctor and he motioned to the big chair. Ben nervously sat. "As you may or may not know, I'm a psychiatrist, a shrink," said the doctor with a good-natured grin. "You've come through quite an ordeal. Tell me about it."

Ben looked at the doctor. He was silent, first with incomprehension, then fear. The doctor's gaze was steady, penetrating. "I can't," sighed Ben.

"Why not?"

"Because, I don't know what I've come through."

"Try, Lieutenant."

"I have tried -- tried like hell. I didn't even know my name until Doctor Williams told me after I came to."

"Where did you live before you entered the Navy?"

"Somewhere near a park, I think," responded the Lieutenant.

"In what city?"

"I don't know."

"Where did you get the park from?"

"From a dream, a real dream. In that dream I think I saw myself. I was called Izzy by my sister, Rebecca, if I have a sister Rebecca, and 'Izzy-you-red-headed-brat' by my father, if I have a father."

"Tell me all you can remember about your dreams," said Gertzman. And Ben Feldman did. When he finished, the doctor calmly inquired, "You father's name is what?"

"I don't know."

"Your mother's name is what?"

"I don't know."

"Do you have any other brothers or sisters?"

"Dr. Gertzman, I really don't know. Truly, I don't," and Ben was beginning to shake.

"Calm down, son, we'll soon make yesterday come back. Tell me anything at all that you remember -- not in any sequence."

Ben lowered his head. He was trying to think, to remember and he was getting more panic-stricken by the moment. The doctor observed him quietly. Ben raised his head as if struggling to keep it above water. "I haven't forgotten how to read," he said pitifully.

"No, you haven't, and that's a help, a real help." The doctor had read not only Ben's health record, but his personnel folder. "Your name is Benjamin I. Feldman. Could 'I' be for Isadore?"

"Could be, Doctor, but you can't prove it by me."

"Before the war, you lived with your parents, Martin and Ruth Feldman, in Philadelphia, Pennsylvania. Do you remember them?"

"Maybe my mom, from a dream."

"You graduated from the Naval Academy in 1938. You were twenty-two years old. Do you remember the Academy?"

Ben was silent, then replied hesitatingly, "Not really, but I do remember something about -- about an Indian head -- a bust -- Tecumseh."

"Hold it, hold it right there, Lieutenant. Don't let that image go. Where was the bust? Concentrate!"

"I don't know. I just don't know. Even that image is so vague and gray," said Ben.

The doctor wrote rapidly, looked up, smiled, and said, "Relax, Ben, we are beginning to make progress.

"Let's change the subject for a moment. What do you know about goats."

"What are goats?" queried Ben.

The doctor laughed, "How about Bora Bora?"

"What's a Bora Bora?" asked Ben.

"You remember nothing about Bora Bora, an island?" asked the psychiatrist.

"Never heard of it in my life, " responded Feldman.

"How are your testicles?" asked the doctor.

"Now that's something I do know about," said Ben with a faint smile. "And only because Doctor Williams defined them to me. They still hurt and are swollen. But, they do feel better."

"How did you injure them?"

"If I only knew," responded Feldman.

The doctor was silent as he scribbled on a pad. He looked up. His eyes seemed to bore into Ben's. "Son, you have an unusual case of Traumatic Amnesia. I am sure that the injuries to your head and groin were the basic causes. How and why this really occurred I don't know and apparently you don't either. But, I think your remembering what happened holds the key to your future. You can read and comprehend much and that's a big plus. Tomorrow I'll let you read your physical record and see if that helps. The magnitude of your amnesia is puzzling. You have much to relearn. From the physical report, your body functions are returning to normal and that's another plus. I suggest you start reading anything and everything you can. Some way, you've got a lifetime to catch up on. I want you back here tomorrow at the same time. There will be a session every day until we land. Bit by bit, we'll try to unravel the problem, your lack of memory. Start getting a little exercise. It stimulates the brain. Try to walk more. Go to the officers' therapy room for a fifteen minute exercise at least once a day. I'll leave word with Bos'n Little, he's in charge and he'll help you with an appropriate workout."

"Thank you, Commander. I appreciate your efforts and interest," said Feldman.

Just as he was leaving the room, the doctor casually asked, "What was it about Nurse Welling that caused you trouble?"

A terrified Ben Feldman looked at the doctor, "I wish to God I knew, Sir," he responded.

11

For the next four days Feldman kept his appointments with the doctor. In addition, he read voraciously, primarily old magazines that were aboard. Some articles he understood, but many he did not. His cabinmate, Karl, was of real assistance in definitions and explanations. Feldman understood that his home was in Philadelphia, Pennsylvania, and that Pennsylvania was a state in the United States. Karl showed him the location of his home city on a map in an old Hammond Atlas. The atlas was in the ship's library. Ben spent hours pouring over the sprawling map book. The world was slowly coming back to him. He even found the island of Bora Bora, but it was of no significance to him. The one name that he recognized was Annapolis, Maryland. For some reason, it conjured the image of Tecumseh. And, then suddenly in his mind's eye, he saw a wet drill field and grey buildings. The name Bancroft Hall came out of the blue. He knew he had been to the Academy. That afternoon when he met with Gertzman, he was excited. The shrink saw the spark in Feldman's eyes. "I know something," blurted out Feldman. "I held on to Tecumseh as you suggested. Yesterday, I was reading a map and recognized the city of Annapolis, Maryland. I saw Tecumseh. I saw a drill field. Suddenly, I remembered the name Bancroft Hall, I must have gone to the Academy."

"And what else do you remember about it?"

"The time was winter and all was gray. The images are still so fuzzy and unrecognizable."

"Keep on reading and looking, that helps. By the way, do you have a girl friend?"

Ben was stumped. He looked helplessly at Gertzman. "Sir, I don't know. I don't think so. The only one I can remember is the one in my dreams, Janice Witherspoon. I was only eight."

"Just trying to trigger a flash," calmly remarked Gertaman. The doctor knew his patient had a long road to cover before he reached full memory, if ever. Knowing Feldman was from the Philadelphia area, the doctor had written in his report recommending that the bedeviled young lieutenant be transferred to the Bethesda Naval Hospital in Maryland for observation and treatment before a final disposition of his case. To him, Feldman was an enigma, for there was no real indication of his previous makeup or personality. When the young lieutenant was brought aboard in his tattered uniform, all that came with him was a copy of his personnel and health record, no wallet, nothing to truly indicate who he really was. Could a couple of ram goats have been the horror, as reported on the officer's health record? Gertzman doubted the report. But, he damned to hell whatever the true cause had been. The guy deserved to know the truth. Gertzman believed that only then would Feldman stand a chance of real recovery. And he so reported in his written summary of the young officer's present physical, mental, and emotional condition. That summary would not be in Feldman's copy of his health record, but would be forwarded separately to the Bethesda Naval Hospital.

12

The hospital ship arrived on schedule at San Diego. Feldman, with other ambulatory officers in PJs and robes, was wheeled off the ship and placed on a bus for the hospital receiving station. Ben Feldman held tight to his Naval records. They were all he had in the world to identify him. He had no idea where he was going or what would happen after he got there. He had been told he would be evaluated at the base hospital. A determination would then be made as to where he would be sent for recovery and rehabilitation. Little did Ben realize that an interested Gertzman had set the wheels in motion to bring Ben close to home for whatever beneficial efforts could be made by the Navy.

13

Ben's stay at the San Diego hospital was only three days. They gave him a new ID card on a chain, to hang around his neck. At 0800 hours on 8 January, 1945, he, with thirty other recovering Naval officers, was whisked to Alameda Naval Air Base, boarded an ambulance version of an R4-D (DC3), and started his journey to Anacostia Naval Air Base just outside of Washington, D.C. Fourteen hours later the tired, recovering Naval officers were loaded into a bus and transported to the towering Naval hospital in Bethesda, Maryland. From his study of the atlas, Feldman knew Bethesda was fairly close to his alleged home. He became increasingly nervous. To just what was he returning?

In addition to the bathrobes they were wearing, each of the officers was given a single Navy grey blanket. The heater on the bus was broken. An older black warrant officer, wrapped in his blanket, was seated next to Feldman. "I wish they had left me in San Diego," he mumbled through chattering false teeth. Feldman nodded agreement. Even with his blanket wrapped around him, he was so cold from the weather and fear, he dared not try to speak. The words wouldn't have come out; only a stutter.

14

The bus stopped at the receiving entrance. Orderlies and corpsmen, each with a wheel chair, seemed to appear from nowhere out of the night, like pushcart vendors rushing to the wholesale truck for merchandise. Order quickly grew out of apparent chaos as the officers' names were called when each disembarked. An orderly knew the name of his patient and made his way through the crowd to the bus door.

Ben Feldman heard his name called as he stepped from the gray carrier. A strapping, black man pushed to the door. "At your service, Lieutenant Feldman," he said with a broad smile. For the first time since Ben had entered the plane for the trip, he relaxed. There was something about the guy that was comforting, maybe it was his size.

"What's your name, Orderly?"

"My name is John Archibald Jackson Smith, Sir. But I'm called Archie. You can call me Archie, Sir."

"Where are we going, Archie?"

"First, I'm going to sneak you into the kitchen behind the officers' mess and get you a steaming mug of java. You look like you are 'most frozen. Then, I'm going to take you to the room you are sharing with Marine Captain Brothers. He's a pretty hurt kid."

"Thanks, Archie. That's very thoughtful of you." And Ben didn't know if he had ever thanked anyone before. He didn't remember ever using that word. Where did "thanks" come from? Some place inside of him he didn't know he had?

Archie wheeled Ben down a corridor and stopped by two large swinging doors. "Just stay calm. I'll be right back." He disappeared between the doors. When he returned, he had a steaming cup of coffee in one hand and two freshly-baked sweet buns on a paper napkin in the other. He gave the cup and one bun to Feldman. "You don't mind if I join you in a snack?" asked Archie. His black eyes were flashing good natured humor as he bit into the other hot bun.

"Not at all. Be my guest," grinned Feldman, who then took a long swig of the warming liquid.

Archie said, "I'll take you to your room now. You better eat that bun. You won't get no more food 'til breakfast. Your plane was late and the rehab officers' mess closed an hour ago." Ben was grateful.

"You surely know your way around here."

"Ought to, been here twelve years," replied Archie. And so began the first real friendship Ben could remember.

Archie wheeled Ben to his room, rolled back the covers on the hospital bed and said, "The head and shower are in there," and he pointed to a door. "You got shaving gear and a toothbrush?" Ben shook his head negatively. "I'll get you some. They ain't the best, but they'll do until you get settled."

On the trip home, a hospital ship corpsman had shaved Ben occasionally. Now he knew why his mouth tasted so nasty. He hadn't brushed his teeth since he had come to. I've forgotten the simple amenities of life, he mused.

Archie disappeared and was back in a few minutes. He went into the bathroom and quickly returned. "Your stuff is on the right-hand side of the shelf. Do you want the side rail up?"

"No, thanks, Archie. I'm fine."

Archie went to the bed across the room, looked over the rail, reached down, patted the blond head, and said, "Sleep well, Timmy, buddy. You need it."

As he reached the door, he turned to Feldman, "That's Marine Captain Timothy Brothers. He had to have his right leg amputated above the knee. He's been through hell, but he's on the way back." Archie hesitated, then continued, "I'm on night duty this week. If you need anything, the buzzer is on the table by the bed, just push. If all goes well, I'll see you around 0800 hours tomorrow. Goodnight, Lieutenant."

"Good night, my friend," quietly replied Feldman. Then, for reasons beyond his understanding, he wept. Emotionally exhausted from his weeping and bone tired from his trip, a strange calm engulfed him, and he slid into the most comforting sleep he had experienced since he had come to aboard the hospital ship.

15

During the first two days following his arrival at Bethesda, Feldman was put through a rigorous physical exam. In the late afternoon of the second day, Commander Henry Adams, M.D., called the lieutenant to his office and gave him the results. Ben was recovering well physically, except for the fact that his right testicle was permanently damaged and would be of little use in procreation. However, his left one had healed and would be sufficient for fertilization in any family attempts. Adams suggested that Ben visit the paymaster and accounting office, get his financial status cleared, draw sufficient pay to get clothing, uniforms, and other necessities of making an attempt at normal living, and limited duty; all, of course, subject to the decision of the psychiatrist's findings.

Ben had ambivalent feelings about the doctor's report. He was delighted that his physical health was improving. He agreed that was so. But, he was increasingly nervous about his mental and emotional well-being. Damn it all, why couldn't he remember the past? He still had that horrible feeling he was floating, not really living.

Ben Feldman read constantly -- even past lights out time. Now it was fiction. There were stories of love, hate, compassion, loss and triumph. Had he experienced those feelings? He couldn't remember. How would he know in the future? At this point all he experienced was what had been defined by Gertzman as fear and uncertainty. Ben wished he could experience and recognize some of the feelings that he read about.

16

At 1400 hours on the fourth day after his arrival at Bethesda, Ben Feldman went to the office of Naval Captain Blandford Reynolds, Chief of Psychiatry, for his first interview. He saw Reynolds as a cheery, gray-haired, fatherly figure. Just before Ben took his seat in front of the Captain's desk, the Captain looked, pointed behind Ben, "I want you to meet one of my therapists, Lieutenant Ann Miller. She's a psychologist." Ben turned to see a tall, black-eyed, brunette in an officer's uniform. She held out her hand. Ben's knees buckled and he fell into the chair. He was gasping for breath.

There was deathly quiet. The chief psychiatrist's eyes never left Ben's face. The associate was looking at the struggling young lieutenant with pity.

"Why, Lieutenant Feldman?" asked the Captain. That was the same question Gertzman had asked. And Ben was sure the shipboard psychiatrist had sent a report to Bethesda.

"I don't know. I honestly don't know, Captain," murmured Feldman.

"Well, son, you had better get used to Anne Miller because she is going to be your therapist while you are here. Doctor Miller, will you please bring up a chair and sit beside Lieutenant Feldman. We have some questions to ask him."

Feldman heard a chair scrape. He knew she was on his right, but he dared not look.

The Captain spoke calmly. "Lieutenant Feldman, I want you to understand that Doctor Miller means you no harm. She is here to help you. You don't have to look at her until you feel comfortable in doing so. Just answer our questions if you can." He paused, then continued. "What caused your emotional reaction when you turned and saw her?"

"I really don't know, Sir."

"Have you ever seen me before, Lieutenant?" asked Doctor Miller.

"I ---- I ----- don't. . ."

"Take a look, Lieutenant. She's not going to bite, I promise," said Captain Reynolds.

Ben slowly turned to the young psychologist. Fear mirrored his blue eyes. That fear lessened as he looked steadily at the brunette. Ben saw she was rather comely, and showed no hostility. He gave a nervous grin and said, "Please forgive me, I didn't mean to embarrass you."

"You didn't embarrass me, Lieutenant Feldman. Make no apology. You embarrassed yourself, but why?"

"If I only knew. If I could only remember, I wouldn't be here," and his eyes implored understanding.

The two shrinks knew that Feldman spoke the truth.

"Could it have been shock at the sudden sight of me, because I am a woman and a brunette?" asked Miller.

Feldman was quiet as his mind strove to pierce the mist guarding yesterday. He looked beseechingly at the therapist. "I honest-to-God don't know. But, could be. And could be something else. At times I think I'm going crazy trying to remember. I try, I try until I think, oh shit, what's the use."

The psychologist reached out and sympathetically put her hand on his shoulder. Feldman fainted.

17

As the Captain and his associate were striving to bring Ben back to consciousness, Anne Miller turned to her boss and pointed to the report on his desk, "Ram goats, my butt, no pun intended, Captain. I'll bet all the tea in China, Feldman's condition is the result of a meeting with a wild, wild nanny."

"I think you are on the right track, Lieutenant. But, the Bora Bora base report says clearly that Feldman's injuries were caused by two ram goats of the flock on the north end of the island, while Feldman, alone, on assigned duty, was inspecting the dismantling of a MASH unit. Unless and until he remembers, there's no use in our torturing him further on that subject. I guess we'll have to focus our attempts at recall on other avenues."

"His parents and older sister would like to visit him tomorrow. We'd better prep him for that," said Doctor Miller.

"He functions well in many ways. I'm inclined to think his chances of recovery would be helped by giving him leave, let him go home for a while, and report on an out-patient basis to the rehab center at the Philadelphia Naval Health Annex. What do you think, Doctor?"

"Let's see how the meeting goes with his family. Then you can make up your mind," said Anne Miller.

The smelling salts soon brought Feldman around. He raised up from his slumped position in his chair and looked in anguish at the two doctors. "I couldn't help what just happened," he moaned.

"I'm sorry," said Doctor Miller. "We had to know what your emotional reaction would be to my touching you."

"Now you know," said Ben. "And what good does that do? Yes, when I suddenly see a tall brunette and she comes near me, you've seen what happens. I've known that, but why? I can't remember. Just like I can't remember much at all except my dreams and I know damned well you have Gertzman's report on those."

"You're right, son. We do have it," said the chief psychiatrist. "I promise from now on we'll not dwell on the brunette problem. There's so much more to work on. By the way, your parents and your sister, Rebecca, want to visit you tomorrow. They'll be in Lounge A at 1000 hours. Are you up to it?"

Again Feldman was fearful. He looked down at the floor. "I don't remember, I just don't remember. But, yes, I'll meet with them. How will they feel if I don't remember?"

"I guess we'll just have to wait and see," said the Captain.

There was silence. "You're excused," said the Captain and then he added, "Lieutenant Feldman, you function well in so many areas. Keep trying and we'll give you all the help we can."

"So long, Lieutenant Feldman. I'll talk with you after your parents leave. You're a gutsy guy. You're on the mend," said a worried Doctor Miller.

"Thank you both," said Feldman as he padded out the room, wrapping his robe close around his shaking body.

After Feldman left the room, Lieutenant Miller looked with concern at her boss. "He's got a long road to hack. Captain, I've just finished reading the current issue of the *American Journal of Psychiatry*. It included the case histories of traumatic amnesia as reported by Elizabeth Geleerd, F. J. Hacker and David Rappaport. They would have a field day with Lieutenant Feldman's case."

"I'm glad I'm not him," said the Captain. "I'm afraid I'd give up. God knows how long his 'fugue' will last."

18

B en had been back in his room about an hour when Archie walked in. "I hear your family is coming tomorrow," he said.

"What are you doing around so early?" asked Ben.

58

"Well, I came a little early to help Timmy. I took him to therapy. He's down there now getting his new leg fitted. He's going to be there a while. Don't you want to go down to the PX and get some decent clothes to greet your ma and pa? You don't want to let them see you in your pajamas and robe."

"That's one heck of a distance from here. I'm kinda' pooped from walking to and from Captain Reynolds' office," replied Ben.

"I know that. That's why I came by. I'll wheel you there. We'll be back here in time for me to get Timmy."

"Archie, how did you know my family is coming tomorrow and that I needed clothes?"

"There's a network. I hear most everything," said Archie. "If we go now, you can get your underwear and stuff and they'll have your winter blues ready by tomorrow morning. Today, I'll show you how to get there quick. Tomorrow, you can take your time and walk."

Ben looked at Archie. Ben became increasingly nervous just thinking about meeting his parents. Archie saw the look. "You gotta' do it, Lieutenant. You gotta' meet with your family."

Ben Feldman looked at the massive, easy-going, black man before him. He smiled and thought, no wonder you've been here twelve years, you're the best damned shrink in the whole bunch.

19

At 1100 hours Ben Feldman, freshly showered, shaved, and in his new Navy blues, arrived at the entrance door to Reception Room A, and stopped. He mused, why should he go in there? He had no feelings about the three people he would meet. He didn't remember any of them, except possibly in a dream. And, was the dream true or were the individuals involved merely characters his subconscious mind had concocted? He wasn't sure. But he was curious, curious about his life behind the gray curtain of lost memory. He thought maybe the encounter with his family would trigger a pin hole peek through that curtain into the past. Maybe it would help him experience something besides fear and uncertainty. He quietly opened the door just enough to see the three occupants seated on a brown leather divan. They were more or less facing a window. The sun beaming through the window clearly revealed them. On the end of the sofa nearest him sat a short, gray-haired, bosomy, past-middle-age woman. She was looking down at her lap, watching her hands fold and unfold, as if they were two little, spotted, gray kittens pawing at each other -- not vital parts of her body. There was a tender look of resignation on her pudgy face. He thought, this is my mother? She's surely not what he remembered from his dream. Next to her was another woman, much younger. She was chiseled-featured, with a prominent nose and a mound of black hair, wrapped in a bun at the back of her head. From where he stood, he couldn't really see the expression on her face. She was in animated conversation with the heavy-set man on her left. There was a certain defiance in her demeanor that caught his eye. Damn, that could be Rebecca, he thought. Then he looked at the man on her left. He was swarthy, powerful in build, and had a slight hint of a paunch. He sat with an arrogance that exceeded that of the young woman next to him. Ben could see the man's face as he talked. Two steely, black eyes pierced from beneath rugged brows. There were bags under those eyes. His face was etched as if rough weather had made crevices on a poorly-chiseled sandstone figurehead. He talked rapidly, displaying several formidable gold-capped teeth. His hands, when he used them for emphasis, seemed like large tarantulas, leaping, crawling, suspended in mid air. A heavy gold chain stretched across his black suit vest, from pocket to pocket. And this is my papa! The very sight of him made Ben uncomfortable. Suddenly the burly male stared at the door. The eyes of the other occupants followed his. Ben knew he had been seen. He entered.

20

The threesome arose abruptly, as if on command. The little gray-haired lady pitter-pattered rapidly toward him. Tears began to flow from her eyes. She reached out, grabbed him by his ears, pulled his face towards hers and planted a big slobbery kiss on his lips. Then she wrapped her arms around his waist, placed her head on his chest and sobbed, "Benny, oh Benny, my baby. Thank God you're home safe and sound."

Lieutenant Feldman now knew what it felt like to be surprised as well as embarrassed. Here was this elderly, little, old lady, he didn't know from a sack of salt, embracing him like he was her long, lost son. Maybe he was after all. But the only thing he truly knew was that she had bad breath. He put his arms around her, and lying like a trooper said, "It's good to be back."

21

By now the younger woman was standing next to him. She kissed him gently on the cheek and said, "Welcome home, Izzy."

For Ben there was a tiny hole in the veil that hid the past. The tone, the inflection, he recognized the voice even though the timber was deeper than he vaguely remembered. "Thank you," he said. A warmth somewhere inside him made him feel a mite more relaxed. By her faint suggestion of a smile, he knew she knew of his problem, and she knew she had scored, had pierced the veil in some small way.

His father was on the other side of him, his black eyes endeavoring to bore into Ben's very soul, seeking to continue the domination he had maintained even after his son had graduated from the Academy. But, for Martin Feldman, the gray veil of his son's amnesia was a stone wall of absolute rejection. He reached out and placed one of his tarantula-like hands on Ben's shoulder. Ben shuddered ever so slightly. "I expect you will visit us soon," said his father in a deep, husky voice.

"That depends on what the doctors say," replied Ben, mustering as much coolness as he could.

In a small adjoining room, and through a one-way mirror window, Ben's therapist, Lieutenant Ann Miller, had observed the family meeting. She decided now was the time for her to make her presence known. She could tell Ben was becoming increasingly nervous. She walked from the observation room to the reception room's main entrance and entered. "Good morning everyone, I'm Doctor Miller," All eyes turned to her. She calmly came to the foursome. "I know Ben," she said. "You must be his mother," and she extended her hand to Ruth Feldman. "And, you must be Rebecca," she said as she turned to Ben Feldman's sister. Martin Feldman was looking at the lady officer with his penetrating eyes, wondering just how in hell did she know when to make her entrance. He, too, had observed his son's uneasiness and was set to take advantage of what he saw.

"Good morning, Doctor, I'm Martin Feldman, Ben's father." Ann Miller gave Ben's father a penetrating glance and shook his hand. Now, there's one source of Ben's trouble. But, it's a source he'll have to learn to handle -- maybe with a little help from me, she mused.

"Please be seated," said Dr. Miller with a smile. "I'm an associate of Captain Reynolds, Chief of Psychiatry. We have been working with Ben. You have been advised, in writing, that he is suffering from Traumatic Amnesia. He knows it and has been co-operating with us in every way to hasten his recovery. We think that a period of home leave might be helpful to him," said the psychologist.

"Oh, it would be wonderful to have my baby back," beamed his mother.

I'm not so sure, thought Rebecca. Papa has no idea what Ben has been enduring. All Papa can think about is how to squeeze another buck a case on the next liquor shipment he delivers. Unless he can use Ben to further that goal, he doesn't give a damn whether or not Ben comes home. Play it cool, Ben, please play it cool.

"Ben, it would be nice to have you home, and you can visit the office every now and then," said Martin Feldman, and Rebecca knew the old man's mental wheels were already turning with some devious idea.

Ben had said nothing, but was seriously gazing from one member of the family to the other. Just what would I be coming home to, he wondered.

His thoughts were interrupted by Dr. Miller. "It'll be a couple days before he will be ready. Can any of you drive down and pick him up?"

"I can, if you'll call me a day in advance," said Rebecca. "Here's my business card. I look forward to seeing my brother alone."

Martin Feldman cast his daughter a stern glance. By that remark, Ben knew his sister wanted to talk to him. Even Lieutenant Miller grasped the significance. She smiled approval. "I'll call you. Now, if you'll excuse us, Ben has a therapy session about to begin," she lied sweetly. Ben was relieved that the meeting was over.

"We'll see you soon, Ben," said his father as the trio moved to the door.

"Oh, Benny, I'm so glad you're coming home," said his still tearful mother.

They departed.

22

"You did well, Lieutenant," said an encouraging Ann Miller.

"How do you know?"

"Because I was watching," said the doctor as she pointed to the one-way mirror window. Ben followed her finger and saw the tinted glass.

"Damn, you don't leave much to chance, do you?"

Not if we can help it, Lieutenant Feldman." And, Ben wondered how many eyes the hospital walls had.

"We don't really have a session now do we?"

"No," said Dr. Miller, "I just figured you'd seen enough of your family for your first reunion."

"Thanks," said a relieved Ben. Slowly, he was beginning to identify feelings again.

"Lieutenant Feldman, the U.S. Navy Band and Sea Chanters will be performing in our main auditorium later this afternoon. I think you should attend. Do you like music?"

Ben looked soberly at the shrink, "I don't know, but I think so."

"I tell you what. I'll meet you at the entrance doors to the hall at 1400 hours. Be there," said Doctor Miller.

"I will," he said with a dour smile. He wondered why she wanted him to go to the concert.

"See you later," said Dr. Miller, as she left.

23

Ben stood in the silent empty room and thought, so I've met my family. They're not what I expected -- except for Rebecca. She, I vaguely remember. How can I ever go to their house and feel comfortable -- at home -- when I don't know them or even myself. For the moment he felt he was in the middle of a deserted desert, with no idea of which way was an oasis. The only present security he had was his room, with his gimp roommate, Marine Captain Timothy Brothers, and his new friend, Archie.

As he left the cafeteria after an unappetizing lunch, Ben was almost decked when a careless young mess attendant swung his four-wheeled dish cart around the end of a table and nicked Ben in the groin with a corner of the cart. The recovering Lieutenant all but bellowed aloud with pain and could have throttled the Filipino on the spot. The young man was embarrassed and pled for forgiveness. He saw the ashen color of the Lieutenant's face, but couldn't understand how the slight bump could cause such agony. Ben finally gasped, "Forget it, I wasn't looking either." The relieved mess attendant hastened away. Ben went to his room to rest until the appointed time for the concert.

24

At 1400 hours Ben met his therapist. They entered the auditorium and found seats. For the first time since he could remember, he was in the midst of a large assemblage of people. He felt odd. Dr. Miller was watching him. He caught her glance and smiled. "I can't remember anything like this before," he said.

"You're doing fine, Lieutenant," she replied.

The house lights dimmed. On stage were the band and singers. Suddenly, "To the Colors" was sounded and a color guard with the American flag and the Navy ensign swept down the center aisle. In front of the stage, they turned to the audience, the crowd arose, Ben followed. The band played "The Star Spangled Banner." Ben didn't remember hearing the piece before. As the color guard returned up the aisle, the band started playing "Anchors Aweigh." For some strange reason that music sent shivers through his body. He knew he had heard that piece before. He remembered "Sail Navy down the field and sink the Army, sink the Army gray." Tears welled in his eyes. The refrain was at least a glimpse. Just another peep hole in the gray curtain.

My God, why can't I remember more? he mused. Dr. Miller empathetically watched her patient during the concert wondering just what was the total effect and hoping against hope that it triggered some recalled images by her patient. Ben seemed to absorb the music. It swirled around and through him. He was moved by it. The audience joined the Sea Chanters and the band in the final number, the first verse of "The Navy Hymn." When the last note died and the audience was leaving, Ben turned to the psychologist. "Besides being a good shrink, you're a thoughtful person. Yes, I did get a peep into the past -- not much, but a little. However, I do realize I have always loved music. I feel as if I've had a warm, comforting bath, inside and out. I feel more relaxed and refreshed than I've been since I first came to on the *Southern Cross*. I can't tell you why, but I do. Thanks, Doc."

That was not the comment Lieutenant Miller had expected from her patient. But, it revealed to her a more complex and sensitive personality than she had previously envisioned.

"I enjoyed the music also," replied Anne Miller.

She found herself wondering about the troubled veteran for she too had felt cleansed by the concert. Somewhere, shackled deep within his psyche, was a guy worth her effort of trying to rescue. He intrigued her. After having met Ben's parents, Anne Miller had her doubts that Ben's injury at Bora Bora was the sole cause of his present condition. Only from his reaction to home leave would she be able to tell the impact of his family on him. So, she would recommend to the Captain that Lieutenant Benjamin Feldman be granted an indeterminate home leave with orders for him to report weekly to the infirmary at the Philadelphia Naval Yard. At three month intervals, he would return to Bethesda Naval Hospital for a complete checkup. If anything unusual happened, he was to report immediately to her at Bethesda.

25

The next day Ben reported to Dr. Miller as requested. He knocked on her office door. "Come in," she said. Ben entered the neat office. She motioned him to an easy chair and took the one across the cocktail table from him. "Lieutenant, do you think you are ready to try home leave for while?"

Ben thought, his physical recovery was almost complete, he had much more energy, but was he ready to leave the secure surroundings of the hospital? Just thinking about it made his heart beat faster. He knew so little of the outside. His clear, blue eyes sought an answer from her knowing, black eyes. Silence became awkward. "What do you think I should do?" he said hesitatingly. Ann Miller tried to be dispassionately professional. Inwardly, for some strange reason, her heart ached for the bedeviled red-head. She had witnessed his openness, his vulnerability, and his obsessive desire to remember. She knew that Ben's attempted return to real living now or later might be fraught with disastrous results. She had a strong urge to protect him from reality. But, that wasn't her job. Her job was to get him on his feet, figuratively and literally, so he could some day return to his duties as a Naval officer, or at least live a reasonable life under disability retirement.

"Lieutenant Feldman, we think, that is, Captain Reynolds thinks you should try home leave. That's one of the easiest ways to see if you can cope with the real world."

Ben's eyes had not left Ann Miller's. "I hear you, Doctor, I hear what you say the Captain thinks. You have been my therapist. I want to know what Ann Miller thinks I should do."

Dr. Miller's countenance changed from calm professionalism to feminine worry. Her eyes were now those of a concerned woman.

"You and the Captain have spent hours probing into every corner of my being, at least as much as I can remember. And you've probably dug deep, even behind my memory, to know how I will react to life and living. I don't want your answer as if I'm a guinea pig. You know me as well as anybody I remember. I want your answer, not just as a doctor, but as a human being with feelings. Feelings I am just relearning by reading and what sensations I've experienced since I left Bora Bora. God knows how far you've dug into me, I think I have a right to an answer from you."

Ann Miller's face was flushed. Damn, the guy is far more discerning than the Captain and I thought he was. She looked down at the pen in her hand that was, without conscious direction, drawing little circles and squares on the paper attached to her clipboard.

"Ben, trying to re-enter the world is going to be tough, who knows how tough, when you leave this hospital. Maybe, you'll have to come back here from time to time. Maybe you'll get your memory back -- or at least some of it. Maybe you won't. But, you gotta' try and live, somehow. I think you stand the best chance of re-orienting your life if you start from home. Rebecca is living at your parents. She has always loved you and knows you far better than I. I have learned at least that much. She will help, without being obtrusive. You can get additional help from your regular visits to the Philadelphia Yard. And," she hesitated, "Ben, you can always call me here if you really need me." She looked up into those trusting blue eyes and felt nauseated at the battles that the game lieutenant might have to wage in endeavoring to make a real life for himself.

Ben smiled at Ann. "That's good enough for me. I'll try. When do I leave."

"Rebecca will meet you at the visitors entrance at 10:00 a.m. tomorrow. Here are your orders." She held out her hand containing the envelope. Ben reached out with both of his, took the envelope with one hand, stuffed it in his inside jacket pocket, holding her hand with his other. Then he held her hand with both of his.

"Archie is the first friend I remember. You are the second. I'm not so sure it's going to work because I remember so little of the past. I admit that at times I'm so damned insecure that I still feel like I'm floating. But, I do trust you and have since the first time the Captain said look. Thanks Anne, Doctor Anne that is. I'll try to report as required."

"Please," said Dr. Miller.

Ben Feldman left the office, closed the door, and returned to his quarters. Ann Miller relaxed, folded her arms on the desk and laid her head on them. Being a woman and therapist was not the easiest job.

26

The next morning, Ben Feldman walked down the sidewalk to the front door of the visitors center, carrying his new Val-pac and another suitcase. Just as he was opening one of the double doors, he heard, "Izzy,

I'm over here, across the street." Rebecca was waving to him from the open driver's side window of her two-doored auto. He crossed the street, opened the passenger side door and flung his luggage into the rear seat, then got in. His sister rolled up the window, drove from the hospital grounds to Rockville Pike, and headed for home.

"I'm glad you decided to try it at home."

"We'll see how things go, but I'm not all that comfortable about coming home."

"I know, it's not going to be easy," said Rebecca.

Ben was silent, then, "You know, you are the only one in the family I even vaguely recognized. I guess it was your voice that helped."

"Kinda' like a hoarse frog?"

"No," said Ben, pondering an answer. "I really don't remember what a frog sounds like, much less a hoarse one. It's just different, recognizable, nice."

"Thanks," said his sister, and for a while they rode in silence.

"You don't mind if I call you Becky do you? I remember that name from a dream."

"No, Izzy, I don't mind your calling me anything so long as it helps your memory. And you used to call me Becky."

After another period of silence, Ben turned his blue eyes to his sister. "Becky, just what was I like before? When I was young, as I grew up and before my injury?"

Becky was surprised by the question, the very frankness of it. She took her eyes momentarily from the road and looked at her questioning brother. She felt that Ben, for the first time in his life, was trying to find out who he was and is. She looked back at the split, white-lined highway, passed a car. "Slow bastard," she mumbled. Then she spoke evenly, "Ben, you were a prick, an unmitigated prick, made so by Papa since the day you entered the world. Underneath, you weren't meant to be one, but Papa had complete control of you, as he tried to do with everybody."

"Did I ever rebel?"

"No, you knew what side your bread was buttered on. You became Papa's alter ego. He isn't as smart as you are, but he's cunning. He uses everybody he can to his benefit. And you, being the only son, he was trying to mold you for his future. Mama knew, but could do nothing about it. She comes from the old school -- submit."

"Did I have any friends? Real friends?"

"Not a one, besides me. You were a loner, a perfectionist with a high ethic value, something Papa wasn't but wanted to be," answered Becky.

"Didn't I have any real friends at the Academy?"

"Not a one that I know of. But, a couple of your peers on the chess team had genuine respect for your ability. You were as cold as a frozen carp to them and everybody. You seemed afraid to admit your feelings. And Papa was responsible for that. He had dreams that someday, when he was tired and old, you would leave the Navy and take over the liquor business. I felt if you did, it would probably ruin you. Papa's a strange man. He was too scared to serve in WWI. How he evaded the draft I don't know. But, he wanted you, his alter ego, to serve, embellish the Feldman name with a Naval rank, retire and take over the business, adding prestige to the business by your service to your country. He may still try to do so."

Ben was silent. Deep within himself, he knew she was right. His meeting with his Papa in Reception Room A had been a disturbing one. He had wondered why. Now he knew. For all his lack of memory, he knew his father would never again control him. He just couldn't live that kind of life. He wondered how far back he had wanted to rebel.

"How about you, Becky? Do you get along with Papa?"

A half smile, half smirk lit Becky's face. "Yes and no."

"What do you mean, yes and no?"

"Well, I guess by nature, maybe by genes, I'm much like him. I understand where he's coming from. Frankly, I've taken advantage of him. I'm in the business with him. But, no, he doesn't run my life. I married Irving Slinsky, his chief rival in

the business in Philly. Irving died before we had any children.
I then consolidated Irving's business with Papa's. I moved
home really to look after Mama and Papa. Mama's beginning
to show her age. Papa's got high blood pressure and a colon
problem. He likes to pretend he's fine, goes to the office every
day and raises hell. By noon, he's pooped. I run the show, but
let Papa think he does."

27

B en thought, how complex the real world is. Will
I ever fit in again? And then his mind bounced
back to the memory of Becky and Ivan Bososcov
in the park. "Do you remember a guy by the name of
Bososcov?"

Becky's whole countenance changed. She became
serious and wistful. Tears brimmed her eyes. Ben thought, for
the first time, she looks lovely and feminine. She turned her
head toward her brother, "Why do you ask?"

"I think I remember him from a dream."

Becky turned her head back to the road, wiped away the
tears with one hand and said softly, "He was the only real love
I ever had."

"What happened?" asked Ben.

"Don't you remember?"

"No."

"Well, when Papa found out he couldn't control me, he
hired Ivan. And Ivan was killed on an illegal whiskey run
across Lake Michigan way back in '37. That was four years
before I married Slinsky."

"Will I ever remember? Will I ever catch up?" sighed
Ben.

"If you do, Brother, you may wish you hadn't," replied
Becky with a wistful grin.

28

B en changed the subject. "I know we're Jewish. I've read much about it. Do Mama and Papa go to the synagogue?"

"Mama occasionally. Papa never."

"Did I go?" asked Ben.

"Regularly," replied Becky.

"And you?" asked Ben.

"I'm a rebel like Martin Luther. Years ago I joined the Lutheran Church. I guess initially to show Papa my independence. Now I'm comfortable with it. We all pray to the same creator. The rest is fill in."

Ben looked at his sister. He just couldn't help but like her, realized he always had. She's a gutsy gal, he thought to himself.

29

F or the remainder of the trip, Ben plied his sister with questions about where they lived. What street? How big was the house? How many bedrooms? Who did the cooking? Where was Papa's office downtown? For him this was a new world he was struggling to enter. Becky understood and patiently endeavored to answer the questions, filling in details where she thought necessary. In the early afternoon, as they pulled into the driveway alongside the solid, three-storied, red brick house with the wide covered front porch, Ben turned to Becky and said, "Will you keep on helping me as I try to identify what's what?"

"As long as you try to find yourself, your real self, I'll bust my gut helping you. You're the most decent breath of air this family has had since the war started." Becky turned off the engine, leaned over and planted a kiss on her brother's left cheek. "But, it ain't going to be easy for either of us," she smiled.

"I guess not," Ben replied.

30

Ben Feldman retrieved his luggage from the rear seat and followed Becky to the house. She opened the front door and held it for him. He took his first step into a strange new world. Ben's only comforting thought was that Becky would be there too. He recognized nothing he saw in the large, ornate foyer. He looked into the living room. A log fire was burning brightly in the fireplace across the room. He saw the Victorian furniture and the big baby grand piano. He noticed the geometrical patterned antique rug on the floor. He couldn't recollect having seen any of it before. Then, a deep resonant tone sounded on the landing of the stairway. He looked up at the large standing grandfather clock. The chimes within the clock sounded two mellow ricocheting notes, 2:00 p.m. Ben suddenly felt a tingle of excitement. He had heard those tones before. He closed his eyes. When he opened them Becky was standing beside him looking questioningly at him. A faint smile lit his face and he said, "My bedroom was the last room down the right-hand side of the hall upstairs."

"It still is, Ben. It still is. Do you remember what was in your room?"

"No. But I remember climbing those stairs in the dark, late at night, with my shoes in my hand, hearing the clock strike and knowing my room was the last door on the right-hand side of the hall." Ben shook his head in discouragement, "Damn it, that's all I can remember."

Becky leaned over and placed her arm around Ben's shoulder. He was surprised that he felt no fear. "Here, I'll take the Val-pac. You take the suitcase. You won't have to make two trips," she said, and they headed for the stairs.

31

His bedroom door was open. The antique three-quarter maple bed was made up. On the maple dresser was a silver-framed picture of a guy in a Naval Academy dress uniform. Subconsciously, he reached for

73

the wall switch and turned on the overhead light. He knew the picture was of him, but how did he know where the switch was?

"Right across the hall from your room is the bathroom. We'll have to share it," said Becky as she headed to her room.

Ben nodded acquiescence. "Thanks, Sis," he said. After hanging his Val-pac in the closet, he decided to rest for a while, took off his shoes and Naval jacket and stretched out on his bed.

32

He was awakened by Becky pounding on his door and calling out, "Libation time, if you want a drink before supper."

"Drink of what?" called back Ben.

"Damn, your memory is bad. Come on down to the den and I'll re-introduce you to one of the more enjoyable sins of real life," she said spiritedly.

Ben arose, put on his jacket and shoes, and washed his face and hands. He combed his hair before the medicine chest mirror above the sink. When he finished, he gazed for a couple seconds at his image and said, "Just who in the hell are you?" Then, he went down the stairway to the hall, stopped and listened. Where is the den? He heard voices in a room whose door to the hall was open. He walked and entered the pleasantly-lit room with its bookcases on one side and small bar on the other. An array of various colored bottles were stacked neatly on the shelves behind the bar. Ben looked at the names on the bottles. They meant absolutely nothing to him. His father had just finished pouring liquid into an ice-filled glass. He looked up, saw Ben enter, "Would you like your usual?"

Ben looked at his father and asked, "And what was my usual?"

His father's eyes narrowed just a mite. "Don't kid me, Benjamin. A man rarely forgets his liquor."

"I'm not kidding you. The only liquids I know are coffee, tea, milk, orange juice, grape juice, and water. And, I learned those aboard the *Southern Cross*."

"Come on, Ben. You don't expect me to believe that pap."

"Hold on, Papa," said Becky sternly, "Dr. Miller told you to be patient, that Ben wasn't faking. Believe her. Believe Ben. He has problems the likes of which you have no idea. Ben, you used to like a Chevas Regal scotch whiskey highball, I'll fix it for you."

Ben glowered at his disbelieving father. He now knew anger and he was experiencing it. "I truly don't give a shit what you believe," said Ben. Martin Feldman's mouth dropped open. Never had his son spoken to him in such a manner and in such a cold voice. This wasn't Izzy, his little, red-headed, controlled brat. This was someone he had never met.

"Both of you calm down," said Becky as she handed her brother the highball, and continued, "Take it easy on this drink. If it's the first you can remember, it isn't like orange juice."

Ben took a sip of the brew. The cold liquid had an odd taste, but from the first sip that crossed his lips, he sensed a warming glow. The further down the sip went, the more widespread the warmth. He consumed the drink in short order as his sister watched. "Izzy, take it slower. That stuff's pretty potent," said Becky.

"I'll have another," said Ben, now really relaxed for the first time since he had stepped through the front door. "Where's Mama?" asked Ben.

"She'll be down in a few minutes. She doesn't approve of your sister's and my cocktail hour," said Martin Feldman.

Becky made her brother another highball. "This is it, no more tonight," said Becky as she looked at Ben, and thought, until now, he never wanted more than one highball before dinner.

33

$\mathbf{B}$en went into the dining room with more assurance than he believed possible. He was ravenously hungry. His mother entered the room. From some long-hidden impulse, he arose and pulled out her chair. As his mother sat, she cast him a weary smile. "Thanks, Benny," she said. Ben smiled. He liked the word "thanks."

Supper flew by with small talk. Most of it was Ben asking questions and his mother or sister endeavoring to answer them. His father was silent, studying his son. He couldn't tell whether Ben was really suffering amnesia or was the cleverest con artist he had ever seen. The questions his son was asking apparently evidenced a desire to catch up on the world in a whirlwind fashion. Or, they were planned as skillfully as if his mouthpiece, Gus Frieburg, was cross-examining a D.A.'s witness. Only time would tell. But, one thing was certain, not a question did Ben put directly to him. And, Martin felt as if he was purposely being ignored. He was irritated at such indifference.

"Benjamin, would you like to visit the office tomorrow?" asked his father.

Ben looked down at his empty dinner plate, then at his father.

"No," he said bluntly. "Before I do anything like that, I want to become familiar with the neighborhood. I want to walk, see the park, learn how to get home from wherever I go."

Becky intervened, "I think you are right, Izzy. Get reacquainted with the area first. Then I'll take you down to see the office."

Martin glowered at his son. Ben's mother sat with her eyes cast down at her lap. Her husband arose, "I'm going to the den to listen to the war news," he said.

Ben Feldman turned to his mother and sister, "I'm going upstairs to read today's *Inquirer*, if you don't mind?"

"You're excused, Benny," said his mother.

Becky's eyes followed him as he left the room. Then she looked sympathetically at her mother. "Ben's recovery is going to take time, Mama."

"So, who's got the time?" responded Ruth Feldman with a wistful sigh.

34

The next day Ben Feldman started walking the neighborhood, carefully noting the street names on the signs so he could retrace his wanderings. The second day, as if by instinct, he found Fairmont Park. Despite the cold northwest wind, he sat on the bench he remembered in his dreams and endeavored to look through the misty gray veil of lost memory, made all the harder to pierce by the snow beginning to fall. He shook his head disconsolately and sloshed home through the wet falling snow.

35

A week after coming home, he wandered out once again. That's when he found O'Brien's Bar and Grill. He stepped from the six-inch-deep snow into the cheery bistro. He recognized the Chevas Regal bottle among those stocked behind the bar. Despite the fact that the wall clock behind the bar said 11:00 a.m., he felt a gnawing thirst as he remembered the nightly highballs he'd been enjoying.

"Please," he said, "I'll take a Chevas Regal highball."

"Lieutenant, the sun's not over the yardarm yet. Ain't it a little early?" asked the chubby, Irishman behind the bar.

"Mr. Barman. . ."

"The name's Mike," interrupted the barman.

Ben grinned. "OK, Mike, for me the sun never gets as high as the yardarm. I might as well drink now as later." Two hours passed and, as the lunch hour crowd was gathering in O'Brien's, Ben almost fell off the barstool. He was intoxicated, delightfully so. "Oops. That was a high wave," he said with a simple grin at Mike.

"Wouldn't you like lunch, something to eat?" asked a watchful Mike.

"Mike, old friend, I haven't felt this good since I came to on the *Southern Cross*," replied Ben with a thick tongue. "Why should I interrupt this little trip with something as nasty as food? I think I'll take another drink."

"No you won't, Lieutenant. You've had four highballs and nothing to eat. You'll never make it back home."

"Home? Home? Who knows where home is?" inquired Ben, as the liquor bottles on the shelf appeared to change place on some hidden command.

"Where do you live, Lieutenant?" asked Mike.

"Damned if I know. I've got the address written on a piece of paper in my wallet," said an increasingly inebriated Ben.

"Let me see the paper." said Mike.

"The hell you say," replied Ben with a little smirk as he peeked into his wallet. And that was the last thing he knew he said until he came to on his bed in his bedroom. Rebecca was washing his face with a cold washrag. She saw him open his eyes.

"What were you trying to do? Drink O'Brien's dry before noon?" she asked in an exasperated voice.

"God, I've got a headache," said Ben. "How did I get here?"

"Mike Spindel, the barman at O'Brien's, poured you into a taxi cab and gave the driver instructions where to bring you. Mama almost fainted when the cab driver helped you into the house. She called me. What's got into you? You no sooner get home than you get stinking drunk?"

"For a while, Becky, just for a little while, I had no worries," replied her bleary-eyed brother. "Now I've got a roaring headache and an upset stomach." He lunged across the hall to the bathroom. Becky heard him gagging, giving his all to the toilet bowl.

"That'll teach you," she hollered, hoping it would.

Ben staggered back to the bedroom and dropped onto his bed. "Oh, Becky, you've got no idea just how lost I am."

"Maybe I do, maybe I don't, but getting drunk is no way to find yourself."

"How would you know?"

"Because I've been there," she replied caustically.

36

So began Ben Feldman's troubled float through the next nine years of his life; bedeviled by his lack of memory, not having any acceptable perception of who he had been or who he now was, seeing himself only as a severely flawed human being unable to focus on the possibility of a future, for no one apparently truly needed him for any reason. What could he contribute? His nothingness? Only the vague memories of gentle Archie's "You gotta' do it, Lieutenant Ben, you just gotta' do it," Dr. Anne Miller's "You're a gutsy guy, you'll recover," and his sister, Rebecca's "It ain't going to be easy for either of us. But you are a breath of fresh air in this family," gave him any hope, and when the small flame of that hope flickered, as it frequently did, he would get potted, stinking drunk, temporarily escaping from where to where, he really didn't know. Suicide, the only other escape, he had considered from time to time. But, his very being rebelled at the idea, maybe cowardice he thought or maybe a hidden basic wish or perception that some day, somewhere, he would find a life. So, he struggled just to float, a piece of flotsam and jetsam, on an ever swiftening stream of life, relearning, but not focused on living. Six months after his first home leave, he appeared before a Naval Medical Board at Bethesda. His condition was reviewed, and he was placed on inactive duty, full retirement for physical and emotional disability incurred in the line of duty. He was to report to the Bethesda Naval Hospital for checkups every six months thereafter. And, he was requested to seek therapy from the University of Pennsylvania Hospital Psychological Center. He went there only spasmodically. He was a loner, spending much of his time at the neighborhood public library in the quiet recesses of the reading room. He read prodigiously trying to catch up, often wondering what he had known before, if anything. Among the items he read about was Traumatic Amnesia. He just couldn't understand why his lack of memory covered such a spread of his life. Most traumatic cases covered a relatively brief period, sort of a protective device of the brain guarding the psyche from the horrors and pain of an injury. He wondered if his horrors had existed since childhood. He knew his present feelings of revulsion toward his father. Could they be part of his hidden tragedy? He didn't know. His unsuccessful attempts at bringing back the past would periodically overwhelm him and he would find escape in getting drunk and staying intoxicated for increasing periods of time. During all of that time, he continued to wear his Naval uniforms. They were his layered cocoon.

37

The senior Feldman was now a reluctant believer in his son's problem. Time and again, he was persuaded by Becky and Ruth to put Ben in a drying out facility. The family was afraid to go to the Navy with Ben's problem, worried that the Navy might revoke his retirement pay. And, Martin Feldman paid his son's expenses for those treatments, not reluctantly, but almost with a subconscious sense of guilt, as if he had contributed to Ben's present condition. But how? He continually asked himself.

38

Martin Feldman had seen a copy of his son's physical record. Not for one minute did he believe that the injury to Izzy happened the way it was reported. Unknown to Rebecca, he had hired David Armstrong, a private eye with armed service connections. That investigator had determined early in 1950 that Reserve Commander Ralph Farqua, his son's CO on Bora Bora, had been placed on the inactive Naval Reserve in 1946, and had received his honorable discharge from the Navy in May, 1949. Shortly after WWII, the former oil base CO had assumed a pivotal role in the Farqua Fishing and Shipping Company. He was divorced and had three children. His home was in Morgan City, Louisiana. For some strange reason, he was seldom in the U.S.

Through his investigator, Martin had learned that an islander named Mary D'Quino had testified at the Naval Board of Inquiry Hearing on Bora Bora. It was she who allegedly had found his injured son. She was no longer on the island. His source could not locate her. Martin Feldman often wondered just what she knew about the so-called accident. He could do nothing but accept the investigator's report and hope something would turn up in the future.

39

In the early spring of 1954, Ben Feldman was at Appleton Health Spa in the western part of Pennsylvania. He was struggling to emerge from the worst drinking episode he had ever suffered. Not only that, but as he was drying out, he caught the flu. His illness was serious. He had been delirious for several days during the worst of the onset. While recovering, he remembered a reoccurring nightmare he had experienced during his illness. In the dream, he was rolling on the ground with a green canopy of trees above him. He was in excruciating pain. Now and then he saw a glimpse of an odd-shaped, small building and a flash of many colors. Nothing more. Where was he? Had the incident really happened? Try as he did, no memory came from the nightmare, but the vague images bothered him.

When he was able to walk and began to regain his strength, he strolled from the veranda of the rambling, white, clapboard main building down the walkway that ultimately led across the sprawling lawn and then alongside the small lake on the property. He found a bench a few feet off the land side of the gravel path. The bench was shielded from the main building by a clump of prebudding Japonica bushes. The bench was facing the lake. Ben observed the relative privacy of the bench and its view to the west across the lake. He decided to sit. For the first time in his memory, he truly enjoyed watching the shimmering water surface and the evidence of returning greenery on the hills across the water. The view was a very comforting sight, an encouraging sight. The sorrow of winter was slowly leaving. Nature was reinventing herself. Looking down he saw new green grass sprouting through the gray stubble of winter kill. Every now and then a robin would light nimbly near him, cock its head, listen, then swiftly pierce the ground's surface with its beak and emerge triumphant with a less fortunate, small, squirming, ebbing life form. And so with all nature, he mused.

Then he watched a small cumulus cloud, high over the hill across the lake, change from a proud unicorn to a delicate butterfly. For the first time since he could remember, he felt a small thrill at just being alive. At last he could see and perceive and he could imagine. He returned daily to the bench. His favorite time was from 2:00 p.m. to 4:00 p.m. In that way, he could avoid contact with his peers who were in the retreat for many different reasons. He didn't want to participate in the so-called group therapy sessions. There wasn't a damned soul there with a background of Traumatic Amnesia. They wouldn't have any idea of his troubles, and he really didn't want to hear about theirs.

40

On the fifth day of visiting the bench, he was sitting quietly, his soul being fed by the signs of returning spring, when he became aware of someone standing on the walkway. He looked and saw a young, trim, petite, blonde lady staring at him. He said nothing, and looked out over the lake. The woman came closer. She smiled at Ben and said, "You've been sitting on my bench for the last five days."

"Your bench?"

What about Feldman?

"Yes, my bench, until you sat on it. Five days ago I was walking behind you when you came down the path and sat on my bench. I've been sitting on my bench in the afternoon for the last month, until you came along."

Ben looked at the girl; her eyes were a deeper blue than his. Her hair was flaxen, down to her shoulders, then a slight curl. Her features were clean cut. She wore a sloppy, light blue sweater that hung over her matching culottes. Even that informal attire didn't hide her trim figure. But, her shoulders did sag a bit as if she was habitually carrying a heavy load. She is pretty, he thought.

"May I sit with you, just for a few minutes?" she asked.

In that split second, Ben saw the dream image of his mother and Sven Olson on the bench in Fairmont Park. "Do," said Ben as he eased to the side of the bench. "I'm sorry, I didn't know I was usurping your bench."

"You're not usurping as long as you are willing to share," said the blonde as she scrutinized Ben from head to foot. "You haven't been here long, have you? I never saw you until five days ago."

"I've been here quite a while, but until recently I wasn't permitted far from my room. Things are on the mend now."

"Same here," said the girl. She continued to look with interest at Ben. "By the way, my name is Khristina, Khristina Koenig."

He smiled and held out his hand. "I'm Ben Feldman." She shook his hand with a firm grip.

"You're a nice looking guy. Why are you in this nuthouse?"

Ben was stumped at the blunt interest of his new acquaintance. He cast her a wary eye. "Because I can't remember," he answered calmly.

"You can't remember what?" asked Khristina.

"Much of anything before I was involved in an accident on the island of Bora Bora in the southwest Pacific."

"You were in the armed forces?"

83

"You'd never know it from this jumpsuit they make me wear here. But, yes, I still am. I'm a U.S. Naval Lieutenant retired for disability."

"All because you can't remember?"

"That, and its follow-up problem -- alcohol," said Ben.

"Oh, I see," said Khristina as she continued to stare at him.

"And you?" inquired Ben.

Khristina's eyes left Ben's and looked across the lake, far beyond the lake. Softly she said, "I'm not a virgin."

"So?" said Ben.

"I haven't been one since I was a child, eight years old."

Ben looked intently at Khristina. Her eyes were now blue ice cold.

"My father raped me repeatedly from the time I was eight until I was thirteen. Then, when I was thirteen, the bastard died in 1936. Thank God I never became pregnant. I doubt that I ever will."

She looked at Ben with an odd look of disgust, disgust for all men. Then her features softened. "I'm sorry," she said. "It has taken me a long time to come to grips with my problem."

"Didn't your mother know and try to put a stop to what your dad was doing to you?" asked Ben.

"She knew nothing about it for years. I'm an only child. My mom worked the night shift at a twenty-four-hour White Tower hamburger joint. My old man was a carpenter. She just didn't know what went on when she wasn't there. My dad threatened that he would kill me and her if I said anything. God, what horrors I lived through. My mom has been most supportive since my dad's death. She foots my medical bills. She says that's the least she can do. But, she really doesn't understand. She sleeps around with a number of guys for free, now that dad's gone. She's like a bitch in heat, released from the confines of a small pen. But, she loves me. I know my problem eats up most of the money she makes. I try to work, but when a guy begins to come on to me, that's when I get panicky."

"What kind of work did you do?" asked Ben.

"I was a keypunch operator in the accounting department of Wannamakers Department Store in Philadelphia," Khristina replied.

"I guess we're an odd couple," said Ben, with a slight grin.

"How so?" asked Khristina.

"I can't remember and you can't forget," replied Ben.

She nodded, "You're so right."

For a while, Ben didn't know why he said what he did. It just came out. "Maybe we can try to help each other solve our problems, or at least help each other to live with them."

Khristina looked at Ben. No longer were her eyes ice blue. They turned the sky blue of a lovely, clear June day. She felt a strange glow. The tone of those words offered a trust she had longed for over the years. This new acquaintance knew the worst of her past. And just like that, he had offered, as a friend, to aid in her future. Suddenly she needed him and she knew, by some hidden instinct, he needed her.

"Ben Feldman, how about us starting now?" and, with tears brimming her eyes, she again held out her hand. Ben enfolded it with both of his.

"You've got a deal," he said gently.

41

Ben and Khristina then discussed, in depth, their individual problems. Khristina soon learned that Ben's lack of memory had caused a real alcohol problem. Her father drank too much but never admitted it. She, too, believed that if Ben were to ever know the source of his injury, he might regain his memory, or most of it. Whether that would be good or bad, she didn't know. In the meantime, she would try and help him make a life for himself, and that concept wasn't altogether altruistic. At least she would, from time to time, be concentrating on someone else's troubles. The nice thing was, they lived in the same city. They could see each other frequently, if things worked out. And, he wasn't coming on to her for sex -- not yet.

Ben's needs were far more subtle. He knew he cared for his sister, Becky, but he still felt he was just floating. Nothing was tying him down to living a real life. No one needed him for any reason. He felt his family and even his doctors just tolerated him because he was a human being, a flawed human being. Now, here was someone who had said she needed help and offered her hand in trust. He now had a reason to live, regardless of his lack of memory. Someone would be relying on him for help. An honest, open, and, to him, already a lovely friend, the third one he had made since he came to aboard the *Southern Cross*.

The two new friends sat in relaxed silence. Each gazed out over the lake.

"If you were to remember, would you stay with the Navy?" asked Khristina.

Ben looked thoughtfully at the bluebird beside him. "No, not a chance."

"What would you do?"

"Tina, can I call you Tina," he asked. Somehow the nickname came to Ben and he thought it was appropriate.

"I like that," she smiled.

"Well, Tina, I've been thinking about what I could do, should do, since the first day I sat on this bench."

Ben looked to each side of the bench at the beginnings of a greening lawn and then pointed over the lake to the deepening green growth on the hillside. "I've no desire to return to my Papa's liquor business. I'm afraid that would continue one of my problems. I know I never really wanted to be in the Navy. My Papa pushed me there. Although I'm light-skinned, freckled and red-headed, and I'd probably suffer much from the sun, I really would like to work in the open on grass, around shrubs and flowers. Even as a kid, I loved to go to the park just to be outdoors surrounded by trees and shrubs."

Khristina's blue eyes bore into Ben's. She wasn't surprised. She almost expected the answer. She said, "Ben, go for it. I think it would help make you happier. And, you know what? Something tells me you would be damned good at such a career. But, making the attempt would be like starting all over again. It's gonna' take time."

"Right now I've got plenty of that," responded Ben. "How about you?"

"I know it sounds stupid, particularly after my childhood experiences, but I would love to learn how to work with disturbed children," said Tina.

Ben looked down at his slack-shouldered new friend and thought what an amazing triumph for her that would be. He smiled at her. "You'd be a natural," he said softly.

42

The outside dinner bell tolled. Supper would be served in fifteen minutes. There were three dining rooms in the main building, the men's, the ladies', and the mixed. Those patients permitted to walk the grounds unescorted could sit in their own gender dining room or in the mixed dining room. "Let's eat in the mixed dining room," said Ben, much to his surprise.

"I'd like that," replied Khristina.

43

The twosome left the bench and strolled toward the front steps. Two staff doctors were standing on the veranda looking out over the lawn and saw Ben and Khristina approach. One turned to the other and commented, "I think we're making progress with those two."

"Could be," was the reply. "Or could be those two are making their own progress."

44

Ben and Khristina were together regularly after that first meeting.

Mornings, they frequently went to the game room, where Tina taught Ben to play gin rummy. He was an apt pupil and soon they were playing a Hollywood three-game score and carrying the score over from day to day. Their conversations ranged far and wide and were mutually beneficial. Afternoons, they took long walks on the grounds.

On 14 March 1954, Khristina brought to their rendezvous bench a copy of a recent edition of the *Philadelphia Inquirer*. She was excited. When she and Ben were seated, she said, "I've been looking at the help wanted section of the paper. I've found something that might interest you." She opened the paper and pointed to an ad she had ringed with her pen.

> *Outside maintenance man wanted for small estate on Philadelphia Main Line. Duties include mowing, grounds maintenance, shrubbery planting and pruning. Quarters on grounds. Salary negotiable. Only real workers need apply. POB 670, Paoli, Pa.*

"Apply, Ben, apply. I even brought a pen and some plain paper so you could write a note. I've got envelopes back in my room." Her enthusiasm was catching.

For the first time since his accident, he became interested in a future. He looked at Khristina. "I don't have the slightest idea about grounds maintenance," he said.

"You're no dummy. You can learn. And, if you truly like outdoors and nature, you'll learn fast," replied Khristina. "Besides that, you've got a little income from the Navy. You can afford to accept less money than most other people, at least at the start."

"Damn, you're clever."

"You just finding that out?" laughed Khristina.

Ben smiled. Something inside of him that had been trapped was freeing itself. He had a strange feeling of attachment for another human being. He couldn't describe the feeling. He couldn't define it, but it was there.

"Here, I'll help you start your application letter," said Khristina. Together they worked out the language; a bit subtle, long on interest, but not much on experience. "When you sign the letter, put your home address and telephone number under your name."

Ben looked blankly at Khristina. "I know my address but through all these years I haven't used the phone yet. I've no idea what my parents' phone number is."

"I do," said Khristina. "I looked it up in the Philadelphia phone book in the library here."

Ben's eyes popped wide open with surprise. "Jeez!" he said.

"Jeez, nothing," said Khristina. "We're both supposed to be leaving this noble institution on Sunday. I wanted to know how to reach you. Here's my address and phone number at home and at work," and she handed Ben a small, folded sheet of writing paper. "Just in case you want to reach me."

Ben was confused and embarrassed. "I. . . I. . . should have been the one asking for addresses and phone numbers," Ben said almost in a whisper.

"Look, my friend, you've got a lot of catching up on life to do. I know that. And, I've got a lot of trusting to learn to accept. We agreed to try and help each other didn't we?"

For the moment Ben was flabbergasted. Then, without even a second thought, he wrapped his arms around her waist, drew her to him, and said, "Thank God you found me."

Khristina shivered slightly as she leaned away from him. The shiver wasn't from fright. It was from a thrill she had never before experienced. He cared for her. She knew and liked the feeling.

Then, they both relaxed.

Ben looked at her and hesitatingly asked, "What are you going to do when you leave here?"

"I've got a job. I got it by phone. I'm starting out as an apprentice helper in the Children's Center at Harmony House in Philly." Ben's admiration for Tina soared.

45

On Sunday, Becky came in her Papa's Cadillac and picked up Ben. Khristina, looking out of her third-floor room window, watched him leave. Later her mother came by with a boyfriend and the threesome headed home in his old Ford pickup truck.

46

"You look much better, Izzy," said his sister as they drove toward Philadelphia.

"Becky, I am better. For the first time, I really am better."

The tone of her brother's voice piqued Becky's curiosity. "What was so different about the place?"

"The place wasn't much different from the others, but the atmosphere was," said Ben with a slight smile.

"Thank God you've met a woman at last," said Becky as she concentrated on the road.

"I didn't say that."

"You didn't have to. For the first time since you came home, you sound like a man looking for a future instead of a lost memory. You're no religious freak, you didn't get religion that made you look to the future. The only other source had to be a woman, maybe a good woman."

"How did you know? I never said so."

"Izzy, I'm your sister and a woman. You didn't have to say a damned word. I wondered if you ever would find one. Tell me about her."

On the way home, Ben told his sister about Tina, downplaying the horrors his new friend had lived through in her childhood. Then he told Becky how Tina helped him write his letter for a job as a maintenance man on a Main Line estate. When he finished, Becky glanced at him and said sternly,

"Don't tell Mama or Papa about your new job until it happens, if it does. When they find out about your new vocation, they're going to raise hell."

"Why?" Ben asked.

"Because their son, a graduate of the Naval Academy, a lieutenant in the U.S. Navy, joint heir to the Feldman estate and liquor business, decides to be an outside maintenance man. At first they're going to shit a brick at such a choice.

"Don't get me wrong, Izzy. I love the idea. That leaves me in charge of the business," she said kiddingly.

"I don't want to be a part of the liquor business. I doubt if I ever did."

"I know you didn't," said Becky. "Papa never gave you a chance to consider what you wanted to do. He took command. Now stick by your guns. You've a life to live. In my opinion, it could be a happier one than any other member of Papa's family has ever led."

"How so?" asked Ben.

"Because happiness isn't controlled by Papa," Becky said with a sigh.

47

They had driven for about an hour. Ben was dozing in the front passenger seat. Suddenly, Becky put on the brakes and pulled off the highway into a filling station. "I gotta' get some gas and take a pee. You wanna' go?"

"No," said Ben, "I'm fine."

"You always were a camel," and she headed for the filling station.

When Becky returned to the car, she paid for the gasoline and said, "Slide over, it's about time to find out if you have forgotten how to drive."

Ben was surprised and a little fearful. "I never even thought about driving before."

"Well, think about it now, buddy, because you're going to try and I'm going to raise hell if you don't do it right."

Ben sat, uncertain as to whether or not he should make the attempt.

His sister opened the passenger side door, "Slide over, dammit. You're going to drive," and she handed him the keys.

Ben slid over to the driver's seat and almost subconsciously put the key in the ignition and turned on the engine.

"Fine," said Becky. "Just remember this bucket of bolts is straight stick shift, no overdrive. The clutch is the pedal on your left."

Ben had no trouble shifting gears and getting the car out on the highway. He was nervous and proceeded slowly. After a few minutes, with cars whizzing by on either side of him on the three-lane, divided highway, his sister was getting edgy. She said, "Izzy, I want to get home before I have menopause. The speedometer is right here on the dashboard." She pointed, and continued, "The speed limit is fifty-five miles an hour. You're going twenty. We're going to get clobbered if you don't go with the flow. Before the war, you had the heaviest foot in the family. We hated to ride with you. You didn't know the meaning of a speed limit. I can tell you haven't forgotten how to drive, just goose it a little, will you?"

Ben's confidence at the wheel returned rapidly. After another fifteen minutes, his sister looked at him nervously. "Dammit, Ben, you don't have to go from one extreme to the other. Slow down. I all but wet in my pants when you passed that last car. You were doing eighty-five."

Ben looked at his sister with a shy grin, "Yep, I'll slow her down. It just feels good to remember something and I do remember how to drive."

"That little Swede has surely turned up your cooker," said Becky with a twinkle in her eyes. Ben smiled.

48

Ben's parents greeted him and Becky at the front door. They looked at him with hope in their eyes. They did so each time he had arrived home from a drying out. Ben greeted his parents with a much more relaxed attitude. They were surprised and looked questioningly at Becky. She pretended not to see their facial expressions. Inwardly, she was enjoying the scene. Now, if only Ben has the guts to stick by his resolve, she mused.

The front door had hardly been shut when Martin Feldman turned to his son, "A James Hedley on the Main Line wants you to call him, here's his number," and Ben's father handed him a small piece of paper. Martin's face wore an expression that openly asked, and what did Hedley call you for?

"Thanks, Papa," said Ben as he put the paper in his wallet.

Becky all but broke out laughing as she watched her brother put the number away and saw the crestfallen look on her father's face as he realized his son had no intention of telling him the purpose of Hedley's call.

"Benny, it's so good to have you back," said his mother and then she added, "I've kept some chicken soup hot on the stove for you and Becky. Would you like some now? I know the drive was a chilly one."

"That would be just the thing," he replied.

"Me, too," said Becky.

Ruth Feldman padded in her house slippers to the kitchen, joyful at being able to meet a need.

49

B en joined his father and sister in the den at happy hour. "What'll you have, Son?" asked Martin Feldman.

"For the present, I'll take a ginger ale on ice," replied Ben. Becky looked at her brother approvingly. His father was surprised, but pleased. This was the first time Izzy had turned down a drink, even on his first day back from a drying out tank. Supper was a much more pleasant interlude than usual.

Martin Feldman studied his son. Something had changed him. He was beginning to be focused. Ben hadn't alluded to his loss of memory during the entire meal. Ruth

Feldman looked at Ben, then caught her daughter's eye. Becky nodded ever so slightly to her mother. Ruth looked down at her plate, to hide the tears of relief that brimmed her eyes. She, too, now knew that Benny had found a woman. What kind? Right at the moment, she didn't care. At last he was showing signs of recovery.

50

B enjamin Feldman slept late the next morning and lolled around his room until he was sure all the family had left. The only other person in the house was Ida, the maid. She was in the basement handling the laundry. He went downstairs to the den and called Mr. Hedley. He made an appointment to meet the estate owner the next day at 11:30 a.m. Then Ben gulped down his breakfast and, after studying the bus routes from the front of the phone book, headed for Wannamakers Store. This was his first trip downtown and he was nervous. He left the house, walked half the distance to the bus stop and realized he'd have to return to the house for a last nervous pee. He was excited. At last he could shed his cocoon.

Once in the store, he was at times befuddled by the crowds that raced through the aisles. Finally, he found the men's clothing section and purchased a couple of sport coats, slacks, turtleneck shirts, sweatshirts, blue demin work pants, work shoes and a heavy lined trench coat. He felt confidence for the first time. He was going to get that job come hell or high water and he was going to be prepared to go to work immediately. He knew he just had to leave his home if he ever was to become self-reliant. When he finished his buying, he felt elated. He had really done something on his own. He even had considerable cash left over so he indulged in an extravagance. He took his purchases home in a taxi.

51

W hen Ben arrived home, none of his family had returned from their forays. He was delighted.

He took his new clothes up to his room and stowed most of them in his closet and dresser. He changed from his Naval uniform to civvies, stretched out on his bed and, from a map of the city, studied how to take the Suburban to the Paoli Station. Mr. Hedley would meet him there. For the first time since he could remember, he was excited about the possibility of a future. And behind it all, he thought, is Khristina. I've got to call her and tell her what's happening. He reached into his wallet and pulled out the slip of paper with her address and phone number. She even had her new work phone number on the sheet. He went down to the den and dialed the number.

"Childrens Center," said a cheery voice on the other end.

"May I speak with Khristina Koenig, please?" asked Ben.

"Sure," said the voice, "Just a sec," and he heard, "Khristina, phone for you."

There was silence then. "This is Khristina Koenig speaking."

Ben was so excited he couldn't talk immediately.

"Anybody there?" asked Khristina.

Ben cleared this throat, "Only Ben," he said.

Khristina giggled. "Only Ben. Who could ask for anyone better?"

"Tina, I need to talk to you, so much is going on."

"What?" asked Khristina.

"First of all, I've got an appointment with a Mr. Hedley in response to my job application."

"When?"

"Tomorrow at 11:30 a.m. I'm so damned nervous I don't know if I can muster the courage for the interview."

"Look, Ben, whether you realize it or not, as a Senior Lieutenant in the Navy, you had to handle a lot of stressful matters. You can handle that interview. And just remember, I'm by your side every inch of the way."

"God, Tina, just hearing your voice is calming." There was silence, then Ben continued. "Until you spoke, I didn't know how much I missed you." And he realized she was the first person he had truly missed since his accident.

"Ben, I have a class to attend after work tonight. But, I'll tell you what, how about meeting me for supper tomorrow night at Bookbinders Restaurant on Walnut Street? I'll be at the front entrance at 6:00 p.m. By then you'll know how your meeting went with Mr. Hedley and we can have a leisurely meal."

"You're one smart apple. I'll have to find Bookbinders on the city map, but I'll be there," replied Ben spiritedly.

"Ben. . ." then there was silence.

"Yes?"

"Promise me you will go to the interview and, whether the results of your meeting are good or bad -- promise me you'll meet me at 6:00 p.m."

Ben knew the reason for her hesitation. "I promise. I'll go and I will meet you. Either way I'll need your help," he said.

There was again a brief silence followed by words he had never heard before, never really expected to hear, and wasn't sure he knew their meaning. "I love you, Ben Feldman," and the receiver on the other end clicked.

Ben gazed into the phone as if it held some magical revelation. Had he really heard those words? What did they mean? So much of his past life was behind the gray veil. If only he could remember.

Right then he decided to walk to the local branch of the public library. It wasn't far from his home. He had never felt this way about anyone. He needed to find something to help him. He desperately wanted this relationship to be a meaningful one. To him, his future seemed to hinge on Tina.

52

Once in the library, whose reading room he had regularly frequented in the past, he headed for the desk and asked one of the librarians how to become a member. Shortly thereafter, he had his card. He asked the same silver-haired librarian where he could find books on human relationships. She escorted him to the shelf area, and quietly left. He browsed. He didn't realize there were so many books on the subject. As he slowly walked the aisle, he saw a small, much-handled, red-jacketed volume, *A Marriage Manual*, by Hannah and Abraham Stone. It piqued his curiosity. He took the volume from the shelf and thumbed through the table of contents. Damn, this will at least get me started, he mused.

Back home, he flopped on his bed, turned on the bedside lamp, and started to read.

53

"Libation time," Becky hollered up the stairway. "Come on down and join us, Ben."

He arose, straightened his turtle neck shirt and put on one of his new sport coats. When he entered the den, Becky exploded, "Who in the hell are you, you handsome bastard?"

Ben's father looked at him in surprised approval. "Son, you really do look different without your uniform."

Ben looked at his father and calmly replied, "I am different."

Becky thought, if Mama and Papa only knew what I know.

54

Supper began pleasantly, but Ruth was nervous. She sensed that her son was up to something, just what she couldn't fathom. Her uneasiness took what little appetite she had.

During supper, Ben's dad kept glancing approvingly at him. Finally, he could contain himself no longer. "Ben, are you sure you wouldn't like to try the office again? There is a spot open for you."

"No, Papa. I wouldn't fit in," Ben replied.

"How do you know that when you haven't even given it a try?"

"I just know," said his son calmly.

"Well, what are you going to do, sit on your ass around here all day, and then go out and get drunk at night?"

"That's not going to happen any more," Ben said sharply.

Ruth Feldman now knew her son was up to something. There was a ring of positiveness in his tone, a part of the Benny she once knew had returned, the better part before Martin had endeavored to suppress it.

Becky was watching the threesome as if she was attending the opening night of a much heralded new play. To her, the opening scene was living up to all the publicity only she knew about.

"And, I promise you, I'll not be sitting on my ass around here much longer," said Ben in cold anger.

"Benny, Benny, Papa didn't mean it that way," wailed his Mama. "You can stay here as long as you need to. Until you're well."

"Hey," said Becky, "This is a supper table, not a free-for-all boxing ring." Becky cast her father a scathing glance. He saw and immediately calmed down.

Much to Ben's surprise, his father turned to him and said sheepishly, "I'm sorry, Benjamin. I get irritated. I just don't understand you."

"I know," said Ben as he looked at his father and for the first time saw an aging, selfish, proud, stubborn, old man who had been a street fighter all his life. But, a man who had at least attempted to hold his family together and thrive against unbelievable odds. Ben now knew sorrow.

His sister changed the subject of conversation. "Where did you get those duds?" she asked.

"Today at Wannamakers," replied Ben.

"You did good, Benny," said his Mama. "You've got a good eye for coordination."

"Thanks, Mama."

Then the table conversation turned to topics of the day, the Eisenhower administration, the Berlin airlift, the current weather and recent sleet storm. Ben headed upstairs after supper to read more of the marriage manual. He read through much of the night. What he read disturbed him for he remembered so little.

55

The next morning at the breakfast table Ben said casually, "I gotta' go in town today. I won't be home until later this evening. So don't expect me for supper." Becky cast him a knowing glance. His Mama and Papa wondered just what he was up to but knew he wasn't going to tell them until he was ready.

"Be careful, Benny," said his mother. "You still don't know your way around too good."

"I'll be careful," replied Ben.

56

Benjamin met Hedley at the Paoli Station. Hedley was a chubby, past-middle-aged man, bald as a coot, but with a definite sense of humor. As they drove toward the estate, he remarked, "My wife is the one who makes the choice of employees at the house. If she is satisfied with you, that's OK by me. But the job is no simple turkey shoot. She's a stickler for detail, with a tongue as sharp as a Gillette Blue Blade. Underneath it all, she's a good gal, just a little bit too much Boston Back Bay. Now that the kids are grown and left home, she has no one to boss except me and the staff help. They generally don't stay long. I keep on hanging around 'cause I love her."

Ben thought, I guess he's trying to tell me his wife is rather demanding.

Benjamin Feldman met Mrs. Hedley. She was tall, stern, but there was a definite twinkle in her hazel eyes. She wore a mannish, tailored, brown, tweed suitcoat and matching trousers. Her silver-gray hair was almost in a boyish bob.

As they entered the house, she said, "Young man, come in, sit before the fire, and tell me about yourself."

Ben was stumped. He hadn't expected such an approach. Before he could open his mouth, she said, "You haven't been using your hands much for heavy work, have you?"

"No, to tell you the truth, I haven't." He just didn't know what else to say.

"Well, what have you been doing, Mr. Feldman?"

Ben eyed the keen woman. "I've been recovering from an injury."

Mr. Hedley was carefully studying his wife's potential employee.

"You're a war casualty aren't you?" he asked.

"Yes," answered Ben, "In the Navy."

"What maintenance experience do you have?" asked Miriam Hedley.

"None, absolutely none," answered Ben.

Miriam Hedley's eyebrows raised a mite at the blunt, honest answers of the young man sitting by the fire.

"Can you drive a car?" asked Mr. Hedley.

"Yes," said Ben.

"Then, you ought to be able to drive the mowing equipment," he said.

"Can you read and write?" asked Hedley.

"Certainly," replied Ben.

"Are you married?"

"No," said Ben.

"Are you divorced?" inquired Mrs. Hedley.

Again Ben said, "No."

"Aren't you a little old not to be married?" asked Hedley.

"That's none of your business, James," snapped his wife. Turning to Ben, she said, "You will have a lot to learn before spring really arrives."

"I can give it a good try," said Ben, and he grinned sheepishly.

"You know what, Mr. Feldman, I believe you can," said Miriam as she maintained her study of the young man before her. "Three hundred and fifty bucks a month to start, less your share of social security, and you will occupy the one-bedroom apartment over the garage, including a telephone."

Ben couldn't believe his luck, "When do you want me to start?" he asked.

"How about tomorrow?" said Mr. Hedley.

"That's fine with me," answered Ben. "I'll bring my gear out tomorrow morning." He arose and held his hand out to Mrs. Hedley. She grasped it in a firm grip.

"It'll be nice to have you," said Mr. Hedley.

Ben's heart was thumping so loud he was afraid the Hedleys could hear it. He now knew elation.

Just as he was leaving the house with Mr. Hedley, Mrs. Hedley touched him lightly on his arm. He looked at her. Her eyes were clouded with sorrow. "You were a Naval officer?" asked Mrs. Hedley.

Ben smiled a little, bitter smile. "Yes, Mrs. Hedley, I was."

"I was sure of it from the minute you walked in the door," she said gently. "The Academy always leaves its mark."

Ben was surprised and saddened for he realized his new employer had lost an Academy son in the war. Suddenly, he remembered a name, Graham Hedley. But where, when? Damn, if only I could remember more, he thought.

57

Mr. Hedley drove him to the station and Ben took the Suburban into central Philadelphia. Despite the sleet that was falling, he walked around and saw some sights including the Republican Club. At 6:00 p.m., he was in front of Bookbinders Restaurant. As he came up to the entrance, he saw Tina hurrying down Walnut Street to meet him. She never stopped until she threw her arms around him and gave him a kiss. Then, she stepped back, looked at him sternly for a second and broke into a big grin. "You don't have to say a word. Your eyes say it for you. You got the job."

Tears filled Tina's eyes. "Ben, I'm so proud, I just knew it would happen. All day long a little engine inside of me kept huffing, I know he will, I know he will. Let's eat, I'm starved."

Arm in arm, the couple entered Bookbinders to have their first real world meal together. The evening flew by. Their conversation ranged far and wide. During a respite, Ben reached into his sport coat pocket and pulled out the used, small marriage manual.

"I've learned so many things from this little volume, not just about sex, but relationships, patience, attempts at understanding. So many things I didn't recall. Would you like to borrow the manual?"

Khristina looked with ever increasing affection at Ben. He's got more innate moxie and decency than any guy I've ever known, she thought. If he's this way now, with little or no memory, just what would he be like with a full plate? "I'd love to share the book with you. There's so much I have to learn also. And to learn it with you is a blessing and opportunity I never expected to have in my life."

Ben reached across the table and took her hands in his. "I don't know if I ever have had such a feeling before. But, now I know I care. I need you."

Khristina's shoulders shook as she sobbed. With the life she had led, had been forced to lead, she had felt dirty and soiled ever since she was a child. What decent man would truly care for her? That question was part of her problem. Here before her was this naive guy who knew her past, telling her he cared for her and needed her. Needed her -- the defiled kid since she was eight -- she knew she was attracted to him the moment she laid eyes on him. She had honestly told him so. And now he had responded in a way that made her heart soar and cleansed her soul. She was a virgin in spirit.

58

After supper the couple walked hand-in-hand through the sleet covered streets of downtown

Philadelphia. The miniature lights in the boxed trees in front of many of the stores made the couple feel as if they were walking among the stars, so far above all other humanity. The blustery wind from the northwest blew down Walnut Street. Khristina moved closer to Ben. "Hon," she said, "Let's catch a cab, I really should go home. It's cold. There's a stand just up ahead. I see a yellow there."

The couple hustled up the street. As they were entering the taxi, he glanced at his watch. "My gosh, it's late. I had no idea. It's 11:30 p.m. and I've got to move my things to the Hedleys tomorrow morning."

Khristina nodded understanding. Once in the cab, Ben gave the driver her address. She snuggled next to him. As she did, he looked at her, placed his right arm around her shoulder, and with his other hand he tilted her face to his. Through the semidarkness of the back seat, two pairs of loving blue eyes spoke more than words could say. He leaned down and kissed her gently on the lips. Her arms wrapped around his neck and pulled him closer to her. She responded in a manner and with a fervor she had feared she would never have for any man. As the cab skidded around a corner, they heard the cabby's retort through the seat dividing glass. "Damn, this here sleet. Who invented it anyway?" The cab stopped for a red light. Ben heaved a sigh, "I know that never in my life, memory or no memory, have I ever felt like this. This is the most wonderful moment of my life I can remember, or want to."

"Ben, oh, Ben," said Tina softly. "This makes up for all those years of horror. I was so sure I would detest all men forever. You've done more than you'll ever know in freeing me from hell."

Ben again tilted the tear-stained face of the blonde toward his. "Tina, I do care so much and I need you in ways I don't even know how to express. But who am I? I don't even know. How long it will take for me to find out, I have no idea. When and if I do, you may find I'm not worth loving at all."

Khristina put her hand on Ben's face, "You may not know who you are, or maybe you just don't think you do. But, memory or no memory, I know and love the real Ben Feldman. As long as you need me, I'll be by your side," and she reached up and gave him a gentle kiss on his lips. Then she leaned back, and with her blue eyes sparkling, said, "Get out your handkerchief and wipe your lips and face." She giggled, "If you arrive home looking like you do now, your family would think either you've turned into a fag or you've been on a smooching party with some wild girl."

Ben laughed, pulled out his handkerchief, wiped his face and lips. "Why am I doing this now? I'll just have to do it all over again after we say goodnight." Tina laughed and snuggled up to her true love.

59

The cab drove up to Khristina's apartment house. Ben told the cabby to wait. When he left the apartment entrance and re-entered the cab, he did wipe his face and lips again. He gave the cab driver his address. On arrival he entered his parents' home, closed the door, took off his shoes, and started up the stairs. As he approached the landing, the grandfather's clock sounded one resonant reverberating tone announcing 12:30 a.m. Ben smiled.

Just as he opened the door of his room, Becky's door opened, casting light into the hall, and she stood in her purple robe, looking at him mischievously. "Hi, little brother. You've really had a long day. And you didn't wipe all the strawberry shortcake off your right cheek."

"You, dog, you," said Ben with a guffaw, and he again wiped his cheek. "What are you doing up at this hour?"

"Watching time go by as usual, and waiting for a report on your action," said Becky.

"Well, you better get some sleep because if you're not busy tomorrow morning, I need your help to drive me."

"Tomorrow's Saturday. I'm not busy, but why do you need my help?"

"I'm moving. I got a job today."

"And that's not all you got," Becky again glanced at Ben's face.

Ben smiled, then said, "I need you to take me and my belongings to the Hedley estate.   I start tomorrow as the outside maintenance man."

Becky's expressive brown eyes opened as wide as small bagels. "You really took that job?"

"Sure did. I start tomorrow."

"Holy cow, the crap's gonna' hit the fan when you tell Mama and Papa -- especially Papa. He didn't think you had the guts to strike out on your own, particularly with your problem. Despite what you said, he still believes he can coax you back under his wing."

"Well, he's wrong, dead wrong."

"I believe you. And, Izzy, in her heart Mama knows you would leave sometime. But, break it to her gently. In her way, she's had new life since you returned." She hesitated. "It's Papa that's really gonna' be crushed. Underneath that rough outside is a soft spot -- you were his tomorrow. Now all he'll have is me and he's too damned chauvinistic to know what he's got."

"Becky, I'm a guy with no memory, but I've been watching. I'm beginning to know Papa and I do know you. Don't ever think Papa doesn't know what he's got. He knows you can outsmart him in business. And you know what, he loves the idea, but he'd never tell you -- not 'til he is on his death bed."

"Enough of this you-kiss-mine-and-I'll-kiss-yours," grinned Becky. "But, I gotta' say, this Tina, whoever she is, has surely turned your face from an unknown past to a glowing future."

"Lay off. I'm just trying to get started."

"Izzy, I didn't mean to sound sarcastic or smug.   I may be a little jealous of you if you have found a good friend. She apparently has made a definite change in your attitude.   I commend her. And if she's a good woman, I'm happy for you."

Ben looked with affection at his sister. "Becky, she is a good woman -- better than I deserve. And she knows I don't know who I am. But she's already proven to be my friend. I need her."

"The remaining question, does she need you?"

"Far more than I ever imagined anyone would. And that's all the questions. I'm pooped," said Ben.

"Good night, little brother, and for all your lack of memory, I envy you tonight," said Becky as she re-entered her room and closed the door.

60

The next morning with all four family members at the breakfast table, Ben broke the news to his parents. "Mama and Papa, I have some news." Martin and Ruth looked at their son. "I have a job. I'm moving to the Hedley estate on the Main Line. Becky is taking me there this morning."

"Oh, dear God, not so soon," moaned Ruth.

A perplexed Martin Feldman scowled. "What kind of a job?"

"I'm going to be the outside maintenance man at their estate."

"You're going to be what?"

"The outside maintenance man at the Hedley estate," said Ben calmly.

"And I spent a pot full of money for you at Bullis Prep and weaseled an appointment for you to the Naval Academy, all for you to become a servant on an estate? I don't give a damn if it was the Rockefeller estate, no son of mine. . ."

"Hold it right there, Papa," and Becky's voice had the sharp resonance of a drill sergeant.

Even Ben looked in surprise at his sister's controlling demeanor.

"Ben owes you nothing. He's served his country and because of that he has suffered. He has never given you or Mama any real trouble. Now he's trying to find himself and it takes guts to do it. More guts than you'll ever know," said Martin's daughter.

"Oh, Benny, must you go now?" moaned his mother.

"Yes, Mama," replied Ben. "I've gotta' make an effort and this is a start. I won't be far away. I'll have a phone and I'll come by frequently."

He turned to his father, "Papa, I'm sorry you spent all that money. I never knew it before. The fact is, I never knew where or if I went to prep school. I still have practically no recollection of the Academy. I know I am a bitter disappointment to you. Right now, I'm a disappointment to myself. If I'm ever going to have a life, I've got to start with something I can handle and want to do. For some strange reason, I really want to try this job. I'm looking forward to it."

Becky was still glowering at her father.

Martin Feldman fought for emotional control. "Very well, Benjamin, if you are sure," he said as he looked at his half-eaten breakfast.

"For now, I'm sure," said Ben. "Who knows what may change if I ever get my memory back."

"Who knows and who's got the time?" replied Ben's father.

"Ben, you better start getting your gear together. I have a hairdresser appointment at 2:00 p.m. This weather has ruined my permanent," said Becky with a wry smile.

"Benny, I'll help you pack," said his still distraught mother.

61

As Ben and his mother were finishing packing his clothes in the suitcase and Val-pac, Ruth Feldman went to the dresser and lovingly caressed the silver frame with her son's full-dress Naval Academy picture in it. Ben watched. "Mama, I'm not taking that, the picture is yours, always has been."

She took the picture off the dresser, placed it against her bosom, and walked over to her son. Holding the picture with her left hand, she reached out her right hand, grabbed him by an ear, pulled his head down, planted a kiss on his lips, and said tearfully, "Benny, you are one big man, bigger even that Papa. God bless you forever."

Ben's eyes filled with tears for now he knew filial love. "Thanks. Mama." And, for the first time, the words came out, "I love you, Mama, and am proud to be your son." Ruth Feldman cried in relief. Her son was back.

62

Ben Feldman settled in to his bare new quarters, a bedroom with a three-quarter bed, dresser and boudoir chair; a living-dining room with a folding sofa bed, an end table, two straight chairs, a cardtable and a Franklin fireplace stove; a small kitchen; and complete bath. The quarters were over the three-car garage and were entered by an outside stairway that went up one end of the garage.

As he finished stowing his gear, the phone rang, "Mr. Feldman, will you please come to the main house? I'm in the den. I'd like to give you some instructions." She must have seen Sis drive up in her car, he thought.

"I'll be right there, Mrs. Hedley," he replied.

Mrs. Hedley was sitting in a lounging chair before the embers in the large fireplace. Ben stood in the doorway and rapped on the wall. "Come in, Ben. You don't mind if I call you Ben, do you?"

"Not at all, Mrs. Hedley."

"You arrived here at a very opportune time for Mr. Hedley and me. We're leaving for our Florida home at Johns Island day after tomorrow. I hate a late winter sleet storm. The equipment shed is behind the garage. I want you to become familiar with all the machinery and tools in there. There are a dozen manuals on the shelf over the work bench. Know what's in them by the time we return, which will be in about six weeks. Please see that the driveway to the entrance gate is kept passable. The snowblade is on the tractor. Learn how to use it, but be careful and don't gouge the macadam. See that the gang mowers are sharpened. The gasoline edger needs a new blade. Whatever blades or small tools you need, get them at Scarfe's Hardware on the Main Line. Just charge our account. But, if anything major happens, call us in Florida. Here's the number. Dora, the maid, in going to stay in the main house. She'll provide your meals while we're gone. Just keep a weather eye on everything. The crocuses and jonquils in the beds lining the driveway should be the first real signs of spring you will see. If we should have another sleet or ice storm and major damage occurs, call Mr. Dougall's Tree Service. Any questions?"

She stopped and waited for a reply.

"I don't expect any problems," said Ben.

"Just one last thing." He waited. "You're an officer and a gentleman. I expect your conduct in your quarters to live up to that reputation," she said.

Ben smiled at her. "Have no fear, Mrs. Hedley, I think as much of my name as you do of yours. I will be discrete."

"That's all, Ben."

"I hope you and Mr. Hedley have good weather and a pleasant sojourn."

"Thank you, I hope so, too," responded his employer. Ben left.

He realized that with the Hedleys in Florida, he would be quite isolated. The nearest bus stop was a couple miles away and about four miles to the Suburban. He needed transportation and then he remembered he had no driving permit.

63

The Hedleys left on Monday. On Tuesday Ben hiked to the bus stop and went to the nearest Pennsylvania Motor Vehicle Office, took the driving tests and obtained a new driver's permit. During the weekend, he had received his savings account bank statement. He had ample funds to buy a decent second-hand car. He went to Paoli Ford, found a used Country Squire wagon in good shape. He bought the car, arranged for insurance and licenses.

As he drove from the dealership, he was excited. He had wheels again. Life was beginning to hold hope. Now he had a job, a woman and transportation -- even if he didn't have a memory of the past. Maybe he didn't need the unknown past.

He drove to his quarters, bounded up the steps to his apartment and called Khristina. When her gentle, calm voice answered, he said, "Tina, this is Ben, I'll pick you up in twenty minutes."

"How?" she asked.

"In my car."

"In your what? I thought I heard you say 'car.'"

"You did. I bought an auto."

Khristina's whole mood changed. She became enthusiastic. "I didn't know you remembered how to drive."

"That's one of the few things I do remember. I'll be by in twenty minutes. I want you to see where I live."

"Oh, Ben, I'd love to. Drive carefully. Have you a driving permit?" she asked with concern.

"Got it this morning, Tina. It's all legit. I'm on my way."

When he reached Tina's apartment, she was out front waiting for him. He stopped, leaned over and opened the passenger side door, Tina eagerly scrambled into the car. He kissed her hard on her lips. "How are you ever going to pay for this? The car is lovely," she said as she looked around the interior of the wagon.

"It's paid for," said Ben. He saw Khristina was looking at him in an odd fashion. "What's the matter? Something bothering you?" asked Ben.

"I -- I didn't know you had any real money."

"Honey, I've been in the Navy since I graduated from the Academy. I know it sounds strange, but I spent very little. Most of it went to my savings account. My sister looked after that while I was away. I had no idea I had any money when I returned home until Becky gave me back my passbook. My dad has charged me no room and board since I've been home. He has footed the bills for my problem -- when the Navy didn't.

Becky has warned me never to offer to repay Papa. She says, as tough as he appears to be, he has a guilt complex about having contributed to my condition. Footing my rehab bills has been a partial relief of those feelings. My family isn't poor. Papa and Becky control the N.E. Wholesale Liquor Company."

"Wow, I had no idea," said a confused Tina. She sat quietly.

"Does that make a difference in our relationship?" he asked.

"I don't know. I guess I thought you were a church mouse like me. It'll take some getting used to."

"Oh, God, Tina, don't play games with me. A little money doesn't relieve my lack of memory. I've no more or less money than when I first said I cared for you and needed you. I'm no Mr. Got Rocks. I'm just a guy who has saved a little. I grew up in a family that knows how to do that. Does that diminish me in your eyes?"

"Darling, no. But I've so little to offer. I haven't ever asked you in to Mom's and my apartment because I was ashamed of how threadbare and worn it is. My Mom has spent all her spare money on my problems. Now, I get a good job and am in love with a guy who knows money, something I don't. Oh, Ben, you should find a woman who knows the kind of life you have lived and is comfortable with it."

"What are you talking about, Tina? The only life I can remember is since I've returned from the Navy. And, the only part of that life that holds the possibility of a happy future is with you. With all the problems that surround me, I know I want you by my side. I need you there. There's just something right about my being with you. If that's what is defined as love -- I -- I love you. I don't even know whether or not I'm a virgin as defined in the marriage manual. I wish I knew. But, for the first time that I can remember, I truly yearn to be wanted -- and by you. I don't give a damn if you haven't a cent. You've made me want to live."

Khristina looked up at Ben, locked her arms around his neck, buried her face on his shoulder, and sobbed, "Ben, my beloved, never let me go."

He gently raised her face toward his. "Don't fear. We're just getting started. The road may be a bit rough at times. God willing, we'll have a long trip together on it." He kissed her teary eyes, then her lips passionately. She responded.

Finally she leaned back and with her blue eyes twinkling said, "Let's go and see your apartment. If we stay here like this, the whole neighborhood might have some real gossip to talk about."

Ben laughed.

64

When the duo entered the estate grounds, Khristina's eyes were saucer round. "The place is beautiful, even with the sleet."

"I thought you would like it. It's not as pretty as the view from the bench by the lake. But, it'll have to do for now."

"And you've got to take care of all of this?" she inquired.

"Yep. I look forward to trying."

"I can see why," she said.

The couple went up to his apartment. She looked over each room carefully. Then they went to the living-dining room and Ben relit a log fire in the Franklin fireplace stove. He turned to a soft music program on the radio and sat by her side on the sofa.

"Ben," she said, "The apartment is kinda' stark, without any curtains, rugs or wall decorations."

He smiled. "It needs a woman's touch -- your touch. I told you I needed you."

"You don't have to worry, I'll work on that," she said and then she inquired, "What's in the fridge? I haven't had any food since breakfast."

"Neither have I," said Ben. "But the refrigerator is stocked. Dora, the house maid, took off over the weekend. She brought the leftovers from the main house."

Khristina was an innovative cook. The couple enjoyed a hearty dinner and shared the dishwashing chores. Cuddled up on the sofa after supper, they listened to big band music on the radio.

"Hadn't you better call your mother and tell her you'll be late?" Ben asked during a station break.

"Darling, by now, if she is home, she's so potted she couldn't even get to the phone. She won't awaken before ten o'clock tomorrow morning. I know her routine."

65

Ben kissed Khristina lightly, "Tina, could we try? A part of me screams for you. And, at the same time that desire truly upsets me. I'm sure my uneasiness has something to do with my loss of memory but what, I don't know."

"Ben, my beloved, I can't imagine you wanting me with all you know about me. And I can't promise you what my reaction will be. But, yes, I want you to be a part of me. I love you."

The couple, with their separate devils, went nervously into the bedroom.

66

The sunlight was streaming into the bedroom as Ben awoke and felt Khristina's warm body next to his.

He looked at the sleeping imp by his side, leaned over and kissed her cheek. She opened one eye and smiled at him. "Last night wasn't a very successful beginning, was it?"

"I wouldn't say that," responded Ben, "We're still here together and, God willing, I hope we stay that way."

"We will, but we both need to reread that damn marriage manual. I do love you so."

Ben turned her to him and drew her closer. "Tina, please marry me -- today. We can go to Elkton, Maryland, be married and back by supper time."

"Are you serious, Ben Feldman?"

"Dead serious."

"You know this isn't a very loving world?"

"And, what do you mean by that?"

"You're a Jew and I'm a Catholic, but not a very good one."

"And I'm not a very good Jew either."

"I've thought about the differences," said Ben. "To me they are insignificant, if we care for and need each other."

"That's true, Ben, for the two of us, but just remember we live in a real world. And that world isn't very united, spiritually. The real world is damned prejudiced, it's going to take a lot of understanding and loving between us for our relationship not to be wrecked by outside influences."

"You're so damned much smarter than you think you are, and I've known that from the first day I met you," said Ben.

"And, despite all my past, I've loved you from the first moment I saw you. That's why I've thought about us," answered Tina.

"I didn't say the road we'll travel would always be smooth," said Ben. "But it will have to be better than the one I traveled before I met you. That road was so rough I can't even remember it."

"I never wanted a big wedding anyway. Come on my husband-to-be, let's get breakfast and then get married," said Tina in high spirits. "And, besides, tomorrow after work, I've got to stop by Wannamakers and get some material for curtains."

"What's your mother gonna' say? How is she going to feel?" inquired Ben.

"She won't say much, but she will be greatly relieved. From now on, the shoe will be on the other foot. I'll have to start looking after her. From time to time, that'll take some doing."

"What about your family?" asked Khristina.

"My sister already suspects we will team together. She'll be happy. When my Mama and Papa first hear about it, they'll shit a brick. . ."

"Ben!"

"'S'cuse me, Tina, they'll be quite upset at first, but they'll come around."

Tina giggled and thought: My, we are already acting like a married couple. She was delighted.

67

Khristina and Ben were married that day. Ben told his parents the day following the wedding. Their reactions were as he had described to Tina they would be. Ben also notified the Hedleys. They were surprised, but accepted the marriage as a fait accompli. The couple could live in the apartment. Khristina's mother was relieved.

68

On Friday evening following the marriage, Ruth Feldman called, introduced herself to Khristina on the phone and invited the newlyweds to Sunday dinner. Once the couple was at the Feldman home, Becky was delighted with Tina. They immediately became friends. Ruth and Martin were polite, but still in a mild shock over the sudden action of their only son. As the group was finishing desert, Martin arose from the table, went to the kitchen and returned with a large mahogany two-drawer chest. He placed it in front of Ben's new wife. Taped on the box was a card, "To Ben and Khristina." The card was signed by Ruth, Martin and Becky.

"Open the chest," said Becky.

Khristina lifted the hinged top and there was the first layer of an eight-place setting of sterling silver. Khristina had never seen anything like it before in her life. "Oh, my God," she said and almost fainted. Even Martin Feldman was moved by the honest emotional surprise of his lovely Nordic daughter-in-law. Becky tearfully leaned over and kissed Tina on her cheek.

Ben felt a lump in this throat. He really didn't know what to say. All that came out was a croaking, "Thank you so much, Mama, Papa and Becky."

"You're welcome, Benjamin," was his dad's reply. Ruth sobbed and blew her nose. The dinner ended with quiet good-byes and Ben lugged the mahogany chest to the station wagon.

69

The couple drove the first part of the way home in silence. Finally, Tina heaved a sigh, "This is a new world for me."

"Me, too," said her husband.

"Be patient with me, Ben, Darling. I've got more adjusting to do than you -- even without your memory."

"Have no fear. I need you as much as you need me," replied her husband.

70

The sleet storm melted into spring. In short order, Ben was thoroughly acquainted with the equipment and tools. He tried them all and could handle them. He had studied the manuals, particularly the ones on lawn care and gardening. In addition, he was enrolled in evening courses in agronomy, held in a University of Pennsylvania satellite not far from Paoli. Khristina went with him to the satellite, taking evening courses in prekindergarten child care.

The couple had little time for socializing, and that was good for them both. They first had to learn to live with each other and be happy and comfortable with that. They struggled.

Becky came by frequently and admired Tina's taste in decor and furnishing. Even Mrs. Hedley would drop by, ostensibly to see how the couple were handling their life, but in reality to marvel at the change in appearance in the garage quarters. Though Miriam Hedley knew nothing of Khristina's background, she became attached to the attractive, calm, blonde of Swedish descent. Mr. Hedley frequently walked the grounds of the twelve-acre estate. He was delighted with the lawn and shrubbery condition. The flower beds never looked prettier.

One Sunday afternoon in early summer, after golf, he was strolling the estate and came upon Ben trimming the azaleas. "Ben," he said, "How about driving over to the golf club tomorrow. I want you to take a look at our fairways. They can't touch this lawn. Maybe you can give the greenskeeper a couple of suggestions."

"I'll be glad to take a look," said Ben, "I've learned quite a bit about grasses of this area from Rick VanHeusen who teaches one of the courses I take. He's almost a nut on the subject. But few people are willing to try his suggestions. I have. He knows what he is talking about. His family has been farming this area of Pennsylvania for generations. In his earlier days, he was a first-rate research agronomist at Penn State. After his stroke, he sank into oblivion for years. Now that he has pretty well recovered, he's not the authority he once was, but he is damned good."

71

B en went with Hedley to the golf course, took soil samples from several areas, and drew a rough map of those areas. Unknown to Hedley, he held a couple of conferences with VanHeusen. The soil samples were carefully analyzed by Ben and his professor. They reached their conclusions and Ben gave Hedley a written report. Though the soil treatment and type of grasses recommended by Ben were much different than those in current use at the club, Hedley convinced the Greens Committee of the club to try them out in several areas. Much to the committee's surprise, the suggestions resulted in almost immediate improvement. Ben, besides being the Hedley outside estate maintenance man, became a consultant to the Greens Committee of Hedley's club, on a very fair consulting fee basis. So started the new career of Benjamin Feldman.

72

Spring blossomed into summer and summer faded to fall. Ben and Tina were happy, but now and then Ben would run into a barricade by the lack of memory. He would become frustrated and nervous. Khristina knew the signs. She would comfort him and remind him how far he had come, they both had come. As time passed, Ben's tenderness for his wife grew in every respect, but his lovemaking was timorous at best. He was hesitant, unsure, as if some hidden fear plagued him. Tina fervently wished her husband, for his sake as well as hers, could completely relax in their intimacy. She asked for him to do so; however, she knew that something about his war injury was the problem. She would try to be patient.

73

In late October, 1954, Martin Feldman and Becky were to attend a wholesale liquor dealer's convention in Washington, D.C. Martin asked his wife to go along. She agreed to do so. One night, while discussing their plans at the dinner table, Becky cocked her head, smiled at her father and said, "Why don't we ask Ben and Tina to be our guests? We've made a pot full this year and can bury the cost in advertising."

"Martin, please do," pleaded Ruth, "We don't have but so much time left. I want to be closer to them. Khristina's made Ben a wonderful wife. She deserves more of our attention."

Becky said, "They need a rest and vacation. They've seldom been off that damned estate since they were married, except to go to night school. They've just got to start living a broader life."

Martin looked first at Becky, then at Ruth. "I wasn't pleased when Ben refused to come with the company and I was

upset as hell when he married Khristina. But, I gotta' admit
he's got guts and she's making him a good wife. I am getting
old and I do love Ben. I agree, they should go, but, Becky,
you'll have to ask him. He considers me a jerk. Let him still
think so. It helps his ego."

"Papa, you're an old fool, but a loveable old fool,"
sobbed Ruth.

74

B ecky called Tina and invited the couple to be their
guests on the three-day visit in the nation's capital.
The fivesome would be staying at the Mayflower
Hotel, one of D.C.'s finest. Khristina had to plead with Ben to
get him to agree to go. Ben finally said OK and made
arrangements with Miriam Hedley for them to be away. Mrs.
Hedley was aware that the couple needed a vacation. She had
even so suggested to Khristina. She recognized that Ben had
been doing a superb job on the estate and had raised his salary
not once, but twice. Ben was now making more than double his
original salary. Miriam Hedley was no fool. The estate
grounds were a show place. And she knew sooner or later Ben
would be approached by someone with a better offer than hers.
She was going to delay the occasion as long as she could.

On 19 October 1954, with the remnants of Hurricane
Hazel deluging Philadelphia, the Feldman families boarded the
4:30 p.m. Metroliner at the North Philadelphia Station. By
8:00p.m. they were ensconced in their rooms at the Mayflower
Hotel. Tina was surprised and excited when she first saw their
room. Never in her life had she seen such opulence. She didn't
even know it existed. But, she was learning how to accept and
enjoy living on a scale way above her mother's. At times she
was saddened by the wide divergence. Already, she was
contributing funds to her mother, trying to ease the earlier
sacrifices her mother had made for her.

75

On the night of their arrival in D.C., at a late supper in the main dining room of the Mayflower Hotel, Martin Feldman announced, "We've been invited by the Sommenbergs to be their guests tomorrow night. We're going to supper at the Occidental Restaurant and then on to the National Theater to see the opening of the Southwest Pacific Dance Ensemble. Sommenberg is president of the Eastern Dealers Association. He's one of the biggest wholesalers in D.C. He has a box at the theater for the show." Khristina was enthralled. Never had she been to an intown major theatrical performance. She had been to the tent theater at Valley Forge and seen several of their productions. She just couldn't wait for the event.

Becky said, "I'll go, but I'm not very interested in seeing some copper-skinned natives in grass skirts shake their parts on a stage. I read in the *Post* that the Mills Brothers are singing at the Casino Royal. They're my speed. I'll take them two-to-one over some unknown fanny-shaking Polynesians."

"Don't be so crude, Becky," said Ruth Feldman sternly.

"The show should be interesting," said Ben and he wondered from what part of the southwest Pacific the dancers had originated.

76

The next night, after supper at the Occidental, the Sommenbergs and their five guests walked from the restaurant down Pennsylvania Avenue past the Willard Hotel to the National Theater. They entered the theater, were given playbills and escorted to Box A on the left side of the orchestra, the box nearest to the stage.

Ruth and Becky Feldman, Anna Sommenberg and Khristina Feldman sat in the forward row of the box. They were the shortest. The three men sat in the chairs behind them. Martin Feldman, for want of something to do before the house lights went dim, began to thumb through the playbill. Ben

Feldman and Mr. Sommenberg were discussing fairway grasses. Sommenberg was telling Ben how all of the clubs in the D.C. area had problems maintaining any kind of decent fairways that didn't become overrun with Poanna Grass. According to Sommenberg, neither Blue Grass nor Bermuda grew well in the metropolitan area. Ben was listening eagerly.

Martin Feldman, looking on a page of the playbill, saw the name of the lead female dancer, Mary D'Quino Montagne. The first two names jarred a memory. He read that she was from Bora Bora and then it hit him. That was the name of the native female contained in private detective Armstrong's report of three years ago. She had testified at the Bora Bora Naval investigation hearing right after the war that his son had probably been injured by the two ram goats. He had Armstrong looking for her for two years. No wonder the private eye couldn't find her, she was dancing around the world with this group of Polynesians. His blood pressure began to rise. He would call Armstrong tonight when he returned to the hotel. He wanted a confrontation with that island bitch. She had to know more than she told the Navy. But, who was this fellow Montagne? He also was from the same island. What in the hell did he know about the episode?

Now was his chance and Martin Feldman vowed to himself to learn the truth of the happenings that had taken his son from under his control, made him the person he was today. The senior Feldman's breath came in short gasps as he fought to control his emotions.

77

The house lights dimmed, the overture began. Ben Feldman, for some strange reason, felt uneasy.

Then the first dance was underway. As the lead female dancer entered from the left wing, Ben felt a shock flow through his whole body. She frightened him. He knew he had seen her before, but where? Her demeanor? Her regal carriage? There was something familiar about her actions. He began to shake just slightly. He coughed and changed position in his chair. Maybe the edge of the seat was impinging a nerve in his legs. He nervously watched the first two dances. The palms of his hands were sweating. He thought, what is happening? In the meantime, his wife, Tina, was absolutely enthralled with the events on stage. Never had she seen such beautifully-trained dancers. The first two routines were lovely.

78

The scene changed. "Taboo," there in a clearing of coconut trees was a partially disassembled Quonset hut, painted Army green. The female dancers entered from the right wing and danced to center stage. They now wore multicolored, calico, ankle-length skirts and white, off-shoulder, linen, slipover tops. The males entered from the left stage wing wearing multicolored, calico shorts. To the soft low strains of the "Hawaiian War Chant," the lead female dancer swirled from backstage through the troupe to front center stage. She wore an even more vividly-colored calico skirt than the other female members of the ensemble. Her hair hung in two long braids with a little white bow at the end of each braid. Ben gasped, tried to breathe evenly. From center rear stage, through the stage mist, appeared a mock-up of a Navy jeep driven by the lead male dancer who wore a takeoff of a U.S. Naval officer's summer fatigue uniform. The lead female dancer leaped toward the jeep. Ben Feldman jumped from his chair as if he had been hit in his butt with an electrical shock. He all but fell over his wife who was sitting in front of him. She looked up over her shoulder in surprise and then horror. Never -- never before had she seen such a look on her husband's face. It was to her an unknown mask of almost demonic rage -- fear -- triumph, all in one. He was trembling uncontrollably. Slowly, like a melting ice cream figure, he began to sink towards the floor. All in the box heard his vehement moan.

"Damn that Mary D'Quino and that bastard Farqua. I'll kill them, so help me, God, I'll kill them both." Ben Feldman was out like a light on the floor of Box A.

Khristina was aghast with fear. Never had she seen her husband so angry before, and such wild anger. Now he was a crumpled figure behind her chair. Mr. Sommenberg had no idea what had caused young Feldman's spell. But, he had the presence of mind to seek immediate help. He left the box to find an usher and request medical assistance for his guest.

Martin Feldman momentarily sat as if glued to his chair. His vision was blurred by his anger and soaring blood pressure. Damn. Now he was sure that native bitch had played a pivotal role in his son's injury and loss of memory. He would get the truth out of her if he personally had to hog tie her and force it from her.

Rebecca, Ruth and Mrs. Sommenberg stood bunched together in absolute shock and dismay.

79

Ben came to, moaned, turned over onto his belly, started to rise, and then puked on the carpet beneath him. He fought to keep from fainting again.

Tina was kneeling beside him, and with her handkerchief, cleaned the vomit from his face. "Beloved, what in the world happened?" she asked. Ben's face was ashen gray as he looked at his wife.

"Tina, oh God, Tina, I remember. I remember what happened. Just get me out of here before I faint or disgrace myself again." And Ben had the dry heaves.

80

Martin Feldman heard his son's comments and thought: What a fool, an unmitigated fool he had been, not to truly believe in his son's honesty. Without hesitation, he knelt on the other side of Ben, placed his still strong arms around his son and lifted him to his feet. And, as if from a far distance, Ben heard his Papa say, "I don't give a shit if you never work for me, you're one hell of a guy, Ben Feldman."

81

Tina grabbed her coat, reached over to Ben's chair and took his topcoat from the chair back and placed it around his shoulders. She turned to Mrs. Sommenberg, "Ben had an injury during the war. Every now and then one of these spells hits him. He'll be all right as soon as he gets to the hotel and takes his medicine." She turned to Martin Feldman, "Papa Feldman, will you help me take Ben to a cab. I can handle him after that."

Martin Feldman was absolutely stunned at the fast-paced cerebration of his daughter-in-law. His affection for her soared. Damn, I never gave her credit for being such a quick thinker. She's almost as good as I am, he thought. Even Rebecca was astonished at the quick recovery and coverup by her sister-in-law. She thought, Ben you really picked the right one.

As Ben, Martin and Tina started to leave, she turned to the three women still standing agape at the happenings. "Tell your husband we had a delightful evening, up until the time Ben got sick. Mama Feldman, you and Rebecca stay here. Ben'll be okay. Drop by the room when you return to the hotel." She turned to Martin, "Let's go now," she said calmly.

82

Ben had said nothing, as he was standing, weaving unsteadily on his feet. He knew where he was, but his mind was acting like a wildly changing kaleidoscope. Scenes were rushing in, changing, dropping out to be replaced by new ones. To him, a movie of his past life was being shown by a projector gone wild. He shook his head to try to gain control of the projector. And, still it ran wild. Scenes of the Academy, blurred into scenes of his childhood. Scenes of his training aboard the battleship, *West Virginia*, ran into scenes in the synagogue. And, then his cocker spaniel, Princess, darted out into the street, was hit by a car, and lay dying at his feet. The ever recurring scene of his Papa telling

Ben to do this and do that, and Ben wondering what would happen if he said to his papa, "To hell with you, I want no part of your dictates." He felt himself being propelled out of the theater with Tina on one side and his Papa on the other. This wasn't that horrible floating feeling he had felt through the years. He knew he was being helped by the two people who truly loved him most, each in such different ways. They were helping him split a wide gap in the veil that hid the past. They were helping him step through that gap. Ben stumbled as he started to get in the cab. His father's arms kept him from falling. Once seated, Ben turned to him and uttered the first words since his comment to Tina. "Thanks, Papa. Tell Sommenberg I'm sorry. I'll be all right in a few minutes." He then turned to his wife, "Good God, what would I do without you."

"Don't think about it now. Everything's going to be all right. You just relax," said Tina.

Martin Feldman looked affectionately at his daughter-in-law. "You're sure you don't need me to ride with you?"

"No, Papa Feldman, I can handle Ben. Go back to the theater. That will lessen the emotional impact of this incident on the Sommenbergs if you do."

With tears brimming his eyes, he stuck his head through the door opening of the cab and gave his daughter-in-law a kiss on her cheek. As he drew back, he looked at Tina and, in a tender, husky voice said, "Welcome to the family, you anointed woman." He closed the door. Khristina gasped. He knew the Swedish meaning of her name.

83

The ride to the hotel was a silent one. Ben had hold of Tina's hands in a strong, almost frantic, grip. Every now and then he shuddered as if some horrible sight had passed before his eyes. Tina decided not to talk in the cab. She didn't know what Ben's reaction might be and she didn't want the cabbie to hear what Ben might have to say. They left the cab and headed into the hotel. Ben was steadier on his feet. Tina had her arm around his waist as they walked through the lobby. To hell with what people might think, she mused, as she helped him into the elevator.

She took the key from Ben, opened the door and reached for the light switch. A soft lamp light glowed. He flopped on one of the beds. "I've never had a worse headache in my life," he moaned.

Tina reached into her overnight bag and pulled out a bottle of aspirin. She quickly went to the bathroom and got a glass of water. "Take two of these and drink the full glass of water," she said.

Ben complied and dropped back on the bed with his eyes closed. Khristina waited quietly. He opened his eyes. Tina leaned down and, with one hand, pushed his hair away from his forehead. "Shall I call a doctor or do you want me to take you to a hospital?" she asked with concern.

"No, Dear, neither. What happened was one hell of a shock, still is. But I'd rather go back to Philly and get help from the University hospital."

When do you want to go back?" asked Tina.

"Tomorrow morning. Now I need some rest and sleep. I'm exhausted. If only the damned images would go away. I've got to sort things out in an orderly fashion. Right now, they're a mess, but a wonderful mess."

Tina smiled, leaned down and kissed her husband on his forehead. "Welcome back to a full view," she said, and she wondered what that view would portend. Then she reached down, took off her husband's shoes, placed them on the floor and covered him with the quilt that had been folded at the foot of the bed. She undressed, put on her gown and robe, and cleaned her teeth. When she came from the sink alcove, she looked at her sleeping husband with thoughtful tenderness. "Sleep well," she said softly. "Who knows what road is ahead for you, for both of us now?" She turned out the light near his bed, went to the table in the far corner of the big room, and turned on the reading lamp. She would read until the senior Feldmans and Becky came by as she knew they would.

84

A couple of hours later there was a soft knock on the door. She asked quietly, "Who's there?"

"The three of us," said Becky.

Tina unlatched and unchained the door. As she opened it, she put her finger on her lips. "He's asleep, thank God. We'll see you in the morning at breakfast, say 8:30," she said softly.

"You're sure he's okay?" asked Martin.

"I'm sure, for now at least. If there's an emergency during the night, I'll call you."

"Good night," said Becky and the threesome left. Tina locked the door, left the light on in the bathroom and crawled into the other double bed. She knew she would get far less sleep than her exhausted husband. Their future was more clouded than she ever thought it would be.

85

At breakfast the next morning, Ben said, "Tina and I are heading back to Philly today. We would like to stay in my old room at Papa's home for a couple of days. I don't want the Hedleys nosing around as to why we came home early." Ben had called and made an appointment with the psychiatry department of the University of Pennsylvania hospital for the following day. He needed help on channeling his memory.

Tina, at the table, was strangely quiet. Martin eyed her. "Do you want us to return today also?"

"No," said his daughter-in-law, "Let Ben and me try to get things sorted out. We need to be alone for a couple days."

Becky said, "Call us if you need us."

"I will," replied Tina.

As Ben and Tina left the table, Ruth said quietly to Martin and Becky. "They didn't eat a thing for breakfast."

"Good, God, I don't blame them," said Becky. "Ben's memory is coming back like a surging incoming tide. They're both afraid they'll be swept out to sea by the undertow. I hope they have the strength to survive the impact of the first waves. If they do, they'll adjust and live better than before."

86

Martin Feldman gazed silently at his half empty breakfast plate. Ruth saw and knew the look. She was nervous. During the rest of the visit in Washington, Martin Feldman was morose, uncommunicative. When he left the dinner table during their last night in Washington, Ruth turned to Becky and said, "He's up to something, I know. This is like old times when things were rough." Rebecca had noticed her father's quietness, but put it to the stress of Ben's episode and the fact that her father was aging. Ruth's warning put a different slant on the problem.

"What do you mean, 'This is like old times when things were rough'?" she asked.

Ruth evaded a direct answer. "I just know your Papa is up to something. Please keep a sharp eye on him. I can't."

Rebecca decided Ruth was right. She would not only keep a sharp eye out, but sharp ears also.

The next morning, as they boarded the train for Philly, Ruth moved close to Rebecca. "Papa tried to reach David Armstrong by phone last night. He thought I was asleep, but I wasn't."

"Who is David Armstrong?" asked Becky.

"He's the private eye Papa employed in 1949 trying to find the truth of Ben's injury on Bora Bora."

"He never told me. Why didn't you?"

"Because I didn't think it was any of your business -- at least until now."

"Did he reach Armstrong?"

"No, I could tell, David is out of town for the next week. But don't say anything to Papa yet. Maybe he'll forget about calling Armstrong again."

"And, maybe pigs will fly," said Becky. "I'm going to keep an even closer eye on him than I originally planned."

What about Feldman?

"Good," replied Ruth.

87

When the trio reached home, they found a note on the front foyer table.

Dear Mama, Papa and Becky,
Tina is at work. I have spent most of the last
two days in conference at the psych clinic at the
university. They have been a real help to me.
I'm better. Thanks for the trip and use of the
house. We'll be at our home this evening.
                                        Love,
                                        Ben

"He's better. I can tell," said Becky.
"Thank God," said Ruth.
Martin looked at both women and said nothing.

Becky helped her mother take the suitcases upstairs. Something about her father's demeanor made her decide to come down and take a peek to see what he was doing. She had kicked off her high heels and slid on a pair of slippers. She quietly padded down the steps, looked in the living room. Her Papa wasn't there. She headed for the den. The door was ajar. She stopped, listened, and heard her Papa's subdued, husky voice. "Jake, this is Martin. I need a favor. What kind of favor? I need you and a couple of your boys to go to Washington, D.C. I have an elimination job for you."

Becky gasped. He must be talking to Jacob Weiner, she thought. That was the name of her father's strongarm man from rum-running days. She had heard her Papa tell tales about the "shiv" artist. She had thought they were tall tales, fantasies. But what she was hearing was no tall tale. Her papa was outlining a proposal of cold blooded killings. Killings for which her father was apparently willing to pay a huge sum. He was identifying the subjects, Mary D'Quino Montagne and excommander Ralph Farqua, both of whom were in

Washington, D.C. according to Martin. And, if Mary's husband, Jacques Montagne, manager of the ensemble, got in the way, take him out too. She heard his last remark. "Call me back when you've studied my plan and give me your answer. Thanks, Jake."

As her father was hanging up the phone, Becky fled silently to her room. My God, she said to herself, what in the world should I do? Should I talk to the old man? Call the police or wait and call Ben before I make another move? She was so frightened, she shook. Never, never did she think her Papa would go this far. I wonder how many times in the past he has called Jake Weiner for such action, she thought. She shuddered for she had no idea her Papa could actually stoop to such depravity. Suddenly she decided she would talk to Ben in person before she did anything else with respect to the conversation she heard. She changed her slippers to walking shoes, freshened her face and went down the stairway.

She walked to the den and opened the door. Her father was reading his accumulated mail.

"Papa, I'm going out for supper. I'll be back by nine o'clock."

Her father looked over his reading glasses. "Aren't you a little tired after our trip from D.C.?"

"Not tonight," she replied, and she left.

88

Thank God Ben's home said Becky to herself as she drove up along side his station wagon at his apartment. She raced up the stairs and knocked on the door. Tina, all smiles, opened it.

"Hi, Becky," she said casually.

"Hi, Tina. Where's Ben? I've just got to talk to him now."

"He's in the living room working on memory information for the psych department. Come on in."

Tina led the way to the living room. "Look who's here," she said to Ben.

Ben looked up, arose, went over and kissed his sister on her cheek. That's when he noticed she was as nervous as a cat. "What's wrong, Becky?"

Becky looked first at Ben, then at Tina. "Good God, Ben, Papa is planning on killing Mary D'Quino, Commander Farqua and maybe even Jacques Montagne."

Ben stared incredulously at his sister. "What?"

"You heard me, Papa is planning on killing Mary D'Quino, Ralph Farqua and Jacques Montagne."

"How do you know?"

"I heard him on the phone talking to Jacob Weiner. He laid out a complete plan."

"I can't believe he would do such a thing," gasped Tina.

"Are you sure, Becky?" asked Ben.

"I'm positive," and then she related the conversation as she had heard it.

89

Ben looked at Tina. "Start packing my suitcase. I've got to go back to D.C. right now. I've got to warn Mary D'Quino and Jacques. I didn't know Farqua was in town. I've just got to try and find out what was behind that whole scheme."

Becky looked at her brother. "You're asking for real trouble, Izzy."

"Why?" he shot back.

"She damned near killed you. And, now, after ten years, your memory is starting to return. Just before you passed out in Box A, you threatened to kill Mary and Farqua. I heard. Everyone in the box heard your vehement remark. You're asking for big trouble if you go back," responded Becky.

"Ben, I don't think you should go," said Tina positively.

Ben glowered at Tina. "I never intended to kill anyone. What I said was a result of pure shock. I remember. At that moment all I could think of was revenge for the years I've suffered. I'm no damned saint, but I'm no killer either. You both know that. I'm going, but Tina you stay here."

"Not on your life," said Tina. "We've stuck by each other this far. If you go, I go."

"Please stay here. I've got to go," said Ben.

"I don't think you should go, but if you go, I go, and that's all there is to it. I'll start packing."

Ben turned to Becky. "After you take us to the station, go home and talk to Papa. Do anything to try and stop him. Threaten to go to the police. If necessary go to the police. Try and find Weiner's number and tell him Papa has gone off his rocker, that he had no idea what he was talking about."

Becky stared as if she was dreaming, watching Ben and Tina hastily pack. "Where are you going to stay?" she asked.

"At the Mayflower if they're not booked solid. I'll let you know if we have to go somewhere else," said Ben.

Ben and Tina packed in short order and Becky drove them to the North Philly station. As luck would have it, a southbound local was due in fifteen minutes.

With tears in her eyes, Becky kissed Tina and Ben and, turning to Tina said, "Keep a sharp eye on that stubborn brother of mine and you be careful too. I want you both back safe and sound."

"I will," said Tina as she gave Becky a squeeze around the neck.

And they were gone.

Part III

What About Farqua?

1

Lorraine and Talbott Farqua had chosen the name of Ralph, if their first born was a son. Ralph for Raphelo D'Farqua, the rascally, great-great-granddaddy of Talbott Farqua. Raphelo had been an assistant minister of finance in the French Revolutionary government. In that capacity, he had assisted the government in making him a very wealthy man. When he died a violent death, he was the owner of a large fishing fleet that was headquartered at Arcachon, south of Bordeaux, France. Knowledge of the fishing industry had been handed down by Raphelo through the generations of Farquas, almost as if by genetics.

On that muggy day, 12 September 1909, and within five minutes after screaming, Lorraine Farqua bore her first child, Ralph, he became slick, not sleek. Marilou Tremaine, a ranking midwife of St. Mary Parish, Louisiana, delivered Lorraine's son at sun up in the Farqua home fronting on the headwaters of Atchafalaya Bay, near Morgan City, Louisiana.

Marilou didn't have to beat his red behind to start him breathing. He was yowling as loud as his mother as soon as his head cleared her body. Marilou tied off the umbilical cord, cleansed the male infant with a warm, wet washcloth, and having nothing better at hand, rubbed him down thoroughly with cocoa butter. Then, she placed the calmed newborn on his mother's belly and lightly dropped a small blue towel over his moist torso.

The graying, wrinkled, almost toothless, Creole grinned at the blonde new mother. "He's a slick 'un. You best hold him fast." Lorraine and her sturdy fisherman husband had struggled to do so from that moment forward.

2

Young Ralph inherited the robustness of his father, the facile mind of his mother, and the voracious appetites for living well of Raphelo D'Farqua, the ancestor for whom he was named. By the end of the first two weeks of breast feeding, Lorraine would howl during feeding time. Her suckling son was bruising her teats with his audacious gumming. She would pull him away for a brief rest and he would scream like a stricken Banshee until his appetite was assuaged. And so, Ralph began his charge through life, taking command wherever and however he could. By instinct and from his genes, he soon learned that he could best achieve his goals by slyness, not overtness. His two younger brothers and sister alternately revered and feared him. He cold-bloodedly assessed the results of his tactics on them as a basis for his moving onward and upward in life. His parents adored him for he was so much like each of them. And yet he was so different. He was both of them in one. That combination neither Lorraine nor Talbott truly understood. In their honest efforts to "hold him fast," they dealt with his shadow, not with the real Ralph. While purporting to comply with their advice, suggestions, and teachings of life, he was always a step ahead or to the side of the thrust of their endeavors. From the time he started talking, and that was at an early age, he hid his contempt for his parents and most mankind by correct and polite mouthings. Then, he would surreptitiously have his way.

He was in the upper ten percent of his grammar school class, but seldom appeared to crack a book. He was a sprint star at high school and maintained an excellent academic rating for the whole four years. He constantly and vocally, behind their backs, found fault with every teacher under whom he studied. Over time, word of his pithy, snide comments reached the teachers' ears and they fumed. They hated the slick, blond bastard's guts. But he was smart and his old man had the biggest fishing enterprise based in the Atchafalaya Bay.

Talbott Farqua also was a local political force to be reckoned with. So, the teachers kept quiet.

3

Ralph had no regular girlfriend but dated several in high school. To him, they were children. At seventeen, he sneaked off to Baton Rouge and, through another high school track star, found Madame Louella's house of relaxation. For some strange reason, Georgette, one of the attractive members of the household, took a fancy to the blond stud. He became her "freebie." In her idle time, she taught him much. More than that, she liked the slick, young rascal. He had all the right moves to go somewhere, be somebody. And, as she said to Iris, one of her house mates, "He's the most articulate young bastard I've ever met. Even when you know he's lying, he sounds believable."

4

During the last week of his senior year at high school, he was offered a track scholarship to Louisiana State University. He turned down the scholarship, but decided to go there for his collegiate years. In the spring of his freshman year, he went out for the freshman track team, qualified for the sprints and made ready for the first meet against the University of Alabama. Friday night before the meet, he went down to the Gilded Parrot in Baton Rouge, got soused and finally rolled into his dormitory bunk at 3:00 a.m. on Saturday, the day of the meet. Freshman coach, Ed Sparrow, heard of the episode and declared him ineligible to run. However, just before the meet began, Ralph had convinced the coach that he had seen the error of his ways. Ralph ran away with the 100-yard and 220-yard dashes, establishing a new freshman record in both events. After the 220 race, Ralph tossed his cookies right in front of the coach. That upheaval was the result of the alcohol of the night before and the strain from the races. Coach Sparrow was upset at the episode. But not Ralph. He toweled his face and smiled, "Coach, I'm ready for the 440."

"Like hell you are. I shouldn't have let you run in the previous races. You're in no condition to try that pace."

"Either you let me run the 440 or I'll never run again for the school," Ralph said laconically in front of the members of the LSU freshman track team.

Coach Sparrow was furious with his new-found, nonscholarship track star. "Suit yourself. But you're in no condition to run a third race. I'm not going to risk what might happen if you do."

Ralph reached for his warmup pants and jersey and slung them over his shoulder. His steely, gray-green eyes seared at the coach. "So long," he said, and grinned at the gathered freshman runners. He never again ran on the track team for the university. He had the coaches tearing their hair. They begged, they cajoled, they ordered him to report for practice. And all he would say was, "Up yours, too." Over the next four years, he would race in the intramural and class track events. His times for the 100, the 220 and the 440 were consistently better than those of the leading varsity runners. The varsity coaches boiled, but that was all they could do. Ralph's grades put him on the dean's list, and his old man was footing the bill.

5

During the summers of his collegiate years, young Ralph worked for his dad's fishing fleet, but not as a deckhand. Early on he had mastered handling the helm of a shrimper. Beginning his freshman year at college, he was the summer captain of the *Marietta*, the smallest and oldest shrimp boat in Talbott Farqua's fleet. The four deckhands of that shrimper were always beginners. Ralph didn't mind. He had complete domination and he trained them well. Somehow the boat always made its fair share of the haul. Talbott watched with pride as his son matured into a competent shrimper.

Navigation, piloting and netting came easily to Ralph, almost by instinct.

6

During his senior year at college, he met Martha Ann Hyde from Charleston, South Carolina. She was a junior English major, quiet, aristocratic and studious. More than that, the brown-eyed, brunette was built. My God how she is put together, mused Ralph during their first meeting. She was lean, but with curves in the right places. She dressed casually, but she consistently looked like a top-flight model about to step out on a runway -- she carried herself gracefully erect. When those calm, brown eyes met his, he all but flipped. He just had to have her, particularly when he learned that her father, Tatum Hyde, was the money source of the largest U.S. cotton brokerage firm on Wall Street.

7

Martha Ann Hyde was no fool. True, she had been reared in the lap of luxury, but old luxury. She knew her way around, had been wooed by many eligible young men and knew how to counter an unwanted advance. But, she was intrigued by this cocksure, arrogant bayou brat. She knew he was smart for she had been in a couple of classes with him. In one on mythology, Ralph had become embroiled with Professor Hetherwaite in a heated discussion over the definition of "Universalism." Much to her surprise, the articulate blond had more than held his own with the prof. She reasoned that the arrogant bayou waterman would have to be a real student of mythology and religion to so forcefully argue his point. Partially out of curiosity and for some other reason, she couldn't then fathom, she didn't discourage Ralph's interest in her, nor did she encourage him. She remained coolly aloof but more or less available, at least for conversation. Her demeanor was a direct challenge to Ralph. On a Friday afternoon in early

May of Ralph's senior year, as they left their last class, Ralph approached her.

"Martha Ann, you got anything better to do than have dinner with me tomorrow night at The Embers in Baton Rouge?"

The trim South Carolinian looked coolly at Ralph, "I'm sure I could think of something in a hurry," she replied.

"Don't try too hard. I really would appreciate your going with me."

Martha Ann's heartbeat quickened. She tried to remain calm. "What time do you suggest?"

"I'll pick you up at your sorority house about 6:00 p.m."

"I didn't say I would go, I was only inquiring about the time, if I agreed to go."

Ralph was caught off guard. For a few seconds he was damned irritated that he had been boxed in so neatly.

"Forget it. I wasn't playing a game. I was merely asking you to have dinner with me."

"Why?" asked the cool coed.

Ralph surveyed her from head to foot. Martha Ann blushed. Almost involuntarily her hands hugged to her bosom the two books she was carrying.

"Because I think you're the most interesting woman I've seen on this campus."

"Why?"

Damn she's tormenting me thought Ralph.

"Have dinner with me and I'll tell you."

"OK, Ralph, I'll have dinner with you, but I have to be back at the house by 9:00 p.m."

Now it was Ralph's turn, "Why?"

"Because I have a late date," said Martha Ann calmly.

Inwardly Ralph fumed. But he at least had his foot in the door. "That's OK. I'll bring you back in plenty of time." Ralph smiled at Martha Ann. "I have a late date also." Not until he spoke those words had he considered a late date. Now he knew he would have one -- with Georgette.

8

For some reason, Martha Ann was perturbed at the smug remark of her dinner companion-to-be. She would have to rush to the sorority house and change her long-standing Saturday dinner date with her steady, Earl Rowen, put him off until 9:00 p.m. by some obvious lie, just to go out with this bayou stud. And, he had the effrontery to tell her he was going out on a late date also. She thought he said it just to irritate her, and it did.

9

At ten to six Ralph pulled up to Martha Ann's sorority house in his silver colored Corvette convertible. Dorothy Winters, her roommate, was looking out of their upstairs, front bedroom window. "I often wonder who owns that Silver Streak. I've seen it around campus for the last two years," she said. Martha Ann came over and watched Ralph, in a summer seersucker suit, vault over the driver's side door.

"That is Ralph Farqua, my date," said Martha Ann.

"I thought you were having your usual Saturday night dinner with Earl," remarked Dorothy.

"He's coming later. I'm having supper with Ralph. I'll be back by 9:00 p.m."

Dorothy could see the excitement in her roommate's eyes. "You take it easy, Kiddo," she remonstrated.

"Have no fear, Dot. He's just a senior I met in one of my classes. We're going to The Embers for supper."

"Well, that ain't exactly like going to the campus cafeteria," said Dot with a smirk.

"No, The Embers is a little different. He's a little different," said Martha Ann as she gave her uplift bra a slight tug of adjustment.

Dot again observed the tinge of nervousness in her generally cool roommate.

10

Mrs. Wanda Smithers, the brooding, middle-aged housemother came upstairs and entered Martha Ann and Dot's room.

"Martha Ann, Mr. Farqua, your dinner date, is waiting in the reception room. My, he's an attractive young man." She continued her gaze at Martha Ann. She smiled, "You're lovely looking tonight, Dear, but should you wear that off-the-shoulder blouse just to go out to dinner?"

"We're going to The Embers," replied Martha Ann quietly.

"Oh!" said Mrs. Smithers as she raised her eyebrows and looked at Dorothy. Dot just shrugged her shoulders.

11

Martha Ann walked confidently down the stairway into the reception room. "Good evening, Ralph," she said.

Ralph arose, looked at the trim brunette, and mused: Damn, she's even more lovely than I first thought. In fact, she's downright beautiful, desirable. "Hi, Martha Ann. I brought a little something to celebrate our first dinner date." He handed her a small corsage of exquisite cymbidium orchids.

"My, what an unexpected surprise," she said as she took the flowers and pinned them on the upper left side of her blouse. "That's very thoughtful of you," she said.

"Shall we go, particularly if I have to get you back before 9:00 p.m.?" Ralph inquired.

"I'm ready," she replied.

As they left the room, Ralph with the courtesy of a trained diplomat, turned to the housemother who was standing in the hall watching the duo. "Mrs. Smithers, it was a pleasure to have met you. I hope I'll see you again soon."

What a polite young man, thought the housemother as the couple went down the outside steps to the car.

12

"Good evening, Mr. Farqua," smiled the parking attendant as Ralph pulled up to the restaurant entrance.

"Hi, Virgil," was the casual response.

Martha Ann was puzzled for she had no idea that her date was a regular patron of the posh restaurant. "You come here often?" she asked.

"Occasionally, when the food on campus gets boring," was the response.

And Martha Ann thought, that food must be boring much of the time for them to know you by name.

As they entered the plush dining room, the maitre-de slid up to Ralph. "Your usual table is waiting."

"Thank you, Henri," replied Ralph, and Martha Ann saw the almost sleight-of-hand passage of an unknown sized tip to the chief servicer. She studied Ralph carefully as they walked to a corner table set for two.

13

The dinner was delectable and the wine appropriate. Martha Ann would later reflect that most of the conversation had been hers. Ralph's questions were casual but elicited from her the composition of her family: her mother, father and two younger brothers. She found herself talking about all of them and as if she were confiding to her best friend. She had found out nothing -- absolutely nothing -- of his background. He even found out what foods she liked and disliked. She realized she had been a real blabbermouth, something she seldom was, but why, she pondered? The evening ended when Ralph looked at his watch and, with a grin, commented, "My how the time has flown. I promised I'd get you home before 9:00 p.m. -- for your real date. I guess we better get going."

Martha Ann was irritated at the remark. First, she didn't want to leave and, second, why did he have to add that little dig -- "for your real date." She looked at her watch and then at Ralph. "I guess so. I've had a lovely time."

14

The couple left the restaurant, entered Ralph's waiting car, and headed back to the campus. For a brief while they drove in silence, then Ralph spoke. "What a beautiful night for a late date," he said as he gazed at the starlit heaven and the new quarter moon.

There he was digging again, thought Martha Ann. She was not amused. "You're going to take the advantage of it too, why act as if I'm doing something wrong?" she asked, her anger rising slightly.

"Oh, I didn't mean to upset you. I was just making an observation for both of us," smiled an elated Ralph. He had hit the mark and he knew it. Martha Ann was upset.

They reached her sorority house. Ralph came around, opened the passenger door and held out his hand to help Martha Ann from the car. She placed her hand in his and it was as if an electric charge raced up her arm. She gasped imperceptibly.

They walked up to the house steps. She didn't want to take her hand from his. When they reached the top of the steps, he dropped her hand and opened the screen door. "What a lovely evening this has been," he said. "Please, let's do it again soon."

"Maybe we can," repled Martha Ann. "Give me a call when you're not busy."

Ralph again stuck out his right hand, "Goodnight, pretty lady. I've enjoyed every minute."

Martha Ann shook his hand with warmth, wondering why he didn't draw her to him and at least try to kiss her. But, he didn't. She was perturbed.

"Good night, Ralph," she said. Inwardly she seethed. Why was this slick senior getting me so upset? He had been the essence of gentlemanly composure, something she hadn't expected. For some reason she had expected some action she could denounce or object to. But if anyone had evidenced the fool, it was not Ralph, but herself. She was more intrigued than ever.

15

As she entered her shared room, Dot, in a halter and shorts, was lounging in an easy chair reading. She looked up. "So, he brought you back on time?"

"Yes, dammit," responded Martha Ann. "He was so much the gentleman, I can't figure him out."

"Isn't that what you wanted him to be?" smirked Dot.

"No -- yes," said Martha Ann. "I just sensed he's really far different than he pretended. He was like a cat toying with a mouse -- me."

"Did you ever stop to think it might be cat-on-cat?" quizzed Dot with a twinkle in her eye.

Martha Ann was silent for a minute as she pondered, then, "Maybe so, Dot. But he's a big, back alley, tom cat and I'm just a lap-sitting pussy cat."

"Man, now I've heard it all. Martha Ann Hyde feeling sorry for herself," said Dot.

"No! I'm not feeling sorry for myself. I just don't understand my own feelings for this guy."

"Well, you better hurry and change into something less formal if you're going out with Earl."

Martha Ann sat on the side of her bed and reflected as she watched a lone fly light on the floor and dash madly from one point to another. "I'm not going out with Earl tonight," she said.

"You what?"

"I'm not going out with Earl. When he arrives, tell him I've come down with a terrific headache in the last thirty minutes, and I have."

"Tell him yourself," snapped Dot.

"No, Dot. Please go down and tell him. I really don't want to see him tonight."

"Are you sure this guy Ralph didn't step out of line?"

"He didn't even put his foot on the line. He didn't do a damn thing but be a perfect gentleman. And for some reason that's got me upset," said Martha Ann.

"Are you trying to tell me you've fallen for that bayou fisherman?"

"Good God, no," said Martha Ann. But suddenly she realized she had. So did Dot.

"Oh, boy," said Dot with anguish. Just then the front door bell rang.

"I'll get it," said Dot. "I'll tell him."

16

Ralph swung away from the sorority house, and headed for Madame Louella's. When he reached there, he heard live music, Saturday night music, New Orleans jazz. He rang the bell. Willifred, the black doorman in a white tux, answered. He peered out and saw Ralph. "You ain't supposed to come here on weekends," he said.

"I know, but could I speak to Georgette?" responded Ralph.

"Well, I reckon so. Stay here, I'll get her."

Shortly thereafter Willifred reappeared followed by Georgette. As the blonde entertainer in a black, low-cut evening gown, approached the doorway, Ralph thought -- she may be older than Martha Ann, but she's no slouch. Georgette looked out and saw Ralph. "What in the name of God you doing here this time of night?" she inquired.

"I need to see you," was the blunt answer.

"My young coquin, I'm busy now," said Georgette.

"I know, but I'll pay too."

"Stop that talk, or I'll wash out your mouth with soap," said an irritated Georgette. She surveyed her young friend from head to foot. "You're disturbed about something aren't you?"

"I guess you could call it that," said Ralph.

"Ralphy," she said, "I'll be through here in about an hour. Come back then. You can follow me in your car to my place."

"You've got a separate home?"

"Sure, I have to get away from this maison de mal fame occasionally. I'd go nuts if I didn't."

Ralph was flabbergasted. He'd never given a thought that Georgette had a separate life away from the house of relaxation. "Gee, I never thought about your living away from the house before," said Ralph aloud.

"Ralphy, you seldom think about anything or anybody that isn't centered in you. You're a genuine narcissistic young stud -- except when it comes to copulation and that I've taught you to my satisfaction."

"How would you know the meaning of narcissistic?" asked a puzzled Ralph.

"Because, you simple jerk, I've had as much formal education as you and a damned sight more empirical knowledge. You do know the meaning of empirical?"

Ralph was absolutely stunned. He was listening to a Georgette he had never heard before. "Yes," he mumbled.

"Well, stud," she said, "Be back at midnight. I'll meet you out front in my car."

17

A confused Ralph drove down to the banks of the Mississippi, parked, pulled out a joint, turned on the radio and thought about the evening so far. Martha Ann would be his in due time. He had no doubts about that. All he had to do was be a little more patient. But, before he made a commitment, he did want to meet her parents and get the lay of the land. They might be of considerable assistance at the appropriate time. But, Georgette was the one who had upset him. She had defined him to a tee, as if she had bored into his soul, found its essence and analyzed it like a medieval alchemist, and then had decided to use her findings to her advantage. He was as disturbed at his feelings about Georgette as he knew Martha Ann was disturbed with her feelings for him.

18

Now it was time to meet Georgette. He flicked the small butt of the joint into the reeds and headed back to the house of relaxation. As he drove up he saw a Ford pickup truck parked at the curb. Georgette stuck her head out the open window. "Follow me," she yelled.

They drove north for about thirty minutes on the highway, then turned right down a narrow, live oak tree lined road. Ralph knew they were approaching the north bank of Lake Maurepas. As they swung around a sharp curve, the headlights of Georgette's car picked up a large cabin on low stilts. She stopped, turned off her lights, left the car, and waited for Ralph to join her. When he did, she flicked on a flashlight and beamed it ahead. "Can't be too careful," she said. "Every now and then a copperhead likes to sleep on the walkway." Ralph followed her up the steps onto a screened porch. The porch completely encircled the residence. She opened the screen door, crossed the porch, opened a back door, reached in, flicked on a light switch, and the room was softly lit. Ralph saw a large comfortable eat-in kitchen, well equipped with all the latest gadgets, modern appliances, and sparkling copper kitchenware peg-hung on the walls on each side of the stove. A round dining table with four ladder-back chairs was at the far end of the room. Above the fieldstone fireplace, was an oak mantel and on that mantle sat an antique Seth Thomas clock. He knew, for his family had one similar to it. Windows with white cafe curtains flanked the outside wall.

She crossed the kitchen, reached inside another door and turned on a mellow, glowing table lamp. She looked at Ralph, "Make yourself at home," and she beckoned for him to enter the room. As he did, she said, "I'm going to take a quick bath and then change into something more comfortable than this exhibition crap."

Ralph looked at the vaulted ceiling and then around the room. He was now even more dumbfounded, because the decor wasn't gaudy or tacky. The large living room was decorated in a most relaxing, comfortable manner. To his left was another big stone fireplace. Over its mantel hung an original misty scene of a bayou. The painting was in a tasteful, muted, gray-washed, cypress frame. He wondered what artist had made the deft strokes? In front of the fireplace was a comfortable-looking three-cushioned sofa with pale blue slipcovers. Behind the sofa was a long, Honduras mahogany table with Queen Ann legs. On the table were a couple of antique, brass, tapered candlesticks with bayberry scented candles. He knew the delicate aroma. Also on the table were two brass clamshell bookends with several volumes between them. He looked to his right. On the opposite side of the room from the fireplace and close to the front of the house he saw a closed door. From that door inward to the back wall were several layers of book shelves that reached upwards from the floor. They were filled with books. Near the book shelves was an easy chair and floor lamp. At the end of the room nearest the door he had just entered was a straight chair and a slanted small plantation desk with a goose neck lamp attached to the desk. On the floor was a gray background antique Chinese rug. Its blue border complemented the sofa slipcovers.

Across the front of the room, facing the lake, he saw another row of windows that opened out onto the encircling screen porch. Light blue sheer window drapes had been pulled back. Those windows viewed the lake. Through them beamed the lake-reflected, eerie yellow light of a descending new moon. Ralph stood as if in a trance. Where in the world was he? Never had he expected Georgette would have such a setting or such delicate taste. He felt as if he was an ant standing on an exquisite painting. He was out of place when he expected to be in full control.

The door next to the book cases opened. Georgette entered. He didn't recognize her. Her blonde hair was flowing almost to her waist. She had on a loose denim shirt and pair of blue jeans. She was barefooted. "What do you think of my shack?" she inquired.

Ralph just stared.

"Hey, Ralphy boy, cat got your tongue?"

"My God, Georgette, I never in my life expected anything like this -- even you -- it's all so different."

"Life is seldom what it appears on the surface, Ralphy."

"But why do you do what you do at the House of Relaxation?"

"My young stud, it really is none of your business. But I'll give you a clue." She was silent. Outside the night peepers called. On the top of one chimney the resident mockingbird, surveying his darkened domain, sang lushly the mimicking trills he had learned from his neighboring feathered friends. Off in the distance, a bobcat wailed. From across the lake came the sonorous howl of a night-hunting beagle. "That's why," she said with a faint smile. "The sights and sounds of nature thrill me. They inspire me." She pointed to the painting over the fireplace. "That's just one result," she said soberly.

Ralph gazed at the delicate, misty art work above the mantle.

He had lost all desire for sex. He was in a different world than he expected to be. He was confused because he wasn't in control. And, he realized he never had been so far as Georgette was concerned. He felt she had treated him as an object to be studied, dissected, maybe even painted in sections and sex for her with him had been a study by her. He wondered if it was so with all her paying clientele. He was almost frantic. He had to get the hell out of there. She knew him too well, had toyed with him -- and now was on the verge of controlling his very being, particularly if the relationship went any further.

"Georgette, I must have eaten something at dinner that has disagreed with me. I should get home before I disgrace myself."

"Ralphy, I understand," she said with a sad smirk. "It's quite a shock to first see the other side of life, particularly one you thought you knew and controlled.

"You're my baby. Come by any old time when you want Mommy to comfort you." And Georgette knew Ralph would never again seek her for he was unable to share, to trust and be comfortable with only partial control. She knew he was truly narcissistic, that he couldn't change and didn't want to.

19

R alph pursued Martha Ann with more determination than ever. There was something about the handsome blond that overwhelmed her. Was it his personal magnetism, his cockiness, his persistence, his apparent affection for her? Whatever it was, she knew she was under his spell. In the spring of the year following her graduation from LSU, they were married in a big social wedding in Charleston. But her father, never an advocate of Ralph, had made sure her estate was protected by a premarital agreement.

Martha Ann made every endeavor to make the marriage work. She and her husband had a large house fronting on Atchafalaya Bay. She quickly became one of the accepted young matrons of the community. She had a child in each of the first three years of marriage. First Ralph, Jr., then Jane C. (for her mother) and finally, Martha Elizabeth. The couple's sex life bore no relation to love. Mostly it was Ralph satisfying an animal appetite, one that could, at times, be rapacious. Never did he give consideration to the feelings of his wife. Slowly, Martha Ann realized that the enormous drive, the soirde-vi, of her husband was completely self-centered. He could be courtly gentle in the presence of others, but only for a purpose of his.

The fishing business was prospering and her ambitious husband was rising through the ranks of his father's far-flung fishing and trading empire. More and more he was away from home on alleged commercial endeavors.

20

It was a sad day for her when Martha Ann's father, on a Florida business trip, happened to see Ralph in the company of a young, ravishing red-head at the Breakers Hotel in Palm Beach, Florida. Her father had quietly inquired and found that Ralph, arrogant bastard that he was, was registered in the hotel under the name of Mr. and Mrs. Ralph Farqua. Her father had, on the spot, hired a private eye. That investigator had uncovered all that was necessary for his daughter to obtain a divorce.

When Martha Ann had at first accused Ralph of infidelity, he lied with the greatest of ease, denying her allegations. When she confronted him with the photographs he said, "So what. You're protected by the premarital agreement. I can live up to the terms of that document. But, you'll not find anyone better than me. You might as well put up with me for your and the children's sake."

Martha Ann, in blind fury, had slapped him across the face as hard as she could. "You self-centered, egotistical prick. I'll see you in hell before I'll spend another night with you," she yelled.

He made no effort at retaliation. "Have it your way. I could care less," he replied with a smirk. The marriage was over.

21

By the time the divorce was final, Ralph was thirty-three and World War II was roaring. The U.S.

draft was in effect but not yet breathing down his neck. However, he decided it would be to his best interest to enter the service of his country.

He conferred with his dad, who agreed Ralph should enter the Navy. A major interest in the business would be Ralph's, if and when, he returned to civilian life. Talbott Farqua, though he didn't understand his overbearing son, loved him dearly. Whatever his faults, Ralph had an instinct for the shipping and trading business. His father knew he was, and could continue to be, a valuable asset to the business. Talbott helped Ralph enter the Navy as a Lieutenant JG. After a ninety-day indoctrination, Ralph was assigned to the Navy Fuel Depot in Mobile, Alabama.

22

Gwendolyn McAllister, wife of T. Crampton McAllister, Captain, U.S.N., raised up on an arm in the big four-poster bed and looked at her drowsing husband. "Perry, turn over and talk to me. You know I can't go to sleep so soon after drinking a scotch highball and a grasshopper after dinner."

"What'd you say, Dear?" questioned her contented, sleepy husband. The former star blocking back of the U.S. Naval Academy football team, squirmed to a more comfortable sleeping position.

Crampton McAllister had been given the name "Perry" in his plebe year by his teammates. "Perry," short for "peripheral vision." And he had it. That's what made him so special as a blocking back. Tousled headed, six foot, 200 pounds, with plenty of speed, he could see trouble coming from almost any angle and cut off the would-be tackler before that opponent reached the Navy ball carrier, particularly on wide sweeps.

"You heard me. Two drinks after dinner don't make me drowsy. They make me jumpy as hell. And, besides that, we gotta' talk," said Gwendolyn, his long-limbed mate of twenty-six years.

"Gwen, at this time of night what do we have to talk about except sleep?" ask Perry.

"First of all, that blond, too perfectly groomed Lieutenant Ralph Farqua, who was seated at our dinner table earlier this evening, the guy on our Susan's right, is a slick animal."

"Just how do you know?"

"Because after you've danced in the line at Radio City Music Hall for more than six months, and met as many stage door Johnnies as I have, you can tell almost instantly who's an animal and who isn't. Besides, Marybeth Neal knows the family in Morgan City, Louisiana. She says he's an arrogant, selfish, divorced bastard, with three kids he never sees. His former wife and children now live in her home town, Charleston, South Carolina."

23

Perry McAllister rolled over, faced his wife and opened his eyes. The night light at the door jamb to the bathroom cast enough of a soft glow to emphasize the exquisitely proportioned features of his wife's face. Even in the semidarkness her eyes sparkled with a delicate dark fire. She was, to him, the same girl he had fallen in love with the minute he first saw her twenty-six years ago. He remembered: Cornell had whacked the hell out of Navy on that cold October Saturday afternoon at Yankee Stadium. He was tired and sore. His nose was scratched. He had a charlie horse in his right calf from the knee he had taken on an off tackle block in the second half. And Navy was supposed to have a good team. This had been their big chance to make up for the last two years.

After the game he and his teammates were to go to the Navy alumni buffet dinner dance at the Hotel Astor in New York City. He went. At first he thought it was sheer stupidity to attend. Then he saw Gwendolyn Horseley. She was tall, graceful, poised and had such flashing black eyes. She was there as a single with other invited alumni and students from Barnard College. He just couldn't keep from staring at her. Her eyes met his, and with that grace of hers, she seemed to float over to him. He had no idea what to say. She did.

"You're Perry McAllister, number 47, aren't you?" And she held out her hand. He responded. Her hand was warm, gentle, but firm.

"What's left of me," Perry grinned.

"And other than Helen of Troy, who might you be?" he asked.

"I'm Gwendolyn Horseley. Just call me Gwen. How's your right calf?"

"You saw that happen?"

"Sure did."

"But how?"

"My little brother, Angie, was the guy from Cornell who speared you. I was watching. He didn't mean to, but you caught him on a bad angle."

"Little, my a...," and Perry stopped before he completed the word.

"I know," she said. "He's a sophomore tackle, weighs 230 and, like you, he plays to win. You've got to meet him sometime. He really is a nice guy. But his ribcage is so sore tonight from the blocks you threw at him today, when I talked with him earlier he said, 'To hell with it, I'm not going out tonight, I'm going to bed.' You both played well."

"And you, where do you go to school?" asked Perry.

"I've finished Barnard as a theater major. Right now I'm on the stage."

"On or off Broadway?" quipped Perry.

"On Broadway at the Radio City Music Hall."

"You're a Rockette?"

"I love dancing. Know a better way to start?"

"Start? Half the aspiring women dancers in this country would give their eyeteeth to be in that line."

"Lucky, aren't I? And, I have tonight off. Mr. Blocking Back, when do you finish the Academy?" asked Gwen.

"Next June, God willing."

And, God had willed a number of good things since then reflected Perry as he looked at his wife. They were in the master bedroom of the Commanding Officer's quarters at the U.S. Navy Fuel Depot, Mobile, Alabama.

"Perry, I'm not kidding. That guy's a slick animal -- he's trouble."

"Yeah, I know," replied Perry. "He's got some enlisted men and civilian dock hands on Pier Two under absolute control. He's told them about an old gas pump behind the tank farm where they can discretely evade gas rationing. He knows every time and how many gallons each of those dumb bastards snitch."

"And how do you know, Mr. Base Commander?"

"Because I've got peripheral vision," jibed her husband.

"Well then, I guess you know that Farqua may be sleeping with our daughter, Susan?"

"What?" Captain McAllister was wide awake. "You're kidding?"

"No, I'm not kidding. And, Susan's divorce from the alcoholic bum she married isn't final yet. I'll bet Farqua's found out her marital status, knows she's vulnerable, and ashamed of the horrible mistake she's made. And, he's playing her feelings to the hilt for his selfish purposes. Perry, there could be serious trouble ahead for Susan." She stopped to catch her breath.

"I don't believe it," said Perry.

"Call the BOQ and see if the animal is in his den," shot back Gwen.

"Dammit, I will," said a thoroughly aroused Captain McAllister. He reached out and took the telephone from the bedside table and telephoned the BOQ. A front-desk Yeoman picked up the desk phone, he heard, "This is Captain McAllister. Will you please send a message to Lieutenant Farqua that I want to speak with him now?"

"Sorry, Sir," said the Yeoman, "But Lieutenant Farqua is not in his quarters this weekend. He's on a forty-eight-hour pass. He left just a little while ago."

Perry's anger was rising. "He's supposed to let the duty officer know where he can be reached. Did he leave an address and a phone number?"

"Just a minute, Captain, Sir, I'll look in his mail slot." There was silence and then the Yeoman continued, "Yes, he did, Sir. He's at his home near Atchafalaya Bay, Louisiana. His phone number there is LI3-7605."

"Thank you, Yeoman."

"You're welcome, Sir."

"Gwen, that son-of-a-bitch is not in his quarters. He's on a forty-eight-hour pass and has gone to his home in Louisiana."

"I'll call Susan's apartment and see if she's home," said Gwen. "But, I'll bet all the tea in China she isn't. And, I'm worried."

Gwen dialed the number of the apartment shared by Dianne Wheat and her daughter. The phone rang.

"Dianne Wheat speaking."

"Dianne, this is Mrs. McAllister. May I speak with Susan, please."

There was a brief silence. "Mrs. McAllister, Susan's left for the weekend."

"Left for the weekend? Where?"

"She didn't say exactly, except it was to be with an old schoolmate."

"Well, doesn't she have to leave a number where she can be reached by her employer, Ashland Oil Company, in the event she's needed in an emergency?"

"Oh, she did that."

"Dear, will you please give me the number."

"Mrs. McAllister, I don't think I should. I was to give the number out only in the event of an emergency."

"I assure you, Dianne, this is a real emergency."

There was a brief silence, then, "Well, okay, the number at Atchafalaya Bay, Louisiana, is LI3-7605."

"Thank you, Dianne."

24

Gwen McAllister hung up the phone. She glared at her husband. "Your peripheral vision isn't what it used to be. I told you that Farqua is a slick animal. She's with him. You've got to do something and fast."

"Gwen, I've already started the wheels in motion."

Gwen eyed her husband approvingly. He's the most principled guy I know, she thought.

Perry said, "Farqua's smart and crafty, but he's no team player. He's already put a number of my base civilian and Navy enlisted personnel on the spot with his gasoline dealings. I won't tolerate that. I've checked his personnel record. In addition to English, he speaks French fluently. There's a little island in the southwest Pacific. An Army MASH Unit is moving out, further west. The Navy is considering taking over the unit pier, enlarging it into a way stop refueling station for small Naval ships as they reach that area. The Navy is trying to fill the officer slots now. I've recommended Lieutenant Ralph Farqua. He knows the depot business. It may work out if he's in charge. Only trouble is, if he's made depot CO, he get's another half stripe. I hate the thought of that."

"I don't give a damn if they make him vice admiral. Just get him away from our Susan." And Gwen sighed in relief at the prospect of the animal leaving.

25

O n 5 December 1943, four days after returning from a delightful liaison weekend with Susan McAllister Smith at his home, Lieutenant Ralph Farqua received orders immediately transferring him to the island of Bora Bora. He read the orders and smiled sardonically. He would be the CO of a small, as yet not completed, fuel depot on the north shore of the island. He thought, at last I'm out of this dump. I was sure the affair with the base captain's daughter would precipitate a move, and, I get another half stripe. But where in the hell is Bora Bora and the French Society Islands?

Part IV

The First Meeting

1

Caroline yelled through the bathroom door, "Greg, Jacques is on the phone. He says it's urgent."

"What the heck, it's only eight a.m. I told him I would meet him at nine thirty."

"I know," replied Caroline, "But he's quite upset. You better speak to him."

Greg, in his skivvies, came in and sat on the edge of the king-sized master bed. He picked up the phone. "Good morning, Jacques. What's the problem?"

Jacques' excited voice was a tone higher than usual. "The problem, Greg, is threefold. First, I am sure Farqua's in town and, for some strange reason, I am being watched by two of his henchmen. I saw them in the dining room earlier this morning. Second, a reporter from the *Washington Post* called at six thirty this morning. He wants to meet with me at noon about what happened to Mary last night. The reporter no sooner hung up when I received a call from Benjamin Feldman. He is also in town. He wants to see Mary and me as soon as possible."

Greg was surprised. "Benjamin Feldman's in D.C. and wants to see you and Mary?"

"Yes, he is at the Mayflower."

"Did you tell him Mary died last night?"

"No, I did not."

"What did you tell Feldman?"

"Nothing, absolutely nothing. I told him I would return his call shortly. Then, I hung up the phone. I had already made up my mind to call you before I talked to anyone."

"How do you know the men you saw were Farqua's men?"

"I have seen them before, overseas."

"Overseas? When?" queried Greg.

"Yes, during the Ensemble's European tour. They were frequently with him. I guess they were acting as body guards. There is much we need to talk about before things get out of hand. I need your advice now."

"Why are you now being watched by Farqua's men?"

"Greg, I don't know unless it has something to do with Mary's death."

"Are they following you?"

"Yes, they are clumsy, but persistent."

Greg was silent for a few seconds, then said calmly but firmly, "Jacques, before we talk further, I have one question to ask. You don't have to answer it, but if you do, I want nothing but the truth."

"And what is that question?"

"Were you, in any way, involved in Mary's death?"

There was a gasp, then silence followed by, "Holy Mother of Mary, I had absolutely nothing to do with her death -- at least not knowingly. But so many unusual requests are being made, I do not know which way to turn. I feel threatened, as well as saddened, by my wife's death."

Greg thought, then he said, "Jacques, do you have a small suitcase or backpack?"

"Yes, Mary has a small backpack I can use. She took the pack everywhere, sometimes with only a pair of dancing slippers in it."

"Well, put three or four days change of clothing in the pack. Is there a back or side emergency stairway on your floor?"

"There is an inside emergency stairway."

"As soon as you pack your bag, take a look-see. When your corridor is empty, take the pack and go down that stairway to the first floor. Don't go through the lobby, find a rear or side exit. Walk through the alley to the first street you come to and take the first taxi you can find."

"Then what?" asked Jacques.

"Have the cab take you to the F Street entrance of the Willard Hotel, the hotel where you first saw Caroline. Leave the cab, go through Peacock Alley, the hotel corridor, and take another cab from the Pennsylvania Avenue entrance, to the Jefferson Memorial. I'll meet you at the memorial. You'll be staying with Caroline and me until I get a handle on what's going on."

"Thanks, Greg, I will start immediately."

"Jacques."

"Yes?"

"If you can tell you're being followed, stop at the first public phone booth you see and call my home. Give Caroline your number. She can reach me on my car radio. Then stay there until I call back."

"I am on my way," and Jacques hung up.

2

Greg Morgan quickly finished shaving and dressed. In the process, he told Caroline of Jacques' message and that he would return home with his island friend as soon as possible.

As he left, Caroline said, "Please be careful."

3

Greg drove his full-sized Mercury station wagon down the George Washington Parkway toward the Fourteenth Street Bridge, an entrance to D.C. As he drove along the river drive, he noticed that the sun was trying to break through the high horsetail clouds that meant a coming colder weather pattern. A chilling northwest breeze was raising goose bumps on the Potomac River surface. He glanced across the river and saw that the trees lining the north shore were shedding leaves, like brown tears, over their sadness at the departure of summer. Above that tree line soared the gray-white spire of the Washington Monument. To him, it looked like a large irritated finger admonishing the sky for the changing season.

He was perturbed by the call from Jacques. Why were Farqua and Ben Feldman in town at the same time? Greg drove to the Jefferson Memorial parking area. There were no cars in the lot. He felt relieved, in the early gray morning, as he walked up the broad main entrance stairway, and looked up at the memorial. No one was in sight, then Jacques appeared from behind one of the massive columns.

"You made it much quicker than I thought you would," Jacques' initial greeting echoed across the colonnade area. He continued, "I was careful. I am sure I left the hotel unnoticed. I saw no evidence that I was being followed." The two men hurried down the steps and entered Greg's car. As Greg drove out of the parking lot, he scanned the area carefully, then said, "Nice going, Jacques. I think you are right."

4

After they had been driving for a few minutes, Greg spoke. "What's this about Ben Feldman and Farqua being in town?"

"I can tell you about Farqua. But, Feldman I do not understand. His telephone call came just after the reporter called. Feldman said it was imperative that he see me as soon as possible. He is in room 712 at the Mayflower. He insisted I call him back within the next hour and set a meeting time."

"Did he say if anyone was with him?"

"Yes, his wife, Khristina."

"Did he say why he wanted to see you?"

"No. Only that it was most important."

"Well, we'll call him when we reach my house. Now, what's this about Farqua?"

"He has been in town since opening night. Wherever the troupe has danced, he has always attended opening performance."

"All through Europe?"

161

"At every single opening night, he has been there. Each time he is accompanied by a good-looking woman, never the same one twice. During each opening night, he brings his current lady friend backstage to show her how 'his' Ensemble works. Most of them are quite impressed."

"Jacques, just what do you know about Farqua?"

"I will tell you as much as I know. But, there are a lot of blanks to fill in."

"We won't worry about the blanks right now," said Greg.

"I did not meet Farqua when he first arrived on the island. I was busy with school chores on the south side of the island. I was having problems recruiting capable teachers for the school there.

"In November, 1943, weeks before Farqua arrived, the Navy group had arrived and started enlarging the compound that was to become the fuel depot. Early on, I met Samuel Gilford, Chief Bos'n's Mate. He was initially in charge of construction. He was a knowledgeable, decent guy. But he did not stay long when Farqua arrived."

"Why?" asked Greg.

"I learned from Gilford that unless Farqua had absolute domination of everyone around him, there was trouble. Sam Gilford was willing to take orders, but would not be dominated and he was more savvy than the new C.O. In no time, Gilford had maneuvered orders transferring him to a more acceptable environment. He left shortly after Farqua's first executive officer arrived on board.

"I met Ralph Farqua the day Senior Lieutenant James Richmond reported to the depot.

"Gilford had been teaching me to drive the jeep left behind by the MASH unit. They gave it to my father saying it was a pile of junk. Gilford's men helped me make the jeep drivable. The base has been supplying me with essence (gasoline) at no cost, one of the benefits of being the Chief's son. One day I took Gilford back to the base after he had given me a driving lesson. We drove to the gate, and saw a small Navy ship docking at the pier. We both wondered what was going on. We left the jeep and went down to the pier. Mary D'Quino was there also. The only person who came ashore was Lieutenant James Richmond. You cannot imagine a more docile, pliable guy in your life than Richmond. He was fat, flabby and sloppy. But, he is an honor graduate in fossil fuels from some U.S. university. Commander Farqua was on the pier. He all but drooled when he saw him. Farqua and Richmond met. Then Gilford introduced me to both of them. I was wary of Farqua from the moment we met."

"Why?" asked Greg.

"Because I know an island ram goat when I see one."

"And, what is that supposed to mean?"

"He exuded craftiness, dominance and plain meanness. He was impeccably dressed, but to me, his uniform was a camouflage of what it covered. As the eldest son of an island Chieftain, I knew I had to tolerate him, but we would never be friends. I determined right from the beginning not to be close enough to him to be dominated by him. But, that slick blond had a way about him. Not long after he arrived, he was controlling most of the elders on the north side of the island."

"Including your father, the Chief?"

"Not him, but before Farqua left the island at the end of the war, he became a very fast friend with Elder Pierre Swarraine. He is the master craftsman who fashioned your wife's earrings and your cufflinks. In addition, Swarraine is truly an accomplished sculptor. He is best known for turning whole coconut husks into the most weird and grotesque head carvings. He uses cat's eyes gems as the pupils for the eyes of his carvings. Sometimes those pupils are flaming red, sometimes blue or black or green. Oftentimes, each pupil would be of different color. Why, I do not know. The complete carvings with the set pupils have, since the war, become objects of art much in demand in Europe and now the U.S. market is beginning to accept them.

"Farqua, during the war, saw several of the carvings. He became intrigued by them. He and I have watched Swarraine work his magic on those husks. The sculptor would rough carve the head figure. Then he would cure each head before he finished the facial features."

"What do you mean by 'cure each head before he finished the facial features'?" asked Greg.

"Well, when he had rough carved the head and knew where the eyes would be located, he would drill from the right eye pupil area through the shell and meat of the coconut. He would let the coconut milk drain out. Then he drilled another smaller hole from the top of the head through the coconut meat. He let each rough carving sit for several days. He could tell when the inside meat was drying by the smell from the eye hole.

"He had a funnel with a spout just a little smaller than the eyehole. He would stick the funnel spout in the hole and pour in a small amount of fuel oil and alcohol, swish it around until it was absorbed by the coconut meat. He would light a taper and stick it into the hole. The interior coconut meat would burn to a crisp and not rot. When the coconut interior cooled, he would fill the void with boiled, dry beach sand and seal the two holes with small hard wood pegs."

"Why would he boil the sand?" asked Greg.

"To kill any organisms that might rot the interior of the husk. Then he would complete the carvings," replied Jacques.

He continued, "Farqua would sit and stare at the finished heads by the hour. It was as if he expected them to speak to him. Maybe they did."

"Why do you say that?" asked Greg.

"Several months after the war, Farqua left the island and returned to the states. I hoped I would never see him again. How wrong I was. About eight months after the war was over,

I learned Farqua had returned to Tahiti on the tramp steamer *Wild Orchid*. Shortly thereafter, he came to the island on a trading schooner and renewed his acquaintance with Mary D'Quino and Swarraine. He placed an order for all the head carvings Swarraine could make. In fact, he insisted the island sculptor hire a couple of helpers to increase his production. Then Farqua returned to Tahiti.

"The completed carvings were picked up every three weeks by the trading schooner and taken to Pacific Island Imports in Tahiti. Swarraine now lives like a king at his home. His house has been doubled in size. He is the next elder in line to become chieftain when my father steps down, which my father may do most any day now because of his ill health."

"Who owns Pacific Island Imports?" asked Greg as he drove north on the George Washington Parkway toward his home.

"I know not," responded Jacques. "But Farqua must have something to do with the company. That is where all the carved coconuts go."

Greg, after a few minutes of silence, asked, "Jacques, who finances the Southwest Pacific Dance Ensemble?"

"Pacific Island Imports," was the immediate reply.

"What!"

"You heard me right, Pacific Island Imports."

"Just how was the Ensemble put together?"

"According to Mary, she went to Farqua before the war ended and asked him to help her organize and find funding for the dance group. He agreed to do so and Mary claimed he secured the financial backing of Pacific Island Imports, a foreign company with offices in Tahiti. Since the time I took over management of the group, my correspondence has been with a Martin DeLange, finance officer of the trading company. All expenses are approved by him. All money transactions are cleared through a branch or affiliate of Chase Manhattan Bank. I have had no trouble."

"Where is this fellow, DeLange, headquartered?" asked Greg.

"In the U.S. In New Orleans, Louisiana."

Greg pulled over to the side of Spout Run Parkway and stopped. "Did you say New Orleans, Louisiana?" inquired an incredulous Greg.

"I surely did. Why?"

"I'll be damned," said Greg, "Either you just filled in a big blank, or created a new one. Did you know that Farqua came from Louisiana?"

"I had no idea where he lived in the U.S.," replied Jacques.

"Who handles the bookings for the tour?" asked Greg.

"Farqua, with the help of the French government," replied Jacques.

Greg drove onto Spout Run Parkway headed for home. "That's odd, odd, odd," said Greg softly. His thoughts were whirling. For him there was a connector missing. As he drove homeward, he remembered back to the afternoon of the taboo, and he recalled his last island conversation with Mary D'Quino and Jacques just before his ship left the lagoon.

"Jacques, you said the other night that there was a Naval Board of Inquiry on the taboo episode?"

"Yes, Greg, there was. It was held on the island not long after the war was over and before Commander Farqua returned to the U.S."

"Were you summoned to attend?"

"No, my friend, I was not."

"Did you attend the hearing?"

"No, I did not. I was called by the colonial government to attend an educational conference in Tahiti. That conference lasted a week, the week the Naval hearing was to be held."

"Was the Naval inquiry actually held?"

"Yes, it was, according to Mary."

"What happened, if you know?"

"Mary said she told the board what had occurred and that somehow she was exonerated from any wrongdoing."

"And Farqua?"

"The board believed her story that the Commander knew nothing of the episode until after it happened, until Mary told him. He received no reprimand and the whole affair was dismissed."

"Do you believe Mary's statement of what happened at the hearing?" he asked.

Jacques hesitated and then said, "She had no reason to tell me a lie. Who would benefit from what she said?" The answer to that question might fill in a big blank, thought Greg.

The two drove silently for a few minutes. Greg looked from the road to Jacques. His island friend appeared weary and worn as he had every right to be. Greg spoke quietly, "I know this is not a very appropriate time for me to ask, but there is so much to learn and so little time in which to do so before we will have to meet with the D.C. authorities. When did Evangeline, your first wife, die?"

"Almost three years ago," said Jacques. "She was pregnant with our second child. She had gone to Tahiti for a medical check up and was returning to the island aboard the trading schooner. The sailing ship ran into an unexpected severe storm, capsized and sank. The only person to survive was Marquis Venture, a deckhand. He clung on to some debris for over two days before he was rescued. I will never feel the same. Nothing has meant much to me since then. Now this," he sighed.

"How did you and Mary get together?" continued Greg.

"After my wife's death and in addition to my educational work, I became interested in the history of my people on the island. Why? I wish I really knew. Maybe to fill in the sensibility of loneliness. I should have been happy just spending spare time with Renee, my daughter. Not so. She reminded me constantly of Evangeline and that kept me ever sad. Besides, my parents and my wife's parents were providing Renee with more affection than I could show. I was desolate. I even climbed the mountain and considered delivering myself to the pagan god, Maui. I guess I had not the inner strength to do it. While on the mountain side I looked down on the village and, for some strange reason, determined to learn more about my people in my spare time. It was a long study.

"When, after my wife's death, the Ensemble returned from the Orient for rest, I knew Mary D'Quino was keeping an eye on me. I could tell. When she learned of my historical research, she became a mother hen. And, as rough as you know she can be, she can also be the opposite. I began to feel very comfortable in her company.

"One evening after dancing in the village center, we both had too much pineapple brandy and the next thing you know we were in bed together. Holy Mother of Mary, she was so much woman. Several days later, she did not suggest, she asked me to marry her. She said she needed no dower from me, never would. She had her own funds. She asked, 'Are you comfortable with me?' I replied, 'Yes, but I am not in love with you.' And she said, 'That is enough for me,' and added a strange comment, 'I am used to not being loved. I doubt if I ever will be.'

"So, we were married. She was not only content, but seemed greatly relieved at the relationship. Soon thereafter, I agreed, with some prodding from the colonial authorities, to leave my post in education and become general manager of the Ensemble at a compensation I never dreamed of before. And though Mary seemed to grow happier in our relationship, I must confess that as much as I admired her, I was not really close to her. I felt a barrier. Just small things."

"Like what?" inquired Greg.

"Her relationship with Farqua."

"What was her relationship with him?"

"That is hard for me to define. It was as if they hated each other, but were strangely drawn together by some hidden force. And, I sensed she was protecting me from Farqua, for what reason I know not. I just felt uneasy."

"Could she and Farqua have been involved in some joint project in addition to the Ensemble?"

"Greg, I am not sure, but she acted as if she knew far more about Farqua and his activities than I did."

"Did you ever ask her if she had any reason to question Farqua about his other activities, if any?"

"I did," replied Jacques.

"And what did she say?"

"The less I knew about that animal the better off we will be."

"Did you ask her what she meant by that remark?" queried Greg.

"She never really answered me. She just said, 'Just let us look after the Ensemble, and worry not about his schemes.'"

Greg swung his car into the driveway to his home. Jacques looked at Greg and said soberly, "I have begun to suspect many things not just about Farqua. All is confusing. I should never have married Mary. I should never have become general manager. I should never have left the island."

Greg looked at his agitated friend. "We'll talk more about that later."

After Greg parked his car and in an effort to divert his friend's emotional upheaval, he turned to Jacques, "Where did the idea of Feldman's taboo originate, if you know?"

"I can tell you it came not from my father. He was against the taboo. But, this was one of the few times when he was overruled by the council of elders. To a man, the other members were in favor of it. My father has made it a policy to tell no one of the private discussions of council. I later learned from Mary that Swarraine was the real impetus behind the idea of the taboo inflicted on Feldman."

"When did you learn that?" asked Greg.

"Long after the Naval inquiry," responded Jacques, "And, my father was in Tahiti when the elders made their decision to place the taboo. Early on the day of the taboo, he returned to our island, was told of the upcoming event, and asked me to secretly attend and to bring a witness from your ship. I asked you to be beside me.

"I had absolutely no idea of what would transpire, only when and where the event would take place. I not only was shocked at what happened, I was deeply ashamed, ashamed for Mary, ashamed for my father, and ashamed for my people. Yet, I could not intervene, for if I had done so, my ultimate fate may have been far worse than Feldman's. I thank God you did not try to stop the episode. No telling what would have happened.

"Never before had I seen Mary's ferocity and strength. My embarrassment at what you saw was so deep I knew not what to say to you on our way back to the base. So, I said nothing."

For the first time, Greg began to understand his island friend's behavior while they viewed the weird event. Greg now had increasing suspicions as to why the taboo happened.

5

As the two men went up the three-step entrance to the house, Caroline, all smiles, opened the door and said, "Welcome, Jacques. We have a guest room ready for you."

"You are so kind, Mrs. Morgan."

"Please don't call me 'Mrs. Morgan,' you may not know me, but I've known of you for years. I'm Caroline and to me you're Jacques."

Jacques looked appraisingly at Caroline. "You are not only beautiful and smart, but thoughtful," said Jacques.

Caroline smiled, and escorted him to one of the two guest rooms in the large rambler.

6

"Has J.R. come home from his overnight stay at Tim's?" inquired Greg as Caroline re-entered the living room.

"No, not yet, he won't be home until after school, why?" asked Caroline.

"For a while I don't think he should mention that we have a house guest from the Society Islands."

"And, why not?"

"Well, I have learned from Jacques that Benjamin Feldman is in town and has tried to reach Jacques. In addition, Jacques says Farqua's in town and his men have been watching Jacques."

"What does Feldman want and why have Farqua's men been watching Jacques?" asked Caroline.

"If I knew, I wouldn't be as cautious as I am now," said Greg.

"Were you followed out here?" asked Caroline.

"No, I'm pretty sure that Jacques gave Farqua's men the slip. But, Jacques is supposed to call Mr. Feldman in the next hour. Mr. Feldman and his wife are staying at the Mayflower. I'm going to call him instead."

"And so the plot thickens?" asked Caroline nervously.

"Just a little," said Greg casually. Inside, Greg's emotions were beginning to churn. The plot wasn't thickening a little. It was beginning to darken like an ominous approaching thunderstorm.

7

A little later, Jacques walked into the living room. Greg said, "Jacques, if you don't mind, I'm going to call Feldman and try to find out why he so urgently wants to meet with you."

"Greg, I leave this whole mess to you. I know little of U.S. culture and nothing of the law. I am in your hands."

171

"You've got the best," said Caroline.

"We'll see," said Greg. "Excuse me a minute."

He went to the den and disconnected the phone from the wall jack. He brought the unit into the living room and called Ben Feldman's room at the Mayflower. Khristina Feldman answered the phone. "Mrs. Feldman speaking."

"Mrs. Feldman, this is Gregory Morgan, a friend of Jacques Montagne. May I speak with your husband?"

"Just a minute, please," said Khristina, and she placed a hand over the phone mouthpiece. She turned to her husband, "Do you know a Gregory Morgan? He wants to speak to you about Jacques Montagne."

Ben Feldman's memory had been tumbling to the present ever since that fateful night at the National Theater. But, he had no clear recollection of a Gregory Morgan. "I'll take the call," he said.

Ben Feldman took the phone and spoke cautiously. "This is Mr. Feldman. Why do you wish to speak with me?"

"Because I'm a friend of Jacques Montagne. I know you called him earlier this morning and asked for a meeting."

"So?"

"Did you know that his wife, Mary D'Quino, collapsed on stage at the National Theater last night. She died a little while later at the George Washington Hospital. I was at the theater. I saw her. I think she was poisoned. The report will be all over the *Evening Star*, D.C.'s afternoon paper. Have you turned on your room radio this morning?"

There was utter silence on the other end of the phone, except for someone breathing heavily. Finally came a gut wrenching, "Oh, my God, no."

"Yes, her death is tragic," said Greg calmly. "Not only am I a friend of Jacques, I'm his lawyer. Would you be willing to chat with me before you meet with Jacques?"

"I don't know, Mr. Morgan, with what you've just told me, I just don't know that I should."

"Before you make up your mind, Mr. Feldman, let me add one more item for you to consider as to whether or not you should talk with me. I saw what happened to you that day on Bora Bora."

"You saw what?" Ben Feldman gasped into the phone.

"I saw what happened involving you and Mary D'Quino on Bora Bora."

Again the phone on the other end was silent -- except for heavy breathing. Then Ben said, "I can't believe it, I just can't believe you saw what happened."

"Mr. Feldman, I think we have much to talk about. I truly would like to meet with you."

"You've more than convinced me, Mr. Morgan, where and when?"

"I'll meet with you and your wife in your room as soon as I can get there. It'll take me about twenty minutes."

"We'll be here, Mr. Morgan," and Ben Feldman hung up the phone. He turned to his wife in anguish and fear. "My God, Tina, Mary D'Quino collapsed on stage last night and died. After what I said in Box A on opening night, I'm sure Sommenberg has already called the D.C. police. Where will all this end?"

Tina tried to hide her rising fear. "Don't worry, Hon. I know you had nothing to do with it. I only hope your Papa didn't."

"You know that's among the reasons I came here, Tina. To warn Mary D'Quino, Jacques and Farqua about what Papa may have set in motion. I better call Becky right now, tell her what has happened and see if she can stop Papa from going any further with his plans."

8

Ben Feldman picked up the phone and called his parents' home. Becky answered, "This is Rebecca Slinsky speaking."

173

"Becky, it's me, Ben. We're at the Mayflower Hotel in Washington, D.C. I'm afraid we're too late."

"Too late for what?"

"Mary D'Quino collapsed on stage last night and died. She may have been poisoned."

"Holy shit, Ben." There was a silence, then, "I don't think it was Papa."

Ben warily asked, "Why?"

"Because, last night I told Papa if he tried to set in motion his plans to kill Mary or Jacques or anybody else, I was going to the police."

"And?"

"Papa swore on Abraham's grave he hadn't gotten anywhere with his plan, but he would still like to," said Becky.

"How about Papa's talk with Weiner that you overheard?"

"Papa said Weiner finally called him back and said he was too old for that kind of crap anymore. Weiner said he would much rather watch his grandson's soccer game than shiv anyone. Besides he said, there are too many smartass cops around nowadays. So Papa said he was still looking for somebody to help him. I told him to forget about the whole idea. This isn't rum-running days. It's 1954. Izzy's memory is coming back. He's his own man now and he has a good wife. What more can you ask of a son that you tried unsuccessfully to make your boot-black?"

"And what did Papa say?"

"He said. . .he said, 'I still love him even if I can't control him. He deserves better than what he got.'"

"Becky, are you sure he wasn't pulling a fast one on you?"

"I'm sure, Ben." But what she didn't say was that she could tell that Papa's health was failing from the effects of his colon problem. He didn't have the heart or drive to head the dirty work he thought should be done.

"Thank goodness," said Ben with a sigh of real relief. "Tell Mama and Papa I've got some things to get straightened out here. Then we'll be back."

"When?" asked Becky.

"In about four or five days."

"Izzy, you be damned careful. I know you had nothing to do with that hula dancer's death and that your memory is on the mend. Nevertheless, you aren't any Sherlock Holmes. Clear your skirts and get your fanny back here where you belong. Tell Tina to watch you carefully."

"OK, Becky, I will," said her brother and he hung up the phone.

9

" My, I'm relieved," said Ben to Tina.

"What did she say?" asked his wife.

"She said she's positive Papa had nothing to do with D'Quino's death."

Khristina heaved a sigh of relief. "You didn't, your Papa didn't, then who did?"

"Right now, I've got no idea. I'm lost. But, I'm determined to try and talk with this Gregory Morgan, Ralph Farqua and Jacques Montagne, before we go home."

"Those conversations can't happen soon enough to suit me. You've got Morgan coming by in a few minutes. What's with him?" asked Tina.

"He claims he saw what happened at Bora Bora. How in the hell he saw I don't know. I didn't see a soul around except Mary D'Quino when I drove up to the MASH demolition site that day."

"Ben, I can well understand why you said what you did that night in Box A. And, I saw a glimpse of a man I never knew -- never want to know. Just why did you come back to the scene of your resurrection, the return of your memory?"

"I can't give you a full answer. Maybe I never can. But, I now understand that before the accident, I was never me or what I intended to be. I can't place all the blame on Papa. I guess I was accepting the easy way to live, by mimicking, by being a puppet, not by thinking or my conscience. Ever since I came to on the *Southern Cross*, even without a memory, I knew I had been given a second chance at living. And, I damned near kicked that away until I met you. For the first time in my life, I became interested in somebody other than myself. I am no paragon, never will be, but whatever happens in the future, you and your caring opened a window, a window with a view. I shall try never to lose that view. I don't want anyone hurt because of what happened to me on the island. I suspected a lot more was going on under the surface of Farqua's domination. But, damn it all, I didn't know how to get to the root of what was happening, nor did I know how to stop any of it, except to be loudly dogmatic."

"What are you driving at?"

"Tina, something sinister was happening on that island. I'm sure of it. I guess one of the reasons I was determined to come here this weekend was to see if I could get a handle on what the hell was, and still is, behind that feeling."

"My God, Ben, you aren't the FBI."

"I know that, but I still want to talk to Jacques and Farqua. They've got to know more than I do."

"Suppose the police find out you're here?" asked an increasingly nervous Tina.

"I'm not worried about that. I've done nothing wrong. I didn't kill Mary. Besides, all the reports say two ram goats caused my injury."

"But Farqua, Jacques, and now that Gregory Morgan coming here, apparently know what happened. Maybe we should call the police," said his troubled wife.

"Not yet, Tina. I'm sure Sommenberg has already talked to them."

10

Greg turned to Jacques, "I must immediately go back into D.C. and try to talk with the Feldmans. I'll return here before long."

"That is OK with me," said Jacques. "If you do not mind, I will call the hospital and see if I can find out the results of the autopsy. In addition, I want to make arrangements to send Mary's body back to the island."

"No! Please don't do that yet," said Greg. The hospital will ask where they can reach you. In my opinion, that could be disastrous. Read, rest, listen to the radio, but don't phone, don't go outside until I return, please."

"I do not understand, but I will do as you say," said Jacques.

Caroline had been listening to the two men. She said, "Jacques, while Greg's in town, why don't you listen to the local radio news. You'll learn that the D.C. police are already looking for you."

Jacques eyes opened wide with surprise. "Mary, mother of Jesus, where will it end?"

Greg left to return to Washington and meet with the Feldmans.

11

There was a knock on the Feldmans' room door. "Who's there?" asked Ben.

"Greg Morgan," was the reply.

Ben opened the door with the chain still in the slide. "Would you please show me some identification?"

"Sure," said Greg and he took his billfold from his back pocket and showed Ben his Virginia driver's license.

Ben scanned it carefully, then said, "Please come in." Before he closed the door, he looked up and down the hall to see if any strangers were in the corridor. Greg observed the move with respect, but said nothing.

"Mr. Morgan, this is my wife, Khristina."

"It's a pleasure to meet you, Mrs. Feldman," said Greg as he observed the diminutive blonde.

"Thank you, Mr. Morgan, do be seated," replied Tina and she motioned to a boudoir chair.

Greg looked at the duo. Feldman was obviously nervous. His wife was wary. "Mr. Feldman, time is of the essence. I will dispense with courtesies. Why do you want to talk with Jacques Montagne?"

"First, I wanted to warn him and second, to talk to him about what was really happening on Bora Bora that triggered my injury on an early December afternoon in 1944."

"Warn him about what?" asked Greg.

"That my father, in the recent past, has been threatening to kill every participant in the unfortunate event that happened to me on that day. He was in the theater with me the night my memory began to return. I did not know Mary D'Quino died last night until you told me earlier this morning. We arrived in D.C. yesterday at 10:15 p.m. on the local from Philadelphia. We have not turned on the radio. The truth is, I didn't remember what happened on Bora Bora that fateful day until I saw the opening night of the Southwest Pacific Dance Ensemble at the National Theater a few days ago."

Greg looked with astonishment at Feldman. "What do you mean, you didn't remember what happened on Bora Bora until the opening performance of the dance group?"

"Mr. Morgan, when I came to on the Naval Hospital Ship *Southern Cross*, I had absolutely no memory of what had happened in my life prior to returning to consciousness. I have struggled from that date in 1944 until the Ensemble's performance on opening night, with a tormenting void that almost ruined me."

"You mean for the last ten years you have had no memory of your life through the alleged taboo on the island?" asked Greg.

"He's telling the truth, Mr. Morgan," said Khristina fiercely. "Not only that, but he was lied to."

"By my Naval record and those who testified at the Naval inquiry on the island shortly after the war," answered an infuriated Feldman.

"How do I know you're not lying to save your old man's skin -- maybe yours?"

Ben walked to the dresser, unzipped a small briefcase, and took out two documents. He walked over to Greg and slapped the documents onto his lap. "Read these before you make any more smartass insinuations, Mr. Morgan."

Greg's cheeks reddened with quick anger at the seemingly snide remark. He picked up the copy of Feldman's physical record and read the report of the accident as signed by Lt. Commander Ralph Farqua, and he read the findings of the Naval inquiry board at Bora Bora. He stared first at Feldman, then at his wife. He felt queasy, guilty as all hell at not having long ago tried to determine the truth behind the tragic event. Just imagining what Feldman had lived through for so long was gut wrenching.

"Mr. Feldman," he said, "God knows how much torture you have suffered. Just thinking about it makes me cringe. Both the physical report and the board findings are based on lies. I was there, with Jacques Montagne, behind some palmetto bushes. We both saw what happened. There were no ram goats involved."

Khristina Feldman began to cry. "Oh, Ben, you really have remembered. Mary D'Quino did attack you."

Feldman looked at the floor and said softly, "When my memory of the event returned that night at the theater, I threatened to kill everyone in connection with the affair. I didn't even know who you were. I didn't mean a word of those remarks. I was so shocked at my returning memory and realizing who was responsible for my injuries, I'm sure my host of the evening, a Mr. Sommenberg, has taken my threat to the police. What the hell do I do now? I came down to warn Mary D'Quino and Farqua of the threat of my father and among other things to assure myself that the memory was true. I have since learned that my father's verbal threat, like mine, was just that, the venting of years of anguish and nothing more. He's no more of a killer than I am. And, I wouldn't put myself in this position if I had something to hide."

There was a period of awed silence.

"I don't blame either you or your father for your outbursts," said an astonished Greg. "Who knows you are here?"

"No one but my sister, Rebecca, in Philadelphia. Why?"

"Mr. Feldman, I apologize for my initial brusqueness. I had no idea what you have suffered all these years. With what these documents begin to reveal, I do believe you." Greg stopped talking, looked out the window and thought it would be a good idea to get Feldman and Jacques together and find as much of the truth as he could before the authorities closed in. He sensed real trouble ahead for both the island educator and Farqua's former executive officer. His gaze centered on the anguished couple. "In my opinion, you are in serious danger."

"From who?" asked Khristina.

"I don't know yet, but Farqua has got to be involved."

"I've always suspected that crafty bastard," said a dour Ben Feldman.

Feldman's usually calm wife was really upset and started to cry. "What should we do? What is going to happen to us?"

"Mrs. Feldman, nothing's going to happen to you if I can help it," said Greg.

12

Ben had been eyeing Greg. He's not as bad as I thought he would be. In fact, he's pretty straightforward. He spoke, "Mr. Morgan, what would you suggest we do?"

"First of all, you can call me Greg," said the young lawyer with a glimmer of a smile.

"Thanks," said Feldman, "I'm Ben and my wife's Tina."

"Second I'm going to call my wife, and tell her to expect two more guests for a couple of days. Did you register in your name?"

"Yes, we did," responded Ben.

"Then we're going to get the hell out of here without you paying your tab at this time."

Greg went to the phone and called his home. Caroline answered. He spoke rapidly, "Hon, I'm fine. We're going to have two more guests. Be there soon," and he hung up.

"My, that was quick," said Tina.

"I don't want it traced if someone was listening," said Greg. "I hope like hell no one but your sister, Rebecca, knows you're here. But I can't take chances. Just take one suitcase. Leave enough clothes here so they'll think you're out for the day."

"Who is they?" asked Tina.

"Anyone looking for you," said Greg.

"You're serious, really serious," said Ben.

"I sure am and have every reason to be. Let's get going."

13

Ben and Tina packed furiously.

"Leave your shaving gear here. I've got plenty extra at home," said Greg. "We're going out the back entrance of the hotel. There'll be cabs at the back entrance as well as the front."

Tina looked inquiringly at Greg, "Where do you live?"

"In North Arlington, Virginia. But, we're not going there by cab. My car is parked in a garage on Twentieth Street,

N.W., in D.C. We'll take the cab to get my car, then we'll head home. Jacques Montagne is already at my house. Hopefully, no one saw him leave his hotel."

"Mary's husband is at your house?" asked a wide-eyed Tina.

"For his protection as well as yours, I hope. He arrived there only a couple of hours ago. Do you remember him, Ben? He is Chief Lorenz Montagne's eldest son, the educator."

"Not by name. Maybe when I see him, I'll recollect. I still have problems of recall. Names are difficult, images help a lot."

"Well, I'm sure that discussions between all of us will bring into focus many useful factors. Factors that I hope will help solve Mary's death and the reasons for your torture," said Greg.

"I hope, I hope, I hope," said Tina.

14

The trio left the elevator on the lobby floor and headed for the 17th Street hotel entrance. Greg eyed the corridor for loungers. There was none. He gave a sigh of relief.

As they left the back entrance, Greg saw one of three parked Yellow Cabs. He motioned. The lead cab drove up. The trio entered. Greg gave the address and the cab drove away from the curb. He glanced behind the cab to see if they were being followed. All was clear.

15

Greg drove homeward, and he was aware of another problem. Here he was with Jacques, his client (a possible murder suspect) in his home. Now he was taking Feldman and his wife to his home (another one or two possible suspects). Legal conflicts of interest flashed through his mind. Jesus, he could be in a mess with the Virginia Bar if there was a conflict of interest or even if there was tension between Jacques and Ben Feldman.

If his instincts weren't right, that neither had committed the crime, and both men were in serous danger, he, Greg, was going to be in an unholy mess. Sweat gathered under his arm pits. He just had to be right. Greg was also beginning to believe he had been terribly wrong in his assessment of Mary D'Quino and Farqua. He had originally thought of them as such strong honorable human beings. And that Feldman was the selfish weakling. Now, he didn't know, but the curiosity that had disturbed him for years, was gnawing at his gut with the fierceness of a starved beaver. He had to have some answers.

16

The silence was broken by Ben Feldman.

"How does Jacques fit into the picture, " asked Ben.

"He was the one who asked me to accompany him to the scene of the taboo."

"Why?"

"Mary D'Quino told me it was to protect Farqua, the base C.O., if he was called on the carpet about the episode."

"How long had Jacques known that the taboo was to take place?" asked Ben.

"Jacques said he was told of the pending event by his father, when his father returned from Tahiti early that morning. And, he told Jacques to find an impartial witness -- one from my ship -- to watch the proceedings. I had met and become friendly with Jacques. He chose me."

"Do you believe what Jacques has told you is the truth?"

"I do believe he has told the truth about what he knows. You're going to have plenty of time to interrogate him, and there's much more I want to know."

"If you think you have questions, wait until he hears mine."

The tone of Ben's voice reminded Greg of the problems he could be making for himself just bringing those two together.

17

"Mr. Morgan -- Greg--" said Tina, "What happens if Ben and Jacques, for some reason, don't get along?"

For a brief period Greg drove in silence, then responded, "I've thought about that. And, it could be a problem. If something arises, and there is a conflict of interest or even a personality conflict between Ben and Jacques, I'll take you two back to your hotel, Jacques to his hotel, and represent none of you, but I'll be a witness to the extent permitted by law. You'll have to fend for yourselves."

Again there was silence. Finally Ben spoke, "I accept your position, Greg. It's a fair one for us, but a risky one for you."

"Agreed, but I, like you, really want to know what was the background, the real reasons as to why the episode occurred. I believe that knowledge holds the key to Mary D'Quino's death."

18

Caroline heard a car drive up, recognized it as Greg's. She went to the door, opened it, and greeted the Feldmans. They were nervous and Caroline, a little irritated, thought, Greg is really doing a balancing act this time. There are times when he can't help but be the white knight on the white horse.

Jacques had gone to his room. Caroline escorted the new guests to the second guest room, showed them the closet and dresser, then discreetly left.

Jacques had returned to the living room. "Did I hear other voices?" he inquired as Greg entered the room.

"Yes," responded Greg. "I brought the Feldmans home with me."

"You what?" asked a surprised Jacques.

"I brought the Feldmans home with me."

"Why?"

"Because they are in as much danger as you are. Maybe even more."

"How could that be? It was my wife who was apparently murdered? And the police are looking for me."

"I'm sure they're not the only ones looking for you, the Feldmans and before long, for me," replied Greg.

19

Caroline entered the room carrying a tray with a fresh pot of hot tea and five cups. She placed the tray on a coffee table, turned to Jacques and said, "Take a sip of this, it'll help calm your nerves."

"I need something," retorted Jacques.

Greg looked at his island friend and said, "Jacques, before the Feldmans come into the room, I've a question to ask that has nothing to do with them."

"Ask," said Jacques.

"When Mary collapsed on stage last night and you were kneeling by her, did you notice an odor, an odd odor?"

Jacques was genuinely surprised, as if the question was awakening a long-hidden memory. "Yes, I did," said Jacques.

"Have you ever experienced that odor before?"

"Oh, Holy Mary. I have."

"When, where?"

"Maybe twice, three times in my life, on the island. But until your question, I couldn't believe that odd aroma might surface in this country," said Jacques.

"What do you mean?"inquired Greg.

"When wading and fishing close to the reefs one has to be most careful of the giant Nohu fish. They are very poisonous. Stepping on the horns of those devils can sometimes mean a slow torturous death. Their poison destroys the flesh, the muscles, the nerves, and sometimes may lead to a paralyzing death, depending on the amount of venom the spines of the dorsal fin eject. I have witnessed two or three such deaths; so had Mary. The victims emanate a horrible stench. Now that you remind me, the same odor wreaked from Mary. My God, how could that have happened?" Then the color drained from Jacques' face. "Oh, no, Swarraine," he moaned.

"What are you saying?" inquired Greg.

"Swarraine, in addition to being a sculptor, was the only islander who knew how to catch the fish and extract the poison by removal of the dorsal fin with its spines and venom sacs. He would cook the venom until it was in powder form. That was done under strict colonial government supervision. They supposedly took his entire production. The process was undertaken only once a year. A small amount of the powdered concentrate, if ingested, would kill a person in no time at all. Oh no -- Mary -- but how?" moaned Jacques.

20

Caroline had been listening intently. She looked at Greg, then at Jacques, coughed nervously and said, "I think I have an idea of how, but not who."

"You think you know how?" asked her surprised husband.

"Yes, I remember something," she said as she arose and walked rapidly to the maple chest-on-stand. She tugged on the drawer and took out the small evening bag she had with her last night when she and Greg had attended the dance Ensemble. She opened the bag and took out some soiled facial tissue.

"What in the world is that?" asked Greg.

"The tissue I used to wipe up the mess I made when I poured the remnants of Mary's Orange Crush back into the bottle from the glass," said Caroline.

"And why did you do that?" asked her husband.

"Because after I called for the ambulance and while I was in Mary's dressing room, my throat was so parched I needed a drink of water. The only glass I could find was by the Orange Crush bottle on Mary's dressing table. The glass had some Orange Crush in it. So, rather than pour the remains into the sink, I poured the orange liquid back in the bottle, then washed the glass before I got my drink of water. As I was pouring the Orange Crush into the bottle, I spilled some drops of the liquid on the dressing table and wiped them up with this tissue. I couldn't find a trash basket, so I just put the soiled tissue in my evening bag."

"Why do you think the tissue has anything to do with Mary's death?"

"Well, I'm not sure it does, but when I came back to get the costumes to throw over Mary while she was on the sofa in Jacques' office, I happened to glance at the dressing table. I remembered, I just remembered, that the Orange Crush bottle was gone. The only person to come into the room while I was there was Linguette. She was taking Mary's place and had to make a quick costume change. Maybe that drink contained the poison. Maybe some of the poison is in the tissue."

Jacques was looking in bewilderment at the Morgans.

"I remember your commenting about the look on Linguette's face during the waters routine. Hon, please let me have the tissue, I've got to call my friend, Dave Springer, Chief Homicide Detective in the district," said Greg.

Caroline gave Greg the soiled tissue. He went to the phone and called the Chief Homicide Detective, a former law school mate of his. After graduation and passing the D.C. bar, Dave had elected to stay in the police department, following the footsteps of his father.

When Dave answered the phone, Greg said, "Hi, Dave, this is Greg Morgan. I need to talk to you as soon as possible."

"Good to hear from you, Greg. What's up?"

"I need to talk to you about an outfit called Pacific Island Imports and a dance troupe, now on the stage at the

National Theater, called the Southwest Pacific Dance
Ensemble."

There was silence on the other end of the phone. Then,
"OK, Greg, but not here. I'll meet you at the bar of the D.C.
Lawyers Club in thirty minutes."

"That's fine with me," responded Greg, and he
wondered why the guarded conversation of his friend and the
necessity to meet out of headquarters.

21

Greg looked anxiously at his wife and then at
Jacques. "I've got to go back into town right now
for a little while. It's important. I may go by the Embassy
too."

"My, you just arrived with our last guests. They haven't
even met Jacques," said a perturbed Caroline.

"I know, I know. Hon, you'll just have to do the
honors. It's urgent that I meet Dave as soon as possible. Time
is really of the essence or I wouldn't put you on the spot." He
turned to Jacques, "Please, no big confrontation between you
and the Feldmans, at least until I get back. Tell them to keep
their cool until I return. I'm sure what I'm about to do will help
us all."

"I hope you are right," sighed Caroline.

22

As Greg was leaving, J.R. came up the front steps.
Greg turned to him, "Hi, Son, aren't you home a
little early today?"

"Yep, Dad, teachers conference this afternoon. We're
gonna' have a long soccer practice."

"Fine, J.R., but so that you know, we have three guests.
Your mother will introduce you to them. Please be pleasant,
but don't -- DO NOT -- mention them to any of your friends --
at least not yet."

"Why not?" asked J.R.

"Because there are some problems I'm trying to solve before their names become public. It might put us all in jeopardy if you do -- understood?"

J.R. was more than mildly curious. "Understood," replied his son. "But, will you fill me in a little later?"

"Absolutely."

"OK, Dad, I'll keep my yap shut," said J.R.

"Thanks, Son. I'll be back soon, I hope."

23

J.R. entered the house. Caroline introduced him to Jacques. Then told him the Feldmans were getting settled in the other guest room. They would be out shortly.

J.R. was puzzled that his family had accumulated three guests in such a short time.

"I'm going to my room to put down my books and overnighter. Timmy and I had a heck of a good time last night. How was the show?"

"Very different," said his mother as she cast a wary glance at Jacques.

J.R. saw the look and wondered what his mom meant by her remark. Then he remembered that just before going to school that morning, he heard Timmy's radio commenting on some dancer who had collapsed last night on the National Theater stage. He just had to know more. He would ask after he returned from soccer practice.

As J.R. passed the open door to Jacques' guest room on the way to his room, he looked in and saw Jacques' backpack stretched across a boudoir chair. He recognized the pack. He wanted one just like it, maybe for Christmas he thought. He went to his room, changed into his soccer togs and came back to the living room where his mother and Jacques were conversing quietly. He stopped. "Mom," he said, "Jacques has the neatest backpack."

"Well?" asked his mother.

"I saw it through the open guest room door. The backpack was lying across a chair. I'd love one just like it for Christmas. Timmy has one. It's neat. Light and strong. They're in many of the sporting goods stores around here. They cost a little more, but they're worth the price. They're from France and called 'Lit'l Trouper.'"

"What did you say they were called?" queried Caroline.

"J.R. is correct," said Jacques. "The backpack bears the brand name 'Lit'l Trouper.'"

"How do you spell 'little,'" asked an excited Caroline.

"L, I, T, apostrophe L," said Jacques.

"I'm gone to practice at the Williamsburg Middle School soccer field, Mom, I'll be home by five thirty," said J.R.

"OK, no later," said Caroline, and her adrenalin was pumping. She remembered Mary's note, "If something odd, untimely, should happen to me during our stay in D.C. or later, tear the Lit'l Trouper apart." She and Greg thought it had reference to some member of the dancing troupe. Could there be something of value hidden in the backpack?

24

Caroline arose and said to Jacques, "Please come with me into the den. That room also serves as Greg's study." As they were leaving the room, Ben and Tina Feldman entered. There was an awkward moment of silence, then Caroline did the introductions. Ben and Tina were coolly polite. Jacques was nervous. Before any of them could speak, she turned to the Feldmans and said, "I think we might just have stumbled onto something, with the help of our son, J.R. He just left for soccer practice. You'll meet him at supper time. Come with me," and Caroline headed for the den and Greg's desk.

"What in the world is she saying, Ben?" asked Tina.

"Beats me," said her husband, "But I guess all we can do now is follow, wait and see. I wonder where Greg is?"

They entered the den. Caroline asked them to be seated. They did in the big easy chairs in the room all facing the fireplace from different angles. She went to Greg's desk and found Mary's note, read it again. Now she was excited. She gave it to Jacques. He read it and was absolutely stumped. He looked at Caroline.

"This is the first time I knew Mary had written a separate note to Greg."

"I know, Greg hasn't had the time to tell you about it. Now that note becomes increasingly important. Would you mind fetching the backpack and let me take a look at it?"

"Not at all," said Jacques, and he left the room.

Caroline turned to the Feldmans. "I know this sounds like Greek to you, but before Mary was stricken last night, Greg sent a note backstage asking if we could meet with Jacques and his wife. He received two responses, one from Jacques and this one from Mary. She handed the note to the Feldmans. They read it.

"So what or who is the Lit'l Trouper?" asked Ben.

"We didn't know until a few minutes ago. Our son, on his way to soccer practice, passed the open door to Jacques' room. When he came through the living room, he said he would love a backpack like Jacques', and then told us the pack carried the brand name, Lit'l Trouper."

"Holy smoke," said Tina. "No wonder you got excited. What in the world could be in it?"

"I haven't the foggiest idea," replied Caroline.

Jacques entered the room carrying the backpack. He gave it to Caroline. "Take a look," he said, "It is empty."

Caroline took the pack, opened it wide, studied it. She flipped back an inner lining fold. Across the inside top edge of the pack was a black tape strip. The pack appeared to have been made that way. She looked at the tape carefully. There was just a small corner of it not stuck to the back of the backpack. She picked at the tape until she could get a grip.

Then she pulled and the strip of tape came off revealing a soft horizontal zipper that ran across the inside back top edge of the pack. She turned to Jacques, "Did you know this pack has a hidden inside compartment?"

"I have never checked that pack in my life. It was constantly in Mary's possession."

"Here," said Caroline and she handed the pack to Jacques. "It's yours to open if you wish to do so."

"I will try," said a somber Jacques.

The Ben Feldmans were watching with intense interest.

Part V

Mary's Diary

Jacques reached into the hidden space revealed by the opened zipper slit and took out an oblong-shaped object wrapped by several folds of white linen. He unwrapped the linen and there was a writing pad, a typical writing pad used by the students at the island schools. He flipped back the front cover. The first page of the pad revealed the neat handwriting of his dead wife, Mary D'Quino. He read a few pages silently. Ben and Tina Feldman and Caroline Morgan waited anxiously. Jacques' nervousness increased as he read. Then he looked up with incredulity and distress at the threesome. "I cannot. Here, Caroline, you read Mary's livre -- aloud please." And he handed the pad to Caroline.

"You really want me to read it aloud?" asked Caroline, as she looked at the first page. "This diary contains Mary's private writings, her thoughts, and reflections."

"I wish that was all," said distraught Jacques. Ben and Tina waited, not knowing what to expect.

Caroline took the pad, turned up the table lamp on the little side table, shuffled nervously on the seat of the large wing chair, looked at Jacques, and said, "Well, okay, here goes." In a calm voice she began to read: *Dated: 21 Feb. 1944. I write the opening of my livre from a retrospective point of view. My entries, whatever they will be, are of my contacts with the American Navy Lieutenant Commander Ralph Dupui Farqua, and what flows after. Until just before this writing, I had never accepted the notion that it would be necessary for me to make these notes. I now realize I must, for I fear in the end, either Farqua will kill me or I will kill Farqua.*

Tina said softly, "What a disturbed lady."

Caroline continued her reading: *I will not make my entries on a daily basis, for that would reveal too much of me. Truly, my life is only pour moi. However, deep within me, I do not trust Farqua. To me he has the beautiful coloring of the coral snake and an equal amount of venom. My maternal grandmere, Tangora, will have a copy of each entry of my livre in her sacred death chest. She alone knows when to use them. If I die first, I must have my retribution; I come not from a gentle breed, but on Bora Bora my family and the Swarraines are the last of the Arioro, the dancing warrior rulers of Polynesia. I am no angel.*

Tina looked at Jacques. His head was bowed and eyes were closed. Just what would the diary reveal she wondered, and felt sorry for Mary's husband.

Caroline cleared her throat and, without looking up, continued her reading: *The MASH unit that came to the island in the early part of the war was under the command of Colonel Henry Javitz, a skilled surgeon. There was no fraternizing by the medic forces, in the sense of cohabitation, with any of the island women. He was a strict disciplinarian. I respected him. When he learned I was a graduate operating room nurse from the Hospital-de-Paris in Tahiti, he gave me a job as nurse assistant in one of the O.R. units. I was, at that time, well paid in francs. I lived in a small cottage behind my parents' home and had no desire for any sexual affair with the GIs. Such times were reserved for my trips to Tahiti where I had comfortable male contacts that ran back to my years of nurse training and even before that, to the Conservatoire-de-Danse.*

When the MASH unit was about to leave the island, Colonel Javitz pleaded with me to go with them. He said I could enlist and because of my medical education and experience, I would have the rating of Master Sergeant and O.R. nurse assistant. I was tempted, but I deferred. I was, at that time, the only medical aide on the north side of the island. The island medical needs are not many. However, from time to time emergencies arise where my services are needed until a docteur can be summoned. And, I am well compensated by the elders. I did ask the Colonel that I be made the onsite manager of the islanders demolishing the MASH unit -- at an agreed compensation.   That arrangement has been most favorable for me in compensation and fourrage.

"She surely was an independent somebody," said Ben Feldman.

Caroline continued the livre: *Shortly after the MASH unit left the island, a small Naval force under the command of Chief Petty Officer Neal Gilford arrived.   That force was to enlarge the pier and ultimately prepare for the installation of a small fuel depot.   Several weeks later, I was standing on the pier when a U.S. Naval oiler pulled in and tied up alongside the pier.   Down the gangplank came Lieutenant Commander Ralph Dupui Farqua.   He was in natty, fresh, brown Navy fatigues.   He looked like an overdressed modeleur, blond and bold.   His sharp face was lightly tanned.   His gray-green eyes were fierce -- piercing, as if he was seeing to the core of every object or creature at which he looked.   Linguette, Pierre Swarraine's youngest daughter, twenty years of age, was by my side.   He glanced at her.   Their eyes met and I could hear Linguette's soft gasp.   He looked at me and, though I was not sexually aroused, I was attracted, as if our destinies could be intertwined. He came up to us and, in fluid French, said, "I am Commander Ralph Farqua.   It is a pleasure to be on your island."   Linguette stared at him speechless.*

I replied, "Commander, we speak English.   We have studied it along with our mother language and schooling is mandatory on this island through our seventeenth jour de naissance.   In addition, I am a nurse graduate of L'Hospitale de Paris in Tahiti."

"And, I can tell you speak English well," he answered.

"Just what does the U.S. Navy really intend to do with the pier?"

"We have the authority to convert it and six surrounding acres into a Naval fuel depot," he responded.

"Has the Army told you that an islander is to be in charge of the workers who are demolishing the MASH unit?" I asked.

His eyes bore into mine. Then he smiled, like a benevolent devil. "Colonel Javitz has informed me that an islander, Mary D'Quino, is to be the onsite boss of the demolition team. I am sure that can be continued," he said. "And your names are?" he asked as he stared possessively at Linguette.

"My name is Mary D'Quino and this is my friend, Linguette Swarraine," I said.

"It's a pleasure, mademoiselles. I'm sure I will see much more of you in the days to come."

Linguette, the simpleton, smiled her sweetest and demurely replied, "Oui, Monsieur."

I thought, you double entendre bastard I know you will try.

"Gosh," said Tina, "She really didn't like him from the start. I'm surprised."

Ben scowled and soberly mumbled, "They were two devils incarnate."

Caroline looked up at Jacques. "Shall I continue?"

"Yes," he replied. "Her story might as well come out now as later. Her livre may enable us to prevent further trouble."

Caroline took a sip of water from the glass sitting on the side table, then said, "I wish Greg could hear this. I'm sure he'd know how to interpret the diary better than we can."

"I'll fill him in on all of it as soon as he returns," responded Ben.

Caroline continued her reading: *Farqua soon knew the inner workings of the Council of Elders for the north side of the island. He latched on to Pierre Swarraine like a 'sangsue.' Swarraine is talented, vain and an idiot. He has a knack for carving and that knack was discovered by the Colonial authorities when Swarraine was quite young. At an early age, he was sent to the only art school in Tahiti. He excelled. When he returned to the island, a young adult, he did all types of carvings and sculpture, for the government, as well as for his purse. His hands are truly precision instruments for crafting art objects, large and small.*

Caroline looked up at Ben and Tina and commented, "He was the one who made the exquisite earrings for me and cufflinks for Greg that were given to Greg by Jacques when Greg's ship left the island."

Jacques shook his head in agreement.

"Why?" asked Ben.

"I'm sure you'll know before I finish reading Mary's diary," responded Caroline.

She continued: *Swarraine wanted to go to France to try his talent there but the Governor General of the island never permitted him to do so. He has had a smoldering hatred of the authorities ever since. Farqua soon found out about Swarraine's contempt and dislike of the powers that be. He has fostered that dislike and has taken advantage of it in every possible way.*

"What is she saying?" asked Tina.

"I'm beginning to get an inkling," said a very interested Ben Feldman. "I just knew something was going on."

Caroline could see that Jacques was humiliated and chagrinned to the point of real despair. She looked at the educator, "Shall I continue?"

"You have to," was his soft reply.

Caroline read: *Not long after Farqua arrived, liaisons between the island women and Navy personnel became apparent, open. Many of the personnel were living with their petite amie in small cottages behind the main family maison. I know that Jacques went to his father and complained about the declining moral fabric of the islanders. The senior Montagne knew the situation, had held meetings of Council in an endeavor to correct the extramarital relationships, only to find out that Farqua had previously contacted each of the elders and persuaded them that it would be in their economic interest, and in the best interest of the island families, to permit such arrangements. He was requiring each Naval personnel so involved to contribute financially to the family of his object-de-amour. The senior Montagne was enraged and had gone to the French civil authorities, only to find out that Farqua had been there before him and obtained their implicit assent, with the understanding that no French civil wedding would be permitted between the consenting parties. The involved island women and any of their enfants will remain islanders when the Navy personnel leave this area. The senior Montagne was beside himself. Jacques has cold contempt for the C.O. and has distanced himself from Farqua, tending to the islander's education and his hobby of fishing.*

"Farqua, that slick bastard, was setting up his realm of complete control. I just knew he was, but had no idea how he was accomplishing his purpose," said Ben.

"I knew, but I could do nothing," said an anguished Jacques.

Caroline continued her reading: *My family's background is of the Ariori. They were the dancing rulers of the Leeward Islands. They ruled by dancing and death. Through their dances, they portrayed the law and a violation of that law, the law of Raiatea was sacrifice, human sacrifice. Though that concept has diminished since French control, my parents sent me to Tahiti to the Conservatoire-de-Danse when I was four. I have studied the ballet off and on ever since, even while attending nursing school. I have learned and mastered the French ballet steps and through my grandmere, Tangora, I have learned many of the routines of the Ariori. For the last four years, I have studied choreography under Ferdinand DeShields in Tahiti.*

I have determined to leave the island. The formation of a dance group seems a way certain if it can be financed. Ultimately that arrogant bastard, Farqua, is going to provide the way, not altogether voluntarily, I admit.

Caroline stopped, looked up at the others and said, "She was truly a talented ballet artist."

"And she was as mean as she was talented," said an irritated Ben Feldman.

Caroline cast a glance at Jacques. He seemed to have grown smaller and more pitiful as the reading progressed. Suddenly he arose and said, "I must get a drink of water. My throat is dry."

As he left the room, Tina looked at the others. "How much that poor man is suffering, I can only imagine. Ben, you be more careful how you speak. From what I am hearing, he was on your side all the way."

Ben cast his wife a sidelong glance. "Maybe, maybe not, we'll see," he replied.

Jacques returned, sipping a glass of water. He stopped, looked at Caroline. "Continue," he said, "Her livre is my purgatory, I will live through it."

Caroline read: *Dated 1 Mar. 1944. I have just learned that Farqua has been rendezvousing with Linguette and of all places in the Catholic church, St. Mary's by the Sea. At the onset of the war, when the old priest was called home, the colonial authorities refused to let the new priest on the island. The church is now used as a storage area, services for all denominations are held in the Base frond-roofed chapel. Until this war, Catholicism, French Catholicism, was the only openly practiced religion on the island. But, deep within me, and many of us, simmers the spirited remains of our ancestral gods. I was working late in an evening at the MASH unit, looked, and through a vista saw Farqua and Linguette leave the church entrance hand in hand. When they were out of sight, I entered the building and passed down the pews loaded with calico, rolls of French linen, palm fronds and grass skirts. There was an odd odor, sickly sweet, yet musty. At first I could not tell where it originated, but I followed my nose. In the little room off the alter, that can be locked only from the inside, I saw two pallets on the floor. The odor I now knew. It was from the smoke of pavot somnifere. I had, during my days at nursing school tried it, but it held no fascination for me. The pipe I did not find. But, hidden in a jar in a far corner of one of the room's many shelves, I did find the source. I let the hallucinogen rest there. Maybe I can use the evidence later if need be. Just where the drug came from, I know not. But, I shall keep a weather eye on Linguette and Farqua.*

"That poor child," said Tina. "He's using her so unjustly,"

"Just as he tries to use everyone he comes in contact with," replied Ben. "He is truly a bastard."

Caroline quickly continued her reading before Ben could say anything more: *Dated: 28 March 1944. This morning I saw a small U.S. Navy freighter enter the harbor. I hastened to the pier to see what cargo would be unloaded. Farqua was there. Just as the ship tied up, Bos'n's Mate Gilford and Jacques arrived. The only cargo from the freighter was a sloppy looking, overweight U.S. Naval Lieutenant. He dropped his large duffel bag onto the pier and carefully crawled down the freighter boarding ladder. The Commander was studying every move of the new arrival. He smiled and salivated like carnivore about to devour a helpless victim. The new arrival, when he saw the Commander, hunched to attention, saluted and said, "Lieutenant James Richmond reporting aboard, Sir. I have been assigned as executive officer of the depot."*

"Welcome," said a smiling commander Farqua. "I've been awaiting your arrival. I understand you have an M.A. in fossil fuels."

"Yes, Sir," was the prompt response.

"Well, then, we'll get along just fine," and Farqua held out his hand. The lieutenant responded. When Farqua shook the wet fish hand of Richmond, he squeezed so hard the new executive officer went pale and all but sank to his knees. I watched and saw the animal glee in Farqua's eyes. He was in complete control. Gilford then introduced Jacques to Farqua and Richmond.

Caroline cleared her throat and continued: *Dated: 16 Apr. 1944. Farqua left this morning by sea plane. I understand he is going to Tahiti to meet with Naval authorities. About what I do not know. Swarraine and his daughter, Linguette, were at the pier when the base small boat took him out to the plane, just beyond the coral reefs. My work on dismantling the MASH unit continues. I now know where to stand to keep the church in constant view. I have had little or no medical work to do, only a few cuts and bruises on the petite ones. Sloppy Lieutenant Richmond is in charge of the base. I am sure he is pede. He is the only Navy man who shows no interest in any island woman. He seems fascinated by the younger male islanders, plays with them every chance he gets. I shall watch.*

I have learned from Linguette that before Farqua left for Tahiti, he had interrogated her father about the Quong family, the ones who ran the general store on this side of the island before the war started. The Quongs returned to China as soon as the conflict erupted, but Quong has a brother in the trading business in Tahiti. Linguette says her father thinks Farqua may try to contact him on this trip.

"Jacques, did you know something was going on between Linguette and Farqua," asked Ben.

"I had no idea of any of these affairs being revealed by Mary. My duties with island education were strenuous. I was on the go constantly between the island's north and south schools. The demands of Colonial authority were severe. Just keeping up with the required paperwork was almost a full time job. I had little enough time to be with my wife. I wanted no part of Farqua, or the base," responded Jacques.

Caroline continued: *Farqua returned day before yesterday. During the evening of his return, according to Linguette, he had a long discussion with her father. I saw Swarraine today. He volunteered that Farqua has personally ordered ten of his head carvings at a very fair figure. They are to be delivered by the next trading boat to a new company in Tahiti.*

"I remember those head carvings," said Ben Feldman.

Dated: 29 Jun. 1944. Today careless, sloppy Lieutenant Richmond met his fate. He was seriously injured while working on the pier. A couple of insecure connector pipeline sections fell from the pier rack, hit him, and broke his left leg in two places. He was in wild pain. I helped the base pharmacist's mate make temporary splints in an endeavor to lessen injury from the fractures. Later this evening a medivac sea plane arrived and he was flown to some hospital area. Farqua seemed quite agitated about the episode. I believe he is worried as to what kind of individual will take the place of his former executive officer. I continue supervising the dismantling of the MASH unit. I am paid regularly. Recently, the first and only time Farqua made a sexual advance toward me, I warned him -- told him bluntly -- I would kill him if he tried again. He laughed and said, "Another Georgette." Since then he has kept his distance. In fact he has been most respectful and co-operative of my efforts in the coconut grove. He knows by instinct, as do I, that there will be times when we can help each other in our mutual or separate goals. And, each day I am laying more ground work to assure that I will achieve mine.

"Damn, I knew she was a bi...."

"Ben," sharply retorted his wife. "For now keep your thoughts to yourself."

Jacques looked helplessly at the trio seated in the den with him.

"Why don't we take a break?" asked Caroline.

"No, I think you should finish," said a somber Jacques. "The whole livre may reveal much that will help us, particularly when we tell Greg what the livre contains."

Caroline took another sip of water and continued: *Dated: 20 July 1944. Today Commander Farqua's new executive officer arrived on an oiler. I saw the ship coming and hastened to the pier to watch its entry and determine its cargo. I had no idea that the new second-in-command of the base was aboard. Apparently, neither did Farqua. He was surprised when the neat, alert, red-headed lieutenant stepped off the gangplank and introduced himself to Farqua. He saluted and said, "I am Lieutenant Benjamin I. Feldman, reporting for duty as executive officer of the depot." The Commander has all the natural instincts of a predatory animal. He sensed challenge the first minute the new second-in-command stepped onto the pier. I could tell. I remember the Commander's opening remarks. "Welcome, Lieutenant, I am Lieutenant Commander Ralph Dupui Farqua, C.O. of the finest little oil base in the Navy." The two shook hands. Feldman's blue eyes were polite but cold. "Thank you, Sir. I will be very happy if it is." And that is when trouble started.*

"How right she was," retorted Ben.

Caroline continued her reading: *Feldman, with Farqua, inspected the base, still under construction. They then went to the MASH site, I did also. When we reached the area, Feldman asked Farqua, "Who is in charge of dismantling?"*

"Mary D'Quino is by agreement with the Army and this base."

And Farqua pointed to me, "This is Mary D'Quino, native in charge."

"Hi, Mary D'Quino," said Feldman with no attempt at cordiality. He looked at Farqua, then at me and said, "A

native woman in charge of a MASH wrecking crew, I never heard of such a thing."

"Well, you have now," responded Farqua with a humorless smile, and he continued, "That is how things are and will be." Feldman made no reply, but shrugged his shoulders. They left and I stayed with the dismantling.

The next day I saw Feldman strolling the whole lagoon area. He had a pen and pad. Occasionally he would stop strolling and furiously scribble on the pad.

"Damn, she was observant," said Feldman. "God knows how many pair of eyes were constantly watching me. I could feel them."

Caroline shifted her position in the chair and continued: *Dated: 10 Sept. 1944. This morning Commander Farqua came up to the MASH area in the base jeep and asked if I would drive with him to a quiet spot. He said we needed to talk. We drove the lane to the church and parked in front of the entrance. Once there, he said, "There is a little problem."*

"Like what?" I asked.

"Well, this Lieutenant Feldman is a graduate of Annapolis, America's Naval Academy. He's chock full of Navy regulations, been sitting on his butt in some stateside office gathering all kinds of irrelevant concepts on how to run a war. He claims the Navy does not condone the open life style being engaged in by some of my personnel and the native women."

And, I thought, including you, you bastard.

"What am I supposed to do about that?" I asked.

"You might try to divert his attention," quipped Farqua.

"How?" I asked.

"By showing him how attractive and alluring a native woman can be and you are alluring."

"Mr. Commanding Officer," I replied, "You must think I am a crazy flying fox. I would no more attempt to seduce that red head than attempt fornication with an island ram goat. I

can tell already that he disapproves of me. And, I can tell you more. He has been scouring this end of the island, absorbing what he learns like a sponge, even been looking inside of St. Mary's by the Sea."

"How do you know?" And Farqua was irritated.

"Because I've had him followed by some of the petite ones."

"What has he found?" queried Farqua.

"I do not know yet. I just want to see what he is up to," I said.

"If you want to head off his complaints, I suggest you talk to the elders. You are the one who made the initial arrangements. But, do not talk to Chief Montagne. He is dead set against the life style you have introduced, even if it seems to be working now. And the Chief truly dislikes you. This is your cause, Celebre, not mine."

As I walked away from the jeep, Commander Farqua quipped, "You have given me an idea."

"Oh, Mary, mother of Jesus, where is all this leading?" said Jacques.

"I think I know where," and an upset Ben Feldman glowered at the threesome.

"Take it easy, Ben. You wanted to hear it," said Tina trying to calm her husband.

Caroline noticed Jacques was breathing heavily, hiding his emotions.

"Hadn't we better take a rest?" asked Caroline.

"No!" said Ben.

Caroline saw Jacques again close his eyes. "Go on," he said.

She read: *Dated: 30 Nov. 1944. I saw the first American amphibious ship arrive in the harbor this morning, U.S.S. L.S.M. 460.5. I know Commander Farqua visited it. From the yard of my family's home, I watched the small boat with Farqua aboard go out to the ship. Before that I saw*

Mary's Diary

Jacques, who had been fishing in the lagoon, paddle over to the vessel and converse with some officer, who was looking down at him. I later learned that is when Jacques met Lieutenant JG Greg Morgan. I also learned from Linguette that day that, according to Farqua, the oil storage tanks on the base are empty. The large oiler heading to the island to refuel the base had developed engine trouble, returned to the Hawaiian Islands, and would not reach the base for another ten days to two weeks. The officers and men aboard the only ship in the harbor are in for quite a vacation.

Yesterday, Linguette, now a beginning second grade teacher in our area school, took quite a tongue lashing from Jacques because of her continued failure of lesson preparation for her students. I heard from a discreet, concealed distance. Little does he know of her affaire with Farqua. And I am sure the base commander is increasing his domination over her by the affair-de-amour and opium. Jacques is such an idealist. He expects the best from everyone, and the only one I know who lives up to those expectations is his wife, Evangeline. And she is good, godly good. She has been in love with him since childhood. Right now she is in Tahiti. She is pregnant with their first child and is being checked over by docteurs in the Hospitale de Paris.

Jacques sobbed and Tina Feldman arose, walked over to him and patted him on his shoulder. The picture she was getting of the island educator aroused her sympathies. He has many of my husband's good qualities, she thought.

Caroline cleared her throat and continued: *Dated: 4 Dec. 1944. I am having increased troubles with Lieutenant Feldman. He knows he is being followed by the little ones. Yesterday, he cornered eight-year-old Rosemarie and scared her witless. She finally admitted she was following him at my behest. She told me so later. Though Feldman has not accosted me about the surveillance, he has been making my life miserable at the MASH site. Just what he is driving at I know*

206

---

not. But, I can tell he suspects much more evil doings than even I know.

"I remember that episode," said Feldman. "I didn't know what D'Quino was up to. I had no idea that Farqua had started the life style on the island. But there was something much more sinister than sexual affairs that just pervaded the whole atmosphere of the area. I couldn't find a clue. I was frustrated as all hell. No native would talk to me. Jacques seldom came to the base, at least not until after the LSM 460.5 arrived. I knew he was the Chief's son and an educator, but that was all I knew."

"What you have said is true," said Jacques. "And now you should begin to understand why I did not come to the base."

"I do," said Tina. "What a stress to live under. I once knew such stress, even worse," she said as she looked at Jacques and then at her husband.

Caroline had stayed out of all conversation. But she was absorbing as much as possible in order to tell Greg. She knew his story in detail and somehow it was beginning to fit into a much larger disturbing picture.

"Shall I continue?" she asked.

"Please do," the threesome responded almost in unison. Tina couldn't help but giggle.

Caroline continued reading: *Dated: 9 Dec. 1944. Last night I could not sleep, I was disturbed, so I took a walk through the village. The elders' meeting chamber was dark. I knew there had been a meeting earlier. I went up to the thatched hut opening and poked my head in the doorway. I was shocked. I smelled the same sickly sweet odor I had recognized in the church. I knew that Chief Montagne was attending a regional conference in Tahiti called by the District Governor General of the Colonial authorities. I knew the Chief abhorred hallucinogens of any kind. Who led the meeting? How long has opium been used in high council? Could it be Farqua's influence and how? I am more determined than ever to leave the island. Also, late last night, a large Navy tanker was escorted into the lagoon by the base tender.*

The import of that entry left the foursome in the room waiting eagerly for the next excerpt. No one spoke concerning the weird episode that they expected Mary's diary to reveal. So many thoughts were racing through their minds. They needed to hear more before commenting.

Caroline continued: *Dated: 10 Dec. 1944. This morning a petite one came by and summoned me to the home of Pierre Swarraine. He was alone in his house when I entered. He told me that last night the Council of Elders had determined that a Taboo was to be placed on Lieutenant Feldman. He told me what they wanted done initially and that I had been appointed the perpetrator. He ended by saying that it was a tribal order.*

I asked, "Did Chief Montagne decree the order?"

Swarraine's answer was curt and cold. "No. The Chief is away on business and besides, he is growing old and senile and we were unanimous in our agreement, except for him."

"Does the base commander know of the order?" I asked.

He retorted, "None of the base commander's business."

"Nevertheless, does he know about it?" I persisted.

"Go ask him," he shouted in fury and then added "The wrath of the God Ari will descend on you if you refuse our bidding."

I did not believe that wrath would descend, but the wrath of the elders could descend and that might be worse. So I determined to seek out the commander for I believe he knows much, much more than he has alluded to. According to Linguette, Farqua has boasted that he and his family are quite opulent. They apparently make their money in the fishing and shipping business. I will soon know.

By pre-arrangement, the Commander and I met that day, in the late evening, near the church. I had determined my approach to him. If he was not involved, he would not comprehend what I would be talking about. If he understood, then I would be sure that someway and for some reasons unknown to me he had set the whole fiendish scheme in motion.

When he arrived in the base jeep, I got in the passenger seat, looked him in the eye and said, "Commander, some day when the current international conflict is over, and it is moving further west each month, I would like to head a dancing troupe to entertain island visitors. I know I can obtain the consent of the French Colonial authorities for such a venture, but neither they nor I have the funds to back such an enterprise. I wonder?"

"You wonder what?" interrupted Farqua.

"If I protect your future, will you provide the funds for my dancing group and provide my future? I think the venture could be mutually profitable."

The Commander was silent, then said, "What if I say no?"

"Neither of us will have a future, not a long one anyway," I replied.

"Just what the hell do you mean by that?" he asked peevishly.

"If at any time, from this moment on, I am put at risk, for any reason, from any source, I have provided that, as sure as night follows day, you will be at risk also."

"And how can you assure that?" he asked.

"Commander, how is my business, but I can tell you, that in the end, the islanders' commitment to protect their own, and in particular the descendants of the Arioras, dedication to retribution for any threats or attacks on them is deeply ingrained, even now."

The Commander was quiet. He remained so for several minutes. I could tell he was reviewing his options, risks and

*possibilities. His piercing eyes sought to fathom my soul, but
they did not go very deep because I am sure that mine is as
black and impenetrable as his appears to be. He made a wry
smile and said, "If you protect my future, I swear on the grave
of Raphelo D'Farqua to provide the funds for the troupe and
assure your future."*

"The deal is done," I said.

*We parted. What physically took place concerning
Lieutenant Feldman at our meeting at the MASH unit the next
day you can best learn from Jacques Montagne and his friend,
Gregory T. Morgan, a Naval Lieutenant J.G. and executive
officer of the LSM 460.5. He was an unwitting witness to the
episode. Earlier in the morning of the event, the tanker, having
filled the base oil tanks, left the lagoon. The following morning
the LSM 460.5 tied up to the fuel dock and commenced
replenishing her fuel supply.*

"Damn, it was all orchestrated by Farqua," moaned Ben.
"But, for what? I hadn't learned much of anything."

"I wish Greg would return," said a nervous Jacques.
"He has to be told right away what this livre reveals. Oh,
Mother of Mary, what an ass, what a dupe I have been. Just
how large an operation it is, is hard for me to imagine. The
islands, Europe, and now the U.S."

"What in the world are you saying, Jacques?" Caroline
asked.

"I am saying nothing more until Greg arrives. I have
had suspicions for a long time. You must wait."

"Shall I wait for him to return before I continue
reading?" asked Caroline.

"No," said a continuously nervous Jacques. "We need
to know as much as possible."

"Thanks," said Ben.

Caroline read: *I don't like Lieutenant Feldman.*

"The feeling was mutual," snapped Ben.

"Ben, please try to control your comments. What you are hearing is what you've wanted to know for over nine years," said Tina.

Caroline continued reading: *He was loud, autocratic and domineering, but underneath it all, I could tell he was unsure. He had found out so little. I felt he had a sense that under the surface of an apparently acceptable life style, something was horribly wrong. And, he was right. But he did not know how to get at the problem. It was my commitment not to let him have a chance. I did what I was ordered to do, and what I determined would be to my advantage. The results were more severe than I anticipated.*

"That island bitch," snapped Feldman.

Tina glowered at him and then cast Jacques a sidelong glance.

Caroline's eyes kept focused on the writing. She coughed then continued: *The only time I felt any remorse was when I talked with Lieutenant Gregory Morgan, the Naval witness, just before his ship left the harbor the day after the taboo. Jacques did not know what was behind the taboo. If and when he does, he will find it hard to accept. Maybe I do not know what truly triggered the taboo order.*

There was something about Morgan that was appealing to me, deep down inside. However, I knew that he would have second thoughts about the reason I gave for my actions. Sooner or later, he will inquire and dig around. I will have to deal with that when and if -- and if I am still able to deal.

"If I had only realized, been willing to see," Jacques said in a choked voice.

Caroline read: *Dated: 18 Dec. 1944. This morning Farqua left for Tahiti by sea plane. He is supposed to be attending another Naval conference. I do not believe it. So, when the trading schooner dropped by the harbor today, I talked with Henri Salvatori, the first mate, gave him two hundred francs and asked him to check on Farqua's activities in the city. He said he would be glad to do so. He said that the ship should reach the central city by tomorrow evening. He knows Farqua, has talked with him several times, and can recognize the blond. Salvatori will report his findings to me when the trading schooner returns here in two weeks.*

Dated: 6 Jan. 1945. Evangeline, Jacques wife, returned on the trading schooner today. Salvatori was also aboard. The docteur says she is doing fine and that her infant is due in three months. I met today with Salvatori. The conversation was most interesting. When I asked him what he found out about Farqua's activities, he said, "Beaucoup et petite."

"And that means what?" I asked.

He said, "Farqua held a lengthy conversation with Chi Quong, our former storekeeper's brother. Chi Quong has been suspected of dealing in pavot somnifere for years, but no criminal action has ever been brought against him. What he and Farqua talked about I know not. Farqua also visited Marselle Simpure, a 'homme de loi,' for what reasons I do not know."

Salvatori related that Farqua was in Madame Surrette's brothel nightly. He also bought a few trinkets in the market place. At no time did Farqua visit the U.S. Naval facility on the island. Several days later, just before Salvatori left the island he said a new trading company had opened an office near the wharf. The sign above the company's entrance door read Pacific Island Imports. He saw both Farqua and Quong go in and out of the office several times. He presumed Quong was doing cloth business, but he had no idea why Farqua was visiting the trading company.

"I think I know why," said Jacques.

"Why?" inquired Ben Feldman.

"The coconut carvings Farqua buys from Swarraine," said Jacques. "They were shipped by Swarraine to Pacific Island Imports in Tahiti. Greg already knows about those things."

"How?" asked Ben.

"I told him. That's one of the reasons he insisted I come here, to his home, before we have discussions with the D.C. police authorities. He suspicioned much more than I did, up until now."

"Gee, I wish you wouldn't talk in riddles," said Tina.

"Mrs. Feldman, I understand your wish, but I was so fully occupied, first with the schools and later with the dance Ensemble, I had little time for conjecture about peripheral matters. I should have, but I did not. And, I sorely missed my daughter and the island. Only Mary's constant urging helped keep me focused."

"Oh, boy, I'll bet that was some urging," Ben said sarcastically.

"Shut up, Ben," and Tina meant it.

Caroline quickly picked up where she had left off and read: *Dated: 11 June 1945. Farqua has returned from Tahiti. He held a lengthy conference with Swarraine at the sculptor's home. When he came out he was in fine spirits, patting the heads of the petite ones he happened by on his walk to the now completed oil base, link fence and all. Work on dismantling the MASH unit is almost complete. I have made plans to go to Tahiti next week and resume training at the ballet school. While there, I will begin to recruit dancers, not an easy task. The war has diverted so many former pupils. However, Madame LeFevre is still maitre-de-dans, and Ferdinand DeShields is the professeur-de-musique. He is excellent at blocking dance with music. I shall depend on his talent.*

Dated: 4 Oct. 1945. I am back on my home island. The war is over. There is much rage here. The Navy personnel are leaving the island, sans their tribal wives and children. The French Colonial government and the U.S. State Department are struggling to find a solution to the mixed family situation.

Yesterday I met with Farqua. "Tomorrow is the day," he said.

"What day?" I asked.

"The day when the Naval inquiry board arrives to investigate the Feldman affair. The hearing will be two days later. All because someone has been inferring that my report of the accident may be flawed."

"Someone from the island?"

"No," he said, "someone from the States."

"Feldman?" I asked.

"No, not Feldman. From the time you brought him into the infirmary, I was sure he would not remember the episode. I learned from Navy medical sources shortly after the accident that he, in fact, had no memory of how the taboo occurred. The medics say Feldman has no memory of what happened before the accident -- not even when he was a kid."

"You are indeed fortunate, Mr. Commander," I said.

"We both are," he replied with a self-satisfied grin.

"What are you going to do about Jacques? He saw the whole episode." I asked.

"Have you not noticed? He is not around."

I realized I had not seen Jacques since the beginning of the week.

"Where is he?"

"Attending an educational conference in Tahiti. He will not return until after the Naval Board has left this island."

"How do you know?" I asked.

"Because I made arrangements with the regional colonial director of education. And, all the natives who had any knowledge have been sworn to secrecy. Even Pierre Montagne dare not talk."

"How about that young Naval lieutenant, Gregory Morgan?" I asked.

"He will never know about the hearing, and besides, he will never give the Taboo another thought now that the war is over. He will have his hands full making a living back in the

States. If he ever thinks about the episode, it will seem like a dream, not reality."

"I am not so sure," I said.

"Trust me, I am an American. I knew the stateside mind set. Just remember, our future is at stake -- your dancing dream and my trading dream."

Somehow I began to feel that the two dreams were more closely intertwined than I originally thought they would be. I determined to keep a sharper eye on Farqua.

"Mary, mother of Jesus, said Jacques. "I had no idea what was taking place. I trusted what my wife told me. When I asked my father, he merely shook his head from side to side, 'You know the official results,'" he would talk no further about it.

Caroline continued the livre: *Dated: 1 Nov. 1945. The results of the Board of Inquiry were as Farqua had hoped. We both lied as to how Feldman was injured. We used my original story of the ram goats -- and those two were long gone, eaten at the Festival of Fathers. Two young new ones have taken their place.*

The Board of Inquiry accepted our version, particularly since it was the version signed off by Farqua on Feldman's medical record. The base C.O. is one slick snake. I was surprised by naivete of the Board. They should have dug deeper into the neighborhood and would have found some troublesome information -- contrary to the elders power. Just what would have happened to both Farqua and me if the truth had been told -- I hate to imagine. Now, I will have my dancing troupe. No doubt about Farqua, I can tell by the flash of those gray-green eyes, he is not only pleased, but is focused on a course of action I know not. I am worried.

"Why, why would she be involved with such a despicable human being?" asked Ben. His rising anger was apparent.

Jacques was absolutely stunned and bewildered.

Tina looked at her husband and said, "Ben, they were two evil counterparts that met and in their mad dreams, left reality behind. Please don't let your emotions run wild over what you are hearing. I came to Washington this time to be by your side when you tried to fathom what really took place on Bora Bora and why. You were the one who wanted to warn Mary D'Quino, Farqua and Jacques of your father's initial intent. Retribution is no dominant part of your nature. For God's sake, keep that perspective."

Ben looked at his wife. His facial features were taut. His cheeks pasty white, and his blue eyes blazed with the emotions that seared through him. Yet, he knew she was right in what she said. "I'll keep the view," he said to her somberly. Her eyes held his. She smiled and he relaxed.

Caroline continued: *Dated: 6 Dec. 1945. Farqua has left the island to return stateside, he said for about four months. He spent the last two days with Linguette. Why Swarraine does not suspicion something is going on between his youngest daughter and Farqua, I can not fathom. Maybe he does, and cares so little. He is so vain, I think he can only see his damned coconut heads and the francs they bring him.*

Farqua and I held a long discussion before he left. My dancing troupe must be ready by the time he returns. Expenses and my compensation will be paid through Pacific Island Imports. We have agreed on a budget, at least until he returns. I am excited. There is only one hitch, he insists that Linguette Swarraine be included in the troupe. I do not object to her dancing ability. She has taken lessons at the ballet school for years, and she is talented and adept. Her family, too, are remnants of the Arioro (dancing lords) but, Farqua's dominance over her makes me uncomfortable. She is so easily swayed.

Caroline continued reading: *Dated: 20 Feb. 1946. I write this in Tahiti where I have spent the last two months recruiting. Now have a company of twenty dancers, two costumers, one makeup artist, two scenery designers, builders and painters, and one lighting technician. I have been acting general manager but will insist Farqua either assume or provide someone for those duties when he returns. He has answered none of my mail to him through Pacific Island Imports but the company has borne the troupe's expenses, which I have kept to a minimum, except for my agreed compensation.*

"I wonder," said Ben, "Just who is behind the trading company, providing the funds?"

"I think it is Farqua," said Jacques. "Who else would take such a risk? The island government could not."

Caroline continued: *Dated: 6 May 1946. Farqua is back in Tahiti. He is in high spirits. He will initially act as general manager of the dance unit and do the bookings. He apparently has an island tour arranged. Jacques has been made island superintendent of Bora Bora education. When he visits each island school, his wife, Evangeline, and his daughter, Renee, accompany him. He is a strong, respected presence on Bora Bora, but I am wary as to what unrevealed events he may stumble on.*

"I did," said Jacques, "but I just did not recognize what I was stumbling on. I was focused on education, not on drugs, massive use of drugs and degradation."

"Just what the hell are you saying?" scowled Ben.

"When Greg returns, I will tell you what I think, not before," said Jacques.

Caroline read on: *Dated: 3 July 1946. The island tour has begun. The* Wild Orchid, *one of the tramp steamers owned by the Farqua trading empire is our mode of island transportation and our home for the island tour. The accommodations are make-do, but meet the necessities of life. Our places of performance coincide with the steamer's ports of call. At each port of call, certain goods are delivered ashore. I have noticed a number of Swarraine's head carvings are* among the items delivered. I had no idea they would be acceptable objects-d-arte out here, but they seem to be.

We rehearse regularly on board. The workouts reduce the boredom. Slowly, the routines, all of which I choreographed with the aid of Ferdinand DeShields are beginning to resemble dance. With each performance our mastery improves. Our performance was viewed by officials of the Colonial Ministry of Tourism when we recently performed on San Jose Island. They were surprised and pleased. There is a chance our area of performing will be expanded. At last I will be leaving the islands for a broader perspective. Farqua is ecstatic. Somehow he seemed assured that the expanded tour would take place.

Dated: 5 Oct. 1952. The tour is over. We have spent almost six years roaming the southwest Pacific islands and Asiatic mainland. During that time, the ensemble has become accomplished. Now and then certain members of the group would return to their homes for a brief respite. But not a single dancer has deserted the troupe. Life has been good to us. Our health has been good, our bellies full and our pocketbooks are bulging. There has been so little to spend it on. The troupe has returned to the islands for a much needed rest. Time has slipped by so fast. I have invested some of my earnings in The Lever Company, the company which has helped to provide a living for so many of my people in the coconut groves.

When I returned to Bora Bora, I was shocked to learn that Jacques' wife, Evangeline, who was pregnant with their second child, lost her life over a year ago when the trading schooner, Mademoiselle Leeward, capsized in a storm as it was returning from Tahiti to Bora Bora. Jacques has been in deep despair. I find that he is researching the history of the island, going from elder to elder to pick up lost background. He has spent considerable time in Tahiti, researching records and conferring with the Colonial Government on his findings. I learned that for some reason, even before his wife's death, he *had been inquiring about the Feldman episode. Why, I know not. Though I·am assured he has learned nothing new, I have determined to get closer to him and find the reason for his inquiry. Farqua is unhappy being tied down as general manager of the troupe, now named the Southwest Pacific Dance Ensemble. After our rest here, there is the possibility of a European tour. If that event happens, I will be pleasured beyond belief. Farqua claims that the other demands of his trading business require that we find a new general manager for the troupe. He will continue to do the bookings.*

"Evangeline, Evangeline, I so wish I had been with you. Then this ordeal would never have occurred," Jacques audibly whispered.

Tina Feldman looked with pity at Jacques. "You're not to blame," she said. "Remember what Mary wrote in the beginning of her diary? 'I fear in the end, either Farqua will kill me or I will kill Farqua.' You, being who you are, could not stop the evil works of either of them. Things may have been a lot worse, but for you."

"You are kind, Mrs. Feldman, but I am afraid that is not so," responded Jacques.

"Should I stop now?" asked Caroline.

She and the Feldmans looked at the anguished islander.

"No," was his soft reply.

Caroline read on: *Dated: 8 Dec. 1952. Farqua has been to the Ministry of Tourism Office in Tahiti. Upon my suggestion, he has persuaded them to seek the release of Jacques Montagne from his educational duties and have him become the general manager for the troupe. I have been inching closer in my friendship with the educator and have continuingly asked that he consider being the troupe manager, that after the death of his wife, he needs a change of scenery to expand his life and help him forget. I have suggested that, for the time being, his daughter will be well cared for by his parents and in-laws, but so far he has resisted all my entreaties. Farqua will be applying the pressure shortly. Dated: 20 Dec. 1952. Today I learned we will have a European tour starting immediately. I am ecstatic. Good bye island life. I have made a determination. I will seek to become Jacques' wife. In that way, I can assuage his questioning of the Feldman episode, stop his historical research, and protect him from Farqua. I shall persuade him to become general manager of the troupe. Farqua has heard that Jacques has been asking questions concerning the Feldman Naval Inquiry. I fear what Farqua might do.*

Jacques nodded his head affirmatively and said, "I did ask questions of the elders because I learned from some petite ones, on my return after a four-day education meeting in Tahiti, that a stranger, an American stranger, posing as a reporter from the U.S., was asking questions about the Feldman episode and Naval Inquiry. I tried to find out his name and what he wanted. No one knew his name or why he was inquiring. I was curious."

"That had to be David Armstrong, the investigator my father hired years ago," said Ben Feldman. "I wish he had found out the truth."

"Would it have done any good if he had discovered at that time what really happened?" asked Tina.

Ben looked with surprise at his wife -- then thought. Finally, he said, "Maybe, maybe not, Hon. I guess I'll never know -- because it didn't happen."

There were a few moments of silence, then Caroline read on: *Dated: 4 May 1953. I am now Jacques' wife and he is general manager of the troupe. I feel real remorse for my actions. Just why he agreed to marry me, I do not know for I am sure he does not have the depth of feeling for me that he had for Evangeline. But, mother of Mary, he is good in bed. And, he is making an excellent general manager. Farqua is exuberant. Beyond all this, however, I have a sad almost numbing sensation. I am falling in love for the very first time in my life. Jacques is just basically decent, gentle and thoughtful, not just to me, but to all whom he meets. It makes me wish I could disavow what I have been, what I am, and what I will be if this route continues. All I can do is protect him, from himself and those who might endeavor to hurt him -- and I know of two who are increasingly alarmed by his quiet perceptions, the answers to which he denies, even to himself.*

"Oh, Mary, mother of Jesus, I can not help but feel sorry for her," Jacques lamented sadly. "And the questions continued to flow into my head."

Ben Feldman looked out the window and wondered how in the hell could two such different people get so involved with each other. Then he remembered his own needs, his finding Tina, and he felt genuinely sorry for the island educator who hadn't found a Tina.

Dated: 13 Oct. 1954. London, England. Our tour of Europe has been a triumph. Our cast now includes a five member musical ensemble headed by Emil Flaubert. That group integrates with the pit orchestra of the theaters in which we perform. There is a full library of orchestra arrangements. Flaubert is the guest conductor wherever we go. And always, Farqua is present on opening night. How long he has been in the area before that time, I do not know. In France and in England, I have seen newspaper advertisements of Swarraine's carved heads (Masques of the Islands) being sold by some fashionable decor shops. How Farqua arranges delivery of those heads, I wish I knew. Just how long before our opening night in each location did those heads arrive in that city? The one thing I cannot comprehend. They are offered at such a reasonable price. How does Farqua make a profit from their sale? That bothers me.

Jacques apparently has not noticed the advertisements for he has not commented on them. His hands are full handling the troupe. What a job that is, keeping lonesome troupers out of trouble, arranging transportation, making sure costumes and scenery are properly cared for, making agreements with music hall musicians, arranging for publicity, even though the Ministry of Tourism helps greatly in this respect. The whole unit rests on his back. He does the job admirably, but I can tell he yearns to go back to the islands. I know I shall never do so and that saddens me.

I know Jacques has never really loved me. I made him try to think so. After his first wife died, I courted and beguiled him until he married me. I did so originally in order that I could keep a wary eye on him lest he learn the truth concerning certain of my past actions and Farqua's evil conspiracies. And then it was I who learned of the goodness that's inherent in the Montagnes, even down through Jacques. As the evil flowed around him, even from me, I am for the first time in my life truly in love -- and with him. I knew his wife, Evangeline, and I know his daughter, Renee. Their love for him radiated from them when he was with them. I now know why. I had to become his protector, for he belongs not to touring the stages of Europe or America. He belongs to what will be the true future of Bora Bora. He is the quiet modern embodiment of Maui, the god who pulled our islands up from the sea bed. I constantly fight the ache in my heart. I would it was possible I could tell him the truth of what has happened, what is happening, beg his forgiveness, then go with him to some unknown island where he could teach and I could listen, love and bear him a child. The results of that chemistry would be noble, I am sure. But it will never happen. Farqua would never permit it. I know too much.

"I noticed the advertisements and a lot more. That's why I wrote an unsigned letter to the French embassy in London," Jacques said quietly. "By then, I knew I could not go to the Embassy in person for I believed that might be placing not only my life in jeopardy, but Mary's also. And, I had no idea how Mary really felt toward me. She seemed to become more and more isolated from me and so entangled with Farqua. Please continue," said Jacques.

Caroline read: *Dated: 21 Oct. 1954. I write this entry in our little suite at the Harrington Hotel in Washington D.C. Jacques is asleep. He has had an exhausting forty-eight hours. Our trip from England was by plane, a large four-engine one. The plane was packed with all our troupe and gear, except the scenery. That had been shipped two weeks ago. When we arrived a La Guardia Airport, we took hours to clear customs. They were merciless in their inspection, as if we carried some type of contraband. Farqua was not aboard. He had flown to the U.S. two days before. Linguette became ill during the inspection and had to be assisted to the ladies room. For some reason, Jacques has begun to suspect that when we have opening night in any city, Farqua has more pressing business there than just the ensemble. When we arrived at the National Airport in Washington, D.C., Linguette was still ill, almost hysterical. Shortly after we reached the Harrington Hotel, Farqua appeared out of the blue and went to Linguette's room. When I went to her room, I found her sleeping soundly. Farqua was there and claimed she was just overfatigued. But I know better. She had received her stupefiant. She must have called Farqua as soon as she arrived. How she knew where to locate him, I do not know. Now I know why she became ill at La Giardia Airport. She was desperate to get rid of the drugs she was carrying. She must have flushed them down the commode. By the time she reached Washington, her need was desperate. I am now sure that Farqua is her complete master. How does he evade the authorities in transporting his spirits from hell?*

Tonight's opening at the National Theater in Washington, D.C. went well. Linguette was a bit unsteady, but her youth keeps her resilient despite her habit. During the Taboo routine, just before intermission, I observed a commotion in a box nearest the stage. No doubt some

*intoxicated American theater goer must have become sick.
They do drink the most vile liquors -- particularly a malt called
bourbon. I have had but one sip of the fluid and it made me
wretch.*

"Holy shi..."

"Ben, no!" said Tina.

"I'm sorry," he said as he sheepishly looked at the
others in the room. "That's me she's writing about. That's the
night when it all started coming back -- my memory. You can't
imagine what a kaleidoscope my mind has been since then."
He stopped, looked for understanding from the others in the
room. Then he looked at Jacques. "I will never be able to
thank you enough for letting me hear Mary's diary. So many
things have fallen in place. A huge weight has been taken from
my shoulders. Now, Jacques, I, like you, believe we are in real
danger. I just wish to hell Greg would return."

Caroline read: *Tonight, as Jacques and I left the
theater, I am sure I saw Farqua with Chi Quong, the cloth
dealer from Tahiti, and a beautiful woman enter a limousine.
I know that Farqua did not see me, but I'm not so sure about
Quong. I could not tell. I grow more suspicious as to
Farqua's activities on the tour. I now believe the Ensemble is
the cover for some nefarious trading by Farqua and Quong.
How can I extricate myself from this quagmire and still protect
Jacques. I am afraid to talk of the matter with Jacques.*

Caroline looked at the writing, saw she was on the last
page. She turned to the group. "There's just a little more, shall
I finish?"

"Yes," said a disconsolate Jacques.

Caroline read: *Dated: 25 Oct. 1954. Linguette has
been my understudy for more than six months. She has become
increasingly obnoxious and constantly evades rehearsals. I
write this in the afternoon because I sense an air of danger, an
air of death lurking for someone. I smell it. Arioros' always
do.*

Linguette stayed close to me at the theater this afternoon. I caught her look several times. It is a strange one, as if she wanted to tell me something but had not the will to do so. I shall try to find out after the show tonight what is bothering "Trouble."

"That's the end; I know what happened after the diary, but I still don't know who killed Mary," said a worried Caroline.

Jacques was quiet, deep in thought looking down at his lap. He moved nervously in his chair. Ben watched him. Jacques raised his head. "Are there any firearms in the house?" he asked.

Tina Feldman quietly drew in a deep breath as she wondered, if Jacques was so morbidly disconsolate that he wanted to commit suicide.

"No," said Caroline. "Greg just doesn't believe in keeping them around. Why?"

"I am sure Farqua and his men cannot be far behind. I wish Greg were here," Jacques said somberly.

"I agree," said Ben. "We're kinda' like sitting ducks if Farqua has found where we're staying."

"I'm sure Greg has us covered," said Caroline, seeking to calm the anxiety of her guests.

"I hope, I hope, I hope," said a doubting Tina.

And the foursome fell silent with their separate thoughts.

Part VI

Exit Linguette

1

The word "trouble" jolted Caroline for she remembered Mary D'Quino's comment in the note the ballerina penned to Greg just last night: "Trouble dances with the troupe."

Caroline broke the silence. She asked Jacques, "What did Mary mean by the word 'trouble?'"

Jacques said quietly, "I am sure, after hearing you read Mary's livre, she meant Linguette."

"Linguette?" gasped Caroline.

"Yes, her name, interpreted in our native tongue means 'trouble.' She was the sixth and last child of Pierre Swarraine's wife. His wife, Medina, died almost immediately after Linguette's birth. He sardonically gave his youngest daughter the name of Linguette (trouble)."

"Holy smoke," said Caroline. "First 'Lit'l Trouper' and now 'Trouble.' Greg and I thought those references were about one and the same person. This whole thing is taking a queer twist."

2

"Where did Greg go?" interrupted Ben. "He's like a jack-in-the-box, now you see him, now you don't."

Caroline smiled, "Jacques gave him some information a little while ago. As a result, Greg has taken the soiled tissue I had in my evening bag from last night and hurried back to D.C. before he could introduce you and Tina to Jacques. He's going to see Dave Springer, his friend and ranking detective of the Homicide Bureau of the D.C. Police. Then I think he's going by the French Embassy for some reason."

"Mother of Mary," said Jacques. "If he goes to that Embassy, we could all be in death's way."

226

"What in the hell are you talking about?" snapped Ben Feldman.

"I have just told you that before the troupe left London, I addressed an anonymous letter to the French Embassy there, suggesting that the appropriate authorities look into the Swarraine head carvings being peddled by Pacific Island Imports. I had noticed they were sold in various decor shops at ridiculously low prices, not only in the Pacific, but throughout western Europe and the British Isles. Something is amiss. I do not know, but I suspect. If Greg goes to the French Embassy concerning the same matter, I am really worried."

"Why?" asked a curious Caroline.

Jacques looked with deepening concern at the listening threesome, then said, "With what I know and what I have just heard from Mary's livre, I feel sure that Farqua has a large criminal drug organization and I am worried that lookouts and informers may be planted in almost every French Embassy you can name. When Greg goes to the Embassy and inquires about Pacific Island Imports, I believe that soon thereafter Farqua would know who the inquirer is and where we are, if he does not already."

Ben Feldman looked at the Polynesian and said, "You're right, Greg shouldn't go directly to the Embassy. Maybe that's why he went to see Springer first." Ben Feldman, for the first time, felt a degree of ease being with the islander. He mused, maybe Mary's smothering attention may have duped Jacques for a while, but he's no dummy.

3

Caroline was becoming increasingly nervous. While her guests watched, she picked up the radio transceiver in the den and called Greg's car. The other three occupants of the room listened intently. Much to Caroline's relief Greg answered. "Greg, have you been to the French Embassy yet?" she asked.

"No, Hon. Traffic has been heavy and I'm late for my appointment with Dave Springer, but I'm right now pulling into the parking garage on my way to the Lawyers Club."

Caroline quickly told him the important parts of Mary's diary, of Jacques' answers regarding Mary's note to Greg. Then she told him of Jacques suspicions and his anonymous letter to the French Embassy in London.

"Why didn't he tell me about his suspicions and his letter to the Embassy?"

"Because he said you asked so many other questions, he never got around to telling you before you took off again for D.C."

There was a moment of silence.

"It all fits," said a relieved Greg.

"How does it all fit?" asked a nervous Caroline.

"From what Jacques told me before, I began to suspect that there is a drug operation headed by Farqua. With what you just told me, I am more convinced than ever. Farqua's operation must be bigger than I thought, maybe that's why Dave won't talk to me in the D.C. Police Headquarters. Sure as hell, he suspects a mole in the department. I'll talk to Dave before I go to the Embassy. Now I feel a lot more comfortable having Jacques, Ben and his wife, at our place. But, tell each one of them not to even stick their head out the door. They're safer inside, at least for the time being. Things are coming together fast. You keep your eyes peeled on the street in front of our house. If you see anything unusual, call Arlington Police headquarters and ask for a patrol check. I've already alerted Arlington Police Chief Salasky."

"Greg, what in heaven's name are you talking about?" asked Caroline.

"Just do as I ask and keep calm. Everything's going to be copasetic," and Greg flipped off his two-way radio switch.

Copasetic in a cat's foot, mused Caroline to herself, and she was more upset than ever.

4

Greg was also perturbed, really perturbed. He thought: if Mary's diary was true and Linguette was controlled by Farqua, Caroline, Jacques, the Feldmans, and he could be in increasing danger. He remembered Caroline telling him she had introduced herself to Linguette in Mary's dressing room last night. Linguette surely had time to relay that conversation to Farqua, and it wouldn't take Farqua long to determine that Caroline Morgan was the wife of Gregory Morgan, the former Naval officer who had witnessed the taboo. Farqua would soon discover Morgan's home address. All he had to do was to look through the telephone books of the metropolitan D.C. area, if he hadn't already done so. Damn, I hope Dave's at the club, Greg mused.

5

Dave was chagrined when he entered the D.C. Lawyers Club, for he knew he might be betraying a good friend. He just hoped that his conversation with Greg would be mutually beneficial. From the few remarks Greg had made on the phone, Dave suspected Greg was, at least, on the fringe of one hellaciously dangerous situation. Also, as a result of previous professional contacts with Greg, Dave knew his former law schoolmate had a knack for privately delving into criminal matters with the single-mindedness of a dedicated ferret. Only when he felt swamped, would Greg call for help. Dave hoped this was the present reason for the call.

6

Greg didn't know that Dave Springer, on the evening following the opening performance of the Southwest Pacific Dance Ensemble at the National Theater, had received a telephone call at his home from an acquaintance, Albert Pfiester. Pfiester, an FBI agent and communications expert, said, "Dave, I'm bypassing usual D.C. Police policy by calling you at home, but we need your help and expertise. I couldn't call you at the department because we believe there is an informer somewhere in your headquarters."

"What kind of help do you need?" asked a surprised Dave.

"Before I tell you, I gotta' couple of questions."

"Fire away."

"What do you know about a Ralph Dupui Farqua?"

"Never head the name before," retorted Dave.

"Well, what do you know about Pacific Island Imports?"

"What's that?"

"You sure you've never heard that name before?"

"I've got no idea what you are talking about," said Dave.

"The last question. Ever heard of the Southwest Pacific Dance Ensemble?"

"All I know is they're on the stage at the National Theater."

"Good, you're our man. Meet me in half an hour in Room 506 at the Carlton Hotel."

"Albert, I can't do that tonight. My son, Rick, is on an Optimist Club junior basketball team. They've got a game at a school gym tonight at 7:30 p.m. I'm an assistant coach of the team."

"You'll just have to beg off. We're on to one of the biggest drug operations in U.S. history," said Agent Pfiester.

"So, how does that involve me?" queried Dave.

"We've learned enough to believe that the dope smuggling of Pacific Island Imports has left a trail of dead bodies from Southeast Asia through western Europe. Wrangling into that market is serious business. We believe the same will be true here."

"How so?" asked an irritated Dave.

"Our sources tell us that Pacific Island Imports, among other ventures, controls the Southwest Pacific Dance Ensemble now playing at the National. We believe that dancing group is a front for the illegal drug activities of Ralph Dupui Farqua. We have learned he owns the major interest in Pacific Island Imports. Wherever the Ensemble dances, Pacific Island Imports opens a warehouse. Increased dope traffic seems to follow, and bodies turn up. We believe that Farqua is trying to get a toe-hold in the District. We need someone with your contacts and expertise on our side. Please, Dave. You've been cleared by the Director. Don't let me down."

"Damn! My son is going to be upset," said Springer.

"You can explain it to him when the investigation is over. He'll understand. He knows you're in a position that sometimes demands quick action. And, believe me, this really is one of those sometimes."

"All right," said Dave. "But, I'm not happy about letting my son down. I see him little enough as it is."

"I understand, I've got two boys," said Albert, and he hung up the phone.

7

When Dave reached the hotel, just up 16th Street from the Hay Adams House, he went to Room 506 and was introduced to the other members of the team.

"This is Agent Robin Younger and Agent Marshall Minor, said Pfiester as he pointed to them. He pointed again, "And this is Captain Henri Stover, a drug interdiction expert from the Suretè Internationale, the French equivalent of our FBI. He's passing as a tourism aide to the French Embassy in Washington. Gentlemen." Pfiester said, "This is Lieutenant Dave Springer, chief detective of the Homicide Bureau of the D.C. Police Force. You can rely on him."

Dave shook hands with the members of the team.

"What's all this about," asked Dave.

Agent Younger said, "We believe that an American citizen named Ralph Dupui Farqua is the purse strings behind the Southwest Pacific Dance Ensemble and that the troupe is a front for Farqua's drug activities. Those activities, we believe, are channeled through Pacific Island Imports which we have learned is also controlled by Farqua."

"How long has the dance group been performing?" asked Dave.

Younger continued, "About eight years, in the Southwest Pacific and Asia. A little over a year ago, the dance troupe started a tour of Western Europe. We suspect that during the Pacific and Orient periods of the Ensemble, Farqua and his Chinese cohort, Chi Quong, reputedly a cloth importer, have put together a vast drug empire. When the operation was well organized, Farqua entered the European scene, using the Ensemble as his cover. Only recently have we begun to suspect how he brings the drugs into the various countries."

"What do you suspect?" asked a curious Dave Springer.

"By the 'Masques of the Islands,' the vividly-colored coconut head carvings done by one Pierre Swarraine on the island of Bora Bora. Those carvings are shipped from that island to Pacific Island Imports in Tahiti. From there, they are transhipped -- wherever.

"Suretè Internationale and the FBI have obtained several of the head carvings from decor shops here and abroad. When these were first inspected, they appeared to contain nothing but sand in the nut void of the coconuts. However, on microscopic examination, traces of opium or heroin have been found near the right eye area on some heads. Just where the drugs were exchanged for sand is now the subject of intense search."

"How much dope could the average coconut head hold?" asked Dave.

Agent Minor responded, "Oh, about a litre, dry measure, and half a kilo in weight, more or less, depends on the size of the void in the coconut," said Younger.

"How many heads are carved each week by Swarraine?" asked Dave.

Agent Minor again responded, "Until recently we had no idea. Now we have a source on the scene. He says Swarraine and four students turn out about forty heads a week. It's quite a production line. The trading schooner picks them up every week. Used to be the trading ship only came by the island once every three weeks."

"We believe the heads first entered the U.S. through Pacific Island Imports at New Orleans," said Agent Pfiester. "Now we believe they also come into the U.S. through Norfolk, Virginia, as well."

"How?" asked Dave Springer.

"Brought in by one of the Farqua Trading Company ships, an old line that's been in the fishing and freighter business for almost fifty years," answered Pfiester.

"That comports with our belief, too," said Henri Stover. "But, that isn't all. Apparently wherever Ralph Farqua had an opening night of the Ensemble in France, a Pacific Island Imports office and warehouse had recently been established in the area. We have quietly examined the contents of several of those warehouses, mostly cloth and 'Masques of the Islands.' We've even purloined a few of the heads from various warehouses. They've all been loaded with sand. However, once the heads begin to appear in the decor shops, some members of various competing drug gangs turn up dead. It's more than a coincidence."

"That's where you come in, Dave," said Agent Pfiester. "We want you to see if you can find out what underlying tensions are spreading in the local drug ranks now that the Ensemble is on stage in D.C. We know that the Pacific Island Imports' newly-opened warehouse is located on the outskirts of Alexandria, Virginia. And, for God's sake, fill us in on every D.C. killing reported, no matter whether or not it appears to be tied in with Farqua. The last thing is, don't mention any of this around your office. We know there is a leak there, but not who. Later on we'll clear your actions with the Chief."

"I'll do my best, guys. Who do I report to?" asked Dave.

"You contact me," said Pfiester. "No one but me. But, do it out of your headquarters. Call CO3-7142. Just say supper will be at 6:00 p.m. That means you'll be at this room, 506 in the Carlton Hotel, in thirty minutes. I'll be here."

"Besides the so-called leak in our headquarters, why all this hush-hush?" asked Dave.

"Because you have no idea how large and widespread we believe Farqua's organization is," replied Pfiester.

"That's all for now," said Pfiester. "But, if anyone stumbles on a new clue, let me know immediately. Our next regular meeting will be five days from now, same place, same time."

Four days after Dave Springer first met with the FBI team, he received his call from Greg Morgan. He was startled when Greg asked him about the Southwest Pacific Dance Ensemble and even more so when his friend questioned him about Pacific Island Imports. Dave wondered just how in the hell his friend in suburban Virginia could be tied in to those suspect organizations.

Dave was already investigating the death of Mary D'Quino, the Ensemble's leading ballerina, that occurred last night. He had reported her death to Agent Pfiester earlier in the morning. At that time, he had no knowledge that Greg had been backstage at the National endeavoring to aid the stricken ballerina. Now he would have to make another call to Pfiester before he met Greg.

When Pfiester learned Dave was to meet Greg at the D.C. Lawyers Club, he said, "Come by right now. We'll wire you. And, we will be in one of the conference rooms at the Club taping the conversation. It's a must. In addition, if you two leave the Club, we'll follow you at a discrete distance and continue to record. You may really have stumbled on to something."

When Dave arrived at the room and was being wired, Agent Minor spoke up, "Listen to this short tape. We don't know the voice on the other end, but the call came from a phone in New Orleans, Louisiana."

They listened.

"Who is Sweeney and what's a Sweeney Report?" asked Dave.

"Damned if we know yet, but obviously, Farqua was upset with the call coming to his Hay Adams suite. He's smart, he suspects a phone tap. It was installed by us just before the call. We do know that Pacific Island Imports has an office in a large warehouse near the New Orleans city docks. That warehouse is now under constant surveillance," replied Younger. "We have observed that the company is primarily a large importer of Western Pacific and Oriental cloth goods of all types."

"We better get going if you intend to set up before Greg arrives," said Dave.

8

Dave was sitting on a stool at the Lawyers Club bar quaffing a draft when Greg slid onto a stool beside him. "Little late," said Dave.

"I know, I'm sorry, but traffic over the Key Bridge was tied up because of an accident," replied Greg.

"I heard on the way over," commented Dave. "What's on your mind, counselor?"

"Let me get a draft, then let's take a corner table. Things are beginning to rapidly fall in place."

The chunky, almost bald, detective with the horned-rimmed glasses and trimmed goatee, seemed more like an English lit college professor than the ranking homicide detective of the D.C. Police Department. His dress code was indifferent, brown pants, a little baggy, white turtle-neck shirt and a mottled tan sports coat. Overall, he gave the initial appearance of a bespectacled terrapin -- and he was one during his undergraduate years at the University of Maryland. Not blinking, he watched as his former law school mate and legal fraternity brother waited for a beer. But, looks are deceiving.

9

"Drinks are on me," said Greg.

"Not this time," and Dave smiled that beguiling way he had, completely destroying the terrapin image. "The last time they were on you was after I damned near lost my job over that Radar Rape Machine episode of yours. They're on me, so we can head in the right direction as we get started on this affair."

Greg laughed, and he remembered: What a weird, delightful episode that had been for him. He had settled a real estate sale in the firm's Washington office. The sale involved D.C. real estate. The seller, Mrs. Fiske, a seemingly quiet, middle-aged, graying widow was a client of Allen Balston, one of Greg's partners. Balston had been called out of town because his sister, living in Chattanooga, Tennessee, had been taken seriously ill. So, Greg agreed to handle the settlement. It had gone well and the widow received almost a half million dollars profit.

Two nights after the settlement, around 2:00 a.m., the phone on the bedside table by Caroline rang. Caroline and Greg awoke with a start. Caroline was fearful something had happened to her widowed, aging father. She, still struggling to come awake, fumbled for the phone, picked it up, cleared her throat and answered, "Hello."

An excited feminine voice on the other end asked, "Is this Mrs. Morgan?"

"Yes, it is," answered Caroline.

"Are you the wife of lawyer Gregory Morgan?"

"I am," said Caroline in a guarded tone.

"Is your husband there?"

"He is," replied a now irritated Caroline.

"Will you please tell him to go up to the attic and turn off his Radar Rape Machine. He's driving me wild."

Caroline was wide awake. She nestled the phone on the pillow beside her husband. Greg heard every word of the conversation. Caroline just couldn't believe her ears.

"What did you say?" she asked.

"I'm Mrs. Fiske. Please tell your husband to turn off the Radar Rape Machine in the attic. The damned device is driving me wild." And the phone on the other end went dead.

An amazed Caroline looked at the phone and then at Greg. "Just who in the hell is Mrs. Fiske?" she asked as she put the receiver back on the stand.

At first Greg was a puzzled as his wife. Then he remembered the quiet gray-haired widow. "Someone for whom I recently settled a real estate sale in the D.C. office."

Caroline was seething. "You having an affair with her?"

"Hon, I never saw her but once in my life. She's Allen's client. He was called out of town when his sister became ill, so I held the sale settlement in our D.C. office."

Caroline was relieved, believed her husband. "Why would she make such a call?"

"Damned if I know," said Greg as he turned away from Caroline and went back to a sound sleep. Caroline slept restlessly.

The next night at 2:00 a.m., the phone rang again. Caroline came awake with a start and answered the call. The same voice said, "Mrs. Morgan, I spoke to you nicely last night and asked you to have your husband turn off the Radar Rape Machine in the attic. Now I'm telling you, have him cut it off right away, I am exhausted from that infernal device," and the phone went dead.

Greg had awakened and, with a grin, was watching his wife. He just knew the call had to be a repetition of the night before. Caroline didn't think it was humorous at all. She was furious. "Who does that crazy woman think she is, calling at this time of night? I want a stop put to it."

Greg hid his grin with an arm over his face, but he knew Caroline meant it. He debated what he should do. Then he said to her, "The next time she calls, I'll handle it."

"You'd better," responded his squirming, agitated wife.

The next night when the call came, Caroline handed the phone to her husband. When Mrs. Fiske heard his voice, she said, "Cut that damned thing off now."

"Mrs. Fiske," asked Greg, "Where do you live in D.C.?"

Mrs. Fiske gave him the address. Greg, with a wry smile, responded, "The Machine must be a little off line. The beam was meant for a secret girl friend of mine in nearby Glover Park."

Caroline's mouth dropped open in amazement.

"I suggest, if the misdirected beam really bothers you so much, you call Dave Springer, chief detective of the Homicide Bureau of the D.C. Police Department. And, since I live in Arlington, Virginia, I suggest you call the Clerk of the Circuit Court of Arlington, the Commonwealth's Attorney of Arlington, the Judge of the Circuit Court of Arlington, the Sheriff of Arlington County and the local FBI office. I'm sure they can help you." And Greg hung up the phone.

Caroline looked in disbelief at her husband. "Have you gone nuts?"

Greg laughed. "No, Hon, I'm just getting us some relief and sleep."

Mrs. Fiske never again bothered Greg and Caroline, but Greg's suggestion to Mrs. Fiske caused an uproar. She began to pester Dave Springer at his office and to harass the officials of Arlington County to the point where rotund Michael Higgins, Sheriff of Arlington and close friend of Greg's sheepishly came by to take a look in Greg's attic. Higgins, standing on a ladder in a bedroom closet, pushed up the small hinged attic trap door, tried to squeeze his broad shoulders through the opening and got stuck in the trap door framework. The attic was not floored, only a couple sheets of four-by-eight plywood had been placed on the attic joists near the trap door. There was no electric light. What light there was came through the screened triangular vents at either end of the attic. In July, the heat up there was searing. The only item on the sheets of plywood was a .25 caliber Japanese carbine in a canvas case. Greg had brought the gun home at the end of the war. The light-weight carbine had been in that space ever since the Morgan family had moved into the rambler. Higgins all but fainted from heat prostration before he was freed from the opening. Shortly after the Sheriff's inspection, a hearing was convened in the District of Columbia to determine whether or not Mrs. Fiske should be sent to St. Elizabeth's Mental Hospital, in D.C., for mental observation. Dave Springer testified at the hearing, as did the agitated officials from Arlington County. Mrs. Fiske was committed to the hospital for a sixty-day observation period. While there, she was a model patient. At the end of her stay, she was released with no finding.

Immediately thereafter, she obtained out-of-area counsel and filed two suits, one in D.C. against the Police Department and Dave Springer alleging, among other things, false arrest, liable, slander and conspiracy. She filed the same type of suit in the Arlington County Circuit Court against the Commonwealth's Attorney, the Circuit Court Clerk, the Judge of the Circuit Court, and the Sheriff of Arlington. No local judges, either in D.C. or in Arlington, were willing to try the cases, so out-of-area judges were brought in. Though she lost the cases in the trial courts, she appealed both. She had plenty of money to cover her costs and fees. Ultimately she lost the cases on appeal and moved from the area.

During the whole episode, Greg's Arlington Courthouse friends were righteously indignant and upset, as was Dave Springer. They accused Greg of foisting Mrs. Fiske on them.

When interrogated by his peers, Greg would only grin and say, "The public has a right to be protected from Radar Rape Machines." The D.C. Police Chief raised holy hell with Dave for the District having to waste so much time and money on the defense of the Department and Dave. Even after Greg went to the Chief and told him how Dave became involved, the Chief was still irritated at his homicide detective leader. Now all involved could laugh at the entire episode as just one of those weird events of life.

Caroline took a lot of ribbing from her female friends who knew the story. Some, with mock seriousness, begged her to have Greg beam the Radar Rape Machine at them saying they needed a lift, a new adventure. Several of Greg's legal peers offered to help him obtain a patent on the device and then form a corporate venture. They were sure they would all be millionaires overnight. Greg would gleefully demur saying he was leaving the device to his son so he could reap the benefits. More than once, when the subject would come up between Greg and Caroline, he would humorously say, "Oh, boy, how seldom the right shoe is on the wrong foot and feels so uncomfortable."

Caroline, her eyes dancing with merriment, would reply, "Greg, you ought to be ashamed."

And Greg would quietly belly-laugh as he recalled some of the more ridiculous court scenes he watched as a spectator.

10

Greg's quirky, offbeat sense of humor was among the attributes that endeared him to his wife. Frequently, he made himself the butt of his humor and he, by instinct, knew how to play that humor to the hilt for the merriment of all -- including himself. The radar rape episode became one of Caroline's favorite memories.

In addition, she had thought: There are some things about men I'll never understand. That weird episode had acted as a bonding agent for her husband and Springer. When it was over, they were closer friends than ever, kind of like a small mutual admiration society. One good result was that she had met and liked Vicki Springer, Dave's wife. Following the end of the bonding episode, the two couples met several times a year in D.C., had dinner at some posh restaurant, then went to the National Theater, and crawled up to the peanut gallery to see a theater guild play. The couples had season tickets. After the first occasion, Caroline had permanently borrowed her mother's opera glasses so she could see the facial features of the actors and nuances of the performance by each of them. Now, as a habit, she carried the glasses to any type of stage entertainment, regardless of where she was seated.

11

When Dave and Greg were settled at a corner table, Dave asked, "What do you know about Pacific Island Imports?"

"Probably not as much as you do," said Greg. "But, if I tell you what I know, will you reciprocate?"

"That depends."

"On what?"

"How much you really know," responded the detective.

"Well, regardless of whether you tell me or not, I've got to tell you what I know, because I'm going to need your help and soon."

"I'm listening," said Dave.

Greg then told him how he had met Farqua and Jacques during the war and what had happened yesterday evening at the National Theater. Then he reiterated Jacques' conversations about Farqua. He told Feldman's story and finally related the important parts of Mary's diary. He ended his soliloquy by saying, "I think Jacques, Ben Feldman and I are in real danger from Farqua. I believe he has a far-flung empire. I suspect that Farqua has been transporting opium and heroin on a large scale by means of the coconut head carvings. How or where he gets rid of the dope before he sells the heads to the general public,

I don't know. But, there have to be transfer points." Before Dave could answer, Greg switched his point of view and said, "If he didn't poison Mary D'Quino, I'm sure he knows who did."

Dave looked at Greg, was silent for a few seconds, then said, "Greg, you are right on target, but you have no idea how extensive Farqua's operation seems to be. It's almost continent-wide in western Europe. Even in this country, Pacific Island Imports has many agents, some dupes, but most are ruthless members of Farqua's underworld organization, and we are learning that organization has eyes and ears in places you wouldn't believe."

"I guessed that when you said to meet here," said Greg. "Were you followed?"

"No, but you must realize your call to me may have been recorded at headquarters. If that call is reviewed by a wrong person, we could both be in trouble."

"You mean Farqua's organization is that powerful?"

"And then some," said a sober Dave.

"How did you get the info?" asked Greg.

"That's my business," said Dave. "The less you know about it the better, but I can tell you that Interpol, the Suretè Internationale, our DEA and FBI have been delving into the operation of Pacific Island Imports for quite a while."

"Since Jacques' letter to the French Embassy in London?" said Greg.

"How did you know about that?" asked Springer.

"Because Jacques has mentioned the letter."

"Where is Jacques?" asked Springer.

"Isn't he in his hotel?" parried Greg.

"You know damned well he isn't. Not only are we looking for him, so are Farqua's men. And they're also looking for the Feldmans."

"Sommenberg has talked to your office?" asked Greg.

"And, how do you know about Sommenberg?"

"Because, as I've told you before, I've talked to Ben Feldman."

"Greg, where in the hell are the Feldmans and Jacques Montagne?"

"I can't tell you right now. They are my clients. They're safe and I assure you, they'll not run away if they are needed by the government to testify."

"Man, I'm not worried about testimony. Sure, Jacques is considered a suspect because he was Mary's husband, but none of us in the know think he killed her and we know the Ben Feldmans didn't. They didn't arrive at the Mayflower until after ten p.m. last night. This morning they, too, disappeared as if by magic. Sometime after the Feldmans left their room, Farqua's men tore it apart trying to find out where they have gone."

"I'll tell you in due time, after we find out who killed Mary," said Greg.

"Who, shit!" said an irritated Dave, "We can't even determine what killed her. We've got the GW Hospital pathology lab and the FBI lab trying to find out."

"I think I can help," said Greg.

Greg reached into his pocket, pulled out a handkerchief, unfolded it to reveal the soiled tissue that his wife had put in her evening bag last night.

"What the hell is that?" inquired Dave.

Greg told him his wife's story of how she wiped up the spilled drops of Orange Crush. Then he told Jacques' story of the giant Nohu fish that lurks near the bottom of the island's coral reefs. He told Dave of the deadly poison the fish releases through the spines of its dorsal fin and how Swarraine was able to cook the poison into a white, tasteless powder. Greg said, "When this tissue is examined, I believe it will reveal traces of Nohu poison that was in the Orange Crush drink consumed by Mary just before she went on stage for the dance routines after intermission. I believe the poison was placed there by

Linguette. Where she got it from and why she used it, I don't know. My wife said that the understudy was truly surprised to find Caroline in the room and Linguette seemed more puzzled than ever when she saw the glass of water held by Caroline."

"Christ, Greg, you could be right about the poison. Let's get the hell out of here and head for the FBI lab. They're the best in town. We'll go in my car."

As they left the bar, Dave asked Greg, "Is Linguette staying at the Harrington Hotel with the others?"

"So far as I know," said Greg.

"After we leave the tissue with the lab, I think we should pay her a visit. Do you mind?"

"Certainly not," said Greg. "I'd like to hear what she has to say -- if she'll talk. The night Mary collapsed, Linguette appeared to be quite shaken by the episode. But from what Caroline has told me of Mary's diary, she could have been putting on an act to cover her butt. I really would like to get to the bottom of this mess in a hurry."

"Why?" asked Dave.

"Because if what I suspect is true, we may not have much time to act before all hell breaks loose, even as far as I am concerned."

"You mean you think Farqua is already on your trail,." asked Dave.

"I sure do."

"And, if he's on your trail, Jacques and the Feldmans, as well as you, could be in real danger."

"Exactly," said Greg. "And maybe you, too."

"Could be," replied Dave. "Let's get going."

12

The two men entered Dave's car and headed for the FBI lab. "Keep an eye out and see if we are being tailed," said Dave.

"I've been looking," replied Greg, "So far, so good."

Dave called the lab on his car radio and advised what they were bringing as well as Greg's suspicions as to the nature of the poison. When they drove in the Ninth Street driveway to the Justice Department building, Dave said, "Give me the tissue. I'll take it to Dr. Mac and be right back. Keep a weather eye."

Greg gave him the tissue.

In no time at all, Dave was back.

"Let's head for the Harrington," he said.

"I doubt that she's there," responded Greg.

"Where do you think she'll be?"

"With Farqua, if she's alive."

"Well, I know where Farqua is staying," said Dave.

"Where?"

"At the Hay Adams House on 16th Street. He's registered there as Manly Deal. He is also registered as Ralph Farqua at the Shoreham Hotel, but he doesn't stay there. Just picks up his social messages."

13

The two men drove to the Harrington Hotel, parked and got out. The doorman started to object to the car in the front entrance no-parking zone, but stopped short when Dave flashed his ID card and said, "Just keep quiet. We won't be long."

"Sure, Lieutenant, anything you say," responded the surprised liveried man as he opened the front door for the duo.

Dave strode quickly to the registration desk. Joe Stedhick, the day manager, was on duty.

"Hi, Joe," said Dave.

"Good afternoon, what can I do for you, Lieutenant?"

"What is Linguette Swarraine's room number? She's a member of the Southwest Pacific Dance Ensemble. They're staying here."

The manager looked at the registry.

"Room 307. She in any trouble?"

"I hope not, but we need to talk to her if she's in. Will you ring her room?"

"Sure," said Joe and he had the hotel telephone operator dial the room number. The phone rang and rang, no answer. "She doesn't answer, I guess she must have gone out."

"Is her key in her room slot?" asked Dave.

Joe looked, "No," he said, "She must have forgotten to leave it."

"I'm not so sure, I need to see if she's there."

"Lieutenant, you know I'm not supposed to provide entry without a court order."

"Cut the crap, Joe, this may be a matter or life or death. I'm not kidding," said Dave. "Why don't you show us the way and watch. All I want to do is see of she is there."

"I hear you, Lieutenant. Just remember it's my butt if anything goes wrong."

"I'll cover it," said Dave and grinned. "Even if it's such a big butt to cover."

Joe cast him a smirk, picked up a set of master keys, and led the way.

14

The trio left the elevator and headed for Room 307. Joe Stedhick knocked on the door, no response. "This is the manager, Miss Swarraine. I'd like a short chat with you," called out Joe. No answer. He slipped the master key in the door and turned the knob. The door started to open and stopped as the night chain became taut. "What the shit?" said Joe. He looked at Dave.

Dave said, "Let me try, move aside."

Greg watched fascinated, but with a sinking feeling in his gut. Something was really wrong, he just sensed serious trouble.

Dave stood in front of the door then, with the agility of a black belt karate expert, he kicked the door at chain height. There was a loud snap as the chain latch flew off the wall and the door banged open. The three men looked into the room and stood for a moment as if transfixed.

"Jesus," said Joe, "I'll call the police."

"I am the police, you fool. Don't you call anyone until I say so," said Dave.

Greg was shocked. There on the bed, clothed in a light blue, silk nightgown, lay inert Linguette. Greg saw the blood froth still dripping from her lips, and he smelled the odor he had first experienced when Mary D'Quino lay crumpled on the National stage. Just what in hell is going on, he wondered.

Dave was in command. "Come in both of you, but don't touch a thing." They entered. Dave went to the figure on the bed. He placed three fingers of his right hand along side of her throat and felt. Then he took a limp wrist and felt for her pulse. He looked with grave concern at the pathetic form, and said, "She's gone, but she's still warm. She must have died just minutes ago. She doesn't appear to have been shot or stabbed. Wonder what in the hell happened?"

"I think I know."

"How would you know?" asked Dave.

"Because I smell the same odor that emanated from Mary D'Quino the night she collapsed on stage. Poison, fish poison, the poison that may have killed Mary. The reason why we left the tissue at the FBI lab."

Dave began to look around the room. His sight settled on the large mahogany bureau. Greg's eyes followed his. There, on the bureau, was an Orange Crush bottle, partially empty with an empty glass beside it. And, something more, a small, open, silver snuff box empty except for a film of white powder on the interior bottom of it. The box was sitting on a folded sheet of hotel writing paper. Dave walked to the bureau, whipped out his handkerchief, and gingerly removed the box from the paper. Then he unfolded the paper. The three men looked at the writing. They read the at first delicate handwriting that, at the end, trailed off to an almost illegible scrawl: *October 26, 1954. 2:00 p.m. To the finder, God forbid it is Farqua. Years ago, when I first met Lieutenant Commander Ralph Farqua, I was as untouched as a new unfolding jasmine blossom. I thought he was truly attracted to me. I was to him. What followed over a period of time has been the continuing nightmare of my life. No harem of Macaco monkeys could have been treated worse by the ruling male than I have been abused by Farqua. He is a depraved animal. I am addicted and have fallen under his complete domination, now it is too late to escape. I should have known -- I should have known, but he said it was only a mild stupefant that would take Mary out of action for a couple of days -- I have been Mary's understudy for more than six months and I so wanted to be the lead for just a little while, before I lose all control. There are times now when I can not remember, can not make my arms and legs do their job, the dancing steps get more difficult each week. I can tell Mary had noticed -- she gloated, the bitch -- but I never intended to kill her, for I believed him.*

Yesterday evening, during intermission, when Mary opened her Orange Crush bottle, she took a couple sips from it, and dribbled on her costume as she was sitting at the table. "I better get a glass," she said and arose, went out to find one. I started to slip the stupefant in the drink and heard her returning. I only used half the contents. Just before she came in the room, I put my thumb over the bottle opening and shook it -- I can't see very well. Mary poured a glassful of the drink and drank most of it as if she had a mighty thirst. I wtched.

When that hapned, I kne I had m chanc.

Now all is fuzzy. I heard the radio nes ths afternoon after I returned from his suite. I must hav fanted. When I recovrd, I look at my wach, it red 1:30 p.m., I called him at the Ha Adas Hous. He said dnt worry, now you wil be the lead and everythng will be OK shortly. I know where they are.

The slick bastrd. I know he intends to blam m for Mary's deth. I have decide to jon Mary. I take the rst of the stupefant. O, Mother of Mary, wat hav I don.

Linguuuuu

15

Dave Springer looked at his watch and then at Greg. He noticed Greg was seething with anger. "Cool it, Counselor. Its two-thirty, we've got to move quickly." He picked up the room phone, dialed his department and said, "Let me speak to Rich. Hi, Rich, send a squad over to Room 307 at the Harrington Hotel. There's a body here. Take her to the FBI lab. No, not the morgue! The FBI lab. Tell them to run the same tests they are running on D'Quino. Check the room for prints and anything else. Thanks," and he hung up.

Dave turned to the manager, "Joe, don't let a soul in this room except members of my detail. Assign a bellhop to this door until they arrive. Go." And Joe left to assume the requested duties.

16

Dave, using his handkerchief, put the top on the snuff box, pulled a small, clear, plastic bag from his jacket pocket and placed the snuff box and note in the bag. "I'm not leaving these here. They might fall into the wrong hands," he said to Greg.

As Dave was putting the evidence in his jacket pocket, Greg cast him a serious look. "Dave, with what we both now know, I gotta' level with you. Jacques and the Feldmans are at my home with my wife. They could all be in hellacious danger, depending on how fast Farqua is moving."

"Greg, knowing you as well as I do, I was sure they would be there. And you're right, they could be in for damned big trouble. Why didn't you call me sooner?"

"Sooner, hell! I've been jumping hurdles since last night's intermission of the Ensemble's program, except for a few hours sleep. The finish line seems to be farther away each time I clear one. I can feel the competition breathing down my neck. I called you just as soon as I had a real inkling of what was happening."

"Okay, okay," said Dave. "But, despite the fact that you're known as a cool, suburban, civil practice lawyer, you do get involved in the damnedest, wildest adventures I have ever known. Some humorous, others not so humorous, more serious than you alone can handle."

"That's when I come to you," responded Greg with a faint smile.

"Well, this one is bigger than you and I can handle. Drug agents from Europe and America are working on the Imports deal. When the international sting is supposed to go down, I don't know. But, we can't wait for that.

"Once you start to move, you're one hell of a ferret. Now, you've chased your quarry, Farqua, right into the open. But, you haven't provided much cover for his intended victims.

"That depraved beast, he not only had Linguette kill Mary D'Quino, he slowly tortured his mistress to death. As soon as I drop off this snuff box at the FBI lab, I've just gotta' go by the Hay Adams House and see if he's there. I have enough evidence to hold him, regardless of the sting operation."

"What, in God's name, are you talking about?" asked Greg.

"Tell you later, Counselor. Right now, let's get rolling."

The duo hurried down the hotel inside emergency stairway, through the lobby and out to Dave's car.

17

While Greg and Dave were at the D.C. Lawyers Club, and Greg was telling Dave Springer of his conversations with Jacques, how the coconut heads were carved and completed by Swarraine, and the cat's eye gems were used for pupils, Agent Pfiester, in a conference room not far from the bar, listened, smiled broadly and whispered to the other two agents, "I've got an idea how the dope heads are identified."

"How?" asked one of the others in the room.

"By the gem pupils in the eyes. I'm sure there is an identification code for the heads that contain the dope. Robin, call the lab and ask them to check the color of the pupils that had dope traces on the eye socket area. I hope to Christ they didn't dispose of those eye gems or at least they made a note of the color."

Agent Younger left the room to find a phone and call the FBI lab. He returned shortly. "They'll let us know as soon as they check it out," he said.

The FBI agents listened as Greg related to Dave, Jacques' story of the Nohu fish poison, the Orange Crush spill, and Caroline's belief that the poison was in the Orange Crush drink consumed by Mary just before she went on stage after intermission. Pfiester and the other men in the conference room were intrigued, particularly when Dave agreed the idea had merit and they should take the tissue to the FBI lab. And they were truly disturbed when Greg told Dave he suspected Farqua was involved in a major drug enterprise, and that suspicion had been heightened by Caroline's call to him when she told him of Jacques' anonymous letter to the French Embassy in London.

"Damn, that guy is a real ferret," said listening Agent Pfiester. "But God, he sure is throwing a monkey wrench into a quiet investigation. This episode could erupt into a battle royal before the day is over. Is there anyway we can slow him down without tipping our hand?"

"Christ, would you slow down if you believed your wife and house guests could be slaughtered before the end of the day?" asked Agent Younger.

Pfiester replied, "You know the answer to that. I guess we better follow the twosome, at a safe distance, keep in touch with the Alexandria District Office and lend help when we can."

18

Dave knew his conversations with Greg were being received and taped by the FBI team members. He prayed to God they recognized the immediate seriousness of the whole affair. The team, including the French Intelligence officer, followed Springer and Greg to the Harrington Hotel. They heard the conversation as to what Dave, Greg and the hotel manager found in Linguette's room.

"What a mess," said Agent Pfiester as he listened. "Robin, call the District Office, have them find Farqua and put a constant tail on him. We should have done it sooner. It's my fault, I didn't think things would come to a head so quickly."

19

As Greg and Dave left the Harrington Hotel, Dave turned to Greg, "What an animal that bastard Farqua is. But, at least, we got here before he did. That sick bastard would have taken the note and the snuff box."

"That's true," said Greg. "But, I'll wager he's not far behind. If he finds out Linguette's dead and we've been to the hotel, he'll know damned well that we're on to him. No telling what he and his buddies will try."

The pair, in silence, once again drove to the FBI lab. "Take it easy, Greg. I'll be back as soon as I can," and Dave went into the building.

20

He returned to the car with a broad grin. "You were right on target. The poison in the soiled tissue matches the poison in Mary's body. They will immediately test the residue in the snuff box. Henri Stover has already requested his government to expedite a Nohu poison sample to the lab."

"Now what?" asked Greg.

"I've got to make a quick radio call," replied Dave.

He picked up the transceiver and called, "Pfiester, you there?"

"Just up the street," was the reply.

As Dave Springer drove from the Justice Department driveway onto Ninth Street, Greg looked north and there, about a half a block away, in a no-parking zone, was a black Plymouth with three occupants.

"I suggest you three try the Shoreham. We're going to the Hay Adams House. I've turned the snuff box over to the lab. But, as you know, I've got a note, enough evidence to hold that bastard, if we can find him," said Springer.

"We're on our way right now. But keep in radio touch. We'll soon be out of the other range."

Greg looked through the rear window of Dave's car and saw a Plymouth pull away from the curb, make a U-turn and head north on Ninth Street. He wondered what other range Pfiester was talking about. Dave Springer placed the red light on top of his car, turned on the siren switch and headed for the Hay Adams House. "I just hope he is in his den. Sting or no sting, I want that bastard now."

"What do you mean, sting or no sting?" asked Greg.

"Tell you later, Counselor," replied Dave and he concentrated on weaving through D.C. traffic.

He drove in the driveway and came to a screeching halt in front of the main entrance. "I'm just going to see if he's in. If he is, I'll come back and radio for backup. In the meanwhile, I'll leave the set on for any emergency." Dave checked his shoulder holster, then left the car.

21

Greg was puzzled. So much was unsaid in Dave's radio communications with the FBI agent. What sting could Dave be talking about? Could his friend be wired? And, if so, why? Greg was growing increasingly nervous about the situation back at his house. How were the Feldmans and Jacques getting along? He hoped there had been no conflict.

And, just how far behind him was Farqua in learning what was happening. He fidgeted.

22

Dave took longer than Greg expected he would. Finally, the detective came out the entrance with a rapid stride. He was serious, yet excited. He opened the door, got in, and looked at Greg. As he started the car, he exclaimed, "Farqua's not there. Lionel, the day manager, says he checked out at least an hour ago. He let me in Farqua's former suite. His luggage is gone. I wondered where he had headed, so first I called your home. The line is dead. I'm sure it has been cut. I think your wife and extended household are in imminent danger."

"My, God, they're completely uncovered," gasped Greg.

Dave stopped his conversation and picked up the car radio transceiver. He raised the Arlington Police Department and asked to speak to the Chief. "Albert, this is Dave Springer. I've got an emergency in your area. I know Greg Morgan has alerted you to a potential problem which may affect the security of his household. That is no longer a potential problem. It's a real one. A major drug kingpin and some of his henchmen may be headed there right now for a multiple job. Greg is with me, but Mrs. Morgan, Jacques Montagne and Mr. and Mrs. Ben Feldman are at his home. They are the prime witnesses to the D'Quino murder in D.C. and to the elimination of a major drug ring. Send a couple of your best to Morgan's house, but be careful. We don't want any fireworks if we can help it. Just see that the house members are safe. We're on our way there from D.C. Tell your men to let us through when we arrive. And, by the way, an FBI swat team is on its way from Alexandria to back you up."

"We've got an inkling what's been going on," replied the Chief. "We'll start moving this minute."

"Thanks, Albert, I owe you one," was Dave's comment as he hung up the radio.

23

Greg gasped at what he had just heard.

"I know its a shock to hear," said Dave as he looked at Greg, "But, if we're going to try to save your wife and guests, let's get moving and now."

Dave turned on the magnetic, flashing, red light, placed it on the top of his unmarked car, and flipped on the siren switch. Greg, in the front passenger seat, placed his hands on the dashboard to steady himself as he and his friend raced toward the Virginia suburbs.

As Dave wove his siren-howling car through D.C. traffic, Greg had no real idea of how much Dave knew about Farqua's enterprises, but he suspected it was far more than the detective had alluded to. While they were crossing Key Bridge from D.C. into Roslyn, Virginia, a part of Arlington County, Dave, with his eyes on the road said, "Greg, I'm wired, have been since our meeting at the Lawyers Club. It was an order by the FBI. At first, I was afraid you might be tied into Farqua's dealings. Then, as the truth came out, I was damn relieved you were no part of Farqua's enterprise, but I was surprised, nearly dumbfounded, at the information you had gathered. So is the FBI team. What you have uncovered has blown the lid off of a quiet investigation.

"I don't give a crap about quiet investigations, I just want to protect my wife, my son and friends," said an irritated Greg.

"I agree, and that's my first objective," said Dave.

With the red light blinking and siren howling, the D.C. detective's car sped west on Lee Highway in Arlington County.

Part VII

Masques of the Islands

1

Divorced shipping magnate, Ralph Dupui Farqua, on the opening night performance of The Southwest Pacific Dance Ensemble at the National Theater, was seated in a box on the opposite side of the theater from the Sommenberg box. In front of him sat comely, thirty-four-year-old Karen D'Quaisselle from Thibodeaux, Louisiana, heiress to the D'Quaisselle fortune, and twice a divorcee. She was visiting relatives in the Sheridan Circle area of Washington, D.C. Now, those two were an item according to a leading society reporter for the *Washington Post*. Word through the social circles of D.C. was that the rather mysterious Ralph Farqua was one of the main financial backers of the dance ensemble, performing on the National Theater stage. But, no word of that had appeared in the local media.

2

Seated on one side of Farqua was Oren Silver, one of the aides to Allen J. Ellender, senior U.S. Senator from Louisiana. On the other side sat Martin DeLange, the comptroller of Pacific Island Imports. On invitation from Farqua, he had flown up in a company plane to witness the opening performance. He would return early the next day to Louisiana.

Silver turned to Ralph Farqua, "I hear you have an interest in the Ensemble."

"I have an interest in any group that has beautiful women," smirked Farqua, evading the question.

"Come on, Ralph, you know what I mean. Word is out that you are the primary financial backer of the Ensemble."

"Where did you hear such crap?"

"From Henri Stover."

"And who in the hell is Henri Stover?"

256

"He's a friend of mine and a tourism attache at the French Embassy," said Silver.

"Well, don't you believe him. Those frogs will say anything to create publicity."

Silver's comments only added to the anxiety Ralph Farqua was already experiencing. He had helped organize the Ensemble several years ago, and backed it financially, not only to cover his butt from the taboo episode in 1944, but to also cover the enterprise that had brought and continued to bring him untold hidden wealth. He was uncomfortable with the ensemble's opening in the U.S.

He had attended every opening night of the Ensemble throughout the Pacific and western Europe. Each such night had marked the establishing of a new outlet for the "Masques of the Islands," the artfully decorated, grotesque, whole coconut head carvings originated by Pierre Swarraine, the skilled artisan on the island of Bora Bora. The outlets were warehouses of Pacific Island Imports. Farqua's dreams concerning those carvings had led him to help organize and finance the ensemble. Throughout the Pacific and western Europe, his dreams, shrouded by the appearance of the dancers, had exceeded his fondest expectations. But here in the U.S., on this opening night, the dance performance might cause problems, real problems. He had taken precautions that those problems would not likely surface.

He knew from his sources that Ben Feldman, his despised former executive officer and victim of the taboo on Bora Bora, was married and living in the Paoli, Pennsylvania, area. Farqua's latest information was that his former oil base exec had not regained his memory and probably would never do so. He also knew from sources within his organization that Feldman's old man, Martin Feldman, had been a crafty rum-runner in his earlier years, but was now a respected large wholesale liquor dealer in Philadelphia. He knew that Gregory Morgan, friend of Jacques and the executive officer of the landing ship anchored in the Bora Bora protected cove harbor on that fateful day, was an unwitting witness to the taboo. According to Mary D'Quino, Jacques had been told by his father, the chieftain, to have an impartial witness attend the episode. Mary had told Morgan he was there to protect Farqua who knew nothing about the event. Farqua was advised that Morgan was a Washington metropolitan area lawyer and lived somewhere in a Northern Virginia suburb, across the Potomac River from D.C.

Farqua had the ticket reservations for the Ensemble's appearance at the National Theater checked periodically in an endeavor to tell whether or not Feldman or Morgan would be attending the show. He found no evidence that either man was. But, he worried. There was always the possibility they would buy at the box office or come as guests. That was a chance he had to accept.

In Europe, he didn't mind the Taboo routine. In the U.S., the idea of that routine made him nervous. He had suggested to Mary D'Quino that she drop the dance number. Her response had been, "No way. It is a show stopper everywhere. Besides, who knows what the dance really depicts, except you, Jacques, Gregory Morgan and I. Jacques has no idea what happened at the Naval Inquiry. Feldman has never regained his memory. And, you say Morgan will never give the episode a second thought. The routine is just a symbolic dance of our way of life. Why worry?"

Mary's increasing arrogance and domination of the dance troupe added to Farqua's discomfort level, even though Linguette kept a sharp eye on the lead ballerina and reported her every action to him. As he watched the show from his box on the opening night of the D.C. run, he thought with his other major enterprise doing so well, he no longer needed the Ensemble. It had outlived its primary purpose for him. The troupe was beginning to demand too much of his time and worry. So, he would end the Ensemble. Despite Mary's island warnings of retribution if her future was not maintained, warnings he doubted from the beginning, he began to formulate a plan that would lead to the breakup of the troupe.

3

Farqua thought: Some way, he had to have Mary eliminated. Then Linguette, the stupid little addict she was, would be easy to handle. With Mary, Jacques' protector, out of the way, he could get rid of Jacques, the quiet island educator. He was a damned thorn. Just how much the chieftain's son knew of his real enterprise, Farqua couldn't tell. Jacques seemed to know nothing about Farqua's main endeavor, but then again, Mary may have confided what she knew to her husband and how much Jacques had surmised from her remarks, Farqua didn't know. That left only one other person stateside who had true knowledge of the Taboo episode -- Gregory Morgan. And Farqua, the supreme egoist, still believed that the young lawyer would be too busy following his career to ever give the strange happening on the island a second thought, even if he saw the show. Now all he had to do was implement his master plan.

4

Bertrand Arville, Farqua's plant in the French Embassy in Washington, had reported that there was no evidence that Farqua's major enterprise was a source of worry to the French Embassy officials. According to Arville, they knew nothing about it and were most laudatory of the shipping magnate's dance ensemble. "The performances of the troupe has a positive tourist effect, encouraging many viewers to visit the Society Islands," said Arville.

5

Linguette, after the troupe's arrival in D.C., but before opening night, had told Farqua that the U.S. Custom officials at LaGuardia Airport had detained the troupe for hours as the customs inspectors minutely examined all luggage and personal effects. Not only that, but they made a strip search of each member of the ensemble. She told Farqua that as she watched, she became increasingly nervous. Before she was searched and by feigning illness, she was allowed to go to a commode and dispose of the heroin she had hidden in her female orifice. Farqua wondered the reason for such close inspection and had determined to investigate.

6

Years ago, on Bora Bora, Farqua witnessed the lethal effect of ingested Nohu fish poison, when Pierre Swarraine, on edict from the elders, terminated the life of an elderly male islander suffering from an advanced case of Elephantiasis. The tasteless powder had been placed in a mildly fermented pineapple drink. When the ill islander drank the potion, death had been certain, but obviously was painful and stinking. Farqua had persuaded Swarraine to surreptitiously cook him a batch of the deadly mixture, for which Farqua paid Swarraine handsomely in American dollars. Both men were sworn to secrecy because, if the Colonial authorities had discovered the illegal manufacture and sale of the potion by Swarraine to Farqua, both men, under French Colonial law, could have languished in prison for the rest of their lives.

Farqua had no problem hiding the substance and later bringing it into the States. After the war, he had used the concoction only once, on a severely injured Columbian crew member of the family's shrimp fleet mother ship. The deadly poison worked. Now he had another relatively unknown lethal weapon, in ample supply, whenever needed. Such possession made him feel more powerful, more dominant than ever.

7

Chi Quong, Farqua's Chinese cohort, was the supplier of the raw opium. He was a wizard in obtaining the stupefant at very low prices and having it carefully camouflaged in delivery of goods, mostly Asiatic cloth goods, to Pacific Island Imports at Tahiti. There was no serious inspection by Tahitian officials of the goods imported and exported from Tahiti by Pacific Island Imports. Farqua had carefully arranged that privilege. But, he knew it would be difficult and more costly than he could afford if he endeavored to make the same arrangements elsewhere. So, he had built his business concept on the "Masques of the Islands," the plan conceived as he first watched Swarraine carve and cure the grotesque coconut husk heads.

Farqua's primary drug loading plant was on the outskirts of Papeete, capital city of Tahiti. A former large allied bunker was hidden in a coconut grove overlooking the city harbor. Pacific Island Imports had purchased the grove. The dope plant was a reinforced concrete structure with only one hidden entrance. The gun slits in the bunker had been sealed by concrete. An electric wire ran underground from a pole almost a half mile away. That energy source provided power for lighting, cooking, and ventilating fans. Fresh air was drawn into the bunker through several small intakes. The prime contaminated air outlet line ran underground to the edge of a cliff overlooking the harbor. At the outlet, the fumes from the bunker were released to the ocean breeze.

Certain of Swarraines carvings delivered to the Pacific Island Imports' warehouse in Papeete would be carried at night by trucks to a footpath that led to the bunker, then backpacked to the bunker. Once there, Sweeney MacCrae, an escaped, American felon with a knowledge of chemistry, was the bunker manager. He took over. Under his close supervision, the gem pupils were removed from the delivered heads. The hard wood plug to the right eye was removed and the sand drained. A condom would be inserted into the right eye area. The edges of the condom would be tacked lightly to the eye area. The condoms would then be carefully filled with either raw opium or its manufactured derivative, heroin. The drugs were gently tamped until the coconut void was filled by the expanded condom. When the coconut void was full of either drug, the eye plug would be carefully replaced, tapped until it held securely. The exposed portion of the condom would be trimmed to the plug, and the required gem pupils would be set. If the right eye had a green gem pupil, that head carving contained raw opium powder. If both eyes of the carving were green, it contained pure heroin. Other color cat's-eye gems used for pupils were inserted in the eye sockets of the decoys. Those carvings contained nothing but sand. When a shipment of the carvings left Tahiti for other Pacific Island Imports ports of entry, they were a mixture of decoys and the dope-filled heads.

On reaching a port of entry, one Pacific Island Imports employee, an upper echelon member of Farqua's inner council, would separate the dope heads from the decoys, arrange a quiet delivery of the dope heads to a nearby secret transfer point. There the heads would be emptied of their contents. The opium and heroin would be repackaged in kilo-sized blocks to be sold to the trade. The empty heads would be refilled with sand and returned to the warehouse. The "Masques of the Islands," including the sand refilled dope heads, would be sold to the art decor stores of the area. In addition, the various outlets of Pacific Island Imports sold hundreds of bolts of cloth manufactured in the southwest Pacific and Asia and delivered along with the "Masques of the Islands." The entire operation was controlled by Farqua.

Profits from the carved heads were enormous. Farqua was an avaricious wealthy man, growing wealthier by the month. His father and younger brothers who helped run the Farqua fishing and trading empire where unwitting participants in a global dope scheme. They knew nothing about the contents of the coconut heads their ships were transporting.

8

Only Sweeney, the bunker manager in Tahiti; the Chinese doper peddler, Chi Quong; and Martin DeLange, the company financial officer in New Orleans, Louisiana, knew who controlled the operation. The layers of employees in the various sectors of the enterprise helped to obscure the identity of the mastermind. To most of the Pacific Island Imports employees, their leader was an unknown, misty figure.

9

Early in the morning, following the opening night performance of the Ensemble in Washington, D.C., Linguette Swarraine telephoned the theater, and begged off from the morning rehearsal, telling Ferdinand DeShields, the directing choreographer, "Ferdinand, I really am ill this morning. I need to rest if I am going to dance tonight."

DeShields agreed reluctantly. He thought to himself: this has been happening too often. The young ballerina, for some strange reason, is losing her edge in dancing proficiency. She needs the practice. He also observed that Mary D'Quino was increasingly upset at the frequent absences of Linguette from rehearsal. When he told Mary that Linguette had begged off from that morning's practice, Mary had acidly retorted, "If that little bag of trouble is going to be my understudy, she better be here for rehearsals. Her steps are getting sloppy."

The choreographer agreed to himself that Mary was right. But what more could he do? He had already spoken to Farqua about Linguette's apparent lack of commitment to the troupe. Farqua had said he would attend to it.

10

Not long after her phone call to DeShields, nude Linguette was stretched out on the white, satin-sheeted, king-sized bed in the major suite at the Hay Adams House. Farqua, in his scarlet bathrobe, entered the bedroom from the adjoining bathroom. He approached the bed, threw off his robe, and, naked, dropped onto the satin sheets. He drew Linguette to him. She looked at Farqua beseechingly, "Ralph, before we start, I do not ask many favors of you, but I do have one now."

"Ask," said Farqua as his lustful eyes scanned her from head to toe. She was his and he intended to keep it that way for as long as he needed her.

"I have been Mary's understudy for more than six months. I have never once danced the lead role. But, I would, oh, so like to dance the lead for just a few nights. Can you arrange that with Mary?"

The request was an absolute surprise, but a welcomed opening for Farqua. He smiled. He had been wondering how to get rid of Mary D'Quino. Now he knew how. "I think that can be arranged," he said as his eyes and now his hands possessively caressed her body.

"Just how, Ralph dear?"

"Well," said her amour, "I know of a little powder that can cause her to be indisposed and incapacitated for at least a couple days. During that time, you could be the lead."

"Who would administer the powder and how and where?" asked Linguette.

"Oh, I'll give you the powder and you can put it in her drink when she's not looking. Doesn't make any difference where. It'll do the job."

"And the effects are only temporary?' asked Linguette.

"Positively," replied Farqua and he thought, I'll never have a better or safer way to get rid of Mary.

"Oh, Ralph," she sobbed, and she kissed him passionately.

Ralph took her, and abused and primitively violated her with his savage lust.

Around noon, as she as leaving, he gave her additional stupefant to take after the evening performance. He also gave her a small silver snuff box and said, "The powder is in there. Let me know when you have laced Mary's drink with it. Use it all."

"I will, my dear," replied a sore and tired Linguette as she closed the door. She headed down the hall toward the elevator, staggered slightly, regained her balance, and moaned aloud, "Holy Mother Mary, I can't take much more of this. If I can only reach my room, take a hot bath to reduce the aches, then rest and grab a bite to each before the show. I will soon be the lead. But, I just have to have a shot before I bathe."

11

Linguette had been gone only a few minutes when the parlor phone rang in Farqua's suite.

"This is Edgar," said a thin disguised voice.

"Yes, Edgar."

"Sweeney wants me to chat with you."

Ralph knew the code. He knew he was to meet Edgar in Farragut Square Park in fifteen minutes.

"I'll be there," replied Farqua, and he hung up his phone.

He didn't know Edgar personally, but the voice would be wearing an Irish walking cap with a white carnation on the brim, and there would be identification. He knew the name. Just for protection, Farqua slipped into a bullet-proof vest, then put on his shirt, shoulder holster, and slipped the snub-nosed thirty-eight into the holster. As he left the front of the hotel, he was nattily attired in a tan, tweed sport jacket, complimentary trousers and a brown short-brimmed fedora, a tourist out for a stroll.

He walked briskly to the park and saw a figure slouched on a park bench wearing a worn gray trench coat and an Irish walking cap with a white carnation pinned to the brim. He went to the bench and sat. "Edgar," he said softly.

"Right on, Mr. Deal," was the reply.

"Show me your identity," and the thin guy in the gray trench coat pulled out a D.C. police identification card with his name and small photo on it.

"Good, what's the message?"

"Last night, the opening night of the Southwest Pacific Dance Ensemble at the National, was attended by Ry Sommenberg and his guests."

"Who is Ry Sommenberg?"

"One of the biggest liquor wholesalers in D.C."

"So what?" asked Farqua.

"The Sommenbergs' guests were the senior and junior Feldmans from Philadelphia."

Farqua was surprised, but kept his cool.

"And?" asked Farqua.

"Just before the end of the first act, Martin Feldman's son, Ben Feldman, became violently ill and fainted. As he fell to the floor, he was heard by Sommenberg to say, 'I will kill that Mary D'Quino and Ralph Farqua. So help me, God, I will kill them both.' When Ben Feldman came to, he and his wife left the theater. Sommenberg says the Feldmans are staying at the Mayflower Hotel."

"How do you know all of this?"

"Because Sommenberg called the Chief early this morning, reporting the incident. I heard it from the tape."

"Is that all?" calmly asked Farqua.

"That's all, Mr. Deal. I thought you would want to know because of your connections with the dance Ensemble at the National," replied Edgar.

Farqua reached into his pocket, pulled out two fifty dollar bills, "Here's a little something extra, Edgar. Thanks. I'll see you the next time," Farqua arose, turned, and walked away.

12

Damn, how lucky can I get. Here I am trying to determine how to close the Ensemble. Not only do I now have an addict for a killer to do the job on Mary, but a fallback suspect in that red-head, Feldman, if I play it right, Farqua thought. He quickened his pace.

Upon reaching the hotel, he went to a public phone in the corridor and called the Mayflower Hotel asking to be connected to the Benjamin Feldman room. The phone rang for quite a while, then the hotel switchboard intercepted the call. "I'm trying to reach the Ben Feldmans," he said.

"Sorry, Sir, but they checked out earlier today," the operator replied.

Farqua then dialed Paoli, Pennsylvania, information for the home phone listing of Benjamin Feldman. He dialed their number. No one answered. Farqua was increasingly perturbed. Where in the hell can they be? he thought. Maybe they've gone to the Bethesda Naval Hospital. He dialed the hospital. No one by that name had checked in to any of the medical departments that day. Now he sensed real danger. He mused, if Feldman had said the name of D'Quino and Farqua last night in the box at the theater, then he must be remembering something about the taboo episode. He would have to get things moving more rapidly than he had originally planned. He called a private source in Washington, D.C.

"Bradley," he said, "It's Deal. I want a tail put on the senior Feldmans. They're staying at the Mayflower. I also want a tap on their room phone. Keep an eye on them while they're here. Follow them home to Philadelphia. When they arrive at their home, let me know through Edgar. Then keep an eye on them. Also keep a sharp lookout for the Ben Feldmans when the old rum-runner goes home. Ben Feldman and his wife live on the Hedley Estate in Paoli, Pennsylvania. Report daily to Edgar. He will reach me."

"Yes, Mr. Deal," was the reply. "We'll get to work immediately."

Farqua hung up the phone confident he had the Feldman families covered. All he had to do now was concentrate on

Mary D'Quino, Jacques, her husband, and Linguette. Now, that won't be too hard to do, he smirked to himself.

13

R alph Farqua sauntered to his suite. As he opened the door, his suite phone rang.

"Hi, Ralph, this is a Sweeney Report." It was the drawling voice of Martin DeLange back in New Orleans.

"Later," said Ralph and he banged down the receiver. He hoped the call couldn't be traced. He suspected his phone had just been tapped. There was an odd little noise on the line when he picked it up. He had heard that type of noise before. He hastily threw on this sport jacket, went back to the public phone in the hotel corridor and called his financial wizard in New Orleans. "For Christ sake Martin, I told you not to call the suite from anywhere."

"I know, Ralph, but I've been trying to reach Edgar all afternoon."

"He was with me for a while. But do be careful. I believe my line is tapped."

"OK, do you want the report?"

"Yes, give it to me now."

"For the last thirty days, Class A goods, one million two hundred thousand. Class B goods, eight hundred and fifty thousand. Two hundred and sixty heads of which one hundred are g. heads, one hundred sixty are g.g. heads. Maurice reports from customs in New York that the Ensemble underwent real scrutiny before they were cleared by the U.S. Customs Inspectors. He doesn't know whether it was because of the new regs or something else."

"New regs," said Farqua. "I've already checked. Thanks, Martin, but don't ever call me again at the hotel. Call Edgar at night, on his private number."

"Yes, Sir," was the quiet reply, and Farqua hung up the phone. He was elated at the first financial report he had received since his return to the States. All was going smoothly -- almost all, anyway.

14

The day after the night Mary D'Quino had collapsed on stage at the National Theater, Linguette, in near hysteria, called Farqua from her hotel room. He answered. She shrieked over the phone, "You bastard, you made me kill her."

"I did what?" asked Farqua.

"I just heard on the radio that Mary died late last night, and that the police are now hunting for Jacques, her husband. He has disappeared. The powder you gave me killed her."

"My dear, Linguette, I gave you no powder. You must be hallucinating, too much stupefant. Maybe Jacques gave you some kind of powder. But, I didn't. Please be ready to take the lead tonight. I also heard the radio report. I'm investigating the matter right now. You didn't poison Mary. No one knows who did. Calm down."

Linguette continued, "Last night after Mary fainted on stage, I went to her dressing room to change costumes. When I reached the room, a woman was there. She said she was Caroline Morgan and had just called for an ambulance. Do you know Caroline Morgan?"

"No," said Farqua. "I've never met the woman. But, I know how to reach her."

"I wonder how she got there. Do you know?" asked Linguette.

"No, my Dear, but I'll check and see, then let you know."

Farqua hesitated, then continued. "I'm sure I know who she was with and where they are."

"Who is 'they?'" asked Linguette.

"Don't worry your sweet head, just be ready to dance tonight," said Ralph.

"Ralph, are you sure you didn't give me the powder?"

"Positive, my dear."

And Linguette, looking at the silver snuff box on her bureau, still half filled with the white substance, became completely disoriented. "Good bye, my dear Ralph," she said and hung up the phone.

Ralph just knew he had Linguette under control. She would be ready to dance by evening. That'll keep her calm until I can finish the job, smirked a satisfied Ralph. Then he mused, Damn! My line is tapped. I just hope my conversation threw them off.

15

He had no sooner hung up from his conversation with Linguette, when his phone rang again. He was nervous. He glanced at the mantel clock. It read 1:40 p.m. He picked up the receiver. "Mr. Deal, it's Edgar, meet me at the trash can in ten minutes. There are several matters you should know," and the phone went dead.

The communications team in the Carlton Hotel had heard both conversations. They were confused about Linguette's call. They would have to talk to Springer. When Agent Pfeister heard Edgar's call, his heart raced. He picked up a camera with a long-distance zoom lens, threw on his fur-lined leather jacket, and headed for the door. "Boys, we'll soon know where that D.C. leak comes from. I think it's Edgar, whoever is Edgar." He strolled out the hotel entrance and walked casually down the street toward the Hay Adams House to put Farqua under surveillance.

16

Farqua quickly pulled on a sport coat, left his suite, and hurried through the front entrance of the Hay Adams House. He walked rapidly to Lafayette Park. Little did he realize he was now under the watchful eye of Agent Pfeister. Ralph, as he approached the park, noticed the glistening elegancy of the White House off Pennsylvania Avenue, imprisoned by the high wrought iron fence. Then he observed the contrast between that elegant protected area and the cluttered park where several homeless sat on benches, bundled in weird assortments of jackets and patched blankets. Their worldly possessions were in dilapidated pushcarts, probably stolen from local grocery stores and remodeled to suit the whims of their present possessors, he mused.

Ralph saw the Irish cap with the white carnation pinned to its brim enter a park walkway. He hastened to meet the informer. Edgar motioned to an unoccupied bench. The two men sat, and unknown to both, were repeatedly photographed by Pfeister from a concealed area on the north side of H Street just across from the park.

"Do you know a Gregory Morgan?" inquired Edgar.

"Yes," said a surprised Farqua. "Why do you ask?"

"I heard a phone tape earlier this morning at headquarters."

"And?"

"It was a brief conversation between Morgan and Lt. David Springer, Chief Detective of the Homicide Bureau."

"What'd they say?"

"Morgan asked Springer if he had ever heard of Pacific Island Imports or the Southwest Pacific Dance Ensemble. Springer said yes."

"What then?"

"They decided to talk about it at the D.C. Lawyers Club. They're probably there now."

"Why not at headquarters?" asked Farqua.

"Beats me. I heard they are former law school buddies. Maybe they want to chat over a beer."

"Doesn't sound right to me. You're sure they're not on to you?" asked Farqua as he glanced around the park.

"Not a chance, Mr. Deal," Edgar said calmly.

But Farqua's instincts told him differently.

"Are you sure you weren't followed?"

"Positive," replied Edgar.

"Thanks," said Farqua, and he handed the officer another C bill. "From now on, don't call me at the hotel for any reason. You'll hear from one of my men how to reach me."

"Yes, Sir, Mr. Deal," said Edgar and he left.

17

Pfeister was delighted. He felt sure he had all the pictures he needed to identify the leak source from D.C. Police Headquarters. He headed back to the hotel room at the Carlton.

18

Farqua hastened back to his hotel, deep in troubled thought. He remembered Linguette telling him that she had met a woman named Caroline Morgan who had, last night, used the phone in Mary's dressing room. Mrs. Morgan said she had called an ambulance for Mary. Farqua thought, that had to be Gregory Morgan's wife. He just couldn't believe that Mrs. Morgan knew any of the Ensemble. She had to be with her husband. For some strange reason, she and her husband, Gregory Morgan, had been backstage at the time Mary was stricken. Now this conversation between Morgan and Detective Springer. He had better hurry and find out what more Linguette really knew about last night.

Farqua entered the Hay Adams House and went to a public phone. He called Chi Quong. "Chi, we may have some damage control to handle. I'll pick you up at the Pennsylvania Avenue entrance to the Willard in twenty minutes." He didn't wait for an answer. He went to his room, put on a shoulder holster, slipped a .38 caliber pistol into it, buckled on a back waist belt holster and slipped in a derringer, just as an added precaution. He packed all of his clothes and gear. Then, he called for his chauffeured limo to be at the front door of his hotel in ten minutes. He took his gear to the lobby, checked out at the cashier's desk, and went over to a public phone. He called the Key Bridge Marriott Hotel in Roslyn, Virginia, and asked to speak to Mr. Finkle in Room 415. Finkle answered.

"Reggie, this is Deal; I'll be there in about an hour. Have the info I requested ready. Alert the boys, we may have a little job to do."

"Yes, Sir. We'll be ready," and Farqua took his suit cases out to the limo, and headed for the Willard.

19

Farqua drove up in the limo, Chi Quong entered. "What is the matter?" asked Quong.

"I'm not sure, but I don't like it. Gregory Morgan was at the theater last night, and today he's meeting with Lieutenant Springer of the D.C. Homicide Bureau."

"So what?"

"That meeting concerns Pacific Island Imports and the Ensemble."

"How do you know?"

"I have ways, Chi. I have ways. And that's not all. Linguette told me earlier today that a Mrs. Morgan was backstage last night when Mary D'Quino collapsed. I'm sure she is Gregory Morgan's wife. Why in the hell was she backstage? And, I just received two other reports. One, Jacques Montagne has disappeared, just vanished. The last my boys saw of him was after breakfast at the Harrington as he entered the elevator headed for his room. He's bound to have gotten off on the fifth floor. They said the elevator floor indicator didn't stop until it reached number five. When they checked his room a little later, he was gone. Second, the Ben Feldmans came in from Philadelphia last night and are registered at the Mayflower. I've sent Don and Carlos over to the hotel to look around."

"Where we headed now?" asked Chi.

"To Linguette. I want to ask her a few more questions about last night. Then, after we check with the boys, I think we will do a little sight-seeing across the Potomac."

"What sight-see?" asked Chi.

"We'll take a look at where Gregory Morgan lives. I know he and Jacques were friends on the island. Morgan witnessed the taboo with Jacques. If he saw the program last night -- damn, I don't know what might happen. I wish I had insisted Mary cut out that routine. That dance has bothered me from the time we landed in the U.S."

20

The limo pulled up in front of the Harrington Hotel and blocked the main hotel access entrance. Farqua noticed a police squad car parked in the alley alongside the hotel. His blood pressure rose like that of a wary carnivore. He sensed danger. When the doorman opened the limo door, Farqua stepped out. "Chi, you stay here. I'll be back shortly." Then, he slipped the doorman ten dollars and said, "I'll only be a few minutes."

"Sure," said the doorman.

As Farqua nonchalantly entered the hotel, he was positive that the two foyer loungers were D.C. detectives. He pretended not to notice. He crossed the lobby and entered a waiting elevator, got off on Linguette's floor, looked down the corridor toward her room and stopped short.

A uniformed policeman was sitting on a straight chair in front of her room door. What in the hell goes on? he mused. Quietly and without causing the bluecoat to turn and observe him, he disappeared around a corridor corner and, seeing the inside emergency stair entrance, went down the steps to the lobby. He slowly and carefully opened the stairway door to the lobby, observed no one in sight, then sauntered to the front desk area. A young clerk was on duty.

"Will you please ring Room 307 and tell Miss Linguette Swarraine that Mr. Deal is on his way up there."

"I can tell you, Sir, she ain't in."

"How would you know, young man?"

"Because I watched as her body was wheeled through the lobby and out the door about an hour ago. She was dead as a mackerel after drying three days on a beach in the sun."

21

Farqua, for the first time, was frightened, momentarily stunned as if he had walked unobservantly into a large, heavy plate glass door. Then, he became curious. How in the name of God did she die? Who or what killed her? He had talked to her earlier and, though she acted emotional, that wasn't unusual. He had assured her she wasn't responsible for Mary's death and would have the lead tonight. She had always believed him before. There was no reason for her to change now. He knew her. He controlled her.

Farqua went over to the most isolated pay phone in the lobby, looked up the D.C. Morgue and called. "This is Earl Deal calling. A distant young relative of mine disappeared last night. She's about five foot two, brunette, with a slight Polynesian appearance. Her name is Linguette Swarraine. Do you have the body of such a young woman?"

The morgue attendant said, "Wait a minute, let me check the index on last night's and today's arrivals." There was a brief period of silence, then the morgue attendant said, "No, no such young lady last night or today. We do have two unidentified homeless men from the Fifth Street area and an unidentified old lady who was killed late last night on Florida Avenue, by a hit and run driver. But, no young lady -- no Linguette Swarraine."

"Thank you," said Farqua. He mustn't panic he told himself. He'd been in worse episodes than this, for instance, in Brussels, where two of his exchange men had been killed by the opposition. Fortunately, the carved heads had been recovered by two guards following the exchange couriers. And in France when a Paris art dealer had dropped one of the masks that had slipped by exchange. It hit the tiled floor with a resounding thunk. For some strange reason, the husk split, the condom broke, and heroin splattered on the floor. Fortunately, the salesman from Pacific Island Imports was on hand. Before the art dealer could determine just what had happened, the error had been corrected. The art dealer's body was found the next day in the Seine River. The papers said he had been depressed for some time and undoubtedly had committed suicide.

22

Farqua walked back to the desk clerk. "You say you saw the body when it left the hotel?"

"Yes, Sir."

"Who was in the lobby?"

"I didn't know any of them, Sir. But earlier I relieved Mr. Stedhick, the day manager, when a D.C. detective and another gentleman asked him to take them to Miss Swarraine's room. That's when they found her dead. Stedhick has gotten potted since then. He says he never wants to see another sight like that."

"Thank you very much," said Farqua and he slipped the clerk a twenty dollar bill. The clerk smiled in appreciation, but wondered why such information deserved a twenty dollar tip.

23

Farqua walked toward the hotel door, then stopped. Damn, he thought, those two men had to be Dave Springer and that snooping bastard Morgan. Morgan must have been backstage last night. Then he had a conversation with Springer earlier today. For some reason, the two of them had visited Linguette. They must have arrived at the hotel shortly after her death. He pondered. I wonder if they found anything? The snuff box? Now he couldn't find Linguette's body, Jacques had disappeared, and he would bet so had the Feldmans. Then it hit him, Morgan, that son-of-a-bitch, was the key. The former 460.5 exec had to have stumbled on even more than his actions revealed. Farqua's anger knew no bounds. He shook with rage, the mad rage of his ancestor, Raphelo D'Farqua. He sensed his whole enterprise was at risk. He had to get to Morgan and fast.

24

Farqua hurried out to the limo. "We've got problems, real problems," he said to Chi Quong as he entered the car. "Take us to the Key Bridge Marriott," he barked at the chauffeur. Farqua's warped mind and animal instincts were aquiver with adrenalin. He reasoned, Gregory Morgan's house and whoever might be there could be the key to saving the enterprise and himself. If Mrs. Morgan was among those in the house, she could serve as a bargaining chip, if need be. He would soon know.

Farqua, with Chi Quong in tow, knocked on the door to room four fifteen of the hotel.

"Who's there?" asked a gruff voice.

"Mr. Deal and a friend," was the response.

Reggie Finkle opened the door. Farqua and Chi entered. The room was occupied by Reggie and two other henchmen, each with his suit coat off, revealing their shoulder holster weapons.

Farqua's cold, gray-green eyes bore into Reggie. "What have you found out?" he asked.

"Mr. Deal, Gregory Morgan is married. His wife's name is Caroline. They have a son about thirteen or fourteen years old, goes by the nickname, J.R. They live in North Arlington, Virginia, on a corner lot. The house, a big rambler, is set back about a hundred feet from the street. The lot is large, with a wrought iron fence across the front. There are two cement posts, one close to each side of the driveway entrance. The driveway encircles the house. The west lot line along the side street is bordered by a six-foot chain link fence. It is so heavily entangled with honeysuckle and wild blackberry bushes, it's damned near impenetrable. The only real access to the house is by the driveway.

"The house phone number is KL5-5760 and the phone line runs to a pole on the street corner of the lot. It will be easy to cut. Just climb the pole and break it at the junction box. I can put in a cross tie when the line is cut so it will appear still connected."

"Who was in the Morgan house when you went by?" asked Farqua.

"Mr. Deal, we stopped near the property and watched for a while. No one came in or out. I don't know who is there at the present. There was a red Plymouth convertible alongside the house in the circular driveway. The car takes up the full width of that little road. If we're going over there, I don't suggest we go into the driveway. It's kinda' tight if we have to back out in a hurry."

"Good work, Reggie," said Farqua. He went over to the room phone and dialed the Butler hanger at National Airport. "This is Mr. Deal speaking. Have the Pacific Island Imports plane ready to take off any time after six p.m. Notify Dawson, the pilot, to stand by from that time on. Thanks, Fred."

25

"Let's get a bite to eat in the grill," the so-called "Mr. Deal" said to his aides. "It may be quite a while before we eat again."

After a quick meal, Farqua said, "Reggie, you take the rental van with Vic and Sweets. Sweets, you handle the walkie-talkie in your vehicle. My friend, Chi, will handle the one in the limo. I'll be wired. Vic, you handle the wire receiver in the van. If I need help when I go into the house, I'll let you know.

"Reggie, you're sure you saw no one?"

"Positive, Mr. Deal."

Victor Yokart, Sweets Mastive and Reggie Finkle wondered who was the quiet chink with their boss.

"Wait here," said Mr. Deal and Reggie watched intently as his boss went to a lobby phone. He saw Mr. Deal dial a number and then heard him say in a gruff, disguised voice, "Sorry, wrong number." He watched as his boss replaced the receiver. He observed the shrewd, sadistic grin that mirrored Mr. Deal's face. He's one cold-blooded bastard. I'm glad I'm not his enemy, thought Reggie.

Just before they entered their respective vehicles, Farqua turned to Reggie, "While my friend and I are cruising the neighborhood in the limo, I want you to climb the pole and cut the Morgan's phone line. Park the van just east of the Morgan's lot line, on the front street. After you cut the phone service, return to the truck and report to me."

"Done," said Reggie.

The truck and limo left the motel headed for the George Washington Parkway that would lead them to North Arlington, Virginia.

Part VIII

Unmasked

1

The phone rang on the little table next to the wing chair in which Caroline sat. She answered and said, "Hello, Mrs. Morgan speaking." A gruff voice said, "Sorry, wrong number," and hung up.

Caroline wasn't perturbed. The Morgans' phone number was much the same as Julie's Laundry on Lee Highway. Every now and then someone misdialed.

2

She turned to Tina, "How about helping me make a few cheese sandwiches? None of you have had a morsel to eat since you arrived earlier this morning."

"I'd be glad to," said Tina, and she arose to help her host.

"I'm kinda' hungry," said Ben.

"I am not, I wish I was," said a nervous Jacques as he carefully studied the den. First he looked at the mirror on the wall between the windows that reflected the den doorway. He thought, if I stood near the wall to the left of the fireplace, I would be hidden from someone partially opening the den door. But, I could clearly see from the mirror whoever is standing in the doorway. Then his eyes focused on the fireside tool set stand. Among other items held by it, was a sturdy log poker with its heavy brass handle. He again glanced toward the den door. He now knew what his course of action would be if it became necessary and he had a chance. From his years of contact with Farqua, and after hearing Mary's diary, Jacques was the one person in the room who truly knew the devious, cunning creature that inhabited the frame of Ralph Dupui Farqua. Jacques was fearful of the immediate future for everyone in the house. He resolved he would die trying to keep the slick bastard from his mad endeavors. He sensed that

Farqua was near. Yet, he didn't want to unduly frighten the others by alluding to his sense of pending danger.

3

Caroline reentered the room with a tray of sandwiches. Tina brought in a tray with a fresh pot of tea, cups and cookies. She placed her tray on an end table, turned to Caroline and asked, "How old is J.R.?"

"He's thirteen and a half," responded Caroline.

"You're so fortunate to have him."

"I know, but I wish we could have had more."

"I wish we could just have one," sighed Tina.

"It's not too late for you," responded Caroline.

"It isn't as if we haven't tried," said Ben with a faint glimmer of a smile. The others tittered.

"Maybe someday, maybe someday soon," said Caroline.

"I hope, I hope, I hope," responded Tina.

As they ate, the conversation became general and trivial.

4

After the foursome finished their sandwiches, were sipping hot tea and basking in the heatilator warmth from the glowing wood embers in the fireplace, Caroline said, "I'm getting worried. I'm going to try to raise Greg on his car radio." She went to the transceiver and tried to reach him. No answer. "I wonder where he can be. He's been a lot longer than I expected."

5

They chatted for a while about the Ensemble. Jacques told how long and hard the dance group had worked to master the dances. He talked about life on the European tour, then life on Bora Bora and how he truly hated being away from home and his daughter. How different the island life style was in contrast to the life style of the major western countries in which the Ensemble had performed, even the U.S. He was attempting to keep Ben's, Tina's, Caroline's, and his mind away from the tensions he could feel mounting.

Then, he too fell silent, but for a reason. All eyes fixed on him.

"I heard a slightly different sound," he said quietly. His hearing, because of his island upbringing while growing to manhood, was more acute than the others.' They held their breath in suspense. Jacques moved with catlike grace to the fireplace set stand. His hand closed around the poker, and he lifted it noiselessly. The cockles on the back of Ben Feldman's neck rose. He, too, sensed danger. Tina stuffed her fist in her mouth, her blue eyes were saucer round with fright. Caroline knew Jacques was right. She reached over and silently picked up the phone receiver from the stand to call the police. The line was dead. She quietly replaced the receiver on the set and sat back as far in the wing chair as she could. Her breathing was labored with fear, not just for herself, but for J.R. She glanced at her watch, it read 5:30 p.m. Dear Lord, she thought, don't let him stumble in on this hornet's nest and why didn't I lock and deadbolt the front door? Please, please make soccer practice a little longer.

Jacques, with stealth developed by early years of island hunting, noiselessly stepped to the side of the fireplace that would be hidden from view of anyone entering the room, until the door was more than half open -- and all waited.

6

The den door slowly and silently opened not quite half way, concealing Jacques from the view of the entrant. Farqua stood in the opening. His gray-green eyes were spitting beams of raging fury. His left hand dropped from the door knob as he viewed the threesome in front of him. His voice was barely audible, a thin hissing snarl. "I should have known, I should have known from the very beginning."

Ben Feldman was aghast at what he saw. Before him sneered a visage even more grotesque than any of Swarraine's

"Masques of the Islands." Farqua's face was contorted with animal rage. Ben thought, my God, he has gone completely berserk.

"You must be Caroline Morgan, Mrs. Gregory Morgan," snarled Farqua.

"I am," she replied as coolly as possible.

"And, where is your husband?"

"I don't know. He went into Washington hours ago."

Slowly and deliberately, Farqua drew his thirty-eight caliber revolver from his shoulder holster. "And you, I know, you red-headed bastard. Even if your memory has returned, you'll never use it."

The muscles in Farqua's face twitched, pulling his lips apart, revealing his teeth, like a maddened dog.

"And this is your old lady?" he asked pointing the weapon at Tina.

Tina, with her fist jammed in her mouth, nodded affirmatively.

Farqua could not yet see Jacques, hidden behind the partly opened door.

"Well, well," he hissed. "What a happy gathering," and saliva drooled from the right side of his mouth. "Don't any of you dare to move."

The viewed threesome sat speechless with numbing fear.

Each was sure that death was imminent.

Farqua's mad mind was trying to evolve a scheme. "You and you," he said, as he pointed the pistol at the Feldmans, "are in my way. Mrs. Morgan, first you will be my shield. You will come with me when I finish with the Feldmans. The authorities will think Jacques has killed the Feldmans as a result of Ben's threats in Box A on opening night, and that Jacques has taken you, Mrs. Morgan, as hostage because you learned how he killed Mary. The police are scouring the area for him, but my men will find him first.

Later, Mrs. Morgan, you will be my air ticket of safe passage out of the country. My plane is waiting for us now. Slowly, Farqua raised his revolver, aiming at Ben Feldman's head.

Ben Feldman held his breath, waiting for the shot.

7

J.R. was returning home from soccer practice with his goalie friend, Tim Polk. As they approached the Polk house, J.R. said goodbye to Tim, crossed the Polk's backyard, and squeezed through their secret opening in the back fence separating the two properties. My gosh, he was thirsty. His coach, Ted Albright, hadn't brought the usual cooler filled with Gatorade or ice water. WHAM! The kitchen door slammed shut behind him, and he immediately headed for the kitchen sink and the much needed drink of water.

8

Jacques could see Farqua's every movement through the mirror.

The completely unexpected loud noise surprised the drug lord. He turned his head and glanced down the hall toward the source of the noise. When he did, Jacques sprang from behind the door and, with every ounce of strength he could muster, brought the poker down on the outstretched pistol arm of Farqua. A shot rang out. Ben Feldman lurched backwards. Tina fainted, and Caroline flinched at the noise, closed her eyes, and started to shiver.

A wild animal-like scream of pain emitted from Farqua. The pistol flew from the hand of his broken wrist, and slid on the floor under the wing chair in which Caroline sat. All heard the shrill howls of sirens as police and other security cars approached the area. Those sounds contributed to the instant confusion.

Jacques took advantage of the moment, lunged at Farqua. So did Ben Feldman, even though blood trickled down his left arm. The two men tried their damnedest to bring down the maddened drug lord. But, even with only one arm, Farqua possessed a wounded carnivore's strength and fury. Completely berserk, he shook off his assailants, raced through the living room towards the front door, screaming, "Reggie, Vic, I need you."

As Reggie and Vic started to leave the van, Arlington County police cars blocked the street intersection, east and west of the house. The two men ducked back into the van. An unmarked black Plymouth, with siren howling and a red light flashing on its top, jumped the curb, swung around a police car, and roared up the Morgans' driveway. More unmarked cars, with sirens howling, arrived near the scene. The FBI swat team emerged from those cars and cautiously headed toward the van and limo.

Farqua, now little more than a wild, unthinking animal, came running out of the house headed for the limo. He saw Dave Springer and Greg Morgan leave the Plymouth. He recognized Greg. His animal instincts howled for revenge against the brunet bastard he was now sure had ruined everything for him. He reached behind his back with his good hand for his second concealed weapon as he lunged toward Greg Morgan.

"Don't," yelled Springer.

Instead, Farqua with a wounded animal's blind fury attempted to draw his derringer as he continued his rush toward Greg. Greg watched, helpless, as if rooted to the spot. Farqua was not near enough for the Arlington lawyer to act. He heard two vicious silencer shots. Farqua pitched forward onto the ground almost at Greg's feet. The drug lord's body quivered, like that of a mortally wounded animal. The inherited madness of his ancestor, Ralphelo D'Farqua, that had festered a lifetime in Ralph, had finally consumed him. That madness left silently to reenter some unfortunate future member of the family.

Dave Springer, with a silencer .38 in his hand, looked with pity at the fallen madman. "God knows, he deserved it.

I hated to do it, but it was the only way. He'd have killed you in another second."

"Thank Christ, you were here," said a shaken Greg. Then he turned and ran toward the house.

Suddenly the van took off. There was a fusillade of shots exchanged by the van occupants and the swat team. The van crashed into one of the large entrance posts to Greg's driveway. An ornamental, gilded, squatting lion on top of the post fell from the pedestal and crashed through the van windshield. The FBI and Arlington Police charged the van and limousine. The van occupants died in the fuselage of shots. A dazed Chi Quong and the limo driver emerged from the limousine with their hands held high over their heads.

Greg ran up the front steps, and at that moment, J.R. appeared in the doorway, "Holy smoke, Dad, what happened?"

"A lot, let's get back inside. I'll tell you a little later. Is your mother all right?"

"She's seems okay, but she's shivering, and Mrs. Feldman has come around. Dad, Mr. Feldman is really bleeding from his arm."

"Anyone else hurt?" queried Greg.

"No. Mr. Montagne is putting a tourniquet on Mr. Feldman's arm. Mom says he should go to the hospital right away."

9

Greg shut the front door, hurried through the living room to the den.

Caroline saw him enter. She raced to his arms. "Oh, thank God, you're here and not hurt." Greg held her tight. Her shivering stopped.

"The madness is over," he said gently.

She took a couple deep breaths, looked at her husband, then at Jacques, and said, "You just can't imagine the bravery of Jacques. I didn't believe he could do what he did."

Greg looked around the room. Tina huddled in a big arm chair, still shaken, had come to, was crying, and with her good hand was rubbing the knuckles on the hand she had bitten into before she passed out. Jacques was tightening the improvised pressure tourniquet on Ben's arm. He saw Greg and said, "Holy Mother of Mary, you arrived in the nick of time. Ben should get to a hospital to staunch his wound. I do not think it is too severe, just a flesh wound. He is one game guy. He tried to help even after he was wounded."

Greg smiled at his island friend. "And you, Jacques, are something else," responded Greg.

"It was the least I could do, after what I ignored in all the years past. If he had killed me, I could have cared less. At least I tried to help."

"That wasn't just help, that was salvation," said Greg.

10

A uniformed Arlington policeman came into the house, walked through the den door, and took one look at Ben's bloodsoaked arm. "Let's get you to the hospital for a little help," he said.

"Please, I'm his wife, can I go with him?" asked a recovering Tina.

"Sure, said Officer Joe Fields, "It won't take long. I'll bring you both back here when they've finished tending to your husband."

11

While the Feldmans were leaving for the hospital, two men, complete strangers to Greg, strode up the driveway to the house, entered, and walked to the den. Greg looked at them in surprise. One was a slim brunet with a definitely French mustache. The other was a solidly-built, wavy-haired blond. "Which one of you is Jacques Montagne?" asked the mustached one.

Greg instantly became cautious.

287

"Don't worry," said the wavy-haired blond to Greg, "We really didn't mean to barge in so boldly, but the door was open. I'm Agent Albert Pfiester, FBI. I know you are Greg Morgan from Dave Springer's description of you." Pointing to the slim, mustached brunet, Pfiester said, "This is Henri Stover, so-called Under Secretary for Tourism at the French Embassy, but he's really a ranking member of the French Sureté Internationale. He just wants to meet and speak with Jacques."

Dave Springer walked in the door. "I see you two have met. I've known Albert almost as long as I've known you, Greg. He's one of the FBI's best communications experts."

Greg and Jacques shook hands with the two men.

"Before we go any further," said Dave to Greg, "Pfiester found out that the mole, 'Edgar,' at D.C. Police Headquarters was our former schoolmate, mealy-mouthed, Manfred Hasty, Assistant Director of Communications for the D.C. Police. He took off after he had intercepted some FBI calls advancing the sting date. He's on his way by commercial plane to Costa Rica. We'll have a welcoming committee awaiting him when he lands. Right now, the sting is in full progress -- wherever. When you chased Farqua into the open, the international sting operation had to move. But -- it's not your fault, you had no idea what we were doing. We now have Chi Quong and many more, thanks to you. How your household escaped with nothing more than an arm wound, I have no idea."

"I bet I do," said a grinning Greg. "A door slam."

12

J.R. was in the background absorbing each step of the most interesting, wild episode he had ever seen in his young life. He watched out the front picture window as Farqua's canvas-covered body and the three bodies of Farqua's henchmen were placed in the Hall's Hill Volunteer Rescue ambulance and driven away. And, he saw the big wrecker tow the van from the driveway entrance. How in the world did my dad ever get involved in this mess? My gosh, it sounded like a war movie what with all the shots and sirens. J.R. had not been told of his dad's World War II episode involving the taboo. Neither Greg nor Caroline had deemed it wise to talk about the event in front of their son. J.R. thought, am I glad I stayed in the kitchen until the fireworks were over.

Eyes peeked out the curtains of front windows up and down the block. Not a single household in the area had ever seen or heard such a fracas. And, their friends, the Morgans, seemed such genteel, quiet, good neighbors.

Will and Frances Barton, Greg's next-door neighbors, watched the unfolding saga from an upstairs window of their house. Will turned to his wife, "When Greg says 'watch,' you can bet your fanny it's gonna' be worth watching. I've never in my life seen such exciting, bizarre happenings as we've witnessed in the last twenty-four hours."

"Will, I've told you, time and time again, if you wanted an exciting life, you should have studied law, not run a men's clothing store. The wildest thing that ever happened to you was when some shoplifter stole two Harris Tweed sport jackets. I thought you would have a stroke."

"Those coats were expensive," said her matter-of-fact husband.

"Bull!" retorted Frances. "I've just got to talk to Caroline."

"Please wait until the police leave."

"Oh, I'll do that. I'll wait until tomorrow morning, but no later than 10:30 a.m. My cup of curiosity is overflowing already."

"Oh, boy," sighed Will. And, they continued to watch.

13

No press photographers or newspaper reporters were permitted on the premises by the police and FBI. The excitement began to subside. Soon most of the police and FBI agents left the scene. Only FBI Agent Pfiester; the French police specialist, Henri Stover; Dave Springer; and Arlington Police Sergeant, Spencer Rappaport remained.

Pfiester said, "I'm going out to my car. I've got some radio reports to make. And, I have to check on the sting. It's in full swing here, in the Pacific, and Europe. I'll be back in shortly."

Spencer Rappaport looked at the group. "How about my going to the Colonels and bringing back some fried chicken, french fries and cokes. You gotta' eat something after all this commotion."

"You're so right, Officer, I'm starved," said J.R.

Greg took a couple of bills out of his pocket. Spencer said, "Wait till I get back," and he was off.

14

Just as Spencer was leaving, Ben and Tina returned from the hospital. Ben was a little shaken, but the injury was not severe. Five or six stitches had done the job and a neat bandage covered the injured area of his upper arm. He saw Jacques and grinned, "Jacques, thanks to you, I'm alive and kicking, but not very high."

Jacques smiled. Henri Stover approached him. "Mr. Montagne, I have received word from the French authorities. The Ensemble will be disbanded here. The French government will pay the expense of the members' return home. The government will also foot whatever leftover legitimate expenses there may be. And you, when you return to Bora Bora, will resume your position as Superintendent of the island schools, if you so wish. Will you please call me tomorrow morning so we can begin to make arrangements." He gave Jacques his business card. Then he added, "Your government thanks you for your services. There will be a ceremony at the Government House in Tahiti upon your return home. And, by the way, your father is still Chieftain and will be until he dies. Your wife's body is being returned to the island for burial. So is the body of Linguette Swarraine."

Jacques' eyes filled with tears of sadness and thanksgiving. He thought, poor Mary, she is no longer tormented by conflicting inner voices. Now, he would, at least, be returning home to his daughter, his father, and his island. His travels had only emphasized his longing to return to the people and way of life he loved. "Merci beaucoup," he said softly.

15

Greg walked with the two officers to the door. As Dave Springer approached the front door, he turned to Greg. "On the surface you are a quiet, unassuming guy, but hidden underneath that rather controlled exterior, you've got more intuition, guts and drive than any guy I have ever known, and I've known quite a few. Call me, Greg, whenever you need me, and I'll be there. And, I'll call you when I need a local ferret and counsel."

Greg smiled, "Thanks, Dave. I'll even let you use my Radar Rape Machine on special occasions." Dave guffawed. He and Henri Stover left.

16

Officer Rappaport soon returned with food. The Morgan family, the Ben Feldmans, and Jacques, each with adrenalin still flowing, attempted to eat, but the only one who appeared truly hungry was J.R. He did a noble job on the fried chicken and french fries.

17

After supper, Tina turned to Caroline, "Would you mind if we returned to our hotel tonight? There's a lot we should do before we leave for home tomorrow. And, I understand from Agent Pfiester our room is a mess as a result of Farqua's men trying to find out where we had gone."

"Heavens, no," said Caroline.

Ben looked at Caroline, then at Greg and Jacques. "I'll never be able to adequately thank each of you." His gaze rested on Jacques. He was committing to memory an unforgettable image. "You saved my life, maybe all of our lives. And, Mary's diary was a revelation to me, a bigger help than you will ever realize! I'll remain in your debt as long as I live." He looked at Greg, smiled and said, "Consider me your friend for life. I will you. These last two days I will treasure forever. I never expected to live through anything like this."

"Neither did I," said Jacques.

Greg grinned at the threesome. "The feeling's mutual," he said.

"We'll help you all get packed," said Caroline.

"I'll take you in town when you're ready. We'll have to go in Caroline's Plymouth convertible. My car is still at the Lawyers Club parking garage," said Greg.

"Gee, it's been exciting," said J.R. after he had downed the last of a second glass of milk. "I'm darned glad I stayed in the kitchen until the fireworks were over."

"So am I," replied his dad.

18

When all were packed, the Morgan family walked with them to the door. Greg opened it. Tina turned to J.R., "Thank you, J.R., it really was you who gave us a chance to live. I hope I have a son like you."

"You're welcome, Mrs. Feldman, but all I did was slam the door. I had no idea what was going on."

"Holy Mother of Mary, that slam was enough," said Jacques. Then he reached over and kissed Caroline on her cheek. "I will never regret having given those cufflinks and earrings. Please visit the Isle of Everyman. The door will always be open."

"Who knows, maybe some day we will," responded Caroline.

The trio followed Greg down the steps to Caroline's car.

19

Greg returned home from taking his guests to their hotels. His house was dark, except for the porch light. The lion had been replaced on the entrance post pedestal, but the figure was slightly askew. A police car was blocking the driveway entrance. Damn, that's a comforting sight to see tonight, Greg thought. He stopped and walked over to the car. The driver's side door opened and Sergeant Rappaport shined his flashlight on Greg. "I just wanted to make sure, Mr. Morgan, I'll pull up so you can enter."

"Thanks, Sergeant, my family will sleep more comfortably tonight knowing you are here. And, by the way, how much was the food?"

"It's on the Department, and so that you know, someone will be around until your phone is fixed tomorrow morning."

"Tell the phone company not to hurry," said Greg as he reentered his car. "Thank the Chief for me, I'll call him tomorrow."

"I'll pass the word," said Rappaport.

20

Greg entered the driveway and drove up to his house. He walked up the front steps, unlocked the front door, and entered.

"I'm so glad you're home. I know you must be dead tired," said Caroline. She arose in the dark from the sofa by the front picture window, went over to Greg, placed her arms around his neck and kissed him. Caroline led him back to the sofa. They sat in the dark and she held one of his hands in both of hers. "I've been sitting here, watching out the window for your return and thinking about a lot of things."

"Like what?"

"Fate and luck, I guess. How we just happened to go to the National Theater, and the Ensemble was on stage. How one dance was the trigger for a series of events I couldn't ever imagine. And how lucky we are that you were right about Jacques Montagne and Ben Feldman. But, most of all, J.R. It was simply fate that he came in when he did. I've been thinking, my God, how lucky we are he wasn't hurt. I know that would have marred both our lives. And you, you're just something different from anyone I've ever known or expect to. However, now and then you really do tempt fate, even if it's for a noble cause. What would J.R. and I do without you? I shudder to think."

Greg was quiet for a few seconds, then, "Honey, I've been troubled for years by the memory of the taboo. Deep down inside, something about it really bothered me. When the past became present, I just had to try to find the real cause of the episode. I hope you'll forgive me for the anguish I've caused you and for the jeopardy I put us all in."

"Greg, you wouldn't be you, if you hadn't taken the action you did. But, sometimes your intense focus on a cause has unexpected, unanticipated results. We've been lucky, oh, so lucky, but how long can that good luck last?"

"Caroline, don't think any more about any of it tonight. It's over and there won't be another like it."

"Seein's believin,' my beloved," said Caroline and she leaned over and tenderly kissed Greg on his cheek.

"Where's J.R.?" asked Greg.

"He's bushed, and gone to bed. You know, he has to get up early tomorrow morning and deliver his papers."

"Yes, I forgot for the moment. This has been quite a day," and Greg slouched wearily against the back of the sofa.

"Not just a day, a wild two days, the wildest I ever hope to spend," responded Caroline.

Greg nodded agreement. "I'm glad the telephone won't be connected until tomorrow. We can try and get a good night's sleep before the calls start."

"I don't care if the phone is never fixed, now that we're safe and unharmed," responded Caroline.

Unmasked

"You know, Hon," said Greg, "Despite the old cliche, sometimes first impressions can be a damned big mistake. For instance, take Farqua, Mary, and Ben Feldman. How wrong I was about each of them."

"I know, I know, I've known the fallacy of that cliche for years," said Caroline tenderly, and she added, "after I really got to know you."

"Thanks, Hon. Let's hit the sack. I'm dog tired, but still wound up like a new spring clock."

"I think I can help relieve that feeling," said Caroline, her brown eyes sparkling in the dark. She rose, held out her hand. Greg stood and put his arm around her waist. The twosome, aided by the soft glow of the hall night light, headed toward their bedroom.

Part IX

The Ending

1

The next morning, in their hotel room, Tina awoke before Ben. She saw his injured arm resting atop the bedcovers. The bandage was holding well. Then she looked at his sleeping countenance. Waves of relief swept over her. He had helped save their lives yesterday. Tears of affection and thankful release blurred her vision. The years of waiting and wanting sexual satisfaction, wanting more desperately than she would consciously admit, had ended. For the first time, she felt completely married. Despite the wild melee earlier yesterday, and the time it took to straighten up their hotel room after Farqua's men had left it in shambles, last night had been fulfilling, really fulfilling, until she was completely spent, physically and emotionally. Ben no longer was timid or unsure in making love. Now, the Bora Bora episode of her husband was really over and, with his memory returning, their world would be opening to many wider vistas. She just knew it had to be.

Almost as if he read her thoughts, Ben opened his eyes, looked at his wife, and smiled. "Ain't life grand," he said. Tina leaned over and kissed him in reply.

As they separated, he moved his arm, winced, and said, "Except for this."

"That'll heal quickly," replied Tina. "You've been through a lot worse."

"I know," Ben said, and was silent for a few seconds. Then he said pensively, "Last night just before I went to sleep, I was thinking I should check by Bethesda Naval Hospital and report on my condition. The Navy has been more than fair with me through the years."

"OK, Hon. But how are we going to get there?"

"We'll rent a car, go to the hospital and afterwards drive home instead of taking the train."

"I'd like that," responded his wife. "On the way home, could we go by the Naval Academy? I've never seen it."

"I should for memory's sake. Sure, when we leave the hospital, we'll drive around the Academy," said Ben and he smiled at his wife.

Before going to breakfast, Ben called his parents' home in Philly. Rebecca answered the phone.

"Hi, Becky, it's me, Ben."

"Me, you wild rascal. I heard all about your adventure on the radio late last night. Thank God it's over and you're not seriously hurt. Papa's been on the phone almost ever since that news broadcast telling everyone he knows what a great guy you are. And, I agree. When are you and Tina coming home?"

"This evening, after we go to the Bethesda Naval Hospital and later tour the Academy. Despite my little wound, I'm feeling much better, better than I've ever felt in my life. I just had to call and say thanks. You, Mama and Papa helped make it happen for me."

"Izzy, kiss Tina for me. She's the one who really deserves the credit, and don't you forget it."

"I will and I won't," laughed Ben. "We'll see you soon, Sis," and he hung up.

On the way to breakfast, Ben stopped by the hotel automobile rental desk and ordered a car to be at the front entrance by 9:30 a.m.

2

He was quiet as the duo drove out Wisconsin Avenue. His facial features portrayed his reflective mood. After a few minutes, Tina asked, "Something bothering you, Hon?"

"No -- not bothering me," replied Ben.

"What then?"

"There's something I should do while I'm at Bethesda."

"And that is?"

"I should try to find and thank Archie."

"Who in the world is Archie?"

"He was the first real friend I made after returning to the U.S., the first friend I can remember." Ben told Tina the story of Archie. For some strange reason, he had never told it to her before.

Tina listened. "Ben, by all means, I think you should try to see him. I'd like to meet him."

On arrival at the hospital, Ben and Tina walked into the Psychiatric Admission area. He gave his name and case number to the receptionist. She went to her index files, thumbed through them, stopped, read, then returned to the counter. "Lieutenant Feldman, your case has been closed."

"What do you mean, closed?"

"The index card indicates you are on permanent disability retirement. Your file has been put in the 'Case Ended Archives.'"

"Is there no one I can talk to about my situation?"

The buxom blonde clerk hesitatingly said, "I really don't know, but I'll call the chief's office and see if he will chat with you."

"Thanks, I'd appreciate it," said Ben.

The clerk picked up a phone, dialed, and after a few seconds said, "Gertrude, this is Mabel out front. There is a permanently retired senior lieutenant, Benjamin Feldman here. He would like to speak personally to the chief about his situation. Would the chief be willing to talk with the lieutenant? Sure, I'll wait." She waited. "He will? Now? Thanks, Gertrude."

The clerk turned to Feldman. "The chief will see you now. Go through that door," and she pointed, "His office is second on the left."

Ben looked at the door, then back to the clerk. "May my wife come with me?"

"I don't know why not," answered the clerk.

3

Ben and Tina went through the door to the corridor. They stopped at the second door on the left. Ben looked at the lettering on the door, then gasped. "Well, I'll be damned," The lettering read: "Frank C. Gertzman, Captain U.S. Navy, Chief of Psychiatry."

"What's the matter?" asked Tina.

"He was the psychiatrist aboard the *Southern Cross* who first tried to help me. What a coincidence. He's the one I've told you about."

Ben knocked on the door, and recognized the voice that said, "Come in."

Ben opened the door and Tina entered, followed by him. A smiling, now almost white-haired, but still beetle-browed, Gertzman arose from his desk chair. He held out his hand. "You must be Ben's wife."

"I am, I'm Khristina Feldman." Tina shook the doctor's hand.

"Welcome, Ben. This is a pleasant surprise."

"For me, far more than for you, Doctor."

"What brings you here?" queried Gertzman.

"I thought I should report to somebody. I know it sounds incredible, but within the last two weeks, I've begun to regain my memory. I now know what happened on Bora Bora. Scenes have been returning like a fast-playing movie." Ben stopped for a breath.

Tina chimed in, "The chain of wild events started when we went to the opening performance of the Southwest Pacific Dance Ensemble at the National Theater in Washington, D.C. The final routine before intermission was a recreation of the episode in which Ben was involved on Bora Bora. And, the female lead ballerina was Mary D'Quino, the native who attacked my husband. Ben nearly got killed as result of his returning memory."

"What in the world took place?" asked Gertzman. He added, "I never did believe the story on Ben's physical record or the Naval inquiry report. I often wondered what really happened."

"If you've got the time, I'd like to tell you, then ask your advice," said Ben.

"Shoot!" said Gertzman, "but wait a minute." The doctor picked up his phone, dialed his secretary and said, "Gertrude, no calls or interruptions until I let you know."

Tina smiled in understanding. Ben Feldman emotionally told his story. Gertzman sat, listened and was fascinated. When Ben finished, he looked soberly at the doctor. "The Navy says my file is closed and I'm on permanent disability retirement. What should I do?"

"My God, what a story, Ben. You should do nothing, absolutely nothing. You've earned your retirement. And, you'll still have problems to unravel. I'll note on your index card 'Major Fugue ended.' Did you say, October 25, 1954?"

"Yes, Sir," said Ben. He hesitated for a few seconds, then, "Sir, do you know or have you ever heard of a hospital orderly here named John Archibald Jackson Smith? He was called Archie by many of his patients."

"I surely do. Poor man," was the response.

"What happened to him?'" asked Ben.

"That gentle giant is dying of cancer. He's in the oncology wing."

"Oh, no," responded Ben. "Is there any chance I can see him?"

"You know him that well?"

"He was my first real friend when I returned stateside," replied Ben.

"He's an institution," said Gertzman.

"He's in Ward C, Station 16. I'm sure he would like to see you if he is awake." The doctor gazed out the window, almost as if he was searching for a peek into eternity, then he scribbled a note on his private letterhead, looked up at Ben and said, 'Take this to Ward C nurses station. They'll honor my request."

Khristina looked at the craggy-faced doctor. "Thanks so much for all you've done for Ben. He has told me you were responsible for him being brought east to Bethesda."

"You're a brave young woman and a discerning one to have committed yourself to Ben."

Khristina's blue eyes sparkled, "It's been worth it, every inch of the way and now things are really looking up," she said.

The doctor walked around his desk, put his hands on her shoulders, leaned down, lightly kissed her on her forehead and said with fatherly feeling, "And you've been better for him than all us medics put together."

"How right you are," said Ben.

"Good luck to you two. Ben, say 'hi' to Archie for me." The doctor stopped, looked at the duo. "Mrs. Feldman, do go with your husband to see Archie. He'll appreciate knowing Ben has found a wife. For some odd reason, he is able to discern much more about people than we doctors can."

4

Ben and Tina left the doctor's office. Hand in hand, with no words between them, they walked to Ward C. Ben gave Gertzman's note to the head nurse. She read it, looked up at the sober couple. "He's awake, I'll take you to him."

Ben felt queasy at the thought of seeing the gentle giant lying helpless on a hospital bed, not being in calm control of any situation. He and Tina walked to the bed number. The nurse drew the curtain back from the foot of the bed. Tina looked at the form, and saw what appeared to be a giant skeleton, covered by a sheet, except for his head. Two enormous bright black eyes, each surrounded by a whitish-yellowish murky pool, gazed out from hollow cheeks at the couple. The remnant of that once deep clear voice rasped,

"Lieutenant Ben, I dreamed you'd come before too late. It just had to be."

Ben was surprised that Archie recognized him after all the years. Archie's eyes rested with glowing gentleness on Khristina. "You're so teeny-tiny to be so brave." Ben and Khristina gasped at Archie's comment.

"Archie, why in the world did you say 'teeny-tiny?'" asked Ben. Khristina's mouth was agape with surprise.

"Because she is so tiny to take on such a big job -- you-- and her name is Tina."

"My God, Archie, how did you know?"

"I still knows most everything, Lieutenant," said Archie with a grin. His eyes brightened at the effect his hidden knowledge had on his former patient and the patient's wife.

"But, how?" repeated Ben.

The dumbfounded look on the face of each of his visitors titillated the ill giant. "There's still a network, Lieutenant Ben, always will be," he said with a knowing grin.

Tina now realized why Ben had wanted to see the orderly. She, too, felt an enormous affection for the gentle giant. Even wrestling with death, he exuded an encompassing warmth for his fellow man. Outwardly, she remained calm. She looked down at Archie and asked, "Is there anything I or we can do for you?"

"You've done it, Miss Tina."

"What do you mean, we've done it?"

"You've found each other and agreed to struggle through this life together. That's what I helped save Lieutenant Ben for. Most of happiness is the struggle for it. The big man upstairs smiles on that. I know 'cause I can see his smile clearer with each passing day."

Khristina leaned down and kissed the brow of the dying black man. Then she turned, and fled the area. In the corridor of the ward, she wept, not just from sorrow of the suffering and pain that mirrored the entire being of the gentle orderly, but also from the shock of relief in learning that the apparently lonely dying giant, wasn't lonely. Archie knew his creator had smiled on him and was his constant friend, the same way Archie had smiled on Ben when first they met. She wiped her eyes and thought, there are times when the creator who saves and renews is in each of us -- at least most of us.

Ben came down the corridor, and with a handkerchief, was wiping tears from his eyes. When he reached Tina, he smiled whimsically, "He's one of God's noble men," he said.

"You were fortunate to have had such a first friend. I was enriched just by meeting him," said Tina.

5

The couple walked to the front door of the hospital and went out on the concrete entrance way apron. They stopped and looked out over the beautiful expanse of lawn and shrubbery.

"Archie was the first to begin stacking the wood for the fire of my life you truly lit. I now realize that wood pile was made ready by so many. He was the first to help want me to nourish this," said Ben as his hand swept the view of the lawn. "And, it was the gentle giant who started me searching for you," he said as he looked at his wife.

"But, how did he know my name?" she asked.

"All I know is that there is some kind of network," said Ben.

The duo headed for their rental car, to tour the Naval Academy and from there on to tour a new life.

6

Earlier in the morning that the Feldmans left for Bethesda Naval Hospital, J.R. arose and slipped into a sweatsuit and keds. He walked quietly through the house heading for this route delivery of the *Washington Post*. But, as usual, he slammed the front door when he left. Riding his bike down the driveway toward the entrance posts, J.R. noticed that the police car he had seen last night from his bedroom window, just before he hit the sack, was gone. Gee, he thought, we're getting back to normal. And, as he rode into the street, he saw a C and P Telephone repair truck at the street corner, near the pole that served their lot. A lineman, high on the pole, was fixing the phone line that ran from the pole to this family's house. "I didn't even know it was busted," he said softly.

J.R. peddled toward the dropoff corner and he thought: Man what a wild time they all had yesterday afternoon. Dad said he would tell me about our guests. I'm gonna' corner him soon and find out. I just know it had something to do with when he was in the Navy. But, he talks so little about his wartime experiences. Maybe it's time I ask him. I really would like for him to tell me more about his life. I kinda' need to know about him as a guy, not just as my dad. He knows all about me, cause he's known me since I was born. I wonder what he was like when he was my age and, if I was grown, would I have done what my dad did the last few days?

J.R. arrived at the newspaper dropoff corner. He picked up the top paper from the bundle, glanced at the headlines and shouted with glee into the morning mist. He and his family were famous. They were front page news. The banner read: "Taboo Avenged." There was the story, told by FBI Agent Albert Pfiester to crime reporter Charles Betts. The agent chronicled the investigations made by the FBI and the events of the last twenty-four hours, including the prominent part played by the Morgan family and Jacques Montagne in the saga. Among the happenings he related was the role of J.R., the Morgans' teenaged son who unknowingly distracted Ralph D. Farqua, the demented drug lord, from killing the Feldmans and his mom at the Morgans' home in Arlington, Virginia. J.R. wondered, why in the world did all the events happen?

Boy, he could hardly wait to finish his route, show his family the paper and then call his girl friend, Cathy. She just had to be impressed.

7

Caroline and Greg came awake with a start when the front door slammed shut.

"He's a great guy, but he's got to learn to close those doors more quietly," said Greg, and he yawned and stretched.

"My, he certainly did maintain his cool yesterday," responded Caroline.

"I wonder where he gets that from?" asked Greg.

"The both of us," replied his grinning wife.

"Let's go to the living room, sit on the sofa by the picture window and watch for his return. I need to tell him just how brave I think he is. Every son deserves that now and then," said Greg.

"Especially now," responded Caroline.

The couple entered the living room. Greg went over to the radio and switched it on. They heard the early morning news. It included quite a segment on the episode at their home the evening before, as well as the drug bust. They waited and watched for their son.

8

J.R. slung the next to last paper on the McDonald's porch. With the last paper, his family's, tucked in his sweatshirt, he raced home on his bike. When he arrived, he didn't bother to put his bike on the stand, he just hopped off, let the bike slide on the lawn, and headed for the front door. As J.R. approached the entrance way, the door opened wide. His mom and dad, each in their night robe, stood in the doorway smiling at him. "Hi, hero," said Greg.

Caroline walked outside, lovingly wrapped her arms around J.R. and said, "We were so strung out last night, when things calmed down, we didn't thank you enough. We can now."

"But," said his dad, with an impish grin, "from now on, don't slam the front and back doors so hard." Greg hesitated, gazed with pride at his young son, and continued, "Come on, let's have breakfast, I'll tell you how and why everything happened. You've more than earned the right to know."

J.R. felt a tingle from head to foot, a warm comfortable tingle. At that moment, he knew he didn't care about being a hero. He didn't care that much about Cathy. His mom and dad were unharmed. They were one heck of a family -- the three of them together -- that's what really counted.